GNOMES AND KNOTS

reading **basics** **plus**

HARPER & ROW, PUBLISHERS   NEW YORK   HAGERSTOWN   SAN FRANCISCO   LONDON

1817

CONTRIBUTORS

ERIC P. HAMP
LILYAN HANCHEY
JOSEPH A. LUCERO
DELORES MINOR
ELLIOTT ROSS
MARIAN SCHILLING
ROBERT SHAFFER
MATTIE CLAYBROOK WILLIAMS

Special acknowledgment to Marilyn Buckley Hanf.

ACKNOWLEDGMENTS

''The Armful.'' From THE POETRY OF ROBERT FROST edited by Edward Connery Lathem. Copyright 1928, © 1969 by Holt, Rinehart and Winston. Copyright © 1956 by Robert Frost. Reprinted by permission of Holt, Rinehart and Winston, publishers.

''Arthur Loveridge Battles with Warrior Ants.'' Reprinted by permission of G. P. Putnam's Sons from TALES OF THE WARRIOR ANTS by Dee Brown. Copyright © 1973 by Dee Brown.

''Aunt Sue's Stories.'' Copyright 1926 by Alfred A. Knopf, Inc., and renewed 1954 by Langston Hughes. Reprinted from SELECTED POEMS by Langston Hughes by permission of Alfred A. Knopf, Inc.

''B.Sc.'' Copyright © 1946, 1970 by Emily Hahn. From TIMES AND PLACES by Emily Hahn, with permission of Thomas Y. Crowell Company, Inc., publisher.

''Bald Eagles.'' Copyright © 1975 by Russell Freedman. Reprinted by permission of Holiday House, Inc., from GROWING UP WILD: HOW YOUNG ANIMALS SURVIVE by Russell Freedman.

''Brightside Crossing.'' Reprinted by permission of Alan E. Nourse and David McKay Company, Inc., from TIGER BY THE TAIL AND OTHER SCIENCE FICTION STORIES by Alan E. Nourse. Copyright © 1961 by Alan E. Nourse.

''Buffalo Dusk.'' From SMOKE AND STEEL by Carl Sandburg, copyright 1920 by Harcourt Brace Jovanovich, Inc.; copyright 1948 by Carl Sandburg. Reprinted by permission of Harcourt Brace Jovanovich, Inc.

EDITOR Judith Putterman

DIRECTING EDITOR Martha Hayes

DESIGN Leslie Bauman

ILLUSTRATION

JACQUELINE ADATO 236–241, 364–371; JAMES BARKLEY 122–129, 133–139, 390; TONY CHEN 66–71; JOSEPH CIARDELLO 160–165, 450–457; JEFF CORNELL 40–53, 392–417; KINUKO CRAFT 94–95, 428–445; RENEE DAILY 140–157; TOM DALY 20–25; ALLEN DAVIS 96–103; DIANE DE GROAT 502–525; TERRENCE FEHR 210–219, 326–333, 420–427; BETTY FRASER 28–37; JOHN FREAS 130–131, 174–195; JOE HARRIS 196–197; GERRY HOOVER 250–257; TAD KRUMEICH 278–279; ERROL LE CAIN 72–87, 478–501; ALAN LEINIER 38–39; FRED MARVIN 300–305; GEORGE MASI 242–247, 280–283; JERRY MCDANIELS 418–419; CARL MOLNO 26–27, 54–55, 120–121, 132, 158–159, 222–223, 248–249, 258–260, 290–291, 322–325, 346–347, 360–361, 446–447, 458–459; ALAN REINGOLD 110–119, 348–359; EMANUEL SCHONGUT 12–19, 334–345; ROBERT SHORE 448–449; FLOYD SOWELL 172–173; KYUSO TSUGAMI 292, 294, 298; JOHN WALLNER 224–227; LANE YERKES 262–277, 306–319; ED YOUNG 198–207, 220–221, 320–321; JERRY ZIMMERMAN 460–461

PHOTOGRAPHY

AICH/SENTY STUDIO 326–333; JEAN-MARIE BASSOT/JACANA 109 bottom; RON BEN-VENISTI/MAGNUM 170 bottom left; SHALMON BERNSTEIN/MAGNUM 422 top; THE BETTMANN ARCHIVE 58, 61, 64, 230, 235; BRADY COLLECTION, NATIONAL ARCHIVES 388 bottom; GUSTAVE BONHOMME/JACANA 106 bottom; COLLECTION OF MRS. FRANCIS CAMPBELL 210–219; P. CASTEL/JACANA 109 top; CHICAGO HISTORICAL SOCIETY 382 top, 384 bottom, 386; CON EDISON 170 second row left; CULVER PICTURES 168, 170 top left, 233, 380; ROBERT DOISNEAU/RAPHO-PHOTO RESEARCHERS, INC. 424 bottom; B. FRITZ/JACANA 105 bottom; GRANGER COLLECTION 228, 229, 231, 232, 384 top, 389 top; COLLECTION OF ROBERT E. GREENE 382 bottom, 388 top; F. B. GRUNZWEIG/PHOTO RESEARCHERS, INC. 421; J. HAUSLE/JACANA 107 bottom; CARY HERZ 88, 89, 90 top left, top center, bottom left, bottom right, 93; DOROTHEA LANGE, WRA, COURTESY CALIFORNIA HISTORICAL SOCIETY 466, 472; MARTIN LEVICK/BLACK STAR 92 bottom; LIBRARY OF CONGRESS 389 bottom; BARRY LOPEZ/PHOTO RESEARCHERS, INC. 92 top; RENE MALTETE/BLACK STAR 422 bottom; DICK MARSHALL 477; ROLLIE MC-KENNA/PHOTO RESEARCHERS, INC. 362; JOAN MENSCHENFREUND 118, 167 bottom; HANSEL MIETH/TIME-LIFE 119; P. A. MILWAUKEE/JACANA 105 top, 106 top, 108 bottom; NATIONAL ARCHIVES, from YEARS OF INFAMY by Michi Weglyn 469; NATIONAL ARCHIVES 475; N.Y. DAILY NEWS 167 top, 170 top center, 426 top and bottom, 427 bottom; THE NEW YORK PUBLIC LIBRARY 56; PHOTO COMMUNICATIONS 169; PORT OF NEW YORK AUTHORITY 170 top right; J. ROBERT/JACANA 104; ART SEITZ/FOCUS ON SPORTS 90 top right, center left; SEPP SEITZ/MAGNUM 170 third row right; ELLIOTT VARNER SMITH 284–289; MARK SOLOMON/RAPHO-PHOTO RESEARCHERS, INC. 171; DENNIS STOCK/MAGNUM 424–425, ERIKA STONE/PETER ARNOLD PHOTO ARCHIVES 170 third row center; RAY TERCAPS/JACANA 108 top; UNITED PRESS INTERNATIONAL 474; BURK UZZLE/MAGNUM 423 bottom; A. VISAGE/JACANA 107 top; GARRY A. WATSON 425 right; COLLECTION OF MICHI WEGLYN 462, 470; SANDRA WEINER 372–377; WIDE WORLD PHOTOS 166, 170 second row right, last row right, 420 left and right, 423 top, 424 bottom, 425 left, 427 top; YALE MEDICAL LIBRARY 60-61.

Contents

Collection **1**

Collection **2**

Collection 3

Collection 4

Collection

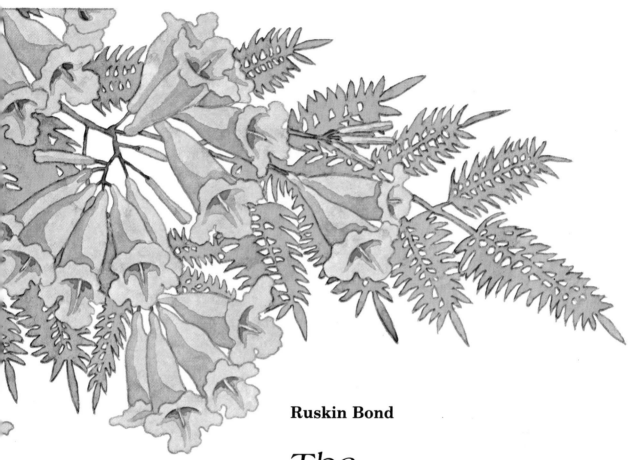

Ruskin Bond

The
Tree Lover

A True Story from India

To date, all of Ruskin Bond's books have dealt with life in India, where he was born in 1934. Bond's stories reflect his love of nature, especially trees and flowers. As you read "The Tree Lover," consider the following questions: What makes Grandfather so memorable to the author? Have you ever known anyone who seemed to "speak" to nature?

I was never able to get over the feeling that plants and trees loved Grandfather with the same tenderness that he showed toward them. One morning, while I was sitting beside him on the veranda steps, I noticed the tendril of a creeping vine trailing across the steps. As we sat there, in the soft sunshine of a north Indian winter, I saw the tendril moving very slowly toward Grandfather. We gazed at it in fascination. Twenty minutes later it had crossed the steps and was touching Grandfather's feet.

There is probably a scientific explanation for the plant's behavior—something to do with light or warmth—but I liked to think that it moved across the steps simply because it wanted to be near Grandfather. One always felt like drawing close to him. Sometimes when I sat by myself beneath a tree, I would feel rather lonely; but as soon as Grandfather joined me, the garden became a happy place, the tree itself more friendly.

Grandfather had served many years in the Indian Forest Service, and it was natural that he should know and understand and like trees. On his retirement from the Service, he had built a bungalow on the outskirts of the city of Dehra, planting trees all around it: lime, mango, orange, guava, eucalyptus, jacaranda, and the Persian lilac. In the fertile Doon valley, plants and trees grew tall and strong.

Grandfather was about sixty, a lean active man who still rode his bicycle at a good speed. He had stopped climbing trees only the year before, when he had got to the top of the jackfruit tree and had then been unable to come down. We'd had to fetch a ladder for him.

Grandfather bathed fairly often but usually got back into his gardening clothes immediately after the bath. During meals, ladybugs or caterpillars would sometimes walk off his shirt sleeves and wander about on the tablecloth, and this always annoyed Grandmother.

Grandmother didn't mind trees, but she preferred growing flowers and was always writing letters ordering seeds and catalogues. Grandfather helped her with the gardening—not because he was crazy about flower gardens, but because he liked watching butterflies. "There's only one way to attract butterflies," he said, "and that's to grow flowers for them. It's a rule of life,"

he went on. "If there's someone or something you really want, then you must prepare the ground well."

Grandfather wasn't content with planting trees just in our compound. During the rains we would walk into the jungle beyond the riverbed, armed with cuttings and saplings, which we would plant in the forest.

"But no one ever comes here!" I protested the first time we did this. "Who is going to see them?"

"We're not planting them simply to improve the view," said Grandfather. "We're planting for the forest—for the birds and animals who live here and need more food and shelter.

"Of course, men need trees too," he added. "For keeping the desert away, for attracting rain, for preventing the banks of rivers from being washed away, for fruit and flower, leaf and seed— yes, and for timber too. But men are cutting down the trees without replacing them. And if we don't plant a few ourselves, there'll come a time when the world will be one great desert."

The thought of a world without trees became a sort of nightmare to me—one reason why I shall never want to set foot on the treeless moon—and I helped Grandfather in his tree-planting with even greater enthusiasm. While we went about our work, he taught me this poem by George Morris:

> *Woodman, spare that tree!*
> *Touch not a single bough!*
> *In youth it sheltered me,*
> *And I'll protect it now.*

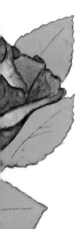

"One day the trees will move again," said Grandfather. "There was a time when trees could walk about like people, but along came an interfering busybody who cast a spell over them, rooting them to one place. They've been standing still for thousands of years, but one day they'll move again. They're always trying to move—see how they reach out with their arms— and some of them, like the banyan tree with its traveling aerial roots, manage to get quite far."

We found an island, a small rocky island in the middle of a dry riverbed. It was one of those riverbeds so common in the foothills—completely dry in summer but flooded during the monsoon rains. A small mango tree was growing in the middle of the island, and Grandfather said, "If a mango can grow here, so can other trees."

As soon as the rains set in, while the river could still be crossed, we set out with a number of tamarind, laburnum, and coral-tree saplings and cuttings, and we spent the day planting them on the island.

The monsoon season was the time for rambling about. At every turn there was something new to see. Out of earth and rock and leafless bough, the magic touch of the rains brought life and greenness. You could almost see the broad-leaved vines growing. Plants sprang up in the most unlikely places. A peepul would take root in the ceiling; a mango would sprout on the windowsill. We did not like to remove them, but they had to go to keep the house from falling down.

"If you want to live in a tree, it's all right by me," said Grandmother. "But I like having a roof over my own head, and I'm not going to have my roof brought down by the jungle!"

When World War II came, I was sent to a boarding school in the hills. During the holidays I went to live in Delhi with my father, who was then serving in the Royal Air Force, and he told me that my grandparents had sold the house and gone to England. Two or three years later I was sent to England to finish my schooling, and I was away from India for several years.

But recently I was in Dehra again, and after first visiting my grandfather's old house (it hadn't changed much), I walked out of town toward the riverbed.

It was February. And as I looked across the dry watercourse, my eye was immediately caught by the spectacular red plumes of the coral blossom. In contrast with the dry riverbed, the island was a small green paradise. When I walked across to the trees, I noticed that a number of squirrels had come to live in them. And a koel, or crow-pheasant, challenged me with a mellow "who-are-you, who-are you."

But the trees seemed to know me. They whispered among themselves and beckoned me nearer. And looking around, I noticed that other small trees and wild plants and grasses had sprung up under the protection of the trees we had planted.

Yes, the trees had multiplied! They were *walking* again. In one small corner of the world, Grandfather's dream had come true, and the trees were moving once more!

Jane Langton

DOLLAR DAY

Officially the Great Depression was over, but money was still hard to come by in Grace Jones' house. This fact had a lot to do with the way Grace decided to spend the money she was suddenly given. How would you spend the first sizable amount of money you ever got?

A quarter for piano lessons—that was the sort of bargain Grace's mother liked. She was a whiz at discovering sales and auctions, and she knew where to find secondhand stores like the Salvation Army. She was always going off shopping and coming back with the DeSoto full of slightly chipped plates or dusty carpets with holes in the middle or old dressers with broken mirrors she had got for fifty cents.

Her mother was clever, Grace knew that. She could make a loaf of bread or wire a lamp or upholster a chair. She could even repair the roof or putty a window or fix the washing machine. She could change a flat tire. She never needed to hire anybody to fix anything because she could fix it herself. Her hands were always green with dye or white with paint or scratched from repairing a screen door. You couldn't help but admire her cleverness and energy. Grace's father would shake his head when he saw the latest broken wreck his wife had dragged home. But then he would be as amazed as the rest of them when she transformed it into a fresh new cupboard for dishes or a record cabinet or a pair of bedside tables.

But Grace and her sister, Sophie, sometimes wished their mother were not quite so thrifty. For them it meant the difference between good clothes from Braunstein's and cheap clothes from Dixon Brothers Dry Goods Store, and that was a big difference. Braunstein's was in the fashionable part of Market Street, way up near the DeForest Building and the library. It was hushed and quiet and expensive in there, with glittering glass display cases and carpets on the floor.

But Grace's mother never went to Braunstein's. She liked the tumble and shove of Dixon Brothers Dry Goods Store, and the cheap prices and the sales. So Grace and Sophie were dressed from head to foot in Dollar Day specials from Dixon Brothers Dry. And their clothes were sleazy, there was no getting away from it. After all the sizing and starch came out in the wash, their new clothes always looked a little limp and out of shape.

There was to be another Dollar Day on Saturday. That Friday evening Mrs. Jones took her daughter aside. There was a look on her face that meant she was going to say something important.

"Grace," said Mrs. Jones, "tomorrow is Dollar Day."

"I know," said Grace.

"I think it's time you learned how to handle money. So I want you to go shopping for some new school clothes all by yourself tomorrow. I think ten dollars would be about right."

Grace saw through her mother's little scheme. Mrs. Jones was trying to charm her away from her middy. Grace had taken to wearing her father's old navy middy in school. She just pulled it on over her school dress and stalked around the school like a sailor striding along the tossing deck of a ship far out to sea.

Mrs. Jones hated the middy. But now Mrs. Jones was hoping that if Grace chose some new clothes for herself, she might want to show them off. She might really wear them and put the middy away.

Well, of course Grace would never do that, but it would be fun to spend ten dollars.

"Would you like that, Grace?"

"Oh, yes."

So the next morning Mrs. Jones and Grace and Sophie all drove into town together to take advantage of Dollar Day. They stood in a tight three-person huddle in the front entrance of Dixon Brothers Dry Goods Store, stemming the urgent riptide of bargain-hunting shoppers. Mrs. Jones counted out ten one-dollar bills into Grace's hand.

"Do I have to spend it all in Dixon Brothers Dry?" said Grace, shouting to make herself heard above the din.

"Why, no, I guess not," Mrs. Jones shouted back. "It's Dollar Day all over town. But of course Dixon Brothers has the best buys. Now you will be sensible, won't you, dear? Ten dollars is a lot of money for one young person to spend all at once."

"Oh, yes. Yes, I will."

"Well, then, meet us right here at noon. Come on, Sophie!" cried Mrs. Jones. "Follow me and hang on tight!"

Grace watched her mother and her little sister plunge into the crowd of shoppers, who were surging eagerly around the big wooden bins. Then she turned away and headed straight up the street for Braunstein's. Whatever she spent her ten dollars on, it wasn't going to be something sleazy and cheap from Dixon Brothers Dry. It was going to be the best there was to be had, the very best.

The shoppers in Braunstein's were better dressed than those in Dixon Brothers Dry, but they were just as greedy and determined. They crowded into the perfumed air of the store, their feet sinking deep into the carpet, their eyes darting this way and that to see if there were any cashmere sweaters marked down

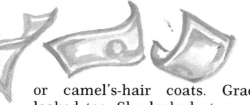

or camel's-hair coats. Grace looked too. She looked at everything. She squeezed between the shoppers. She studied the prices. She read the labels. But she couldn't seem to make up her mind. How could she know whether or not something was the very best of its kind? If it was marked down, didn't that mean there was something wrong with it?

Squeezing her way out of the store again, Grace ambled back down the street in the direction of Dixon Brothers Dry, glancing at the store windows as she went by. Whatever she bought that morning, it had to be like twenty-four carat gold, the very best of its kind, the furthest thing from being marked down. Unique! One of a kind! Something that would last forever. Grace's hand in her pocket felt hot, clutching

the folded dollar bills. Somehow that dirty Dollar Day money had to be transformed into something wonderful and beautiful, something to keep forever.

By this time Grace was floating high above the greedy pushing and pawing of Dollar Day. She felt sorry for the shoppers hurrying past her, their faces hungry for merchandise. *She* would not be like that. She would buy something precious, something beautiful—not at Braunstein's, not at Kennard's, not at the Rexall Drug Store, not at—

Then Grace's floating feet came down to earth. The next store was Plummer's, the silver and jewelry shop. There was no big Dollar Day sign in the window. Plummer's was above such low commercial practices.

And it was at Plummer's that Grace found what she wanted.

"I'll take that one," she said, peering into the glass case, pointing at a gold locket.

It was the smallest one they had, but it was also the most expensive, because it was solid twenty-four carat gold. It was the best.

On the way back to Dixon Brothers Dry Goods Store, Grace ran into her neighbors Dot and Teenie Moon. They had been to the Dollar Day sale at Braunstein's. Proudly Grace opened her precious little package and displayed her prize.

"Why, Grace," gushed Dot, "you're in love."

"I am not," said Grace in hot denial.

"Henry Tonjer?" suggested Teenie in a cheery shout. "Donald Waldorf? Grace is going to put Donald Waldorf's picture in her locket and wear it next to her heart."

"Oh, stop it," said Grace. She stuffed her locket back in the bag and hurried away to Dixon Brothers Dry, worrying about what her mother would say when she saw how the ten dollars had been spent. She wouldn't like it, decided Grace. She wouldn't like it at all.

Grace was right. Her mother was dismayed. Her good idea for improving Grace's appearance hadn't worked at all. But then she laughed, and she didn't scold Grace. (But it would be a long time before Mrs. Jones tried *that* trick again.)

When they got home from their morning of shopping, Sophie ran to try on her new school dress and patent-leather shoes, and Grace began looking around on her desk for the latest issue of the school paper. She wasn't in love with Henry Tonjer or Donald Waldorf, but it did seem a waste to have a locket and not put anybody's picture in it. Carefully she snipped out a tiny face from a photograph of the school orchestra, and wedged it into the gold frame inside the locket. It was a picture of Mr. Chester, the good-looking music teacher. Grace might sneer at things like boyfriends and crushes and falling in love, but she had to admit to a slight weakness for Mr. Chester. She didn't spend much time thinking about it. Mr. Chester was as far away from Grace as Clark Gable was from Dot Moon.

She strung the locket on a ribbon, tied it around her neck, and showed it to her brother Will. (Only the outside, of course, not the inside.)

Will shook his head. "I call that a waste of money," he said.

But it wasn't a waste of money for Grace. It was twenty-four carat gold. It would last forever. It was the best there was.

What's the Connection?

If you didn't know what the word *doleful* meant, how could you tell from the picture? Well, first of all, the boy's expression tells you that he's pretty sad. But often you don't have pictures when you're reading. So let's look at the clue in the girl's statement, "Things can't be that bad." This clue shows that she's talking to someone who's feeling pretty sad or depressed.

When you don't know the meaning of a word in your reading, you can often figure it out by seeing what connection it has to the words surrounding it. *Context* comes from a word that means loosely, "woven in together." Therefore, to find the meaning of an unfamiliar word, you look to see how it is used in context, how it is woven in with the words around it.

Sometimes you can find synonyms in the sentence, words that mean the same thing as the unfamiliar word. In the sentence "The adults frowned on their shenanigans, but the children enjoyed their pranks," what word tells you the meaning of the word *shenanigans*?

What does each underlined word mean in the following sentences?

My uncle is so persnickety that my aunt laughs at him for being too fussy.
That meat is really rancid; even the dog dislikes its awful smell.

Often there are no synonyms to help you with an unfamiliar word, but the rest of the sentence describes or explains the word in some way. Can you figure out what the underlined word in this sentence means?

The desert nomads changed homes frequently to find new food supplies. Did you guess that nomads are people who travel, wander, or who are often on the move?

What do the underlined words mean in the following sentences?

The politician refused to discuss her fiscal policy because her adviser on financial matters was not present.
Mary Lou has a ruddy complexion because she spends so much time out in the wind and snow.

On a separate sheet of paper write the definitions for the underlined words in the following sentences.

1. The zoo ordered several new dingoes when two of their older wild dogs died.
2. That blanket will be superfluous because I brought enough for all of us.
3. I know I'm surly today but I always get crabby in hot weather.
4. Will Sue renege or will she keep her word this time?

Which other words in the sentences helped you? What is the importance of good connections?

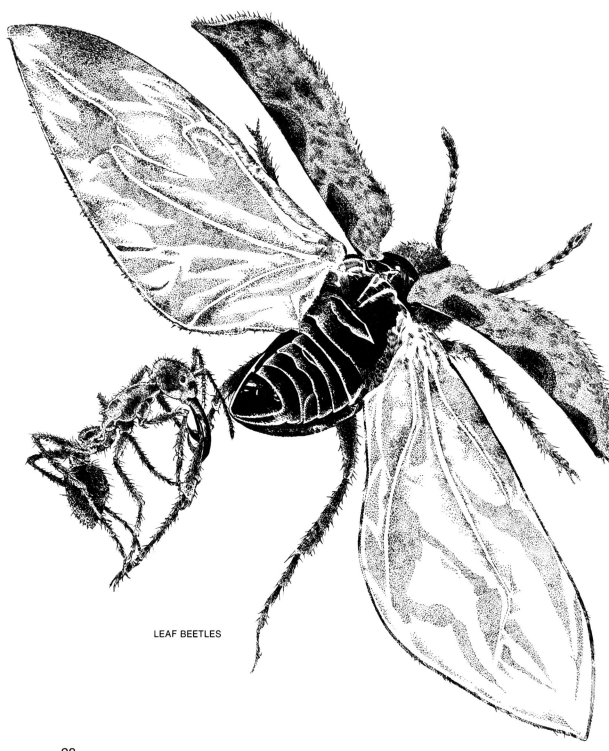

LEAF BEETLES

28

Dee Brown

Arthur Loveridge Battles with Warrior Ants

Arthur Loveridge's battle began one July morning in Tanganyika, Africa. About eight o'clock, he stepped outside his house and noticed large numbers of beetles flying in the air. Loveridge was a naturalist especially interested in insects, and so he observed these flying beetles rather more closely than the average person would have done. He was surprised to see that fierce, reddish-colored ants were attached to many of the beetles, biting at their hind legs.

Immediately afterward, Loveridge discovered half a dozen long lines of the same ants marching over the ground and into cracks at the base of his house. All along the lines of march, skirmishing parties were attacking crickets and grasshoppers, slashing off their legs and tearing at them with large, powerful jaws. As he studied the marching formations, Loveridge noted that the ants were of varying sizes. The majority, or worker drivers, were half an inch or less in length, but along the outer edges of the columns huge winged ants marched up and down like officers directing an army. From his knowledge of insects, Loveridge guessed at once that he was being invaded by a small army of driver ants.

He did not at first, however, realize the seriousness of his situation. Like a true naturalist, he spent the morning observing the army rather than attempting to fight it. He was fascinated by the military precision of the drivers. In addition to the "officer" ants who seemed to be directing the formations, sentries were stationed about two inches apart along both sides of the columns. These sentries stood with the foreparts of their bodies raised and with their powerful jaws wide open as if to repel any disturbers. Loveridge teased the sentries by inserting tiny sticks into their opened jaws, and as soon as they clamped down, he would lift them a few feet away, drop them, and then watch them scurry about until they found their proper posts again.

He knew that a number of ant lions made their homes around the sides of his house, and he went to observe how these natural enemies of the drivers were meeting the invasion. (The ant lion is a flat-bodied insect about the same size as a worker driver. Attached to its large head is a pair of jaws like long, sharp scissors. To set its trap, the ant lion digs down into loose sand, moving in smaller and smaller circles until it has formed a funnel-shaped hole about two inches wide and an inch or more deep. The ant lion then hides under the sand at the bottom, awaiting its prey.)

Loveridge noticed that only the small worker drivers were falling into the pits of the ant lions. They were quickly seized by the ant lions, squeezed and slashed and drawn down into the shifting sand until they disappeared forever.

Returning inside his house, Loveridge was startled to find that the invading drivers had already worked their way into his kitchen and were roaming about the place in search of household prey. His first thought was of his valuable collection of butter-flies, birds, tortoises, crocodiles, and other African species which he had spent months in assembling. Deciding to fight off the army ants, he soaked balls of paper in prussic acid and stuffed them in the outer holes where the columns were entering. With a broom he swept the drivers which had already pene-trated his kitchen out into the yard. Then he piled grass over the heap of ants, poured kerosene upon the grass, and set it afire. Within fifteen minutes, only a few scattered army ants were left around his house.

Congratulating himself upon his victory, Arthur Loveridge retired inside to relax. Had he known the habits of driver ants, how the main body of their army frequently marches after dark, he would not have been so confident.

"About 9 P.M.," he later recorded, "as I was reading, I became gradually conscious of many small noises, making alto-gether quite a volume of suppressed sound. Some time later, on

ACTUAL SIZE

30

taking up the light and going to my bedroom, the reason was obvious. The white-washed walls were a moving mass of driver ants. They swarmed upon the books in the bookcase, overran other shelving, a chest of drawers, etc. The sound was made by the feet of the countless multitide."

WORKER MINOR

While he danced up and down to keep the ants off his feet, Loveridge discovered what this second army of drivers was after—a great host of plant beetles which had flown into his bedroom, evidently fleeing the drivers. When molested, the plant bugs gave off a powerful odor. Ordinarily this odor served as a repellant against ant attacks, but to the drivers it was only a challenge and seemed to excite them to more violent battle.

For two days Arthur Loveridge fought the invaders. With the help of several Tanganyikans, he began fighting them with fire and water and oil. The men shoveled hot ashes down into their holes. They set out meat baits, and as soon as the meat was covered with ants, they drowned them in oil-filmed water. "We thus destroyed several thousand in a few minutes with the greatest ease."

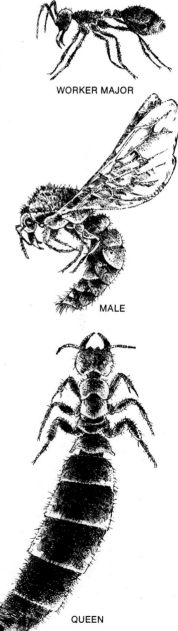

WORKER MAJOR

MALE

QUEEN

At the end of the second day, the tide of battle appeared to have turned against the drivers, and Loveridge decided he could safely return to sleeping in his bedroom. But he did take the precaution of filling washbasins and soap dishes with water and placing them beneath the four legs of his bed. He also raised a fine-meshed mosquito net over the bed.

About two-thirty in the morning he was awakened by the splashing of a crocodile in its pen. "Most of my creatures I had moved outside the previous day, but I thought that the young crocodiles in the tank could defy drivers. The tortoises had also been left in their pen, since it was outside, though against, the house." Deciding to go to the rescue of his live specimens, Loveridge untucked his mosquito net and stretched forth a hand to turn up the lamp on his reading table. An ant was on the lamp handle. When the light flared up, he saw that the walls and floor were a crawling mass of drivers.

But what concerned him most was a group of ants on his pillow and two single lines moving up the mosquito net, one line outside and the other inside!

"By turning up the mattress and giving the net a more generous tuck-in, I stopped the inside stream. Then, jumping up, I got

out onto my slippers, around which ants were swarming. First I examined the pans of water in which the bed legs were standing. Across one of them at the head of the bed, a company of sappers had thrown a bridge composed of living ants upon which their comrades were crossing and so up the net. Unscrewing the cap of the lamp container, I hurriedly splashed out enough oil on the bridge to cause its collapse, and also to form a film of oil on the water beneath."

After treating the other pans under his bedposts in the same manner, Loveridge hurried outside to look after his young crocodiles. He found one of the cages filled with drivers, and the crocodile inside was turning around and around in the water, flipping alternately from back to belly and thrashing the water with its tail. The edges of the rectangular pen were lined with ants, and whenever the crocodile's struggles brought him near a side, they would hurl themselves upon him.

When Loveridge reached one arm inside the cage, a shower of drivers leaped upon it. But he managed to catch hold of the crocodile's tail, lifted the young reptile out, and tossed it several feet away. Immediately a swarm of ants upon the ground surrounded the unfortunate crocodile. Once again, Loveridge hurried to the rescue, removing the crocodile to a drinking tank some distance away where there were no drivers.

Returning to the cage, Loveridge discovered that his other crocodile had already been killed by the drivers. Hearing quite a commotion in his tortoise pen, he hurried in that direction, staying clear of the shrubbery since every leaf was crawling with ants and the ground beneath was teeming with them. Noticing one dense heap of ants, he turned them over with a stick and discovered that they were devouring a large chameleon. "The ground that lay between me and the tortoises," he recorded afterward, "was so alive with drivers that I very respectfully turned back." He also realized that the tortoises probably had crawled under the rocks in their pen and that he would not be able to get at them.

By this time, after two days and nights of battling, Loveridge had grown so accustomed to living with the warrior ants that he decided to return to the battlefield of his bedroom and seek the shelter of his mosquito net. He tore off all the bed clothing

CHAMELEON COVERED
WITH ANTS

33

which might be harboring his foes and then sat down in the center of his bed beneath the net to review his situation.

"The enemy column that had entered the net was wandering to and fro on the ceiling of it, while a score or more of individuals were frantically rushing about on the sheet or sides of the net. Armed with my entomological forceps, I picked these off one by one, killing them as I did so." In a similar manner he disposed of the column on the ceiling of his mosquito net. He then shook off what were left outside the net.

Loveridge knew that it was three hours until dawn, and he dared not fall asleep. He lay there through the tortuous hours, listening to the whispering movement of the drivers, to the darting, slithering sounds of gecko lizards being pursued in the roof, and to the flight of bats. Once he heard the frightened squeak of a rat, which escaped to the outer roof, then lost its footing on the galvanized iron, and rolled down to land with a thump on the ground outside.

As soon as first dawnlight showed, he escaped from his mosquito netting, hurried outside, and summoned his employees to begin an attack on the drivers before they could gain cover in their holes at daybreak. Meat baits set in the outer yard the previous evening were each a mass of ants. "It is difficult for one who has never seen drivers," Loveridge said, "to conceive of the way in which they pile themselves, one upon another. When the baits had been dropped into the basins, we fired the hay in the crocodiles' cage, which was a seething mass of ants. With handfuls of blazing grass we swept up the lines of ants proceeding to my tortoise enclosure, continually moving our feet to frustrate attacks upon ourselves."

Loveridge was relieved to find all of his tortoises alive, though some were suffering badly. The box tortoises had drawn in their armor-plated forelegs, thus protecting their heads, and it was the soft-shelled land tortoises that had borne the brunt of the drivers' fury. A score or more ants were attached to each one of them, biting at their eyelids. He dropped the tortoises in water drums, and put one of the Tanganyikans to picking ants off them with a forceps.

Wondering if his collection of mounted birds and butterflies still survived, he went back into the house. Early in his war with the drivers, Loveridge had taken the precaution to stuff all the

cracks of his largest insect case with cotton. But when he entered the specimen room that morning, he could hear the rasping of the drivers' feet on the gauze mesh, and he knew they had broken through his defenses.

For once, however, he received a pleasant surprise. Only one of his bird specimens had been molested, and only such butterflies and mantises as had not dried thoroughly had been destroyed. There was not enough fresh meat on the others to attract the flesh-eating drivers.

During his long war with the drivers, Loveridge had learned that their main attacks came late in the day, and he spent the afternoon preparing new defenses for an expected evening battle. At the first sign of a skirmish line, he and his helpers began annihilating the ants with hot ashes. When a large reserve force rushed out of a ground hole, he poured in a charge of cyanide powder, covering it with hot ashes. He also continued to put out poisoned meat baits some distance from the house and in some of the unused rooms of the house.

By dusk it looked as if Loveridge had won that day's battle. "Then came the shock," he said. "In every direction from east and south ants were arriving in countless thousands. Quite thirty of these steady streams were moving toward the house."

It was as if all the driver ants in Africa had been summoned to do battle with this single human being who had dared to defy them. While Loveridge and his frightened employees waited, wondering if they should flee while there was yet time, the vast armies halted in the grass some thirty feet from the cleared yard, their ceaseless whispering movements sounding across the deepening dusk.

But they never came any closer. Why they did not, no one can say. Had these new armies been summoned by the drivers who had been battling for days against Loveridge's resistance? Had there been a council of war? Had the destructive tactics of hot ashes and cyanide powder proved so deadly in the final battle that the soldier leaders decided to retreat? No one will ever know, of course.

But when Arthur Loveridge entered his house late that night, he found not one single driver ant in the building. And the next morning, the besieging armies had vanished from the lonely African landscape.

Langston Hughes

Aunt Sue's Stories

Aunt Sue has a head full of stories.
Aunt Sue has a whole heart full of stories.
Summer nights on the front porch
Aunt Sue cuddles a brown-faced child to her bosom
And tells him stories.

Black slaves
Working in the hot sun,
And black slaves
Walking in the dewy night,
And black slaves
Singing sorrow songs on the banks of a mighty river
Mingle themselves softly
In the flow of old Aunt Sue's voice,
Mingle themselves softly
In the dark shadows that cross and recross
Aunt Sue's stories.

And the dark-faced child, listening,
Knows that Aunt Sue's stories are real stories.
He knows that Aunt Sue
Never got her stories out of any book at all,
But that they came
Right out of her own life.

And the dark-faced child is quiet
Of a summer night
Listening to Aunt Sue's stories.

The Rivals

Nick Pease

"But what—ouch!" cried Steve Pasqual, scalding his mouth on a slice of pizza, "—what are you going to *do* all that time up there, Linda?"

Linda Perez finished sipping her lemonade and asked, "What do you mean?"

"Well, look," said her friend, "you're going to be up at your cousin's, in the middle of nowhere, for two solid weeks. I mean there's no surfing, no skateboarding, probably no movies—what're you going to do all day, chase butterflies?" He put his feet up on the coffee table and pointed to a framed photo on the wall. It showed Linda and her cousin Carmen, both mugging for the camera from the patio behind Linda's house. "Just look at that goofy kid," he went on, "pigtails and freckles and baggy blue jeans—a 'country cousin' if I ever saw one."

"Listen, Stevie, Carmen is no hick!" Linda said defensively. "She's a really nice girl, and we had lots of fun during her visit. Besides, that picture was taken two years ago, when we were both eleven. I'm sure she doesn't look like that anymore."

"Well, I don't know," he mused ironically, "all I can say is you'd better get used to the idea of spending two weeks in the backwoods."

The boy's mocking outburst really had nothing to do with Carmen Perez. In fact, he'd never even met her. He was just angry that Linda was going away for the best part of the summer. But later that afternoon, as her long, sleek bus rolled along the California highway, Linda peered through the green-tinted window with a dampened enthusiasm. She was still excited at the prospect of her first long stay away from Los Angeles, but now doubts were filling her mind. What *would* Carmen be like? And what about her little town of Woodlake? Though the girls had exchanged letters over the months, Linda suddenly felt as though she were calling on a complete stranger.

Her anxiety quickened as the bus turned off the main highway and headed north on a country road. In what seemed like minutes it reached the main street of Woodlake and wheezed to a stop in front of the station. This is it, thought Linda, as she stepped onto the hot pavement and handed the driver her luggage ticket. Just then she heard her name called.

"Linda! *Hola*, Linda, it's me—Carmen!"

Shading her eyes from the sun, Linda could see a green station wagon across the street and a slender, smartly dressed girl getting out. The voice was familiar, but the sight of Carmen astonished her. Gone was the awkward, ungainly youngster, replaced by a girl as tall and athletic-looking as Linda herself. Trying to hide her amazement, she returned Carmen's delighted grin as the two met. Carmen's parents followed her, and Linda recognized them with relief. They, at least, seemed not to have changed at all.

"Aunt Maria! Uncle Toby!" she cried, as they exchanged hugs and kisses.

"Hurry up, let's get your things into the car," Carmen said, "we've got chicken and frijoles cooking for supper, and I can't wait to hear your news!"

As they climbed into the station wagon and drove through the cool, tree-lined streets of the town, Linda winced a little, remembering Steve's words. But soon she began to relax and enjoy herself. What a nice, quiet town, she thought. I don't think I'll miss the big city at all.

As they chatted about family matters, Aunt Maria was half-turned in the front seat, looking back and forth at the two girls. Finally she exclaimed, "You know, I just can't get over how much you two look alike!"

Linda stiffened. It was true, and she knew it. Back in Los Angeles she had fancied herself the more attractive and sophisticated of the two, and she was hardly prepared for a Carmen who could almost pass for her sister. She didn't reply and was grateful when the car just then pulled into the driveway.

Her luggage was unloaded, and she was shown to the sunny, comfortable guest room. Soon the four Perezes were seated around the dining-room table enjoying a hearty meal. Recent family history was the topic of conversation. Uncle Toby had been promoted to vice-president of his electronics firm, and Aunt Maria, having returned to college, was finishing a Master's degree in marine biology. Linda was asked about her ambitions.

"I don't know," she said, trying to sound casual, "my grades in English have been pretty good, so I think I might like to be a writer or a reporter."

"Isn't that nice!" said her aunt. "Carmen's been getting straight A's in English—and history, too."

"Oh, Mom!" said her embarrassed daughter.

"In Woodlake I suppose that's easier than in L.A.," Linda answered quickly, "but I go to one of the city's toughest schools.

43

My teachers say I should go on to a special high school for literature and the arts.''

"Woodlake's not so easy!'' Carmen snapped, but just then her father cut in.

"Speaking of schools,'' he said, "Carmen, how about telling Linda about tonight and tomorrow?''

Feeling a bit stung by Linda's remark, Carmen explained that that evening five of her friends were coming over for a party and the next day the group would be going to the mountains for a camp-out, under the direction of their biology teacher.

"Why a teacher?'' asked Linda.

"Oh, it's part of a Summer Studies program at school. We visit a certain area three or four times during the summer and take notes on the plants and animals we see, and later we study the ecology of the area in class. The school gives us all the camping stuff we need, so I got an extra sleeping bag for you.''

"That sounds like fun,'' murmured Linda, "staring at trees and counting mosquitoes. . . . Do you get extra credit if you're bitten by a snake?''

"Don't you worry about snakes or anything else,'' Uncle Toby said before Carmen could react. "Carmen knows a thing or two about life in the forest—she'll take good care of you.''

Carmen just gazed absently out the window.

A few hours later, everyone was busy setting out snacks and getting the house ready for the party. Despite her uneasiness with Carmen, Linda couldn't help liking the house enormously. It was a large, comfortable, old-fashioned sort of home, with a wide porch in front and wonderful oak woodwork throughout. Linda lived in a modern, ranch-style home, but she found the overstuffed furniture and generations-old woven rugs strangely appealing. As she paused to admire the family portraits on the wall, the guests began arriving.

Bill and Julio and Grace and Alicia and Carlos met Linda one by one, and soon the friends were buzzing about the next day's camp-out. They were to reach their area in the early afternoon, pitch camp, and then do a three-hour "observation'' before dark. Then everyone would gather around the campfire for songs and discussion. Three of Carmen's friends asked to be her partner on the observation, but she said that would be up to the Yungs, the two field-trip directors.

After a while the conversation turned to Linda and Los Angeles. Feeling the spotlight shift from Carmen to her, Linda was eager to flaunt her big-city background.

"Do you live anywhere near the movie studios?" asked Alicia.

"As a matter of fact, my neighborh—, my *barrio* is right on the edge of Beautiful Downtown Burbank. (It's really 'Yecchy Downtown Burbank.') That's because my mom and dad both work for the studios. Mom's in wardrobe work and Dad's a film editor. It's nice for me because I get free passes to all their films."

"Wow, neat," said Carlos. "Do you have a swimming pool?"

"Not yet," she said, "but my friend Steve Pasqual does, so I get to use it whenever I want. We go surfing a lot, too. There are some great beaches near L.A."

"Yes, but I bet you don't get to go field-tripping in the mountains," Carmen said challengingly.

"Not in the *mountains,* naturally," Linda retorted, "but my class goes to the shore a lot to study tide-pools and things. And when we do, we don't just sit there and look at things, we bring back specimens. Right now I've got a whole aquarium full of crabs I caught myself."

That brought a few oohs of admiration, but not from Carmen. She was furious. After a moment she stomped into the kitchen to cool down. Her father was there and, seeing the scowl on her face, he asked what was the matter.

"*Ay caramba!*" growled the girl, "that Linda just burns me up! She's such a conceited little know-it-all—everything she has is bigger or better or newer or nicer than mine. She's always putting me down. I wish she'd go back to 'L.A.,' as she calls it, and stay there!"

"I know you two are having a rough time," her father said gently, "but there are bound to be adjustment problems. Remember, you haven't seen each other for a long time, and Linda's a long way from home. Besides, . . ."

"Besides, what?" the girl asked crossly.

"Well," he said carefully, "there might just be some jealousy, too, on her part."

Carmen was stunned. "*Her*—jealous of *me?*" she asked incredulously. Her father nodded.

"I was just looking at these pictures of you two during your last visit," he said, "and if you ask me, she's got something to be jealous about. You've grown up a lot in the past couple of years—look." He handed her the snapshots, and Carmen had to smile at the impish, gawky poses she'd struck.

"Why don't you give her a couple of days to settle down?" he continued. "I think once she's seen you on your own turf, especially up in the mountains, she'll show you a little more respect. So what do you say to a two-day truce?" He held out his hand.

The relaxed girl shrugged and gave him a "right-on!" handslap. "It's a deal."

The next morning, as the Perez car wound its way up the narrow back roads of the Sierra Nevadas, Carmen was feeling positively exhilarated. She waved to their followers in the Yungs' car and chatted breezily with Bill and Grace as she loaded her camera. Even Linda couldn't spoil her mood, even though the two girls were avoiding one another. As the car turned the bend, it entered a cluster of sequoia trees, and everyone began murmuring about their gigantic size.

"Carmen," remarked her father, "aren't sequoias the trees you were telling me about that thrive on disaster?"

"I've heard they're the tallest and oldest trees in the world!" Linda blurted out.

Carmen winced at the interruption. "Actually, they're neither," she said coolly. "Lately they've discovered that the bristlecone pine is older, and the redwoods of the Big Sur region are taller by an average of thirty or forty feet. I suppose you could say these are *bigger*, because they're much fatter and heavier, but they're not the biggest. These sequoias are plenty old, too. That one may be over three thousand years old."

Darn it, there I go again, Linda thought to herself, always trying to top Carmen. I wish I could keep my big mouth shut!

"What do you mean, sequoias thrive on disaster?" Bill asked Carmen.

"Well, first of all," she said, "their bark has no pitch in it, which makes them practically fireproof. When a forest fire comes through, it just burns off the other trees and leaves more growing room for the sequoia. It's the same when there's an insect attack, because sequoia bark is full of tannin, which bugs can't stand. Also, new sequoias don't need rich humus soil the way other trees do. They grow better in blasted areas, where mineral deposits have been churned up by

road builders or some natural catastrophe. The worse the disaster, the better they like it.''

Thanks for the nature lecture, Linda thought sullenly. But even so, she couldn't help noticing how attentively the others listened to her cousin. Later, as they pitched camp in a picture-postcard mountain meadow, she brought it up with Grace.

"Carmen sure seemed to know a lot about sequoia trees," she remarked. "Where'd she pick up all that stuff?"

Grace looked surprised. "Didn't she tell you?" she said. "Ecology is her hobby. She's practically a walking encyclopedia on the subject. Oh look, Ms. Yung is announcing partners for the observation. Let's go find out who we'll be with.''

They ran to the directors' tent in time to hear the woman say, "Carmen, since your cousin is new to the woods, I think the two of you should go together.''

Just my luck, thought both girls simultaneously. Glumly they shouldered their cameras and canteens and set off on a footpath to the west. Padding along behind, lost in thought, Linda was all but oblivious to the forest, with its banquet of sights and sounds and smells. They trooped along until the trail petered out, and Carmen

began noting landmarks in her book for the hike back. After an hour's passage through the trackless woods, she called a rest stop. Linda was puffing and panting and angry.

"Isn't this far enough?" she demanded. "If we cross one more hill we're going to meet the Abominable Snowman!"

"Now, look—" Carmen snapped, but she checked herself. "Now, look," she began again, "our spot is only about five minutes farther along, so relax. Once we're there you've got to keep absolutely still, or we won't see anything, understand?"

"And just sit there?"

"And just sit there. Nothing will happen for the first half-hour or so, but then it should start to get interesting."

Linda shrugged and they set off again. Soon they reached their area, a sun-speckled clearing with a fallen tree to sit on. Taking up positions about ten feet apart, they got out their books and began taking notes.

Well, here we go with the Big Observation, thought Linda. Let's see: That's a tree . . . and that's a shrub . . . and that's it. Oh wow, wait'll I tell Stevie I sat on a rotten log and did tree-watching!

As her attention wandered, Linda became conscious of the

soreness in her feet, legs, and back. Tiny ants crawled onto her thighs from the log, and she tried not to squirm. Resentment churned within her at the thought of this stupid, boring observation where there was nothing to observe. After fifteen or twenty maddening minutes, she turned toward Carmen with a look that said "Let me out of here!"

But the sight of the other girl surprised her. Carmen was sitting as still as an Indian scout, her chin cupped in one hand and her large, dark eyes probing restlessly through the vegetation. Her face, far from being bored, wore a look of the keenest concentration. Suddenly her gaze fixed on something, and Linda looked to see what it was. For a minute or more she scanned the trees in vain. She turned again to Carmen, who silently mouthed the word "porcupine" and pointed with a slow, careful motion. Sure enough, the round, burrlike rodent was descending from its perch in a maple tree. Linda's face lit up with delight, her anger and discomfort suddenly forgotten.

A short while later she heard a low "Psst!" from her cousin, who was pointing to a movement at the edge of the glade. A brilliantly colored red-, black-, and cream-banded snake slithered into the sunlight for a moment and then was lost again in the gloom. Linda grimaced, but Carmen smiled reassuringly. "Mountain king snake," she whispered. "Harmless."

Linda jotted down the sighting, feeling excitement grow within her. Another feeling was growing, too: admiration for Carmen. Gee, she thought, no wonder all her friends wanted to be Carmen's partner— I'd never see a thing by myself. I guess there's a lot more to this "tree-watching" than I thought!

Thanks to additional cues from Carmen, the entire forest soon seemed to throb with life. Gophers scurried through the underbrush, and overhead flying squirrels made spectacular tree-to-tree leaps. Unusual birdsongs warbled through the sweet, humid air, and Carmen identified them with astonishing frequency. All of Linda's senses tingled with expectancy. She even had one triumphal moment of her own, when she spied a set of black-and-white stripes shambling past the clearing behind Carmen's back. "Psst!" she signaled, casually hitch-hiking the direction with her thumb: "Skunk!"

Finally Carmen motioned that it was time to go, and Linda felt a pang of reluctance. She was just closing her notebook and pocketing her pencil when Carmen suddenly faced her and held her with a peculiar look. "Linda, wait a minute," she said, "I'm going to take

your picture, so hold real still." Changing her mind, she said, "I'm going to take *two,* so don't move."

Linda smiled obediently, and after a long pause Carmen clicked off the first shot. Then there was an even longer pause until the shutter clicked again. "Whew," said Carmen, letting out a breath, "got you just right."

"Good," said Linda, standing and stretching. "Boy, Carmen, this was really terrific. I didn't know there *were* so many kinds of plants and animals. And *you* were amazing. You've got eyes like a—an eagle!"

"Why, shore," drawled her cousin with a grin, "that's why in these parts they call me Ole Eagle-Eye Perez. Waal, c'mon, pard, let's hit th' trail. It's a-gittin' late and Ah'm a-gittin' hongry." Laughing and joking, the two girls set out for the campsite.

That night, and in the days following, Linda's respect for Carmen continued to grow. Realizing how much talent and knowledge it took to know the mountains, she stopped judging her by the standards of the city, and all their competitiveness vanished. With the return of their old friendship, the remaining days of the visit flew by like one nonstop picnic.

As the hour of her departure drew near, however, Linda thought she detected something mysterious in Carmen's manner—something mischievous. Finally she asked about it, as they drove down to catch the bus. "Carmen," she said, "lately you've been acting like the cat that swallowed the canary. Are you up to something?"

"Well," said Carmen slyly, "I do have a little going-away surprise for you."

"I *thought* so, you little sneak—out with it, then!"

Carmen waited till the car rolled to a stop, then stepped out into the sunlight. "Climb out," she said. "I want to see if you can take this standing up."

Linda got out, feeling a little foolish, and Carmen thrust two photographs into her hand. They were the ones taken during the observation. Linda squintingly scanned the top photo, then did a pop-eyed double-take: There she was, sitting comfortably on the log, and on the ground before her, about four feet away, was an enormous rattlesnake moving in her direction!

"*Dios mío!*" she sighed, sagging onto the car seat. "You knew that thing was there?"

"I only noticed it when I got up," said Carmen, "but I knew it hadn't seen you because it didn't coil. I thought if I could keep you still it would move on."

"But what—what happened then?" Linda croaked.

"Brace yourself and look at the other picture."

Linda studied the photo and went limp. The snake's rattled tail was disappearing into a hole under the log right between her feet!

"Bus is here," announced Uncle Toby, coming around with the luggage. "You about ready, Linda?"

"I guess so," she said, wobbling to her feet and getting hugs and kisses all around. "You sure were right about one thing, Uncle Toby. Carmen knows a thing or two about life in the forest—and now I do, too! Bye-bye, Uncle Toby . . . Aunt Maria. . . . And Carmen: *hasta luego?*"

"Yes, *very* soon," said Carmen.

WHAT WAS IT LIKE?

The civil defense officer above is interviewing several people after a tornado has passed through their town. The first person describes the sound the storm made by comparing the storm to freight trains. The second person tells us how the funnel cloud looked, and the third person describes how it felt to be surrounded by the storm. Look at the way each person describes the storm. Each one uses a simile—a figure of speech that compares two things by using the words *like* or *as*.

Look at the sentences below. Which ones contain similes? Write each simile on a separate sheet of paper. Beneath each simile write down the two things that are being compared.

1. The new road tunneled into the mountain like an ambitious mole.
2. My cap blew off just as I left the concert.
3. When we unleash our dog, he runs around like a kid out of school.
4. "You're as slow as a frozen river in winter," he said.
5. "I don't like this movie, it's too violent," complained Ray.

The poet in the picture doesn't seem to be doing too well with his love. It seems that she simply isn't interested in either him or his poetry. In his grief he uses a metaphor to express his feelings. "My heart is a stone." What do you suppose he means by this? That his heart is a diamond or a piece of granite? Hardly. He means that he is sad and despairing because he is being rejected. Poets, good and bad ones, often use metaphors involving the heart.

But what is a metaphor? It is a comparison between two objects without using the words *like* or *as.* Instead, one is said *to be* the other. For instance, the simile "Jake is as stubborn as a mule" can be changed to the metaphor "Jake is a stubborn mule." Do the simile and the metaphor about Jake mean the same thing?

Pick out the metaphors in the following sentences. What does each one mean? Rewrite these metaphors as similes.

1. The baby's laughter was a stream bubbling over the rocks.
2. The hockey team members were tigers, attacking from all sides at once.
3. The ship plowed the waters.
4. Sam is a fish out of water when he has to leave his farm.

A Dairymaid Gives Jenner an Idea

Katherine B. Shippen

Many terrible diseases that killed thousands of people in the past have been practically wiped out today. Advancements in medical science over the years have made this possible. In the story that follows, you will read about a doctor who made an important medical discovery almost by accident. What do you think is the greatest scientific discovery ever made? What do you think will be the most important discovery in the future?

Sometimes medical discoveries are made after long study and research—perhaps they are most often made that way. But sometimes they are made almost casually, as the result of observation of facts that people have known all along but have not heeded. It was in this way that Edward Jenner made his great discovery of vaccination to prevent smallpox. He listened to the talk of country folk in Gloucestershire, where he was learning to be a country doctor.

Up to Jenner's time smallpox was one of the most terrible scourges that afflicted people. It was known in China and India, in Turkey and Egypt and Europe. It was especially virulent in the American colonies. Sometimes the disease struck lightly, leaving the patient with a face scarred with pockmarks. Sometimes it left the patient blind, deaf, or insane. One person out of every five or six stricken with smallpox died—it was no wonder that people of all ages everywhere dreaded and feared it.

Particularly in the East, doctors had made efforts to prevent or lessen the impact of the disease by inoculating healthy persons with lymph taken from those who had already suffered from it. Lady Mary Wortley Montagu, wife of the British ambassador to Turkey, saw this done when she was in Constantinople in 1716 with her husband. She wrote an enthusiastic letter to her friend, Mary Chiswell, describing how the inoculation was done.

I am going to tell you a thing that I am sure will make you wish yourself here. The smallpox, so fatal and so general amongst us, is here entirely harmless by the invention of grafting, which is the term they give it.

There is a set of old women who make it their business to perform the operation every autumn, in the month of September, when the great heat is abated. People send to one another to know if there is any in their family has a mind to have the smallpox; they make parties for this purpose, and when they are met (commonly fifteen or sixteen together) the old woman comes with a nutshell full of the matter of the best sort of smallpox and asks what veins you please to have opened. She immediately rips open that you offer to her with a large needle (which gives you no more pain than a common scratch), and puts into the vein as much venom as can lie upon the head of her needle, and after binds up the wound with a bit of shell; and in this manner opens four or five veins. . . . The children or young patients play together all the rest of the day, and are in perfect health to the eighth. Then the fever begins to seize them, and they keep their beds two days, very seldom three. Every year thousands undergo this operation. . . . There is no example of anyone that has died in it; and you may believe I am very well satisfied of the safety of this experiment, since I intend to try it on my dear little son.

After Lady Mary Wortley Montagu returned to England in 1718, she used her influence at court to continue her campaign in favor of inoculation. Partly because of Lady Mary's persistence, a great many English doctors began to inoculate their patients with smallpox serum. But the procedure was not so harmless as it appeared, and the cases so induced were not always mild ones—in fact, a number of inoculated persons died. Moreover, it appeared that even the mild cases were contagious; there were soon more cases of smallpox in England than there had been for years. Inoculation against smallpox was obviously not the way to stop its spread.

While these grim discoveries were being made, Edward Jenner was growing up in Gloucestershire. The son of a clergyman, he had been carefully educated in the classics by his father. But his real interest lay in the life of the country—in the doings of cuckoos, robins, bats, and porcupines. He liked to write verses, and he was especially proud of one called "Address to a Robin" and of another called "Signs of Rain." Poetry and music were equally attractive to him. He loved to sing and could play both the violin and the flute.

When the time came for young Edward Jenner to choose a career, he decided that he would not leave Gloucestershire. He would be a country doctor who practiced among the farmers. In Gloucestershire, Jenner began working as an apprentice to Dr. Daniel Ludlow, and it was then that Jenner's idea occurred to him. In 1790 a dairymaid came to the surgery for treatment and young Jenner heard her say, "I couldn't have the smallpox because I have had cowpox."

The remark stayed in Jenner's memory, and he began to investigate further. There was a general belief among the country people that anyone who milked a cow infected with cowpox was rendered immune to smallpox. Yet cowpox, when it was contracted, was a very slight illness and, so far as Jenner could find out, it could not be communicated from one person to another.

For several years Jenner thought the thing over as he rode through the country, paying calls with Dr. Ludlow, or helped with the patients in the surgery.

In 1796 he tried his first experiment in vaccination.[1] A girl

[1] The word *vaccine* comes from the Latin *vaccinus*, meaning "of or from cows." In Latin, *vacca* means "cow."

named Sarah Nelmes came to the surgery, with her hand infected from milking a cow. Jenner examined the skin of the hand and found small circular elevations that were filled with a clear, watery fluid. It was evident that Sarah Nelmes had cowpox.

Carefully the young Jenner extracted a little of the watery fluid and put it into two small scratches on the arm of a healthy boy, James Phipps. Then he waited for several days.

But James Phipps did not become sick. The two small scratches Jenner had made were circled with a red ring—then they healed.

In July Jenner inoculated the boy with lymph from a vesicle of a smallpox patient. To his great satisfaction he found that the boy was immune to smallpox.

It was May 14, 1796, when Jenner made that first vaccination. Soon afterward he wrote: "The joy I felt at the prospect before me of being the instrument destined to take away from the world one of its greatest calamities . . . was so excessive that I sometimes found myself in a kind of revery."

He talked continually of his discovery—but to country people it was no surprise, and the medical men were completely uninterested. In fact, they became so tired of hearing him harp on the same subject that they threatened to put him out of the Convivio Medical Club, as the local medical society was called.

In 1798 he decided to stop talking and publish his discovery in a pamphlet. Its title was given as *An Inquiry into the Cause and Effects of the Variolae Vaccinae. A Disease Discovered in the Western Counties of England.*[2] The pamphlet was seventy pages long and had a number of illustrations. In it he explained that cowpox, swine pox, and the disease called "grease" in horses were the same thing, and that lymph developed in these diseases might be used in the prevention of smallpox. He showed, most importantly, that a person who had been "vaccinated" was not infectious to others and that matter from a pustule developed in this way could be used to vaccinate others.

Later that same year Jenner went to London to try to find a patient that he could vaccinate and, therefore, attract the interest of the London doctors. But in three months he could not find a single patient who would let himself be vaccinated.

[2] *Variolae vaccinae* was cowpox.

61

Then, accidentally, he succeeded. There was a boy in St. Thomas's Hospital in London who was suffering from hip-joint disease. His physician had tried, unsuccessfully, every treatment he could think of. Jenner had a quill filled with cowpox lymph that he had kept for three months. The physician decided to inoculate the boy's hip with that—thinking, probably, that he would leave no stone unturned.

Jenner's vaccine did not, of course, cure the hip-joint disease, but some time later they inoculated the boy with small-pox and found to their great satisfaction that he was immune.

Recognition came after that. Gradually Jenner was accepted by the medical profession in England, was given an audience by the king and queen, and was receiving letters from various parts of England telling of successful vaccinations. One letter from a doctor in Hadleigh, Suffolk, is typical.

I am happy to inform you that in spite of ignorant prejudice, and wilful misrepresentation, this wonderful discovery is spreading far and wide in this country. The first people we vaccinated in Hadleigh were pelted, and drove into their houses, if they appeared out. We have now persuaded our apothecary to vaccinate the whole town (700 or 800 persons). . . . A physician at Ipswich has taken it up in a very liberal manner.

In America the idea spread faster than it did in England. At first there was some doubt. Some of the lymph that Jenner sent to America was spoiled in transit, and people ridiculed the idea of using matter from a cow to prevent a human disease. One cartoonist drew a picture of some vaccinated children who had the faces of cows. But Vice-President Thomas Jefferson became interested in Jenner's discovery and had himself and all his household vaccinated. He wrote:

Medicine has never before produced any single improvement of such utility. . . . You have erased from the calendar of human afflictions one of its greatest. Yours is the comfortable reflection that mankind can never forget that you have lived; future nations will know by history only that the loathsome smallpox has existed, and by you been extirpated.

Now in America there was a great rush for the new preventive treatment. Everyone wanted to be vaccinated at once. The process was not always successful. Sometimes the lymph, which was kept in quills, was carelessly prepared and ineffectual. But this was the exception to the general rule. Usually the vaccinations achieved their results: the vaccinated people were immune to smallpox. People in larger and larger numbers were using Jenner's vaccine. Before Thomas Jefferson retired in 1809, millions of people around the world had been vaccinated.

In Canada the Indians of the Five Nations, who inhabited the Eastern woodlands and who had suffered terribly from smallpox, discovered the new process of vaccination with joy. They held a special council to compose a letter of thanks to Jenner and sent him presents. The Indians wrote:

We shall not fail to teach our children to speak the name of Jenner, and to thank the Great Spirit for bestowing upon him so much wisdom and so much benevolence. We send with this a belt, and a string of wampum in token of our acceptance of your precious gift; and we beseech the Great Spirit to take care of you in this world and in the land of the Spirits.

Faster and faster the news of the smallpox vaccine spread around the world, and eager men, women, and children bared their arms for the scratch that would provide an opening for the vaccine. Sometimes Jenner was haunted by the fear that carelessness and the "extreme ignorance of medical men in vaccination" would prevent the world from reaping the full benefit of his discovery, but on the whole he had good news from wherever it was tried.

In 1801 the British government had the whole fleet and garrison at Gibraltar vaccinated. And after that all the soldiers and seamen on Sir Ralph Abercrombie's Egyptian expedition were vaccinated.

In Spain, under the king's orders, a fleet was fitted out to sail to all the Spanish colonies in the Old World and the New so that every subject of the Spanish king might have the boon of vaccination. The ships of this fleet carried twenty-two children aboard who had been inoculated, to keep up the strain of lymph, since Jenner had found that the lymph need not necessarily be taken directly from the cow. The expedition was gone three years and visited, among other places, Buenos Aires, Mexico, and the Philippines. In every harbor the vessels were greeted with excitement and hope.

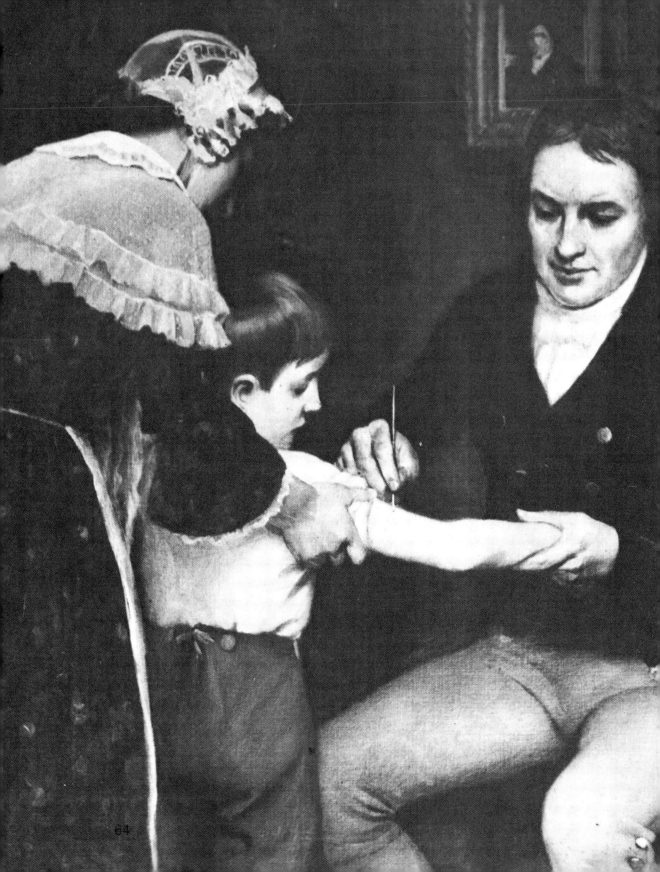

Jenner's reputation continued to grow, and his discovery was considered to be the most important medical advance of all time. The empress of Russia sent him a valuable diamond ring, with a laudatory letter.

The great Napoleon wrote: "Ah, it is Jenner. I cannot refuse Jenner anything."

Jenner had not wanted to make any capital from his discovery. What he desired most was to follow a quiet career as a country physician. But he must have been pleased when the British government gave him a grant of ten thousand pounds (later another twenty thousand pounds was added to this). In characteristic fashion he wanted to use part of this money to fit out a ship that would carry vaccine to India and Ceylon—an undertaking that proved unnecessary, for the governor of Bombay had already applied for sufficient vaccine through Lord Elgin, the British diplomat, who was touring India.

Always, as time passed, there were detractors who said that Jenner had made no discovery, that vaccination amounted to nothing. And always the practice spread and spread. A great sheaf of letters arrived in Jenner's mail from everywhere.

One of them, from a country parson in England, was typical of all the rest. "A few years ago I was in the habit of burying two or three children every evening in the spring and autumn who had died of smallpox, but now the disease has entirely ceased."

So the village doctor who had written his "Address to a Robin" and his verses on "Signs of Rain," the young man who had loved to play his flute and his violin, who had chatted with farmhands and listened to the talk of dairymaids, had made his contribution. It is said that there are doctors now who have never seen a case of smallpox, and credit for this fact may be given to Edward Jenner.

Yet when this is said, it must be added that Jenner never truly understood the cause of the disease that he was seeking to prevent, nor did he contribute anything toward its treatment. What he did was to stumble on a preventive for the dreaded sickness and to persuade the public that they had a responsibility for using it. Those scientists and doctors who followed him were to pry deeper into the causes and thereby discover principles that would apply to many kinds of virulent disease.

Russell Freedman

Bald Eagles

She was hungry. Her parents had stopped bringing food to the nest, and for two days she hadn't eaten. Now she felt restless and irritable. She opened her wings, flapped them noisily, and rose several feet into the air. Then she dropped back down to the floor of the nest.

Her brother chirped and jumped to one side. They were the same age, nearly three months old, but she was bigger than he and bolder, too. He tried to keep out of her way.

Soon they saw their mother's white head gleaming in the sun as she flew toward them over the treetops. Clutched in her talons was a large fish. Excited, the two eaglets hopped up on the edge of the nest and chirped loudly, calling out to their mother.

She circled above them, calling back with throaty cackles—
carruck, carruck, carruck—but she didn't land in the nest.
Instead she flew twice around it and settled in a nearby tree.
Holding the fish with her talons, she tore off chunks of flesh
with her curved yellow beak, lifted her head, and gulped down
each piece. The hungry eaglets leaned over the edge of the
nest, crying and complaining as they watched their mother eat.

When she finished, she picked bits of food from her scaly
yellow legs and toes. Then she cleaned her beak, rubbing it
against a branch, and flew away.

The male eaglet hopped back into the nest. He pounced on a
twig and jabbed at it with his beak. Then he fluffed his feathers
and started to preen them. His sister remained, perched on the
edge of the nest, staring at the wilderness valley far below.

The nest, or eyrie, was a massive platform of branches and
sticks perched high atop a cottonwood tree, one hundred feet
above the ground. It had been built years before by the eaglets'
parents, who were lifetime mates. In this remote valley, far
from the dangers of civilization, they had raised several broods
of healthy young.

Every spring the adults returned to their nest and repaired
and enlarged it with more branches and sticks. By now it was
taller than a standing man and just as wide across, with walls
about two feet thick. Pine needles, feathers, and down padded
its spacious floor.

The eaglets had hatched in May. Now they were almost as
big as their parents. From tip to tip their outstretched wings
measured nearly six feet. But they still didn't know how to fly.
They had never left their gigantic treetop nest.

Several times that morning their parents had circled the nest
with food, trying to coax the eaglets out. Now the young female
leaned forward from her perch, watching the river that rushed
through the valley below. With her sharp eyes she could see
fish leap from the water, then disappear in the swirling rapids.

She leaned forward a bit more. The wind rippled her sooty
brown feathers; her dark eyes glowed. Suddenly she jumped.
As her feet left the nest, she stretched her neck, opened her
wings, and flapped them hard. She was flying through the air.
For the first time in her life, the eagle was flying!

A rising current of air swept her over the treetops, carrying her higher and higher. Now she hardly moved her wings at all as she glided easily across the river and over a grassy meadow beyond.

Then she began to lose altitude. She found herself sinking, and again she flapped her wings. She zigzagged up, then veered sharply down. The ground came closer and closer; a strong wind pushed her from behind. Pumping her wings frantically, she bumped into the meadow and tumbled head over claw through the grass.

Where was she? She scrambled to her feet and looked around. In the distance, on the other side of the river, she saw the nest. Overhead, circling and calling, she saw her parents. She shook herself, fluffed her feathers, and settled down on her stomach to rest.

She sat there for quite some time, poking about in the grass. Her parents perched in a nearby tree, standing guard.

After a while she stood up and tried to take off. She flapped her wings and jumped, but she rose only a few feet. She tried again and still dropped back to the ground. Finally she began to run across the meadow, flapping hopefully, and this time her wings carried her into the air.

Heading home, she made short, uncertain hops from tree to tree. When she finally reached the nest, her tired wings drooped heavily at her sides.

Her brother was gone. He had flown as far as a neighboring tree, where he sat, calling.

From then on, she and her brother left their nest every day. As they practiced flying, their muscles grew stronger and their flights longer. Gradually they learned to steer by using their fan-shaped tails as rudders and by adjusting the flight feathers on their broad, sweeping wings. They learned to land against the wind, pointing their tails down and pulling their wings back as brakes. And they learned to catch long, lazy rides on the warm air currents that drifted upward from the ground.

At first they stayed close to their parents, flying just behind them. Although they were nearly as big as the adults, they didn't look exactly like them. Their parents had sooty brown plumage and pure white heads and tails. The young eagles were dark brown all over, except for whitish patches on their wings. They would not develop the distinctive white head feathers of mature bald eagles until they were four or five years old. Their eyes and beaks were dark instead of yellow.

When they weren't flying, the young eagles spent most of their time in the nest. Once again their parents brought food, but they were also learning how to hunt.

One morning the young female followed her father to a lookout post, a tall tree beside the river. From their lofty perch they watched fish leaping and darting in a shallow pool at the river's edge.

Suddenly the father eagle dropped from his branch. He opened his wings, swooped down toward the river, and turned sharply. Water splashed up against his belly and wings as he skimmed over the surface, reaching down into the water with his talons. When he flew up again, he clutched a wriggling fish.

The young female tried fishing for herself, but at first she had little luck. The fish moved swiftly; as she swooped down on them, she had to check her speed and strike the surface with perfect timing. Otherwise she grabbed nothing but clawfuls of water. Sometimes she hit the water with such force that she tumbled over and drenched herself.

While they preferred fish, the eagles also hunted other prey. The young birds learned to search for wild ducks among the bushes and reeds of the river marshes. They followed their parents beyond the river, scouting meadows and mountains for squirrels, rabbits, and other small animals. Their vision was about eight times sharper than a human's, and they could spot a rabbit from a mile away. They learned to watch and wait, hovering in the sky until their prey was out in the open. Then they would fold their wings and plummet toward earth as the frightened animal ran for cover.

As birds of prey, the eagles needed meat to survive and usually spent the morning hunting, satisfying their appetites by noon. If the day was dark and overcast, or if there were no winds, they might spend all afternoon perched silently in trees. But in good flying weather they rode air currents for hours, until it was time to roost.

At dusk they settled down for the night. The young eagles no longer slept in the nest. Instead they perched on branches. Standing on one leg, with their heads buried in their shoulder feathers, they slept until dawn. Like most bald eagles, they often snored.

As autumn arrived, the young eagles spent less and less time with their parents. They were nearly six months old now, and they were expert hunters—catching all their own food.

One morning, when the young female woke up, her brother was gone. Her parents had flown upriver several days earlier and hadn't returned. A light snow had fallen during the night, dusting the trees and ground with white. Thin crusts of ice glittered along the edges of the river.

The eagle called loudly to greet the morning. She shook herself, fluffed her feathers, and combed them carefully with her beak. When she had finished her preening, she dropped from her perch, spread her wings, and flew upward into the sky.

She flew over the treetops, past the nest where she had hatched, and across the river she knew so well. When she had climbed high above the valley floor, she banked and made a wide turn. Then she headed south, following the path of the river. Her strong wings carried her toward the unknown mountains in the distance beyond.

The Gift Pig by Joan Aiken

Joan Aiken remembers that her home in England was filled with what she has called "an immense supply of books." Reading aloud was also an important activity in her family. Always wanting to be a writer, she began her career at the age of five. Some of her later stories came out of the tales she had told a younger brother on their walks together in the English countryside. Her first work was published when she was seventeen—a story broadcast on a children's show produced by the British Broadcasting Corporation.

Once upon a time there was a King whose Queen, having just presented him with a baby princess, unfortunately died. The King was very upset and grieved, but he had to go on with the arrangements for the christening just the same, as court etiquette was strict on this point. What with his grief and distraction, however, and the yells of the royal baby, who was extremely lively and loud-voiced, the invitations to the christening were sent out very carelessly, and by mistake the list included two elderly fairies who were well known to loathe the very sight of one another, though when seen alone they were pleasant enough.

The day of the christening arrived, and at first all went well. The baby princess was christened Henrietta and behaved properly, crying a little but not too much. Then the guests strolled back to the palace for the reception, and the King noticed with horror that the two elderly fairies were walking side by side. They seemed to be nodding and smiling in the most friendly way, but when the King edged nearer to them, he heard one say:

"Really, my dear Bella, do you think it wise for you to come out in this chilly weather? You walk with such a limp! I wish you had asked me to wheel you in your chair."

"How sweet of you, my dearest Gorgonzola, but could you manage it? Didn't you celebrate your hundredth birthday last week? And in any case, I don't have a wheelchair."

"No? You surprise me. And what surprises me still more is to see you in the palace of this commonplace King—can it be that you are now so poor you have to go anywhere on the chance of a free meal?"

"Hardly that, my dear Gorgonzola. I came out of politeness. I confess I didn't expect to see *you* here. I understood the King only invited intelligent and progressive people."

The poor King made haste to cut the cake in the hope of sweetening these acid ladies.

Presently the guests, fairy and otherwise, began to bring forward their gifts. The baby, pink and good in her cradle, was given silver and coral rattles, bonnets and bootees by the basketful, mountains of matinee jackets and mittens, stacks of embroidered smocks and knitted socks. Besides these, she was endowed with good health, a friendly disposition, a cheerful nature, intelligence, and a logical mind.

Then the fairy Bella stepped forward and, smiling sweetly at the King, said, "You will forgive me if my gift is not quite so pleasant as some of the preceding ones, but meeting such low company in your palace has made me forget myself a little. Let the princess rue the day that someone gives her a pig, for when that happens, she will turn into one herself."

"Moreover," said the fairy Gorgonzola, "she will marry someone with only one leg."

"Wait a minute, you insolent person. I hadn't finished. The princess will lose her inheritance—"

"I was going to say that there will be a revolution—"

"*Will* you please be quiet. There will *not* be a revolution—at least the princess herself will be lost long before that occurs—and she will be poor and unknown and have to work for her living."

"And she will marry someone who has spent all his life in the open."

"Oh, for goodness' sake! Didn't I just say she would marry someone with only one leg?"

"The two things aren't mutually exclusive."

"You don't very often find agricultural workers with only one leg."

"Ladies, ladies," said the King miserably, but not daring to be too abrupt with them, "you have done enough harm to my poor child. Will you please continue your quarrel somewhere else?"

The feuding fairies left, and the King hung with tears in his eyes over his beautiful pink baby, wondering what, if anything, he could do to avert the various bits of evil fortune that were coming to her. The only thing that seemed to lie within his power was to keep a strict watch over her presents, in order to make sure that she was never given a pig.

When Henrietta was five years old her cousin Lord Edwin Fitzlion came to stay with her. He was a spoiled, wild boy of about the same age; he was the seventh son of a seventh son, but his brothers were all much older and had gone off into the world, his father was a big-game hunter and never at home, while his mother had grown tired of looking after boys and had gone off on a three-year cruise. Lord Edwin had been left in the care of the butler.

He was very beautiful, with dark velvety eyes and black hair; much better-looking than his fat pink cousin, he was inclined to tease her.

One day he overheard two footmen discussing the fairies' pronouncements about her, and he became consumed with curiosity as to whether she would really turn into a pig if she were given one. He longed to give her a pig and find out. There were difficulties about bringing pigs into the palace, but at last he managed to buy one from a heavily bribed farmer and smuggled it in, wrapped up in his jacket. He let it loose in the nursery and then rushed in search of Henrietta.

"Henry! Come quick, I've brought a present for you."

"Oh, where?"

"In the nursery! Hurry up!"

With rare politeness he stood aside to let her go first, and heard her squeak of joy as she ran through the door:

Then, there was silence, except for squeaks, and when he went in he found two dear little pigs, absolutely identical, rubbing noses in the most friendly way.

Lord Edwin was sent home in disgrace. His parents were still away (in fact, they never again came home), and he ran wild and spent all his time in the woods, riding his eldest brother's horse Bayard and flying his next brother's falcon Ger. One day when he was in the forest he saw a large hare on the bank of a pool. Quickly he unhooded the falcon, when the hare suddenly spoke:

Don't do it! You'll be sorry if you do.

"Oh, who cares for you," said Edwin rudely, and he loosed Ger. But the falcon, instead of towering up and then dropping on the hare, flew slantwise and then turned and made for home. Edwin's eyes followed the bird in annoyance and disappointment. When he looked back he saw that the hare had become a little old woman.

"You are a spoiled, disobedient boy," she said. "I know all about you, and what you did to your cousin. You can stay where you are, learning better manners, until a Home Secretary comes to rescue you."

No one had been fond of Edwin, so no one missed him or asked where he was.

The King was heartbroken when he learned what had happened to his daughter. Many tests were carried out on the two little pigs to try and discover which was the princess. They were put in little beds with peas under the mattresses, but both rummaged out the peas and ate them during the night. Two dishes, one of pearls, one of potato peelings, were placed in front of them, in the hope that the princess would prefer the pearls, but they both dived unhesitatingly for the potato peelings. The first pig breeders in the land were brought to gaze at them, but with no result; they were two pink, handsome little pigs, and that was all that could be said about them.

"Well," said the King finally, "one of them is my daughter, and she must receive the education due to a princess. Someday she will be restored to her proper shape (we know this because she is going to marry a one-legged man)—"

"The fairy didn't actually say a *man* with one leg," someone pointed out.

"Well, what else could it be—you've never seen a *pig* with one leg. Anyway, she must have a proper education. It would be terrible if she were restored to human form and only had the knowledge of a child of five."

So the two little pigs sat seriously and attentively side by side on two little chairs and were taught and lectured by a series of learned tutors and erudite schoolmistresses. No one could tell if any of the teaching sank in, for they merely sat and gazed. If they were asked questions, they grunted.

One day when the pigs were about fifteen the King came into the schoolroom.

"Hullo, my dears," he said, "how are you today?" He patted his daughter and her friend and sat down wearily in an armchair, to watch while they had their lunch. Affairs of state were becoming very tiring to him.

A footman brought in two little blue bowls of pig mash on a silver tray. The pigs' eyes gleamed, and they let out piercing squeals and began to rush about frantically, bumping into tables and chairs and each other. Their governess firmly collared them one at a time, tied a frilly bib around each neck, and strapped them into two high chairs. Their bowls were put in front of them, and instantly there was such a guzzling and a slupping and greedy slobbering that no one could hear a word for five minutes until the bowls were empty. Then the little pigs looked up again, brimming with satisfaction, their faces encircled by rings of mash.

The footman wiped their faces clean with a cloth-of-gold facecloth. Then they were let out into the garden to play and could be seen whisking around and around the trees and chasing each other up and down the paths.

The King sighed.

"It's no use," he said. "One must face facts. My daughter Henrietta is not an ordinary princess. And her friend Hermione — whichever of them is which — is a very ordinary little pig. I am afraid that no prince, even a one-legged one, would ask for Henrietta's hand in marriage after seeing her eat her lunch. We must send them to a finishing school. They've had plenty of intellectual education — at least I suppose they have — it's time they acquired a bit of polish."

So the two pigs were packed off (in hampers) to Miss Dorothea Foulkes' Select Finishing School for the Daughters of the Monarchy and Aristocracy.

At first all went well. The King received monthly reports which informed him that his daughter (and her friend) had learned to walk downstairs with books on their heads, to enter and leave rooms gracefully, get in and out of motors with dignity and elegance, play the piano and the harp, waltz, embroider, and ride sidesaddle.

"Well, I always heard that Miss Foulkes was a marvel," said the King, shaking his head in astonishment, "but I never thought anyone could teach a pig to ride sidesaddle. I can't wait to see them."

He had to wait though, for Miss Foulkes strictly forbade the parents of her pupils to come and visit them while they were being put through her course of training. The reason for this was that she had to treat the girls with such frightful severity in order to drill the necessary elegance and deportment into them that, if they had had the chance, they would have implored their parents to take them away. Letters home were always dictated by Miss Foulkes herself, so there was no opportunity of complaining by mail, and at the end of the course the debutantes were so grateful for their beautiful poise that all was forgotten and forgiven.

Miss Foulkes nearly met her Waterloo in Henrietta and Hermione.

She managed to teach them tennis and bridge, but she could not teach them flower arrangement. The two pigs had no taste for it — they always ate the flowers.

One day they had been spanked and sent out into the garden in disgrace for eating a large bundle of roses and sweet peas instead of building them into a table center. Sore, bewildered, and miserable, they wandered down the dreary gravel paths, and then simultaneously the notion came to them—why not run away? They wriggled through the hedge at the bottom of the garden and disappeared.

Instead of a final report on deportment the King had a note from Miss Foulkes saying:

"I regret to announce that your daughter and her friend have committed the unpardonable social blunder of running away from my establishment. The police have been informed, and will no doubt recover them for you in due course. Since this behavior shows that my tuition has been thrown away on them your fees are returned herewith. (Check for £10,000 encl.) Your obdt. srvt. Dorothea Foulkes."

In spite of all efforts the police failed to trace the two little pigs. Advertisements in newspapers and on radio and television, pictures outside police stations, offers of rewards, all brought no replies. The King was in terror, imagining his daughter and her friend innocently running into a bacon factory. He gave up all attempt at governing and spent his time going from farm to farm gazing mournfully at all the pigs in the hope of recognizing Henrietta and her friend.

The two pigs had not gone very far—in fact, no farther than the garden of the house next door to Miss Foulkes. They were rooting peacefully (but elegantly because their training had stuck) near the front gate when they saw a young man in a white coat coming down the path from the house escorting a young woman.

"And don't forget," she was saying earnestly, "all the last experimental results are in the stack under the five-gram weight, and the milk for the tea is in the test tube at the left-hand end of the right-hand rack, and the baby amoeba wants feeding again at five. Now I must fly or my fiancé will be worrying."

"Good-by, Miss Sparks," said the young man crossly, and he slammed the gate behind her. "Why in the name of goodness do all my assistants have to quit? I haven't kept one longer than three months in the last three years."

Then his eye fell on the two pigs, who were staring at him attentively.

"Pigs," he mused. "I wonder if pigs could be taught to do the work? Pigs might not be so apt to quit. Pigs, would you like a job as research assistants?"

The pigs liked his face, which was a friendly one, and followed him into his house, where he proceeded to instruct them in the research work he was doing.

"I shall have to teach you to talk, though," he told them. "I can't put up with assistants who grunt all the time."

He left his other work and devoted himself to teaching them. At the end of a week he had succeeded, for he was a scientist *and* a philosopher, besides being a very brilliant man. Nobody had ever considered teaching the pigs to talk before.

When they could speak, the professor asked their names.

"One of us is Henrietta and one is Hermione, but we are not sure which," they told him.

"In that case I shall call you Miss X and Miss Y. Miss X, you will look after making the tea, feeding the amoeba, and filing the microscope slides. Miss Y, you will turn away all visitors, polish the microscope, and make notes of my experiments."

The two pigs now found their education most useful. They could carry piles of books on their heads, curtsy to callers as they showed them the door, write notes in a neat little round hand, and play the piano to soothe the professor if the experiments were not going well. They were all very happy together, and the professor often said that he had never before had such useful and talented assistants.

One day, after several years had passed by, the professor raised his eye from the microscope, rubbed his forehead, looked at Miss Y industriously taking notes and Miss X busily putting away the slides, and said, "Pigs, it occurs to me to wonder if you are really human beings turned into your present useful, if unornamental, form?"

"One of us is," replied Miss X, tucking her pencil behind her ear, "but we don't know which."

"It would be easy enough to change you back," the professor remarked. "I wonder I never thought of it before. I'll just switch on the cosmic ray and rearrange your molecules."

"Which of us?"

"You can both try, and I expect nothing will happen to one of you."

"Shall we like that?" said the pigs to each other. "We're used to being together."

"Oh, come on," exclaimed the professor impatiently, "if one of you is really human, it's her plain duty to change back, and the other one shouldn't stand in her way."

Thus admonished, the pigs walked in front of the ray, and both immediately turned into young ladies with pink faces, turned-up noses, fair hair, and intelligent blue eyes.

"Dear me," remarked the professor, "that ray must be more powerful than I had thought. We seem to be back where we were."

As the young ladies still did not know which of them was which, they continued to be called Miss X and Miss Y, and as they were very happy in their work, they continued to help the professor.

One day Miss Y saw a large number of callers coming to the front door, and though she did her best to turn them back, they poured in and overflowed into the laboratory.

"Professor," said the spokesman, "we are the leaders of the revolution, and we have come to ask you to be first President of our new republic, as you are undoubtedly the wisest man in the country."

"Tut, tut," said the professor, frowning, "why have you revolted, and what have you done with the King?"

"Oh, we revolted because it was the fashionable thing to do—all the other countries have done it already—and the King has retired already and taken to farming. But now please step into the carriage, which is waiting outside, and we will take you to the new President's residence."

"If I accept," said the professor, "I must have unlimited time to pursue my own research."

"Yes, yes, you will have to do very little governing—just keep an eye on things and see that justice and reason prevail. You can appoint anyone you like to whatever government positions you wish."

"In that case I shall appoint my two assistants, Miss X and Miss Y, to be in charge of home and foreign affairs respectively. No one could be more efficient."

The professor and Miss X and Miss Y were driven to the new President's residence, which turned out to be none other than the ancestral home of the Fitzlion family, where Edwin had once run wild in the woods. After drafting some very sensible acts, Miss X, the Secretary of State for Home Affairs, took a stroll in the woods, for when she was a pig she had been very fond of acorns, and she still took an absent-minded pleasure in putting them in her pockets.

She had not gone far when she stood still and listened attentively. It seemed to her that one of the trees was sighing and sobbing.

"Are you in distress?" she said to the tree kindly. "Can I help you?"

"Oh, if only you could!" the tree lamented. "Many years ago I was turned into a tree as a punishment for my bad behavior, and I am so terribly bored in these woods! But only a Home Secretary can help me."

"I am a Home Secretary."

"You! You are much too charming to be a Home Secretary," said the tree in astonishment. Miss X beamed. No one had spoken to her like this before.

The new President was looking through his microscope that evening when Miss X came to see him, starry-eyed.

"I've fallen in love," she announced.

The professor sighed. "It was bound to happen sooner or later. With whom?"

"With an enchanted tree in the woods. I wish you would turn your cosmic ray on him and change him back into a human being."

"By and by," grumbled the professor, "when we've got this present series of experiments finished." He wanted to make sure of his assistant for as long as possible.

However, Miss X and the tree were so much in love that they got the archbishop to come and marry them, and when the professor saw that they were in earnest he trundled his cosmic ray projector out into the forest and turned it on the tree, which at once became a handsome young man, while a raven who had been sitting on one of its branches turned into an elderly fairy.

"Tampering with the laws of nature, I call it," she said, looking sourly at the ray projector. "Anyway, at least Lord Edwin's learned some manners now, though that princess is still as plain a person as ever I saw."

Muttering crossly to herself, the fairy Gorgonzola flapped away, and now, of course, Henrietta knew who she was, and also realized that she had fulfilled the prophecies by marrying a man with one leg who had lived all his life in the open.

Arm in arm the happy couple went off to visit the old King, who was perfectly contented on his farm and thankful to have left off governing. He was delighted to see his daughter again.

"I am sure that you young people can manage very well without me, and Henrietta will make just as good a Home Secretary as she would a Queen. As for me, I have got into the habit of looking at pigs, and I much prefer to go on doing so." And he scratched the back of a large black pig.

So Lord Edwin became Prime Minister (having learned tact and diplomatic manners during his long spell as a tree). Miss Y, who was now known to be Hermione, married the professor, and they all lived happily ever after.

THE GREAT CRAWL FORWARD

"I've been a boxing promoter for over thirty years."
"I demonstrate equipment in a sporting goods store."
"I'm a newspaper sportswriter."
"I head the largest basketball scouting service in the United States."
"I am a baseball umpire."
"I produce TV sports programs."
"I train race horses."

What do the speakers have in common? First, they all love sports and hold jobs in this field. Second, they are not athletes. Third, they are all women.

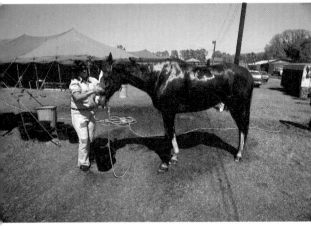

For years, sports jobs were held almost exclusively by men. Then, some twenty years ago, this all-male stronghold began to crumble. From buyers of sports equipment in department stores to coaches to TV sportscasters, and from university to professional sports fields, women began entering the ranks. And the trend continues today. But the change has been slow to take place—as one woman sports pioneer describes it, "It has been like a great crawl forward." Heated controversy still surrounds women entering the sports world. Some people oppose women. Others welcome them. Both sides offer reasons.

For example, those who oppose the idea of women in sports say that sports is a specialized field and that women lack the necessary training and experience. They stress that since many women have never played basketball or football, they don't really understand these sports. "How can a woman interview a football player without knowing the game—inside and out?" asks a sportswriter. "To be respected in the field means having the facts at your fingertips in order to make decisions and give expert comments." "It takes years to acquire these skills. Women simply don't have the background." Such comments are made by people in the field who regard women as intruders. They add that women just can't take the physical punishment of some sports. It's not unusual for a baseball umpire to get hit with a flying bat or a ball speeding at 100 miles per hour. It's tough and dangerous work for a man. Can a woman take this kind of abuse?

No, a woman can't. But a man can't take that kind of abuse either. Being hit by a speeding ball would slow down any human being. And as far as having facts at fingertips, there are thousands of dedicated female sports fans all over the country who can quote football and tennis and baseball statistics as well as any male.

There are many people who strongly favor women entering the sports field. They know that women can grasp sports basics as well as the veteran men have. "Anyway," comments a well-known newspaper sportswriter, "too many men consider sports a matter of life and death. Many women don't. So they lend a refreshing point of view to sports." In addition, more women in sports jobs will likely mean that more attention will be paid to female athletes and women's sports events.

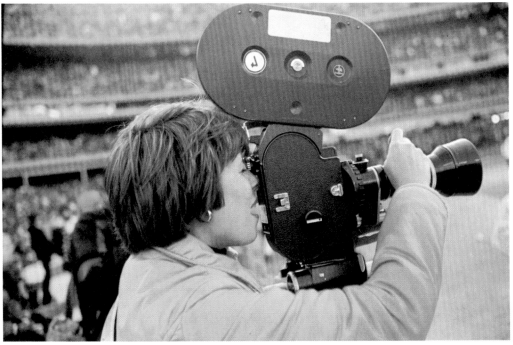

The women in question, those who have made it into the field as well as those who are still trying, speak of prejudice all along the way. "I always feel I have to prove something because I am a woman and everyone's eyes are on me. I feel a double responsibility," comments a sports magazine editor. "At first coaches were reluctant to ask a woman about pressure defenses," says a basketball scout. "It's changing gradually, though." Women also complain of being paid less than men in the same jobs. Yet all agree that, in spite of the hardships, a real love of the game gives them the determination to stick with the job.

Do you have a love of the game? Do you feel the lure of a nonathletic sports career? "If so," says a woman TV sports producer, "get as much basic training in your field as you can." If you want to report sports, learn the basics of writing and public speaking. If it's TV producing that interests you, develop a background in communications. If you want to sell sports equipment, study marketing and selling. A business background would be invaluable to someone interested in professional sports management. Today it is even possible to obtain a college degree in sports administration, qualifying people for jobs in colleges, high schools, parks, and community centers as well as with professional teams. Or if you would like to be behind home plate calling the strikes, then play the game and study it. You may feel like you're "crawling forward" too, but one day, unexpectedly, it may all pay off.

Daria Witt

i should have caught my unicorn when i was

i should have caught my unicorn when i was
sixteen
because to catch a unicorn you have to
trust
and believe
and love
all with an astonishing measure of innocence.
they're crafty beasts, unicorns,
with thin legs and thick manes
and some people say
their horns are gold.
i've lost my chance to catch my unicorn
now
I'm too old
and too
caught
myself.

James Thurber

The Night the Ghost Got In

The ghost that got into our house on the night of November 17, 1915, raised such a hullabaloo of misunderstandings that I am sorry I didn't just let it keep on walking, and go to bed. Its advent caused my mother to throw a shoe through a window of the house next door and ended up with my grandfather shooting a patrolman. I am sorry, therefore, as I have said, that I ever paid any attention to the footsteps.

They began about a quarter past one o'clock in the morning, a rhythmic, quick-cadenced walking around the dining-room table. My mother was asleep in one room upstairs, my brother Herman in another; grandfather was in the attic in the old walnut bed, which once fell on my father. I had just stepped out of the bathtub and was busily rubbing myself with a towel when I heard the steps. They were the steps of a man walking rapidly around the dining-room table downstairs. The light from the bathroom shone down the back steps, which dropped directly into the dining-room; I could see the faint shine of plates on the plate-rail; I couldn't see the table. The steps kept going round and round the table; at regular intervals a board creaked, when it was trod upon. I supposed at first that it was my father or my brother Roy, who had gone to Indianapolis but were expected home at any time. I suspected next that it was a burglar. It did not enter my mind until later that it was a ghost.

After the walking had gone on for perhaps three minutes, I tiptoed to Herman's room. "Psst!" I hissed, in the dark, shaking him. "Awp," he said in the low, hopeless tone of a despondent beagle — he always half suspected that something would "get him" in the night. I told him who I was. "There's something downstairs!" I said. He got up and followed me to the head of the back staircase. We listened together. There was no sound. The steps had ceased. Herman looked at me in some alarm: I had only the bath towel around my waist. He wanted to go back to bed, but I gripped his arm. "There's something down there!" I said. Instantly the steps began again, circled the dining-room table like a man running, and started up the stairs toward us, heavily, two at a time. The light still shone palely down the stairs; we saw nothing coming; we only heard the steps. Herman rushed to his room and slammed the door. I slammed shut the door at the stairs top and held my knee against it. After a long minute, I slowly opened it again. There was nothing there. There was no sound. None of us ever heard the ghost again.

The slamming of the doors had aroused mother: she peered out of her room. "What on earth are you boys doing?"

she demanded. Herman ventured out of his room. "Nothing," he said, gruffly, but he was, in color, a light green. "What was all that running around downstairs?" said mother. So she had heard the steps, too! We just looked at her. "Burglars!" she shouted intuitively. I tried to quiet her by starting lightly downstairs.

"Come on, Herman," I said.

"I'll stay with mother," he said. "She's all excited."

"Don't either of you go a step," said mother. "We'll call the police." Since the phone was downstairs, I didn't see how we were going to call the police—nor did I want the police—but mother made one of her quick, incomparable decisions. She flung up a window of her bedroom which faced the bedroom windows of the house of a neighbor, picked up a shoe, and whammed it through a pane of glass across the narrow space that separated the two houses. Glass tinkled into the bedroom occupied by a retired engraver named Bodwell and his wife. Bodwell had been for some years in a rather bad way and was subject to mild "attacks." Most everybody we knew or lived near had *some* kind of attacks.

It was now about two o'clock of a moonless night; clouds hung black and low. Bodwell was at the window in a minute, shouting, frothing a little, shaking his fist. "We'll sell the house and go back to Peoria," we could hear Mrs. Bodwell saying. It was some time before mother "got through" to Bodwell. "Burglars!" she shouted. "Burglars in the house!" Herman and I hadn't dared to tell her that it was not burglars but ghosts, for she was even more afraid of ghosts than of burglars. Bodwell at first thought that she meant there were burglars in his house, but finally he quieted down and called the police for us over an extension phone by his bed. After he had disappeared from the window, mother suddenly made as if to throw another shoe, not because there was further need of it but, as she later explained, because the thrill of heaving a shoe through a window glass had enormously taken her fancy. I prevented her.

The police were on hand in a commendably short time; a Ford sedan full of them, two on motorcycles, and a patrol wagon with about eight in it and a few reporters. They began banging at our front door. Flashlights shot streaks of gleam up and down the walls, across the yard, down the walk between our house and Bodwell's. "Open up!" cried a hoarse voice. "We're men from Headquarters!" I wanted to go down and let them in, since there they were, but mother wouldn't hear of it. "You haven't a stitch on," she pointed out. "You'd catch your death." I wound the towel around me again. Finally the cops put their shoulders to our big heavy front door with its thick beveled glass and broke it in: I could hear a rending of wood and a splash of glass on the floor of the hall. Their lights played all over the living-room and criss-crossed nervously in the dining-room, stabbed into hallways, shot up the front stairs and finally up the back. They caught me standing in my towel at the top. A heavy policeman bounded up the steps. "Who are you?" he demanded. "I live here," I said. "Well, whattsa matta, ya hot?" he asked. It was, as a matter of fact, cold; I went to my room and pulled on some trousers. On my way out, a cop stuck a gun into my ribs. "Whatta you doin' here?" he demanded. "I live here," I said.

The officer in charge reported to mother. "No sign of nobody, lady," he said. "Musta got away — whatt'd he look like?" "There were two or three of them," mother said, "whooping and carrying on and slamming doors." "Funny," said the cop. "All ya windows and doors was locked on the inside tight as a tick."

Downstairs, we could hear the tromping of the other police. Police were all over the place; doors were yanked open, drawers were yanked open, windows were shot up and pulled down, furniture fell with dull thumps. A half-dozen policemen emerged out of the darkness of the front hallway upstairs. They began to ransack the floor: pulled beds away from walls, tore clothes off hooks in the closets, pulled suitcases and boxes off shelves. One of them found an old zither that Roy had won in a pool tournament. "Looky here, Joe," he said, strumming it with a big paw. The cop named Joe took it and turned it over. "What is it?" he asked me. "It's an old zither our guinea pig used to sleep on," I said. It was true that a pet guinea pig we once had would never sleep anywhere except on the zither, but I should never have said so. Joe and the other cop looked at me a long time. They put the zither back on a shelf.

"No sign o' nuthin'," said the cop who had first spoken to mother. "This guy," he explained to the others, jerking a thumb at me, "was nekked. The lady seems historical." They all nodded, but said nothing; just looked at me. In the small silence we all heard a creaking in the attic. Grandfather was turning over in bed. "What's 'at?" snapped Joe. Five or six cops sprang for the attic door before I could intervene or explain. I realized that it would be bad if they burst in on grandfather unannounced, or even announced. He was going through a phase in which he believed that General Meade's men, under steady hammering by Stonewall Jackson, were beginning to retreat and even desert.

When I got to the attic, things were pretty confused. Grandfather had evidently jumped to the conclusion that the police were deserters from Meade's army, trying to hide away in his attic. He bounded out of bed wearing a long flannel nightgown over long woolen underwear, a nightcap, and a leather jacket around his chest. The cops must have realized at once that the indignant white-haired old man belonged in the

house, but they had no chance to say so. "Back, ye cowardly
dogs!" roared grandfather. "Back t' the lines, ye lily-livered
cattle!" With that, he fetched the officer who found the zither
a flat-handed smack alongside his head that sent him sprawling. The others beat a retreat, but not fast enough; grandfather grabbed Zither's gun from its holster and let fly. The
report seemed to crack the rafters; smoke filled the attic. A
cop cursed and shot his hand to his shoulder. Somehow, we
all finally got downstairs again and locked the door against
the old gentleman. He fired once or twice more in the darkness and then went back to bed. "That was grandfather," I
explained to Joe, out of breath. "He thinks you're deserters."
"I'll say he does," said Joe.

102

The cops were reluctant to leave without getting their hands on somebody besides grandfather; the night had been distinctly a defeat for them. Furthermore, they obviously didn't like the "layout"; something looked—and I can see their viewpoint—phony. They began to poke into things again. A reporter, a thin-faced, wispy man, came up to me. I had put on one of mother's blouses, not being able to find anything else. The reporter looked at me with mingled suspicion and interest. "Just what is the real lowdown here, Bud?" he asked. I decided to be frank with him. "We had ghosts," I said. He gazed at me a long time as if I were a slot machine into which he had, without results, dropped a nickel. Then he walked away. The cops followed him, the one grandfather shot holding his now-bandaged arm, cursing and blaspheming. "I'm gonna get my gun back from that old bird," said the zither-cop. "Yeh," said Joe. "You—and who else?" I told them I would bring it to the station house the next day.

"What was the matter with that one policeman?" mother asked, after they had gone. "Grandfather shot him," I said. "What for?" she demanded. I told her he was a deserter. "Of all things!" said mother. "He was such a nice-looking young man."

Grandfather was fresh as a daisy and full of jokes at breakfast next morning. We thought at first he had forgotten all about what had happened, but he hadn't. Over his third cup of coffee, he glared at Herman and me. "What was the idea of all them cops tarryhootin' round the house last night?" he demanded. He had us there.

NOSY ANIMALS

You may think that there is a lot of variety in the shape of human noses, but animal noses come in even more assorted sizes, shapes, and colors. Some animals have long muzzles, short snouts, or noses so small that you have to look hard to find them. Many animal noses may look peculiar to people, but each nose suits the special needs of its owner.

The most striking feature about the elephant, besides its great size, is its trunk. Not only is it used as a grasping instrument, but it is also used as a weapon, for touching objects, for smelling, for breathing, and for obtaining food and water. An elephant's trumpet, which it sounds when startled by predators, serves as a warning to other members of the herd.

The name aardvark is Afrikaans (South African Dutch) for *earth pig*. The aardvark has an elongated muzzle ending in wide nostrils that can be opened and closed.

The anteater is one of the strangest and most remarkable-looking creatures, and its feeding habits do nothing to deny this impression. Its long, tapering, tubular snout houses a wormlike, sticky tongue. By keeping its long nose to the ground as it walks, the anteater can smell the hidden ants and termites on which it feeds.

The doglike muzzle of the mandrill is an intense red, and the ridged skin of the cheeks is a vivid blue, making this animal one of the strangest-looking of all monkeys. The red and blue colorings can be seen at their brightest in the adult male.

The adult male sea elephant (bull) has a pendulous nose that can grow up to twenty inches long. Bulls inflate their noses with air, and when they let the air out, the loud sound of the escaping air warns other males to stay away from that bull's territory.

The elephant shrew resembles a tiny kangaroo. It has an elongated, tube-shaped snout, which is moderately flexible. The snout is movable but can't be retracted as can the trunk of an elephant.

The elongated, shaggy head of the bush pig ends in a movable snout. Because of their extraordinary sense of smell, bush pigs are able to find food quickly, even in deep ground. They grub the ground with their snouts, and they particularly like to eat roots, herbs, mushrooms, leaves, and sprouts.

Greater horseshoe bats owe their name to the shape of their "nose leaves." Nose leaves are the peculiar, fleshy outgrowths that surround the nostrils. The horseshoe bat uses "echo-location" in flight to find prey and to avoid obstacles. It emits squeaks through its megaphonelike nose instead of through its mouth, as in other species of bats.

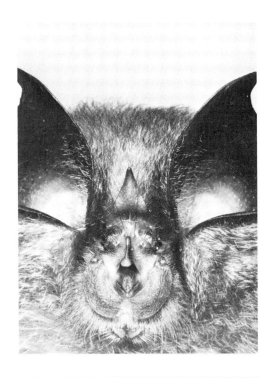

The mountain tapir lives high in the Andes mountain range. At first glance, this animal looks like an enormous pig. Tapirs are plant eaters, and they use their grasping, trunklike muzzles to pull a variety of leaves and fruits.

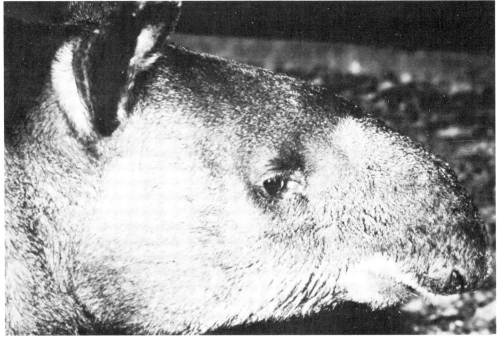

This De Brazza's monkey is about the size of a house cat and is distinguished by the yellow and blue markings on its face.

The habitat of the echidna, or spiny anteater, extends from New Guinea to Tasmania, in the South Pacific Ocean. This nocturnal, egg-laying mammal measures about eighteen inches long. The echidna, which has no teeth, probes for ants and termites with its highly sensitive, long, cylindrical muzzle and with its long, sticky tongue.

The young girl, working intently in the clay pit, seemed unaware of the hot midday sun. From a distance she appeared to be
playing with the soft, red clay, perhaps molding it into the bricks
that the town of Green Cove Springs, Florida, was so famous for.
The tall woman watched her for several minutes; then she started
to walk across the pits, careful not to step into the mounds of wet,
red clay.

"Hey, Augusta," the woman yelled. "Shouldn't you be in
school with the other kids? I don't recall hearing they were hiring
nine-year-old girls to make bricks."

Augusta looked up sharply. Startled, she jumped to her feet,
preparing to run and hide among the tall trees that bordered the
pit.

"Oh, Bertie, it's only you," the girl said, looking relieved.
"Gosh, you scared me."

"What do you mean, *only you?* You should be thankful it's only
Bertie Williams and not your father, or you'd get the scolding
of your life for playing hookey to play in the mud."

The young girl smiled and looked down at the small red figures
that lay scattered around her feet.

"Oh, I know you're right," she said. "But there's a reason why
I play hookey all the time. Come over and look, Bertie. You'll
understand, I know you will. Someone has to," she said.

Augusta Savage

Cynthia Benjamin

110

Augusta Savage carefully held up one of the small clay statues to show her friend.

"Why, it's a duck," the older woman said, carefully examining the tiny figure. "I believe it looks as if it could fly away, doesn't it? Who taught you to do this?" she asked.

"I taught myself," Augusta answered proudly. "And look here, there's lots more. See?"

The older woman looked around the clay pits. There were clay ducks everywhere. Some with gracefully molded necks, others with their wings spread, as if they were preparing to take off. Under one of the large trees that bordered the pit, Augusta had placed a group of clay figures that included a mother duck being followed by a group of baby ducks.

"Why, how did you do these statues?"

"Oh, it's not really that hard. See, first you take a lump of clay, just like this," Augusta said, scooping up some of the soft, red clay in her hands. "Then you roll it in a kind of oval and give one end sort of an upswing. Next you squeeze another piece into a long neck and you stick it on the first piece. And look, you have a duck."

Bertie looked down at the smiling young girl and laughed. "Well," she said good-naturedly, "I guess it sure beats learning how to add. But I bet your father won't be too pleased about what you're doing."

"Boy, you can say that again," Augusta said. "You know, I have to hide everything that I make from him. You've lived next door to us for three years, Bertie, and you know how mad he gets. He

just keeps saying that the daughter of a minister shouldn't be doing things like this."

"Well," Bertie said, "things are pretty tough for him, too, Augusta. You shouldn't forget that. With thirteen mouths to feed, he and your mother have a pretty hard time of it, believe me."

Suddenly there was a clap of thunder. For an instant Bertie and Augusta looked frightened. Then they laughed uneasily as they ran to an old shack at the edge of the clay pit. Even as they ran, they could feel the first drops of rain fall.

"Oh, Augusta," Bertie cried as they ran, "your beautiful statues. They'll be ruined by this rain."

The young girl just sighed. Turning, she watched sadly as the beautifully modeled ducks were reduced to clumps of red clay before her eyes.

"That's O.K., Bertie, it's happened before. Maybe things will change and one day I'll be able to work in stone or even bronze. You know, like a real sculptor does. Maybe," she added softly.

Several years later, Augusta was riding in the school wagon with her high school principal as he moved some materials to a storehouse. Things had changed for Augusta and her family. Her father had been transferred to a larger church in West Palm Beach, and she liked her new school much better than her old one. Augusta had stopped playing hookey and had started attending classes every day. The school principal, Professor Mickens, who had been told about Augusta by one of her teachers, had taken a special interest in his bright new student. He was hoping that Augusta would go on to a teacher's college, and he decided to talk to her about her future while they rode to the storehouse together. However, their talk didn't last long. As they passed the Chase Pottery factory, Augusta suddenly became excited.

"Professor Mickens," she said, "did you see that factory we just passed? Please, stop the wagon, I have to get down."

Before he could say anything, the girl had jumped from the wagon and rushed inside the old factory. She ran along the rows and rows of dusty pottery wheels and large barrels of clay. Suddenly she stopped and scooped up some of the moist clay, carefully fingering it. After she had stared at the clay for a few minutes, she sat down at one of the empty benches and started to mold and shape the soft clay. Her eyes glistened.

Professor Mickens found Augusta several minutes later, busily sculpting the figure of a small dog. She was so engrossed in her work that she didn't even notice the principal standing next to her.

"Augusta," he said, "I never knew you were a sculptor. Why didn't you let us know about this back at school?"

For the first time Augusta looked up from her work. "I had almost forgotten myself. Until I saw this pottery factory. Then I remembered how I used to play hookey when I was younger so I could work in the pits near home. Oh, Mr. Mickens, I want to be a real sculptor. I *have* to be a sculptor. But I need fine pottery clay like this to work with, not mud."

The factory owner, Mr. Chase, had approached Mr. Mickens and Augusta and overheard the girl's story.

"Well," Mr. Chase said, scratching his head, "the idea of using this stuff to make dogs doesn't make much sense to me, but then it doesn't make much sense to see a young girl upset for want of it, either."

When Augusta and Professor Mickens left the pottery factory that afternoon they were carrying almost twenty-five pounds of clay, which Mr. Chase had given to Augusta so she could begin her work.

And work she did! One day Professor Mickens called her into his office. What could it be, Augusta thought, as she waited nervously for the principal. I did much better in math this past semester. But her thoughts were interrupted by the professor's booming voice.

"Great news, Augusta. Now, come on," he added, patting the nervous girl on the shoulder, "don't look so troubled. Forget about that math for a minute. I think I have a job for you."

"A job," Augusta said in disbelief. "But, what kind . . ."

"Just listen to this," Professor Mickens continued. "I persuaded the school board to offer a class in clay modeling and you're going to be the teacher. We can pay you a dollar a day for every day you teach for the next months. Mr. Chase has agreed to donate the clay."

But Augusta was no longer listening. A dollar a day, she thought. I'm going to be paid to teach something I love — sculpting. I can't believe it. But I can sure use the money.

That's how Augusta's teaching career began while she was still a high school student. But Augusta's main ambition was to be an artist. Although teaching was important to her, at this time in her life she was more interested in learning all she could about art. She sculpted all the time now, and her room at home was full of clay animals. Her father had finally accepted her decision to become an artist and, as Augusta became more skilled, he encouraged her to work. One day, while Augusta was modeling a figure on the front porch of their home, she heard the screen door bang shut.

"Augusta," her father shouted excitedly. "Have you seen them?"

"Seen what, Daddy?" Augusta replied.

"The posters for the Palm Beach County Fair. It's opening in another six weeks, you know. There will be almost fifty booths where people will sell paintings and jewelry and clothes and . . ."

"And sculpture," Augusta said suddenly. "Daddy, I'm going to get a booth at that fair and sell some of my figures."

"That's not going to be easy for a young black girl to do," said her father.

"I'll find a way," Augusta said, returning to her work.

A few days later, when the superintendent of the fair, George Graham Currie, came to work one morning, he found a strange sight. On his desk were a chicken, several ducks, two dogs, and a cat. What's this, he thought to himself, someone's idea of a joke? Next to his desk stood the owner—and maker—of this strange menagerie, Augusta Savage. The animals were not alive, of course. They were examples of the sculpture that Augusta hoped to sell at the fair.

"Look, young lady, I don't know who you are, but I have a pretty busy morning ahead of me. Do you mind clearing this stuff away?"

"Mr. Currie, my name is Augusta Savage, and this 'stuff' is some examples of my work. I'm a sculptor, and I want to sell my work at the fair. I'd like to have a booth, Mr. Currie."

Mr. Currie was impressed by Augusta and her work. He examined each clay model carefully. As he handled each piece, Augusta never took her eyes from him.

"You're as anxious as a parent when a stranger picks up the baby," Mr. Currie said.

"These are my children," Augusta said forcefully.

Mr. Currie looked at her. "All right, Miss Savage, you will have your booth at the fair. Just remember, make something for every pocketbook."

Augusta remembered his advice. She worked long hours arranging her booth. Although some of the county fair officials were upset to learn that George Currie had let a young black girl have a booth, they changed their minds when they heard tourists praise her exhibit. When the fair was over Augusta had earned $175. In addition, she received a ribbon and a special prize of $25 for the most original exhibit.

On the last day of the fair, George Currie came to see Augusta. They talked as Augusta packed up the few pieces of sculpture that had not been sold.

"Augusta, are you really serious about wanting to become a sculptor? Because if you are, I have a friend, Solon Borglum, who may be able to help you. He's a famous sculptor and you will have to go to New York to see him. He can introduce you to important people in the art world and make suggestions about where to study."

Was she serious about wanting to become a sculptor, Augusta thought to herself. She remembered playing hookey from school to work in the clay pits. She remembered hiding her work from her father. She remembered Mr. Chase giving her clay so that she could continue her work. And she remembered the most rewarding times of her life—the hours she spent making statues.

"Yes, Mr. Currie," she said quietly, "I am."

Here are examples of Augusta Savage's sculpture.

Augusta Savage (1900–1962) was a world-famous black sculptor. Born in Florida, she had her first formal art training in New York City at Cooper Union, the school recommended to her by Solon Borglum. While she studied, she supported herself by doing odd jobs, including clerking and working in laundries. In 1926 she exhibited her work at the Sesquicentennial Exposition in Philadelphia. That same year she was awarded a scholarship to study in Rome. However, she was unable to accept the award because she could not raise the money she would have needed to live there. Eventually, she did study in Europe. When she returned to the United States, she exhibited her work at several important galleries. In addition to her own work, Augusta Savage taught art classes in Harlem. During the Depression, she helped black artists to enroll in the Works Progress Admiminstration arts project. Throughout her long career, she was an active spokesperson for black artists in the United States, and she was one of the principal organizers of the Harlem Artists Guild.

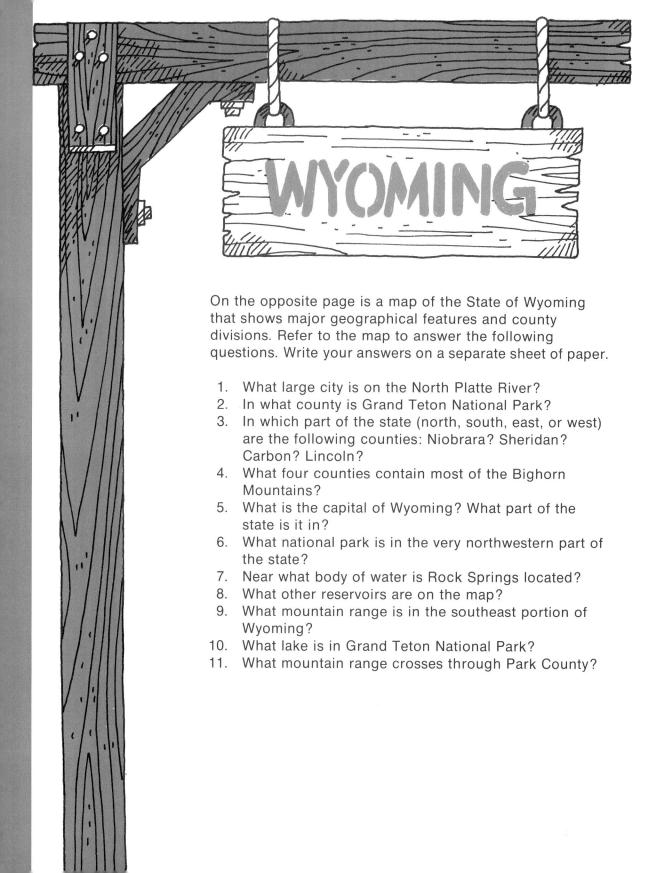

WYOMING

On the opposite page is a map of the State of Wyoming that shows major geographical features and county divisions. Refer to the map to answer the following questions. Write your answers on a separate sheet of paper.

1. What large city is on the North Platte River?
2. In what county is Grand Teton National Park?
3. In which part of the state (north, south, east, or west) are the following counties: Niobrara? Sheridan? Carbon? Lincoln?
4. What four counties contain most of the Bighorn Mountains?
5. What is the capital of Wyoming? What part of the state is it in?
6. What national park is in the very northwestern part of the state?
7. Near what body of water is Rock Springs located?
8. What other reservoirs are on the map?
9. What mountain range is in the southeast portion of Wyoming?
10. What lake is in Grand Teton National Park?
11. What mountain range crosses through Park County?

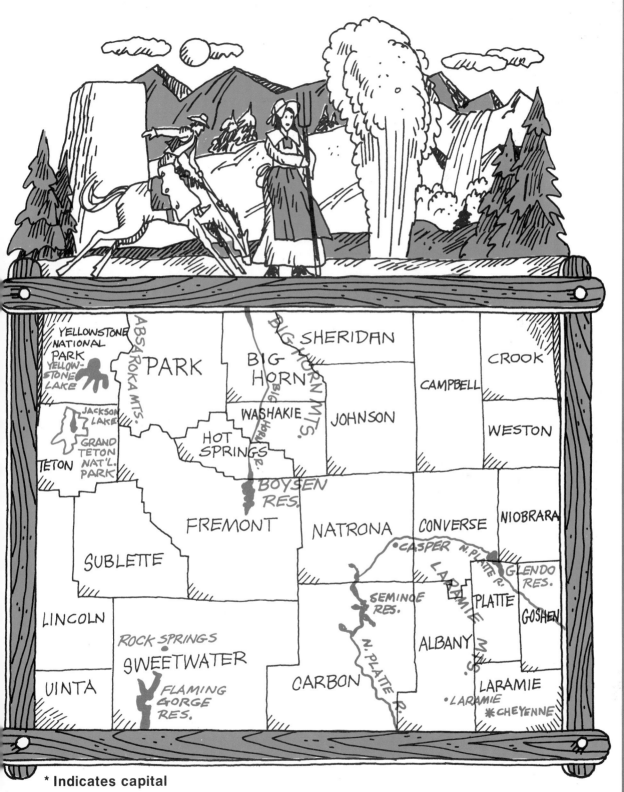

YELLOWSTONE NATIONAL PARK

YELLOWSTONE LAKE

ABSAROKA MTS.

PARK

BIGHORN MTS.

BIG HORN R.

SHERIDAN

BIG HORN

CROOK

CAMPBELL

JACKSON LAKE

GRAND TETON NAT'L. PARK

TETON

WASHAKIE

HOT SPRINGS

JOHNSON

WESTON

BOYSEN RES.

FREMONT

SUBLETTE

NATRONA

CONVERSE

NIOBRARA

•CASPER

N. PLATTE R.

LARAMIE MTS.

N. PLATTE R.

GLENDO RES.

SEMINOE RES.

PLATTE

GOSHEN

LINCOLN

N. PLATTE R.

ALBANY

ROCK SPRINGS

SWEETWATER

FLAMING GORGE RES.

CARBON

LARAMIE

•LARAMIE

✱CHEYENNE

UINTA

* Indicates capital

121

Sylva Mularchyk

A SEARCH FOR FORTUNE

The day Fortune and Sam rode away from the O'Donnell ranch, spring was in the air. The hearts of John and Martha were heavy as they watched their sons disappear in the distance.

"It's a brave thing our boys are doing," John O'Donnell said.

"Brave, yes," Martha answered, "but foolish, too. They are too young to travel alone into the Indian country. They are just boys—not yet sixteen!"

"You're forgetting, Martha, Fortune is an Indian." John turned to enter the house. "Besides, when a boy takes it upon himself to find out who he is, perhaps he has become a man."

"But is it so important?" Martha cried. "Is it so important to know who you are?"

"To a proud boy it is," John said simply.

Martha sighed. It had always been this way with Fortune— ever since he had been a small child he had wanted to know about his own people. He had asked her hundreds of questions she could not answer.

"Tell me again how I was found and where," he had asked her time and again. "Maybe you'll think of something you haven't remembered before."

123

And so she would begin, "We had joined a small wagon train at Fort Laramie and were going into the Montana Territory to settle. Sam had been born in Laramie while we waited for the wagons to leave. At Fort Laramie we turned off on the Bozeman Trail to the north, passing the Big Horn Mountains. We were families of farmers and ranchers seeking new lands to build our homes. We thought the Indian troubles were over.

"It wasn't for us to say who was right or wrong—the Indians or the whites. Perhaps we should not have come to the Indians' lands. But John and I had no hate in our hearts for the Indians. We only wanted to live in peace among them.

"We were camped along the banks of the Rosebud, and John went with a group of men into the hills to bring in meat for the camp. Game was hard to find, and the men were gone for two days. By accident, their search took them near a small Indian village. Scouts from the encampment must have thought the white men had come to destroy the Indian settlement. The women struck camp in fright. They packed their children and belongings into travois tied to their ponies and fled into the hills. A party of warriors ambushed our men, and they had to fight for their lives. Someone had to get back to our wagon train and warn the people of the attack, and it was John who broke away first.

"He galloped through the deserted encampment, but his horse shied, and John fell. As he struggled to his feet and ran to catch his horse, he stumbled over a blanket-wrapped bundle lying near a clump of brush. He took the bundle in his arms, lifted a corner of the blanket, and saw an Indian baby so small that it could not have been more than a few weeks old.

"John cradled the bundle in his arms, mounted his horse, and rode—more slowly now—back to the wagon train. When he came to me and laid the baby in my arms, he said, 'Martha, this is one of the fortunes of war.' And that, Fortune, was how you were given your name.

"I loved you as my own from the first minute I set eyes on you, and although we never stopped asking, we never heard of an Indian family seeking a lost baby. Finally we believed that your parents must be dead.

"The beadwork designs on your baby clothes were flowers with long trailing stems and pointed leaves. Each flower had five petals, and each was blue with a yellow center. Never in all these years have we seen a beadwork design to match it, and no one we asked could tell us what tribe worked such designs, or what tribe had lived in the village."

Fortune was thoughtful. "So they might have come from the far north, or from the Shining Mountains in the west. They might have been strangers in the Rosebud country, having traveled a long way in their search for game. You said game was scarce that year—"

"I'll bet that was it," Sam exclaimed. "Why, they might even have come down from Canada!"

Martha sighed, "I don't know. It is possible."

"I will take the baby clothing and search myself," Fortune had decided at last. "Somewhere I will find someone who knows the design, someone who can tell me who I am!"

Sam would not hear of Fortune's traveling alone. They had grown up together; they would travel together. And so they left home that spring morning.

Neither Fortune nor Sam knew any Indian languages. Yet they traveled among many tribes and villages and made their mission clear by using sign language, common to all tribes.

They did not know how many miles they had ridden. They had visited Cheyenne and Cree, Gros Ventres and Arapaho, Assiniboin and Crow, and many others. They were always met with blank stares and thinly veiled hostility until Fortune untied the bundle of baby clothing. Then the Indians were anxious to help. But they could only shake their heads. The beadwork was not like any they had ever seen, and it was certain that Fortune could not belong to their tribe.

Weeks passed, and Fortune was becoming discouraged. Then one day they came upon a Crow encampment in the Sweet Grass Hills. As they sat around a council fire that evening, the chief spoke through a young brave who acted as his interpreter. "He says you have come far. He wants to know what you are seeking."

"Tell him I am searching for my father and mother, but I do not know who they are." The chief did not wait for the interpreter to repeat Fortune's words. He answered swiftly in his own tongue.

Sam whispered to Fortune, "The chief understands English. I wonder why he won't speak it."

The interpreter heard him. "Chief Spotted Horse has vowed that no foreign words shall ever cross his lips."

Sam felt himself grow small before the stern eyes of the chief.

The interpreter said to Fortune, "He asks, now, how it is that you do not know your own people."

Fortune told his story. As the chief listened, his eyes softened. He looked thoughtfully at the doeskin garments and studied the floral pattern, then he shook his head.

Again the interpreter translated, "He does not know the pattern. There is, however, an old woman in the camp who was captured many years ago from a Blood tribe of the Blackfeet people. He will call her and see if she recognizes the designs."

The old woman came, and Fortune handed her the bundle of baby clothing. His heart was full of hope until he saw that the old woman was blind. The interpreter noted his disappointment and touched Fortune's arm in a kindly gesture. "Old Bear Woman has eyes in her fingers. Do not despair too quickly."

Tenderly Bear Woman's fingers traced the beaded design. She sat cross-legged on the ground for a long time, lost in thought. She asked a question, and the interpreter answered her. "She asks the color of the flowers," he explained.

At last the old woman pointed at Fortune. "Piegan," she said, then she reported her conclusions to the interpreter.

"Bear Woman says she is sure these designs were worked by a Piegan woman. The Piegans are a tribe related to the Bloods, and both are of the Blackfeet nation. There is still another tribe of the Blackfeet people, the Siksika, but Bear Woman believes these garments are Piegan. Her first husband was a Piegan, and she lived with his people until he was killed and she was captured

by the Crows. She says there was a woman among the Piegans who often used blue and yellow in her work, and her flower designs were famous."

Fortune's heart leaped. But Bear Woman was very old. She could not have known his mother—but—perhaps his mother's mother.

"This woman—what was her name?"

"She was known as Many Feathers, and she was the wife of Tall Chief. Bear Woman says she cannot help you further. She hopes you will find your people."

Fortune thanked her and turned back to Chief Spotted Horse. "Where will we find the Piegans?"

The chief turned to the west and lifted his arm toward the blue haze of the Shining Mountains.

As the boys rode away from the Crow encampment, Fortune said, "The Crows have always been enemies of the Blackfeet tribes. How strange that an enemy of my people would help me to find them!"

It took many days of hard riding to find the Piegan people. They were camped along Beaver Creek in the foothills below the mountains. They made the boys welcome and listened to their story with great interest.

Yes, they recognized the floral designs done in beads on the baby garments. Many of their women worked these same designs. Look. They pointed to their moccasins and leggings and to the trappings on their ponies. There were flowers of all kinds and colors, with long trailing stems and pointed leaves.

When Fortune asked about Tall Chief and Many Feathers, they told him that this man and woman had been dead for many winters. There had been a daughter who had married a Siksika warrior. It was said that this daughter had traveled with her husband far into the rising sun and had borne a child. But no one knew what had become of them.

"The daughter of Many Feathers and Tall Chief, what was her name?" Fortune asked.

She had been known as Blue Star. She was named for a flower that grew on the mountain slopes—larkspur—the same flower that had been stitched so carefully on Fortune's baby clothes.

Was it possible that Blue Star had been his mother? Fortune asked the Piegans, but they did not know. How could anyone know such a thing? No, they could not remember the name of the Siksika warrior who had taken Blue Star for his wife. It had all happened long ago, and it was not good to speak of those who had passed into the Great Beyond.

Fortune sat lost in thought. He had reached the end of the trail. He would never be sure who his parents had been. He knew only that he was of Piegan descent, and that perhaps his father had been a Siksika. He was not certain that the small bit of knowledge he had gained had been worth the hardships of the past weeks. But how uncomplaining Sam had been! During all these months of searching, riding in the hot sun, stinging winds, and chilling rains, Sam had never once lost hope or his good spirits. Harassed by mosquitoes or hunger when game was hard to find, Sam had never mentioned turning back.

Fortune started from his thoughts as Sam called to him. "The Medicine Man wants to talk to you."

Fortune uncrossed his legs and stood up. The holy man was very old and stooped, his leathery face was lined with many wrinkles, and his eyes were sad. He chose the foreign words with care and spoke with difficulty. "You have searched long, my son. It may now seem a search without an end, but you have found your people, and we welcome you. We wish to offer you a place here among us, as one of us. We would give you the name of 'One Who Seeks Himself.'"

Fortune bowed before the Medicine Man. "I am proud that I have found my people, and I am grateful for your kindness, and for the name you offer me, but I will not stay, for I am needed elsewhere."

Across the flickering flames of the fire, Fortune caught Sam's eye. His search had come to an end. It was not a name that counted. It was the goodness in a man and in a woman. The Piegans had proved this, the Crows had proved it, and Sam and all the O'Donnells had proved it again and again. He was Fortune O'Donnell, and he was satisfied. He had found himself.

from you
loving sis...
Cla...

Nina Payne

Toni's Shoe Repair

I'm taking shoes
to Toni's Shoe Repair.
I like it there,
the sound, the smell, the air,
the shelves of shoes
not going anywhere.
I like to stare
at all the pictures
on the walls, a baby
on a blanket, bare,
the dressy lady "From
your loving sister, Claire."
Toni asks to see the pair.
She chalks them there, and there,
says "Ready Tuesday,"
leaves them on a chair
and halves the ticket.
"Thank you. Call Again
at Toni's Shoe Repair."

PAYING UP

This bill was recently received by Samuel Brown. On a separate sheet of paper answer these questions referring to the bill.

1. What is this bill charging Samuel for?
2. Whom does Samuel have to pay?
3. How much does Samuel have to pay?
4. How much of the total bill is sales tax?
5. If Samuel has a question about this bill, what should he do?
6. What is Samuel's account number?
7. What is the period covered in this bill?
8. What is going to happen on September 27?
9. How many units of gas did Samuel use in this period?
10. How soon does this bill have to be paid?

Collection 2

Like so many writers, Yevgeny Yevtushenko began his career when he was a child. When he was ten years old, Yevtushenko wrote his first novel, and at twelve, he wrote lyrics for some well-known Russian folk songs.

As a boy in the Soviet Union, he was fond of sports, especially soccer, table tennis, and cycling. He even thought about becoming a professional soccer player. But poetry appealed to him most, and he began his serious career as a poet when he was sixteen years old. He wrote enough after that so that he could publish a book of poems, which he did—at age 19. While he was studying literature in Moscow, Yevtushenko became a leader among Soviet young people and poets in particular. He was openly critical of some aspects of Soviet society, and he contributed to the renewal of interest in poems about love and people and social injustice in the Soviet Union.

In the selection that follows, Yevtushenko writes about a period in his life when he felt he needed to prove his maturity. When have you felt this need? What is maturity? What do you think makes a person independent? Is it more important to prove something to yourself or to others?

On My Own

Yevgeny Yevtushenko

I quarreled with Mother and ran away to join my father. I traveled on the roof of a train all the way to Kazakhstan.

I was fifteen.

I wanted to stand on my own feet. At that time my father was working as chief of a geological expedition.

When I arrived, ragged and skinny, he looked me over and said: "So you want to stand on your own feet. . . . Well, if you really do, no one here must know you're my son. Otherwise you'll be favored whether you want it or not, and that isn't going to make a man of you."

I joined the expedition as a laborer.

I learned to break the ground with a pick, to split off samples of rock as flat as my hand with a mallet, to use a razor blade to make three matches out of the only one we had left, and to light a fire in driving rain.

I couldn't swim. And I lived in fear of being found out and disgraced.

One day I was walking with a geologist along a narrow mountain path above a noisy stream. We both carried knapsacks filled with specimens of rock. Suddenly the geologist took a false step and the ground gave way under his feet. He tried to catch hold of a bush, missed it, and fell headlong from the steep bank, down into the river. Within seconds I saw him thrashing about in the foaming water, struggling to keep afloat, but his knapsack was dragging him down.

I flung mine off my shoulders, whipped my knife from inside my belt, and jumped in.

It was not till I had swum up to the geologist, cut the straps

of his knapsack, and we had both scrambled ashore that I remembered I didn't know how to swim.

And from that day on I have known that the best way of learning something is to take a leap into the unknown without looking back. That way, you either learn or perish.

I learned not to be squeamish.

We had a Kazakh cook with us.

One of his daily duties was to harness an old horse to a cart with a wooden barrel and fetch water from a stream four or five miles away from our tents. In this water he cooked our tinned soup and cereal; it was the water we drank and the water we used to wash ourselves and our shirts.

Every day we went off as the sun was rising and stayed out till sunset. All day long we wandered over the parched Kazakh steppe under the molten sun, looking for minerals, and by evening we were bent double by the weight of our knapsacks. I remember that at first my back, cut by the sharp edges of the rock samples, had open sores on it — they later hardened into calluses. But we kept on until our sacks were full. However, one day we gave up and decided to start for camp earlier than usual.

The sun blazed mercilessly.

Our canteens were empty and our lips parched.

We were walking back, our minds filled with vivid images of the deep, long gulps of water we would drink on our return, scooping it out of the barrel with a pitcher.

Suddenly we heard the sound of a strange song coming from beyond a hill. We exchanged puzzled looks and quickened our pace. Coming around the hill, we saw our horse slowly pulling the cart with the water barrel. No one seemed to be driving and no human being was in sight. Where could the song be coming from?

The sound was growing louder and louder.

Suddenly we saw the cook's head sticking out of the barrel. Up to his neck in cool water, with the hundred-degree heat outside, he was splashing about like a baby in a tub, thoroughly enjoying himself. And flooded with *joie de vivre,* he was singing in his guttural voice a song of joy and triumph.

We wasted no words. With grim determination we set off at a run for the barrel.

The cook saw us and closed his eyes in horror.

We pulled him out of the barrel and he stood before us in all his primordial beauty.

We didn't hit him. We only shook him by the shoulders and asked him: "Have you been doing this all the time, or is this the first time?"

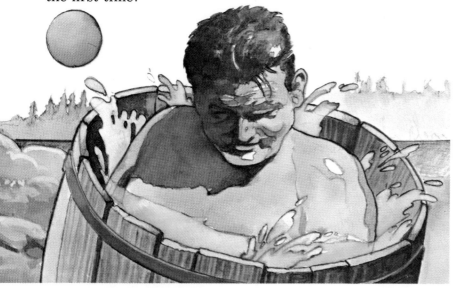

"It's the first time! It's the first time!" he cried, his teeth chattering with terror.

We let him go and looked at the water, torn between thirst and revulsion.

The river was far away and we lacked the strength for another journey.

At last one of us said grimly: "Nuts, it's still water," and dipped his canteen into the barrel.

He tipped it up and drank greedily. I drank that water too.

Life was knocking the city squeamishness out of me.

After Emily Hahn earned her degree in mining engineering, she found out that because she was a woman, the only job open to her was as a file clerk in a mining firm. She left this dead-end job and began traveling and writing. Many of her books deal with her travels to countries all over the world. People of other nations fascinated Emily Hahn, and she taught English for several years at various colleges in China. She now lives in England.

B.Sc.

Emily Hahn

My career as a mining engineer has this much in common with many success stories — it was founded on an accident. Otherwise, there is no comparison, because mine is not a success story. As an engineer I have been a flop, but there were a few glorious weeks, back in 1926, when it might have been otherwise. Flushed with the glory and the triumph of my B.Sc., excited by the publicity which I received as the First Woman Graduate in Mining Engineering from the University of Wisconsin, and generally on top of the world, I completely forgot the reason for my acquiring that extraordinary diploma and actually took a job with a mining company. Yet the facts are simple and stark. I never meant to be a mining engineer at all. The whole thing was a complete misunderstanding.

At the age of seventeen, I was an earnest, plump young woman, much annoyed by my parents' insistence on my going to college, because I felt that I was destined for Art. Once installed at the University of Wisconsin, though, I had to study something. At first I enrolled myself in the College of Letters and Science, where I really belonged; it offered that mixture of language, literature, history, and science that made, I thought, for Culture. It was the required science course which led me astray. A half-year term of freshman geology stirred me up to try chemistry. I had heard that among the chemistry professors at Wisconsin there was a really good teacher, Kahlenberg, but when I tried to get into his class, I ran into a small difficulty. Kahlenberg's course, the dean explained, although it exactly paralleled that of the Letters and Science brand of chemistry, was usually taken only by engineering students.

"Well, that's all right," I said. "I'm sure I can persuade Professor Kahlenberg to give me special permission to go to his lectures. Since they cover the same ground, what's the difference? May I do it that way?" Now, the dean may have fought with his wife that morning, or maybe he was worried about his bank account, or perhaps it was necessary that he say no once in a while, just to prove he was a dean. I'm sure that he never intended thus carelessly to mold my future life with one hasty word, but that is what he did. "No," said the dean rudely, and turned back to his desk.

His manners hurt my feelings, but that alone wouldn't have done the mischief. Like many young people in my day, I was bristling with principles, eager to find abuses in the world, and burning to do away with them. In five seconds I had condemned the dean's decision as an abuse. He was wrong in saying no—wrong on technical grounds, because Professor Kahlenberg's consent would have been enough for any dean in a reasonable mood, and wrong in principle, because students should be allowed to select their own teachers. Anyway, those were my feelings.

I was mad. Boy, was I mad! I couldn't have remained in the same college with that dean for one single day more. Before the registrar's office closed that afternoon, I had transferred myself to the College of Engineering, enrolled for the chemistry course I wanted, and sent off a confused letter of explanation to my parents. There, if only anybody in the Engineering College had had a grain of sense, the great revolt would have ended. I would have listened to Kahlenberg's chemistry lectures, shaken hands with him, and transferred myself right back to Culture at the end of term. The engineers, however, were not wise.

They were stunned when they discovered me, a seventeen-year-old female freshman, enrolled in the Engineering College.

The university had a long-standing tradition, as well as a charter, for being a coeducational institution. Women studied medicine at Wisconsin, and the "pure science" courses were full of girls; the Agricultural College, too, had them. Nobody argued about that. But nobody had yet heard of a female engineer. The engineers' immunity through the years had bred in their ranks a happy confidence that it could never happen there, and I was a horrid surprise. They lost their heads and went into a panic and, in the following weeks, actually appealed to the state legislature to heave me out. After due consideration, the legislature regretfully refused. It couldn't heave me out, it explained, much as it would like to as a group of red-blooded he-men, because the university was a coeducational, tax-supported institution, and if a woman wanted to study any course it offered, and if she fulfilled the requirements and behaved herself, you couldn't turn her down.

Even then, if the engineers had only known, all was not lost. They couldn't keep their mouths shut, though. They were the engineers — hearty, simple folk. All of them, faculty members and students, tried to live up to the college pattern — the awkward guy, the diamond in the rough. To a man, they wore stiff corduroy trousers, smoked pipes or chewed tobacco, and looked down haughtily on the other colleges, which they condemned as highbrow. It was not in them to be diplomatic, and I maintain that they brought upon themselves what followed.

The custom in college is to assign each student to a professor, who acts as the student's adviser. In the College of Letters and Science, my adviser had been a fragile person who taught French literature, but my new adviser in the Engineering College was a mining engineer. I had elected mining engineering as my particular course. Professor Shorey was not tactful. My first advisory hour with him was given over to a violent argument.

"But why?" he demanded. "Why should a woman want to be an engineer? I never heard of such nonsense!"

"Why did *you* want to be an engineer?" I retorted. I was still talking in a more or less academic spirit, of course. I meant to leave engineering in peace, and before long. Sooner or later I intended to break down and explain the circumstances to Professor Shorey and reassure him, but in the meantime his attitude interested me. I wanted to hear more about it.

"It's not at all the same thing," he said. "In the first place, you'll never get a job, even if you should take your degree, which is very doubtful. If I were running a mine, I'd never hire a woman in any technical capacity. You wouldn't have the practical experience, and you'd be a nuisance around the office."

"Why wouldn't I have the experience, Mr. Shorey?"

"How would you get it? Who's going to let *you* go down a mine? Why, the miners would go on strike. They'd call it bad luck and expect a cave-in. It's too foolish to discuss. It's all a waste of time, anyhow—your time and mine—because you won't get your degree."

I moved closer to the desk, all alert. "Why won't I get my degree?" I said.

Shorey sighed. "The female mind," he explained carefully and kindly, "is incapable of grasping mechanics or higher mathematics or any of the basics of mining taught in this course."

That remark, quite simply, is why I am a Bachelor of Science in Mining Engineering. From that moment until graduation, I completely forgot that I had not always, from my earliest youth, intended to become a mining engineer. Every day offered fresh reason for forgetting. I was awfully busy for the next three years, up to my neck in mechanics and drafting and calculus. It was enough to make anyone forget a little thing like Art.

One afternoon, soon after my argument with Shorey, I attended my first class in surveying. We met indoors to get our instructions. I sat on a separate bench a little way off from the men, and none of them looked at me. The instructor, too, avoided my eye in a sulky manner. He explained, with chalk on a blackboard, the simple rules for running a line with a hand level. Then he announced, "We will now go to the instrument room and take out our equipment. You people choose your partners for the term—surveyors always work in pairs. Go ahead and divide yourselves up."

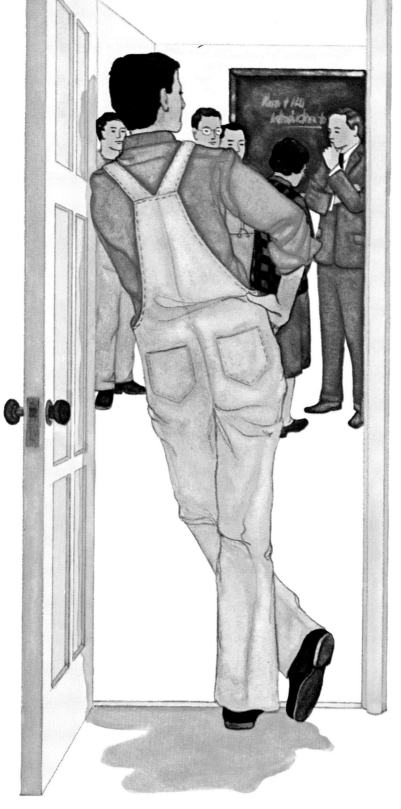

He leaned back in his chair behind the desk. There were fourteen men in the class, and in two minutes there were seven pairs. While the other students got up and scrambled to make their arrangements, I just sat still, wondering where I went from there.

"Well," said the instructor, "let's go and get our instruments."

We straggled after him and waited as he unlocked the storeroom. The levels we were to use, the type called "dumpy" levels, are heavy, metallic objects on tripods. Seven men stepped up and took one apiece, and then, as the instructor hesitated, I walked over defiantly and picked up an eighth. The instructor rubbed his chin and looked at me furtively. I looked at my feet.

"Hmm, I was sure we had an even number in the class," he said. "I guess Bemis has dropped out."

Fourteen men and I stood there tongue-tied, impatient to bring all this to an end. Then I noticed a tall, lanky boy, who had not been in the lecture room, leaning back against the door looking on, a good-natured sneer on his freckled face. He now gathered his bones together and shambled over.

"Aw," he said gruffly, "I'll take her."

"Oh, there you are, Bemis. O.K.," said the instructor, loud in his relief.

Bemis picked up my level and tripod and, with his free hand, waved me toward the long rod which one member of a surveying pair always carries. "Come along," he said. "I know these things. I've already run a few, working in the summer." He turned and started to walk out, and after a second, during which I stared at him, registering eternal devotion, I scampered after him. Behind me there was a loud general exhalation of relief and wonder.

Reginald Bemis—for Reginald was his name—found out all too soon that his responsibility was not temporary. Whatever whimsical impulse of kindliness had pushed him into his offer vanished when he realized that he was stuck with me for the term. But once he learned this bitter fact, he decided at least to bring me up the way I should go. He had worked in open-pit mines before coming to the university, and it was typical of his scornful attitude, that of a veteran miner, that he hadn't come to the explanatory lecture. He was one of those gangling, undernourished boys who work their way through college; he waited on tables at a hash house when he wasn't in class, and got good marks and had a future. As a surveyor he knew his business as well as our instructor did. By the time we graduated from the dumpy level to the transit, Reginald and I had the best record of any pair of engineers for our reports and drawings. None of this excellence, obviously, was due to my talents.

Not that I didn't do my share of the heavy work. I did. We took turns carrying the instruments. Sometimes our trail led us to a very public spot, and when passersby suddenly noticed that I was a female—that took a moment or two, for I wore khaki coveralls most of the time—Reginald became very touchy. The minute a stranger paused to take another look at me holding up the rod or squinting laboriously into the transit, Reginald would make such ferocious noises and wiggle his fingers at his nose so insultingly that the passersby would soon move on. His attitude was brutal but right, and I tried to show him that I appreciated it.

One evening, near the end of the surveying course, as we plodded along through snowdrifts toward the instrument room to turn in our equipment, I said to Reginald, "Excuse me for saying so, but you've been awfully nice. I don't know what I would have done that day if you hadn't said you would take me along for a partner."

"You was all there was left," said Reginald gruffly.

"Yes, but you didn't have to go on with me after that day. It must have been very hard sometimes."

"You ain't kiddin'," said Reginald, with deep feeling. "You know what they was calling me all year? Her Choice—that was it. Once I hadda fight a guy."

"It's a shame," I said. "But anyway, I've learned how to survey."

"Oh, you ain't so dumb," he admitted. "Only trouble with you is, sometimes you don't think straight. It's like you was dreamin'. Like today, when we couldn't find that bench mark. You just stood there with your mouth open while I went around kicking snow up, trying to find it. Lazy, that's your trouble."

"I'll try to do better," I said.

"Anyway," remarked Reginald cheerfully as we entered the door, "the worst is over. I got only one more week with you."

"You've been *awfully* nice," I repeated.

I knew one of the geology professors socially, as it happened, and though I never crossed his orbit in an official way, I did drop in on him once in a while to unburden my soul. He gave me a piece of advice early in the game. "These boys are just afraid you'll interfere with their daily routine," he said. "As soon as they realize you don't, it will be all right. They've got some idea, for instance, that they'll have to be careful of their talk when you're around."

"You mean," I asked, brightening, "that there are words I don't know?"

The professor ignored this and said warningly, "Don't pay any attention, no matter what they say. Don't expect special privileges just because you're a woman. Try to let them forget you're a woman. Pretty soon everything will be all right."

As a result, I trained myself to keep very quiet and to maintain a poker face wherever I was in the college. The mining-engineering course was a stiff one, and we were all too busy to indulge in any feud, anyway. Now and then, however, some complication cropped up. I was excused permanently from one lab course because there was no ladies' room in that building. I was also formally excused from the gymnasium classes the other female students had to take because I got enough exercise just learning to be an engineer. The khaki coverall garment I wore for surveying and ore dressing had to do for more orthodox classes as well, and I could see that my French teacher didn't like it, but she never complained.

It was at this time that I acquired the name Mickey as a permanent label. It was a nursery nickname of mine which had been more or less forgotten by everyone but Mother. The engineers heard it and adopted it as a more acceptable, masculine-sounding name than my real one, which was hopelessly ladylike. Of course, there were brief flareups and resentments now and again. Some of the boys were unfair, I felt. At the beginning of a math course, one of them yelled at me, "You'll never be able to get through this! You're a girl!" Yet at the end of term, when he asked me what grade I had and I replied exultingly that I was in the first five on the list, he said, "Huh, that's just because you're a girl you got that mark." It was irritating, but after all I *had* stuck my neck out. I continued to keep mousy quiet, and our mechanics instructor finally said to a friend, "You know, I've been dreading the day that girl would have to come to my lectures. But now that she's here, she's — why," he said in astonishment, "she's quite a lady."

As I look back on it now, I am amazed that I passed any of those examinations. Half the time and energy I should have given to my work was used up in the effort to prove that I could hold my own without being in the way. I was painfully self-conscious. My professor friend's words had sunk in so deep that I couldn't get them out of my head or my behavior. I took it as an insult when some absent-minded engineering student so far forgot himself as to hold open a door for me or stood up and offered me a chair. In time, though, most of these little frictions wore away. The one serious problem was the matter of field trips.

Field trips are study journeys into the country. Students, both of mining engineering and geology, go out with instructors and wander about looking at rock formations, geographical features, mines, or whatever they are interested in at the time. Of course, I went out on the small trips that were over in one day, but from the longer trips, including one expedition to mines in the West, which took up a whole summer and taught the boys how to work in the tunnels, I was barred. It was simply impossible to overcome that obstacle. The Wisconsin state legislature couldn't help me this time because the State of Montana would have kept me out of its mines. How, then, was I to qualify for my degree?

I figured something out at last as a substitute for the mining experience. I went up that summer and stayed with relatives who had a farm in Michigan. Every morning I went out with a hand level and a Brunton compass and ran lines back and forth at half-mile intervals, straight across the township, until I had made a respectable contour map of the region to take back to the college. The authorities studied the map, smoked a few pipes over it, and unanimously voted to give it the status

of the summer's field work the boys had put in. Perhaps this really definite triumph went to my head a little. Perhaps the summer of walking alone under the Michigan sun had sweated out of me my hard-won humility. Anyway, that autumn, the beginning of my final year, I was in a mood to fight my great, all-out battle with the Geology Club.

Again, it wasn't my fault. I didn't start it; the men did. They should have known that the sign they put up on the bulletin board in Science Hall would be enough to knock me off balance. A stranger would not have understood. All the sign said, in formal lettering, was that the Geology Club was holding an extra-special meeting that night for two purposes — first, to introduce the semiyearly crop of newcomers to the group, and, second, to hear the highly respected visitor, Professor Such-and-So, world-renowned expert on volcanoes or coral reefs or something, deliver the first of his series of lectures. But someone had added a significant line in red pencil: "Women not invited."

I recognized this as an insult aimed directly at me. No other woman would have been crazy enough to want to go to a Geology Club meeting. The sign was the worse for being unnecessary. I knew perfectly well I wasn't invited; I had not been invited, repeatedly, for three years. They had thrashed the matter out many times. I always pretended not to know, but it was an old grievance because all members of the mining-engineering courses had always automatically been invited to become members of the Geology Club. Once I showed up, though, the Geology Club members maintained that they were not a formal institution of the college but a social organization, and, as such, didn't have to abide by the cruel law of coeducation, which forced open their lecture halls to the female sex. True, I did belong to the Mining Engineers' Club — we held our meetings in the ore-dressing laboratory and cooked hamburgers in the blast furnace — but that club, said the geologists, was different, somehow — more entangled in the web of the educational setup. The geologists claimed that their taking mining engineers into their club was a voluntary courtesy, and they said that they preferred not to extend it to me. Inviting me would, they said darkly, establish a precedent.

For three years I had silently accepted this argument, because there didn't seem to be any way around it. This red-penciled message, though, affected me strongly. I was as angry as I had been that long-ago day in the dean's office, back in those prehistoric times when, for some reason, I wasn't yet studying engineering.

It wasn't fair. I hadn't been bothering their old Geology Club. Yet there the men were, jeering and making faces at me in this bulletin-board announcement. Rub it in, would they? I'd show them!

My eyes narrowed as I read the sign through for the fourth time. Somebody had slipped up. Professor Such-and-So had been invited by the college faculty to give that series of lectures, and, as one of the college students, I was, of course, entitled to hear the entire series. Entitled? Why, I was probably *required* to hear them. Not that I had ever felt any particular emotional yearning for information about volcanoes or coral reefs or whatever it was. That was not the point. The point was a matter of principle. The point was that the Geology Club, in thus selfishly acquiring this lecture for their own session, sacrificed their standing as an amateur social organization. They had made themselves, at least for the time being, one of the college classes. That class I was entitled by law to attend. I decided to visit the Geology Club that night.

The most painfully uncertain people are the ones who seem poised and self-assured. I walked into the club meeting as bold as brass, but the slightest push would have upset me, and my old pal, the friendly professor, quite unwittingly almost administered it. As I made my way past the rows of dismayed, silent men, he shouted in a whisper, "Bravo!" It took a gigantic effort to finish the walk, to sit down in an empty chair, to pretend that nothing at all extraordinary was happening. This was my first open rebellion. Just when I had almost captured the good will of the college, too, and was so near to graduation and release. Just when they were about to confer on me the ultimate honor, indifference.

The visiting lecturer saved my face, though he couldn't have known that, by climbing to the platform and breaking the tension. The ensuing hour must have gratified him, for the whole roomful of young people sat in a dead hush while he told us about volcanoes — or was it coral? And after a vote of thanks he said good night and left us alone to wash our dirty linen.

The club president, a kindly soul named Clyde, took the floor and went through a few formalities — minutes of the last meeting and a brief résumé of the club's aims for the benefit of the new members. Then he said, "It's our custom, just to make things less formal, to ask the men who are new to the club to introduce themselves. I'll call on them in order of seating. Mr. Blake?"

"Class of twenty-eight," mumbled a scarlet Mr. Blake. "No other clubs. Transferred this year from Michigan College of Mines. Majoring in petrology."

Everyone grew quieter and quieter as the introductions proceeded. I wasn't just quiet; I was rigid. Were they going to pretend that I wasn't there? If Clyde skipped me, I would have to make a demonstration of some sort. I would *have* to. I held my breath until I nearly strangled. Clyde's eyes fell on me and he cleared his throat.

"Since our friend Miss Hahn has taken the bull by the

horns," he said, "I will call on her to introduce herself to our new friends."

Everybody let out his breath a little; the crisis was postponed. I stumbled to my feet and duly made my recital. The meeting proceeded without interruption. Clyde finished up the official business of the meeting by announcing that it was the evening for collection of dues. If the members would kindly pay their dues—a dollar a head—to the treasurer, he said, we would be able to proceed with refreshments—the customary coffee and vanilla wafers.

We stood in line, with our dollars in our hands, and that was when the trouble started. When I reached the collection table, the treasurer shook his head. "Can't take it," he said.

"Why not?"

"Well, uh . . ." The unhappy boy swallowed hard, and then in desperation raised his voice. "Clyde! Come over here, will you?"

It had all been arranged in advance, evidently. Clyde came over and took my arm with a sort of reluctant affection, and said, "Come on out in the hall, Mickey. I want to talk to you."

I pushed his hand away. "Talk to me here," I said.

"Come on, Mickey. Do me this favor, won't you?"

We marched out between the ranks of embarrassed young geologists.

"It's this way," said Clyde miserably. "A bunch of us tried to—I mean, this thing came up again, the way it always does, last week, and though I personally, and some of your other friends, tried to persuade the fellows, the thing is—"

"All right," I said abruptly. "Here's my dollar, anyway. Take it for wear and tear on the bench. Nobody wants to—" To my horror, it suddenly became urgently necessary to be alone. My unhappy nature had played me false. Whenever I am keyed up to violent anger, tears begin to flow. I ran down the hall, completely routed. This was disaster. I had committed the one unforgivable sin: I had shown my feelings. I wanted to kick myself for shame. I wanted to die.

What happened after that is public knowledge. Clyde walked slowly back into the clubroom and shook his head in misery when the boys asked him what had happened. "Was she awfully sore?" they asked. "Did she make a scene? Did she say—"

"Oh, gosh," said the president, "don't talk about it. She—she *cried*."

"Cried?" Appalled, they stared at each other. Cried! They lowered their eyes, unable to meet each other's gaze.

Somebody proposed a vote. There and then they voted.

A half hour later I was sitting in the study room at Science Hall, huddled in my chair, despair clutched round me like a blanket. There Clyde found me and brought the news. Practically unanimously, I had been elected a member of the Geology Club. One lone man who still stood out against me, admitting that his attitude spoiled the record, was yet unable to give up his convictions, and so he had left the room while the vote was taken. Public opinion had demanded that he do this.

"And in conclusion," Clyde said to me, "permit me to say that I'm sure all the fellows are *awfully* sorry it all happened."

Though stunned, I managed to say a few gracious words of acceptance so that Clyde would leave me the sooner. I needed solitude; I had a lot of reorienting to do. I sat a long time at my desk, looking backward at a three-year program of mistaken strategy. It was the friendly professor, I realized, who had started me off on the wrong foot. Well, it was all right now. I knew better now. Just in time, too.

I blew my nose and started to search my briefcase, diving far down, trying to find a long-forgotten pocket mirror.

CLASSIFIED INFO

What is your favorite subject or course in school now? Which one do you like least? What kind of work would you like to do when you finish school? What jobs would you *not* like to have?

On a sheet of paper, make a chart that lists your likes and dislikes. Use the sample below or change it to fit your needs.

SUBJECT		CAREERS	
LIKE	DISLIKE	WOULD LIKE	WOULD NOT LIKE

While you fill in the chart, try to think of jobs or careers that your favorite courses might lead to. For instance, an interest in math might lead to a career as an accountant or a career in computers; an interest in art could lead to a career in design.

What you have just done in filling out the chart is a form of *classification.* You have put things into *categories.* The chart below is another way to use classification. It has more specific information than the one you just did for yourself, and it can be used in more ways.

This chart has been started for you. You can add more items in both *courses* and *careers.* Here are two ways to start using the chart.

1. Along the top of the chart, fill in all the courses that you take. Then, on the side, list many different careers. Put a check in the box when a career and a course seem to go together.

2. Start the same way as in step 1, only this time put an asterisk (*) under the courses you like best and next to the careers that interest you. See if any checks and asterisks overlap.

COURSES→	MATH	ENGLISH	SOCIAL STUDIES	SCIENCE	ART	TYPING
CAREERS↓						
TEACHER	✓	✓	✓	✓	✓	✓
FILM EDITOR		✓*	✓		✓*	
ELECTRICIAN	✓*			✓*		
WELDER	✓			✓	✓	

If you like one thing, does it mean that you can't also like something else? If Mickey from "B.Sc." were to do this chart, it might look like this:

	MATH	ENGLISH	SOCIAL STUDIES	SCIENCE
MINING ENGINEER	✓	*	*	✓

Did Mickey start out planning to be a mining engineer? Do you think Mickey liked her career choice?

Sometimes career choices are not left completely to us. In the story "Snow Magic," which follows, look at One-hand's choices. Why are his choices limited? What was he able to do? What did he accomplish?

159

"It was in the beginning—" said Oldman. The children hugged their knees and pulled closer to the fire as strange shadows ran into the caves. Will he tell how dog came to stay with us, thought Onehand, or will he tell how the old ones stole fire?

Three women drew closer, enjoying the children and the fire. Rahmoon, Onehand's mother, thought fearfully of last winter, of the sickness that killed many people and left Onehand's arm paralyzed, hanging stiffly and lifelessly at his side. With last year's snow had come fever and death.

Oldman began his story. "Long, long ago two children were alone in the newness of the world. The Spirit Father gave each child a moon for a toy. At first they played together; then one became bored and said, 'I can throw farther than you can.' The other laughed and replied, 'No farther than a rabbit hops.' The first threw his shining toy into the sky, where it stayed to become our moon, and the second threw hers so hard, it broke against the sky and became our stars. The children were unhappy at losing their beautiful toys, and they cried and cried. Their tears became the lakes of our valley. And because the Spirit Father was angry with them for wasting his gifts, he changed one into Mountain-of-snows and the other into Mountain-that-smokes." Oldman paused, smoke curling around his head. "Treat the Spirit Father's gifts with care," he said at last.

Mary Bigger

Snow Magic

Onehand crawled into his sleeping skins, warm from the fire and the story. What gift did the Spirit Father give me, he wondered. How can I hunt with only one arm? It's now my time to join the men. The hunters call even younger boys to help with spears and skins and game.

Every year, in the time before snow, the young men would go to Mountain-that-smokes seeking spirit power. Onehand's fingernails bit into his palm as he thought of this. Last year, when I had two good arms, I was too young, he remembered bitterly. This year they will need everyone. Surely, even with my frozen arm, they will call my name. Watching Rahmoon weave his sleeping mat for the spirit journey, Onehand drifted off to sleep.

Morning came boxed in by fog. Onehand saw Oldman building the spirit fire, and quietly he helped him. Only straight wood, only smooth cones; so many sticks must point to the rising sun, so many to its resting place; some must point to the Mountain-that-smokes, some to the Mountain-of-snows. In the center must be many cones for the hot, straight blaze of spirit power. Onehand toiled up and down the rocky trails, finding the right wood to feed the fire. Oldman said little, but he did not make him go berry picking with the women and children.

That night the hunters gathered at the fire. Slowly they sang, as if their spirit power were low. Oldman suddenly stood up and the song died. He was wearing the spirit robe. Woven into his white hair were strings of shining bone beads, and around his neck were strings of wolf and bear claws. With great dignity he began the song of the hunt. Only hunters who had returned from Mountain-that-smokes could sing this song. Now, thought Onehand, now comes the calling.

"Hardfoot."

Hardfoot stepped forward with his sleeping mat.

"Hungry-one."

My friend, thought Onehand. The sickness had not marked him.

While five more were called, Onehand thought his ears would burst with listening. Now, surely now! But the hunters were already singing the song of dreams. Those called were carrying sleeping mats and torches, lighting their way to Mountain-that-smokes with the spirit fire that Onehand had

162

labored so hard to build. He felt as if he were burning, too. Now he knew that his name would never be called—he would be neither child nor man, belonging to no one, having no place in his tribe.

From then on, Onehand kept to himself. Sometimes he helped Oldman to collect special leaves and grasses required for medicines, but he no longer went with his mother to gather roots or nuts. He struggled alone to climb the high, rocky trails, with his one good arm pulling his slim, hard body out onto the cliff edge. Again and again he thought, why do I live if I am dead among my own people? What is the purpose of my life?

In his solitary wanderings Onehand watched the elk trails. He observed the small digging animals. He noted how the strong and the weak lived, and he saw the slow, the crippled, and the old choose cover and survive. Where is cover for me, he thought bitterly.

The first snows came, but Onehand continued his solitary walks. Onehand's friends, now burdened with the responsibilities of the hunters and disturbed by Onehand's sullenness, gave up on him. Only Oldman seemed to understand.

As the snows deepened, the hunters stayed close to the caves. Only short forays were possible; walking through the deep, drifting snow was exhausting work. When the lakes froze, the snow would be hard enough to walk on; but until then the tribe would have to conserve the little meat they had.

Every day Onehand watched the men go the short distances, something working in his mind as he watched them labor through the snow. Slowly, like gathering wood for a spirit fire, an idea was growing. Animals adapted to winter—Onehand had watched them—they changed their habits; hunters should, too.

Every day Onehand's mother watched him leave the cave. When he came home at night, he was wet, tired, and covered with scratches and welts. As Rahmoon watched Onehand brood unhappily, she worried that some new sickness had claimed her son. He did not complain, but he did not smile. He ate as if he were somewhere else and slept as if he were dead. At last she went to Oldman.

"Onehand has a new sickness," she told him. "It makes him a stranger in his own body."

Oldman threw a few leaves on the fire. As he watched them

burn fitfully, Oldman said, "We must wait for a full moon. Neither smoke nor leaves give us a sign."

Rahmoon went home as troubled as she had come, and Onehand kept to his solitary ways. Then one evening he did not come home. Again Rahmoon went to Oldman and again Oldman threw leaves on the fire. This time the burn was clean, the smoke was straight.

"What does it mean?" asked Rahmoon. "Is Onehand dead?"

"No, some magic walks . . ."

Oldman was interrupted by dogs barking and people shouting. "A ghost! A ghost upon the snow!" Everyone gathered at the cliff edge, children pushing through their parents' legs for a better view, then hiding again for safety. The hunters stood with spears ready.

The ghost did not stumble. It did not sink into the drifts, nor was it caught by soft spots. On it came, walking smoothly over the snow, singing a song full of the power of winter. No one had ever seen such a thing.

Suddenly a child yelled, "It's Onehand!"

It was indeed Onehand. On his feet were strange woven mats, not heavy like sleeping mats but open and curved with a strong branch at each edge. As Onehand walked up to the circle of people, the hunters lowered their spears and stared at these strange "wings" for snow.

Oldman spoke. "Not since dog came to our fire has a greater gift come to us from the Spirit Father." He lit the spirit fire and gave Onehand a torch of the hunter.

Questions poured at Onehand from all sides.

"In the fall I watched animals prepare for winter," he explained, noting the interest and excitement on the faces of the people who surrounded him. As he continued to speak, he felt a closeness to his tribe that he had forgotten. "As the cold times approached, the animals were transformed to match the snow. Animals changed their homes to be ready for the arrival of winter. And I realized that as animals were transformed for the coming of snow, so hunters must adapt. I remembered duck, whose wide feet kept him from sinking into the mud, while deer on his thin legs sank to his knees. I tied branches to my feet, but the snow grew heavy on them. Some snow mats were so wide that I could not move. It took many tries to find branches

light and strong, to find cords that would not break in a few steps. Each day the Spirit Father showed me a little more, and now never again will we sit hungry around our fires, waiting for the snow to freeze."

Oldman stepped into his cave. He brought out the spirit robe and carefully placed it over Onehand's shoulders. "Today Onehand has shown that his magic is stronger than the great sickness. He can see from high places and walk over the snow. I name him Winter-eyes, and he will be our medicine man."

Onehand stepped out of his snowshoes and warmed himself by the spirit fire. Winter-eyes, a good strong name. He was content.

NEW YORK UNDER-GROUND

Mention New York City, and most people think of skyscrapers towering many hundreds of feet above the ground. But New York also has a vast underground city consisting of the city's lifelines—its subways, water pipes, electrical system, telephone cables, gas mains, and sewers.

In this city people can go beneath the streets to buy books and flowers. They may shop in department stores, have their hair cut, and eat lunch—all underground. They can travel underground to work, to a movie, or to the park. Many people go underground to their jobs as track inspectors, signal circuit designers, porters, locksmiths, welders, typists, dispatchers, and so forth.

Workers called gandy dancers keep 830 miles of subway tracks in good repair. They got their nickname from equipment made by the Gandy Manufacturing Company. Thanks to the gandy dancers and 30,000 other subway workers, trains make 7,500 trips a day. The trains carry three and a half million passengers—as many as live in the entire state of Alabama—every 24 hours.

For your fare you can travel nearly 90 miles without going over the same subway rails twice. You can even ride a train ten stories below the streets. Fast-moving escalators will get you back to the surface. But in some places you have to walk down to catch a train.

Upper levels of New York's subways were dug out of the ground. Some of the deeper ones had to be blasted through the city's base of granite. Exhaust fans circulate air throughout. Powerful pumps push drainage water back up to sewers on the top level.

Eight million city residents use one and a half billion gallons of water a day. The water reaches them through 6,000 miles of pipe and leaves the city—with waste materials—through as many miles of sewers.

Manholes—750,000 of them—are entrances to the underground for thousands of workers. Some

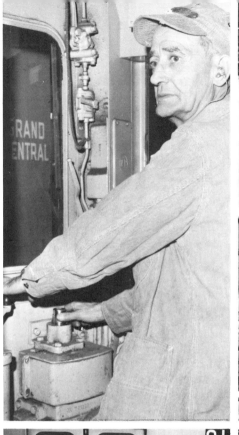

manholes are always full of water. It takes specialists known as mudsuckers as long as eight hours to pump one out before work can start. The reason: Manhattan—the island heart of New York City—has rivers on all sides, and water lies close to the surface. Once a manhole is checked for flooding and for leaking gas, a portable exhaust system is set up to clear the air that the workers in the "hole" must breathe. Through the manholes they can work on:

- Copper wires running through the city's telephone cables. These wires could stretch from the earth to the moon and back again 109 times.

- Electric cables that could reach around the earth three times.
- Gas mains and steam pipes that could reach across the United States and back three times.

When workers go down to repair pipes and subways, they sometimes find passages made by burglars. Once, a would-be thief was discovered, overcome by gas, within a few yards of his target—a check-cashing office. His pickax had hit a gas main.

New York, like many other large cities, has almost as much going on beneath its streets as above them. Think about that when you are walking in a city—there is a lot going on under your feet.

I've Got a Home in That Rock

Ray Patterson

I had an uncle, once, who kept a rock in his pocket—
Always did, up to the day he died.
And as far as I know, that rock is still with him,
Holding down some dust of his thighbone.

From Mississippi he'd got that rock, he'd say—
Or, sometimes, from Tennessee: a different place each year
He told it, how he'd snatched it up when he first left home—
Running, he'd say—to remind him, when times got hard
Enough to make him homesick, what home was really like.

Leigh Brackett

COME SING THE MOONS OF MORAVENN

Before you read this science fiction story, think about these questions. Are there things that can be learned only through experience, or can all things be learned from books? When have you had to "learn something the hard way"?

The Vanguard Foundation people told us that Moravenn was a young person's world, and they were right.

I'm eighteen. My name is Art Farrell.

I was seventeen when we landed. *Vanguard Beautiful* stood off-planet in a stationary orbit while the shuttles brought us down — two hundred of us, with an age limit of twenty-two, sponsored by the Foundation. And we stood looking at this world where we hoped to spend the rest of our lives building a new civilization, fresh and clean and untainted. We would start anew, with respect for each other and the land.

Moravenn's primary is a topaz-colored star way out in the Vela Spur. There are four other planets, either too close to the sun or not close enough to be habitable. Nature is very wasteful. The site chosen by the Vanguard survey for the colony was a wide plain between two rocky mountain ranges. The soil was rich, the climate dry and healthful, with enough seasonal change to keep us alert. The water in the small river ran clear as glass, humming over glistening stones, the day we landed.

Marta took my hand and we stood close together, breathing in the alien air, feeling the alien ground beneath our feet. Our hearts were pounding, and I could see joy and excitement in her eyes.

"It's wonderful," she whispered. "So empty, so . . . innocent."

That night we saw for the first time the moons of Moravenn.

There are three of them. One is almost as large as our own Luna. The other two are smaller and closer to the planet. They rose one after the other and spanned the sky like three great dusky pearls, drowning the starshine. I think we were all awed by the beauty of them, because of the two hundred voices raised, none was much more than a whisper.

Then I heard someone say that we ought to name the moons, and Jamie Hunter said, "They may already have names, you know. The survey party said there might be people here. Of some sort."

We looked at the mountains, eerie and still in the moonlight, and listened to the silence, wondering whether there was somebody out there and how it would be if we met. We were not frightened, only curious. We had no prejudices and no warlike impulses, and we were certain that we could get along with anybody. But we were all Earth children and we had never met any extraterrestrials, but we had seen plenty of them on the Tri-D.

Marta reached over and took my hand again, comfort for both of us against the strangeness. I know it was very late before I fell asleep.

The shuttles brought down our tools and supplies: the field hospital, the microlibrary, the seeds that would be our crops, the animals that would be our companions, enough food to keep us until harvest time. There were no weapons and no power sources to pour out their poisons into the air. We would use animals and our own unpolluting muscles. *Vanguard Beautiful* went away with six hundred more colonists to plant among the starworlds. For the next two years we would be on our own.

We set up camp on higher ground midway between the east bank of the river and the abrupt red-gold scarp of the mountains. We would live in pre-cut shelters provided for us until we could build permanent houses. With all hands working, it didn't take long to survey the campsite, lay out the streets—which followed the contours of the land so as to be pleasing to the eye as well as functional—and set up the metal frames of the shelters. The plastic panels slipped easily into place, and we had our first town, all our own. There was no single shelter large enough to hold all of us, so our community meetings were in the open. I can still remember the first meeting, the immense feeling of strength and pride and dedication we had.

We were all specialists, of course, trained by the Foundation. My own field is agriculture, and so I was glad when the next phase of our settlement began, the laying out of the fields. Then it was my turn, to test the soil and say which areas were best for root crops, legumes, leaf crops, and the all-important grains. A large area had been set aside for grazing, and our animals seemed to be thriving.

Those were hard days. This alien spring was already well along and it was important to get the crops in the ground as rapidly as possible. Everybody worked. Those who were trained in irrigation methods showed us how to prepare the fields, and then they went up into the mountains with the carpenters, to cut timber for well sweeps and waterwheels.

We broke the sod, and we broke our backs. We were city-bred and found that our gymnasium courses hadn't fitted us for plain, hard manual labor. By the end of the day we were too tired for meetings or cultural events. We ate our rations, fell into our cots, and slept.

I had a lot of responsibility here. Jamie Hunter was agricultural coordinator and I consulted with him, but the decisions were mine.

We got the planting done and then rested our aching muscles. Every day I walked among the fields, searching impatiently for the first signs of green. I had never grown anything before except in the Foundation's training plots, and the sheer size and importance of this operation scared me.

We got two good rains. That and the warm sun brought everything leaping up. We watched our growing crops and loved them, and reckoned we could start thinking about building our houses. We had a big meeting on that, to decide whether to bring down timber from the mountains or to make bricks. We decided against the timber because we would have had to cut too many trees, and that was against our beliefs. We hunted around for a good deposit of clay instead.

We found one, and the construction experts got busy. The weather turned hot, which was good for drying the adobe bricks, but the river began to shrink and I had to call for extra help to keep water coming into the irrigation ditches.

One afternoon, looking northward where the lines of the mountain ranges converged, we saw enormous clouds pile up. They were purple-black and we could see the distant flicker of lightning. The thunder came muffled, like a distant growl, rumbling on the threshold of hearing. Jamie Hunter looked at the beasts walking their patient circles around the creaking waterwheels, and at the people working the well sweeps.

"It's got to be raining up there," Jamie said. "Maybe that'll help us."

We went to bed hoping that the river would rise.

In the middle of the night all two hundred of us tumbled out. By the glorious moonlight of Moravenn we watched a foaming wall of water come down our valley, carrying uprooted trees and great booming boulders. The river had risen, all right. We ran from it, and in the morning we saw that half of our fields had been torn away and half of what was left was flooded and one shelter house was gone.

All that work!

All that time and loving care.

All that irreplaceable food. Our supplies wouldn't last us to another harvest.

This wasn't fair. We felt betrayed. Outraged. And frightened.

"It's your fault!" somebody screamed. "You, Jamie Hunter! And you, Art Farrell!"

Jamie bristled. "What do you mean, it's our fault? Our job was to get the crops in and growing. We did it. Who can help a flood?"

"You ought to have done your planting somewhere else," shouted another voice, and a lot more chimed in. I looked at all those faces, black, white, brown, yellow, Indian bronze, every one hostile and accusing, glaring at Jamie and me. And we were all brothers and sisters! I took a step forward, my fists doubled. I felt hot all over.

"We had to have water, didn't we?" I yelled. "Where else could we have done our planting?"

"Hold it, hold it," said Tom Chen. He was the elected president of our council, twenty-one years old. He climbed up on a rock. "Listen, all of you! We've taken a hard blow, we're in trouble, and it isn't going to do any good to start fighting among ourselves." He turned to Jamie and me. "We must salvage as much as we can. Get to it. The rest of you, start cleaning up the camp."

One girl cried out, "Are you giving us orders, Tom Chen?" But the others kept quiet, and we all went grumbling off to see what had to be done and where to start it.

Marta spoke to me, worried. "You were ready to hit somebody, Art."

"Yes, I was," I said, ashamed. "But they made me angry, blaming Jamie and me. They ought to blame the river."

"It's only a river," Marta said. "It doesn't know what it's doing."

I couldn't find much charity in my heart for the great slop of muddy water that was drowning my young crops.

"Rivers," I said, "can be tamed."

The water went down, leaving big raw gouges and piles of debris behind. For days we worked in the mud, digging and hoeing, desperately trying to save what we could. But when, in our first full meeting after the flood, Tom Chen asked me how much we had saved, I had to admit I didn't know. "I've done everything I could think of, but this is all new to me. We'll have to wait and see."

"A great ag expert you are!" somebody said.

"Let it be," said Tom Chen wearily. "None of us has any real experience. We've read the books, and that's it, and there aren't any books for Moravenn. We'll have to write those ourselves." He was beginning to get lines and shadows in his face that had not been there before. "Anyway, what are you crying about? They told us at the Foundation that this would be hard."

Sure, they did. But how could we have imagined an existence bordering on nightmare?

Tom Chen went on. "We've inventoried the food stocks. It must be obvious to all of you that we'll have to go on reduced rations in order to stretch our supply as far as we can. And I warn you right now, we may have to start killing things."

"You mean, eat meat?" a horrified voice said.

"Start getting used to the idea."

The animal husbandry team jumped up and began making a lot of noise.

"Of course not your animals!" said Tom Chen. "We need them for other things. I'm suggesting hunters and wild game." We had seen animals from time to time, but they were shy and stayed away from us. Perhaps they didn't like our alien scent. "I won't put it to the vote now. But consider it."

"That's silly," Marta said. "We couldn't kill game if we wanted to. We haven't got any weapons."

"We can learn to make some. Art Farrell?"

I was standing up, asking for the floor. I said, "We've got to dam that river. Control it. Otherwise, every dry season we'll hurt for water, and every time there's a storm in the mountains we'll get washed away."

"That's interfering with the environment," said Antelope Woman, the head of our ecology team.

"We've already interfered with it, haven't we? We plowed up

181

the land. We planted seeds, we introduced animals that don't belong here, including ourselves. Where do we stop? And there are the fall crops to think about."

Everybody started talking at once. Finally, when he could make himself heard, Tom Chen said he wouldn't put that to a vote either, but he would appoint a committee of engineers to make a feasibility study.

Some more of the young wheat yellowed and died. Then we had another flood. It wasn't as big as the first one, but it got people to start thinking. At the next meeting the engineers said they could build a dam, and when it came to a vote the ayes had it.

There was a place where the river came through a canyon. The canyon narrowed at one point, and there was a natural basin there to form a big reservoir. The engineers, with all the labor that could be spared from other duties, started work on the dam.

In all this time we had never seen any native humans or humanoids.

Now, suddenly, they came.

I don't know who saw them first. I was carrying a basketful of stones on my head, and the silence seemed to close in around me. People were stopping whatever they were doing, putting down their loads and just standing there. I stopped, too, and set my basket on the ground.

And I was scared. Gut-scared. These were *aliens*.

They weren't doing anything frightening. They were just watching us. They were stockily built and very agile, about the same size as ourselves, taking a median height. Their skin was a ruddy bronze-pink. They had arms and legs, feet and hands — the hands held weapons — and heads.

The heads were what curdled me. They were perfectly human — two eyes set frontward, a small nose, a largish mouth — but the bone structure was so oblong and blocky, the jaw so enormously squared and elongated, that they looked like horses' heads. The resemblance was carried even further, in spite of little close-set ears, by the tight white curls that grew on the tops of their heads and continued on down the back of the neck to the shoulders.

About thirty of them, looking like so many ponies with their hides off.

Tom Chen, who had been toting stones with the rest of us, said,

"Everybody stand easy." He beckoned to the two other council members who were there. The three of them stepped forward, their hands raised in the universal gesture of peace.

Universal?

We hoped so.

One of the aliens courteously laid his weapons aside and came to meet them. I judged he was an old man. He was weathered and wrinkled, and his eyes had an expression of patient wisdom. These people did not strike me as being savages.

Our representative and theirs stood face to face, gabbling and making gestures. The gabble was useless so they dropped that. The old man did a series of things with his hands, pointing to the river and then to the dam, and then making a motion of *going*. He repeated this several times, and finally Tom Chen said, "I think he's telling us that water must be free to run."

He imitated the old man. The old man's face brightened, and he wagged his huge chin. I noticed they seemed to talk a lot with their chins. The ones in the background were having a busy discussion about us.

The old man trotted over to our embryonic dam. He picked up a stone and threw it away. He looked at Tom Chen to see if he understood.

He did. "He wants us to tear it down," Tom said, and stared at the old man in baffled annoyance. "How do you explain to him?"

"Why not invite them to our camp?" I said. "Let them see why we want to dam the river. Let Sammy have a crack at them." That was Sam Agatelli, our extraterrestrial anthropologist. "Maybe he can communicate with them." Sammy had been filling in on everybody else's work; it was time he had his chance to show off.

And for all our sakes, we hoped he knew his business.

It was no struggle to get them to come with us. They were curious, and I guess they felt strong enough to take us on, if it should come to that. We all marched back to the camp together.

On the way, I found myself walking next to a young native about my own age, as near as I could guess. His skin was still fresh and glossy, and his blue eyes had a bright sparkle to them. He seemed to want to strike up an acquaintance, and so I smiled and said my name, pointing to myself. He bared a set of big white teeth in his equine face and made a noise that sounded like *Hrrng*.

"Hrung?" I said, pointing to him.

He wagged his chin and laughed. He shifted spear and throw-ing stick to his left hand, reached out his right hand, and touched me three times on the chest, over the heart. I couldn't help flinch-ing a bit, but I guessed it was a ritual gesture indicating friendship, and so I reached out and touched him the same way. This time we both laughed, and some of the feeling of strangeness began to ebb.

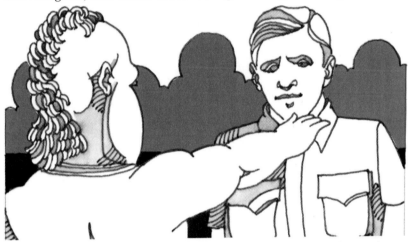

There was big excitement in the camp when we showed up. Tom Chen had sent a runner ahead to warn them. Sam Agatelli was out to meet us, quivering like a puppy. People were setting out food at the meeting ground. They were falling over themselves to make our guests feel welcome and at the same time trying to hide their own nervousness.

We did the hospitality bit. The natives — they called themselves the R'Lann, as nearly as Sammy could make it out — were grave and courteous. They examined all our off-planet things with less amazement than we expected. Then we took them down to the fields and showed them what the river had done.

Very carefully Sammy drew pictographs in the dust. He drew the immature crop, then the mature grain, then a picture of a man eating it. The old man rubbed them out impatiently with his foot.

"I guess they know about agriculture," Sammy said, and drew a picture of the river. He set two stones to be the cliffs and he built a little earthen dam between them. He drew a lake behind the dam. He indicated how the water would flow through a floodgate, nice and tame and well behaved. He indicated the fields. He smiled and made gestures meaning "good."

The old man shook his head. He took Sammy's stick and began to draw pictures of his own. First he drew a big circle and stamped on the ground; the circle was Moravenn — our name, not his. Then he drew a moon. He drew two more moons, in the positions where we now saw them. He erased the two smaller moons and redrew them, in different positions. He did this rapidly three or four times, until the smaller moons were superimposed on the big one. He said something sonorous and very emphatic, and kicked over Sammy's little dam. He threw the stick down and called his people together and they marched away. Hrung looked back and wagged his jaw at me, and I waved.

Then we stared at the old man's drawing.

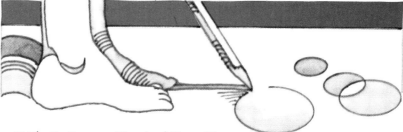

"What's it mean?" asked Tom Chen.

Sammy shook his head. "When the three moons are in line, the dam goes out? I don't know. Maybe. Or maybe it's a symbol of some kind, something to do with their worship. Everybody's got moon myths."

"When the three moons are in line," said Tom Chen, frowning. "Gravitational pull? If it's strong enough, it could make trouble. But how often does that happen — if ever?"

Nobody could answer that. And we had no computer to do the enormously complicated math that might have told us the answer.

Thoughtfully Tom Chen erased the old man's picture. "We'll build the dam anyway."

"Maybe we ought to think about that, Tom," said Sammy. "This is their world. They might know something we don't."

"Bunch of bare-backed savages," somebody said. "What would they know?"

"Besides," said Antelope Woman, "if it is something to do with their worship, and we break a taboo, they might get angry enough to attack us, and they're armed. We're not."

186

"And we don't know how many more of them there may be," somebody said. "We ought to do something—"

"Make some clubs!"

"Pile up stones!"

"Build a wall around the camp!"

In a minute everybody was quarreling about what we ought to do. Tom Chen waved his arms and shouted.

"You want to eat, don't you? Then we've got to build that dam!"

Through the clamor of voices I said to Tom, "Looks to me as though there's only one way to find out for sure what they mean. I'll go and stay with them for a while, learn the language."

"Do you think they'll let you?"

"I can try."

Tom nodded and turned again to the crowd. I said good-by to Marta. She wasn't at all happy. Neither was Sammy, but he didn't make any offers to go himself. I picked up my bedroll and hurried after the R'Lann.

I had a time catching up with them. They really traveled. But I finally did. They stopped when they saw me. I didn't know what they might do, but I held up my hands and smiled and prayed. Hrung said something to the old man. The old man nodded, and Hrung came, wagging his chin and grinning, and led me into the group.

We all went on at a loping trot, up over some cliffs and along a ridge, with the sun hot on my back and my legs aching, and then down some more cliffs into a red rock valley with its own stream and its patches of green and gold where things were growing. The patches were irregular and looked natural, and there were no houses. That was why the survey people had not been sure, on their flyover, whether anybody actually did live here.

I learned later that the different bands of the R'Lann—this was only one of them—moved from place to place according to the seasons, and they were somewhere else when the survey crew had a look at their valley. Otherwise they might have seen the women and children tending the garden patches or dressing game.

The R'Lann live in caves, neat rooms cut into the soft rock and walled up in front with stones. I found out that a cave is pretty nice—cool in summer, warm in winter, and if you want to heat it, a tiny blaze, hardly more than a lamp flame, will do. If you keep the front wall in repair, a cave is impervious to weather. There's no better place to be at night when a thunderstorm is trying to pound the world apart. The R'Lann decorate their dwellings with carvings outside and bright wall paintings in the rooms.

It was a strange new life I settled into. Hrung seemed to have adopted me as his special property. He spent hours teaching me the language, and I felt the old man was anxious to have him do this as quickly as possible.

So the dry, hot days were spent in learning, and at night we watched the moons.

I mean, *watched*. There was a special place high on the cliff, where a very elaborate diagram was incised into the rock. There were three stone counters on the diagram, and someone had to sit up there all night long moving the counters as the moons moved. Normally, Hrung told me, this was done only once a month. But now something was about to happen. I could feel the undercurrent of excitement and the fear. You could smell the fear in the air of the valley. Something was coming.

When it was Hrung's turn to watch, he let me sit up with him. The floor of the watching place was worn smooth and hollow, and it was strange to touch it. It was as though I touched time.

The moons seemed to be lower and brighter and more beautiful than ever.

"They will build the Ladder of Souls," Hrung said, "so the spirits of our dead may climb to the holy sky. It is a time of judgment." His voice was very quiet, as if he feared the moons might hear him. He didn't look real, either, sitting like a statue with his massive head bent forward and the shadows on his long face. "I am unlucky."

"Why is that?"

"Unless I die very soon, which I don't want to do, my soul will have to wait many years for its turn at the Ladder. My father has not seen it before. The oldest of the old people has not seen it."

"How long is it between these — these happenings?"

Hrung shrugged. "The old people say words, but I don't know what they mean. A long time." He swung his head around and the moonlight burned on his white curls. "There are no old people in your band."

"No."

"But the elderly keep wisdom alive."

"The elderly keep war alive, and lies, and greed," I said. "We do not trust them."

"Well," said Hrung, "perhaps it is so on your world."

The moonfire died in the west. The old R'Lann — his name was Kladth and he was chief of the band — came and looked at the markers. Then he motioned with his chin, and we followed him down to the floor of the valley and far along to a desolate and lonely place I hadn't seen before. There was a cave opening and we went to it. The path was worn hollow like the watching place.

It was a natural cave. The walls had been smoothed for the paintings that covered them. Thin strips of limber bone were set into cracks in the floor and stood up like white wands. Kladth led me around to study the paintings. Hrung stayed by the opening. I think he didn't like this place. There was a coldness in it.

I couldn't believe what I saw there. I wasn't even certain that I understood. R'Lann art is very stylized and full of symbols.

Kladth pointed to the floor. "Down," he said. "Look. Feel."

He made me lie down on the rock with my nose almost touching one of the bone wands. I wondered what I was supposed to feel.

Deep down beneath me there came a groaning and stirring, as though Moravenn moved in her sleep. The bone wand bent from side to side.

"It begins," Kladth said.

We left the cave, with all those white wands quivering.

"Your band is still building," Kladth said to me.

"The dam?"

"And houses. This world does not consent to buildings. Go and tell them. Tell them to stop or they will die."

Hrung led me back over the ridges to where my people still sweated on the dam. It was higher than I had thought possible. Water had already backed up behind it, a blue lake shimmering in the sun.

Hrung said, "I will stop here." I went on alone.

Tom Chen and some others met me. The others went on working. They looked thin and sullen; the short rations were telling on them.

"You look fat enough," said Sam Agatelli.

"I've been eating meat," I said. "It was that or starve."

"Savage," somebody said, and spat.

Tom Chen told everyone to shut up. "What did you find out, Art?"

"They say you must stop building or die."

"Tear down the dam?"

"And the houses."

"Or they'll kill us, is that it?"

"Kladth said, 'This world does not consent to buildings.' I think he meant the planet will kill you. Tom, they have a cave, with strips of bone set in the floor. Sort of primitive seismographs. Something is happening, deep down in the rock. I felt it. And there are paintings. Pictures of cities, and how they were destroyed. Quakes and tidal waves. It's the moons, I think. They watch. They have a diagram —"

"How can you be sure of all this?" asked Sammy. "You're not a trained anthropologist." He was sulky because he knew he ought to have gone instead of me.

"According to anthropologists," I said, "their name ought to mean something like The People, right?" Sammy nodded. "Well, R'Lann means The Survivors. They believe they were colonists themselves long ago. Their legends say they came from the stars, and there was a picture of a great ship in the cave. At least . . ."

"At least what?" asked Tom Chen.

"That's what Kladth said it was."

Word had spread now that I wanted them to pull down the dam. More people came. Some carried stones or clubs.

"We've worked too hard on this to destroy it because of a legend," Tom said, and the crowd growled. "Our winter crops depend on it, our lives depend on it. Have you any better evidence?"

"The moons," I said. "When the three moons are in line, that's when everything breaks loose. It doesn't happen very often. There's time enough for people to forget and build again. That's why they have the paintings and the diagram at the watching place."

"Is that all they told you?"

I thought I had to be honest and tell them everything. Maybe if I hadn't. . . . But I told them what Hrung had said about the Ladder of Souls.

"Moon myth," said Sammy contemptuously. "Just myth."

"And I can tell you this," somebody shouted. "If your hammer-headed friends come here looking for trouble, they'll get it. We haven't sweated our hearts out for nothing."

Hands waved sticks and stones. Tom Chen sighed and sent them back to work. "We have to go on what we know and believe," he said. "Don't hold it against them, Art. We're tired and hungry. What's worse, we found that somebody's been stealing from the food supplies. I've had to post guards." He shook his head. "Where did it go, Art? Everything we started with — love, brotherhood, faith . . ."

"I guess," I said, "things just aren't as simple as we thought."

"Simple!" Tom said bitterly. "No. Art, will you go back to the R'Lann and find out for certain about the moons? They make me uneasy, too."

I went back to the red valley with Hrung. And that night the Singing began.

In every cave the sacred bundles were taken from the niches and opened and the sacred garments taken out. Only the stars know how old they were. They were woven of a silvery thread that looked like finely drawn metal, and they weighed a lot. I don't know what the cloth had been used for originally. Shelter tents, perhaps, for the colony. I knew now that that legend was true. The R'Lann reverently clothed themselves and marched in solemn procession up the cliff path, past the watching place, to the highest point, where there was an altar cut from the living rock.

Those who had no garments came behind, and sat down modestly at the back of the space below the altar. The robed men gathered around it. Kladth mounted the low step and laid a wrapped object on the altar. He undid the wrappings, and I saw without too much surprise that the object was a small telescope. The robed men chanted. Kladth stepped down. The chant continued, with halts for our responses.

I whispered to Hrung, "What are we doing?"

"Singing the moons," he said. "Telling them how to make the Ladder of Souls, reminding them to spare the living who obey their laws. The Singing is very important. You see, in so much time, the moons may have forgotten."

So we sang. Night after night we sang, and the moons came closer together, and the trouble of the world increased. The small river in the valley began to behave strangely. It rose and fell, overflowing its banks and washing back again. The women and children hurried to harvest the last of the crops, and there was no joy about it, only a furtive haste. People hardly spoke during those days. The oppression of fear and holiness was stifling. I wanted to leave it, but Tom Chen had told me to find out for certain.

Then came a night when the innermost moon took a large bite out of the middle moon, which was almost touching the outermost moon. I looked down from our rocky platform and saw the river stand straight up out of its bed, shining in the wild light, and I knew for certain. I touched Hrung and said good-by, very softly so as not to disturb the Singing. I went down the path with the mountain shaking under me, and the standing river fell suddenly apart in lashing coils of water. Some of it wetted me, and I was cold enough already.

I knew the way back now, and the beautiful, gliding, deadly moons gave me light enough. The sound of the Singing followed me for a long while. When it faded I could listen to the stones knocking together whenever the world shook.

I found Tom Chen sitting above the dam, watching the lake. I sat down beside him. The water had a life of its own. We could hear it moving, talking to itself, searching for a way to freedom. The moons were calling it, and it wanted to go.

"How long do we have?" asked Tom Chen.

"I don't know," I said, and told him about the standing-up river.

"Not long, then," he said, and rose. "We'll do what we can."

Day was breaking as we came into the town. I don't think anybody had slept much, tired as they were. People who had moved into permanent houses were out looking at them to see what damage the night's quakes had done. Tom called them all.

Marta came to me, but she treated me like a stranger. Her face was hollow and her hands were scarred with work.

Tom Chen spoke. "I think now the R'Lann were right. I think we made a mistake. The pull of the moons has been getting stronger and stronger—you can feel that. When they come into line, everything on this side of the planet that isn't nailed down will be obeying that pull. That includes our lake. And I think we had better get out."

"Just leave all this? Everything we've worked for?" The pinched, tired faces squinted at him in the morning light.

"You're only guessing," said Antelope Woman. "You don't *know*."

"Of course I don't know," said Tom irritably. "We have no past on this world. But the R'Lann—"

"You've been listening to Art Farrell," said Sammy. "He's been swallowing everything those people fed him. Legend, superstition . . ."

"The quakes aren't superstition," I said. "'The river came up out of its bed. I saw that. The lake will do the same thing."

"Let the water out!" somebody shouted.

Gust Clausen, our chief engineer, said, "We can't. The floodgate's not finished. All we could do is blow the dam, and the whole lake would come down on us anyway. We weren't counting on anything like this."

The voices rose, blaming Tom, me, the engineers, the Foundation, and the survey for getting them into this mess. Tom finally quieted them.

"Those of you who want to gamble that things won't really get that bad are free to stay, though I don't advise it. Those of you who want to come with me, get busy. Take the animals up into the hills, except for the draft teams. Food supplies, tools, hospital, library, anything we have time to move, we'll move." Somebody protested, and Tom snarled, "If nothing happens, we can bring them all down again, can't we?"

So we took refuge, such as it was, among the hills. Eighteen people elected to stay behind.

On the night of the Ladder of Souls, when the two inner moons eclipsed the outer one and the sky turned dark and coppery, and the stars blazed bright, we lay hugging the ground that rumbled and shook and sent the loose rock crashing down. And we saw a great pillar of water rise up above the dam and then slowly, slowly lean over, with tatters of itself shredding away around it. It fell

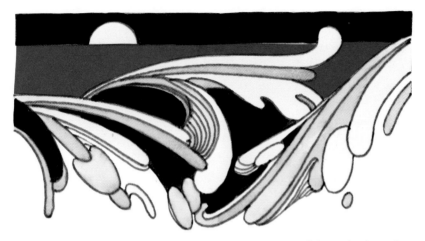

into the valley with a roar like the end of the world, and when the night cleared we could see nothing at all below but a glistening wetness.

So here we are, one hundred and eighty-two of us. The R'Lann have been good friends. They helped to feed us until we learned how to make spears and hunt, and they're helping us cut caves in the cliffs. They helped us to bury our dead, the eleven we could find, and I'm listening to Kladth explain agricultural methods. We'll make it.

But it's strange. Nothing worked out the way we expected, not even ourselves. Tom Chen and I haven't got many friends now. People seem to blame Tom for bad leadership, even though we all voted on everything. And the dam was my idea. I *thought* I was right, I was doing the best I knew how at the time, and I did try to warn them. It's not my fault they wouldn't listen. But they thought they were right. As for the eighteen who died, they made their own decision, and I'm finding out that if you make a wrong one, nothing can protect you from the consequences.

Some of our people are determined to go home when *Vanguard Beautiful* comes again. This wasn't what they bargained for, and they've had it. Most of them, though, seem to be taking up the challenge. They're beginning to think of Moravenn as their world. We have a past here now—and a burying ground and the beginning of a legend—and I think the colony will stay. Perhaps in time we'll even get recruits to come.

And I will stay, of course. Someone has to teach our children how to sing the moons of Moravenn.

Eve Merriam

A CHARM FOR OUR TIME

HIGHWAY   TURNPIKE   THRUWAY   MALL
DIAL DIRECT   LONG DISTANCE CALL
FREEZE-DRY   HIGH-FI   PAPERBACK
JET LAG   NO SAG   VENDING SNACK
MENTHOLATED SHAVING STICK
TAPE RECORDER   CAMERA CLICK
SUPERSONIC   LIFETIME SUB
DAYGLO   DISCOUNT   CREDIT CLUB
MOTEL   KEYCHAIN   ASTRODOME
INSTAMATIC   LOTION   FOAM
ZIPCODE   BALLPOINT
—BURN BURGER BURN!—
NO DEPOSIT
NO RETURN

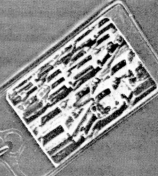

Nick Pease

TAI CHI TURNABOUT

Donna Wah Kee growled at her brother.

"You *said* I could use it!"

"That was *last* week!"

The two glared at one another, gripping opposite ends of a skateboard.

"But mine's broken!" protested Donna. Her glasses slid down her nose, and she pushed them back up impatiently. "Besides, you're not even going to use it today."

"So what?" Jim Wah Kee shouted. "It's still mine, and I don't have to let *anyone* use it. You broke your own board—how do I know you won't break mine, too?"

"But that was an *accident!*"

"Phooey—you're just careless with things," scoffed Jim. He tugged harder on his end. Donna suddenly gave up.

"Okay, Selfish," she said, letting go of the board. Her quick release almost toppled her brother over backward. "Keep your stupid skateboard. Who wants it? I'm sure I can borrow one at the tournament anyway." She made for the doorway. "Only, next time you need a favor don't come whining to me!"

"Oh, yeah? Well, don't do me any fa—"

But the door slammed on his word, and she was gone.

Donna stomped down the front steps and onto the leaf-strewn sidewalk. It was an overcast and windy fall day in Skokie, Illinois. The girl glanced at the slate-gray sky, then looked up and down the street. No friends around. With a sigh of frustration, she started northward toward the schoolyard.

As she walked along, she fumbled with the buttons of her cardigan. One tore loose in her hand. She muttered something and thrust it into her pocket, kicking angrily at a pile of leaves. At the corner she waited impatiently for the green light. When it came, she stepped abruptly into the street, failing to notice a car turning in her direction. The driver slammed on the brakes and the frightened girl jumped.

"Sorry," she said meekly. The driver just glowered and drove on.

"Wow, what's the *matter* with me today?" she thought to herself. "First I have a screaming match with Jim and then I almost get myself killed." She reached the schoolyard and saw that it was deserted. Glumly she started across the baseball field.

But the yard wasn't entirely deserted. Out of Donna's sight, behind an equipment shack, three other eighth-graders were also arriving. Alan Bergman spotted Donna first, and a mischievous gleam came into his hazel eyes.

"Hey, there's Donna," he said. "Wait a minute. Let's hide here and pounce on her when she comes past!" The others, Sherry Pulaski and Ron Robinson, grinned in agreement.

The three flattened themselves against the wall, stifling giggles, as Donna approached. She came abreast of the shack, and Sherry gave the signal. With a whoop she broke from cover and aimed a flying leap at Donna's back.

What took place next happened almost too quickly to tell. A split-second before Sherry's hands reached her shoulders, Donna doubled over in a reflex action and took a half-step backward. The attacker's hands found nothing but empty air, and the force of her leap carried Sherry into a midair somersault. With a deft pivot on her left foot, Donna stepped smoothly under the charge and left her friend sprawling in the grass.

Instantly, another surprise. Alan was running right on Sherry's heels, and when she tumbled he was about to run headlong into Donna. Instead, Donna continued her graceful turn and avoided him. At the same instant, her foot shot out and caught the boy's ankle. It wasn't a kick—in fact, he barely felt it—but it was enough to spin him around and throw him on his back. Without breaking the flow of her motion, Donna turned to Ron.

The boy was totally at a loss. He was off balance, his friends were flattened, and suddenly it seemed a wildcat was pouncing on him. Up came Donna's foot toward his stomach, down came her hand toward his nose, and from out of nowhere one of her elbows whipped toward his throat. Donna didn't touch Ron, but the boy's legs went out from under him anyway. A half-second later he sat on the infield, gaping up at her. Donna's face had been calm during the counterattack, but now she smiled in amusement.

"What're you doing down there?" she teased. "I never touched you!" To Ron's amazement, she was right. Not a blow had been struck. She had bluffed him right off his feet!

"Oh, wow!" Sherry laughed, dusting herself off, "that was fantastic, Donna—how'd you do all that?"

"Yeah," said Alan, "what was that, karate or something?"

"Nope, it was tai chi," said Donna. (She pronounced the words TYE-GEE.) "It's a kind of exercise I do."

"Some exercise!" growled Ron. "You could hurt someone doing stuff like that, you know."

"Oh, Robinson," Sherry chided, "it's only your male ego that got bruised. Here, let me help you up."

"No thanks," sniffed the boy, getting to his feet.

"Tai chi is sort of like karate and kung fu," Donna went on, "but it's not meant to hurt people except in self-defense. Most people study it just for the exercise."

"But how does it work?" Alan asked. "You seemed to be everywhere and nowhere at once!"

Donna smiled. "That's one way of putting it, I guess. It's just a matter of not being where another person is at a given time, and vice versa. See what I mean?" He didn't.

Donna tried again. She pointed to an emblem on the front of her T-shirt. "Well, look: This is the tai chi symbol. It's round, see? That means it's something whole. It's also divided into halves by the two colors. But here's the important thing: The halves are not *opposite* each other, as they are when you divide them by a straight line. They're separate, but they're together. And see these two dots? They show how each of the two sides also contains the other side. Each completes the other side, so the figure is whole even though it's not all the same."

"Pardon my ignorance," Ron remarked, "but what has that got to do with fighting?"

"I was coming to that," Donna said patiently. She pointed again to the symbol. "Look—here's Sherry and here's me, the two different colors. When she jumped, she was using force in this direction. All I had to do was move out of her way and let her motion complete itself."

"That's right, I never laid a hand on you," Sherry added.

"See, we're used to thinking that if things are opposite they're *against* each other. But tai chi says that opposites are really *part* of each other. Here, I'll show you." Donna stepped facing Sherry and held up her palms in front of her. "Now, Sherry, when I say *go* you push against me as hard as you can,

okay?'' With an embarrassed half smile, the other girl nodded and placed her palms on Donna's.

"One-two-three-*go*!"

The two girls strained hard against each other, their feet skidding in the soft dirt of the infield. After a few seconds Donna motioned to stop.

"There," she said, puffing and panting. "That's what we usually do. When someone uses force on us, we try to fight it, to *resist* it by pushing in the opposite direction, right?"

They nodded curiously.

"And where does that get us?" Donna asked. "Nowhere, that's where. We're both pushing, our motions are incomplete, and we're wasting a lot of energy. But now watch again." She signaled to Sherry and they took up their positions. "Ready? One-two-three-*go*!"

Again Sherry pushed, but this time Donna pulled back and down and Sherry ended up falling on her face.

"You okay, Sherry?" Donna asked, helping her up.

"I'm fine," Sherry panted. "But Donna, would you please tell us how you *did* that?"

"It's very simple," she replied. "I just didn't resist you.

Instead of working against your force, I just changed its direction a little and got out of the way. Then your force could complete itself, and when it completed itself you fell flat on your face."

"Hey, I think I get it," said Alan. "You use the other guy's strength against him!"

"—or *her*," corrected Sherry.

"But you moved so fast," Ron said. "How did you figure out where to go?"

Donna pondered the question as she cleaned her glasses. "Well, I don't really *think* about it anymore. I've been doing the exercise for so long that it just works like a reflex."

"Show us the exercise, Donna," said Alan. "Do you break bricks with your hands or anything?"

Donna laughed. "No, Goofy. I *told* you there's no violence to it." She glanced at her watch. "The whole exercise takes about twenty minutes, but I have to be home pretty soon. So I'll just do a little right now. This takes a lot of concentration, so don't interrupt me, okay?"

Her friends sat on the grass to watch Donna perform the slow, graceful exercise. Starting from an erect posture, she smoothly glided into a series of circular motions. Her arms described circles, sometimes moving together and sometimes in opposite directions. At the same time she made careful pivots on her heels and toes, moving constantly and shifting her weight easily from one leg to another. Occasionally she thrust a hand or a foot out, as she had done against Ron. But the pace of her movements was so slow that it looked more like a dance than a means of attack. Throughout the exercise her face wore a look of effortless concentration. Finally she straightened up again and turned to the others.

"Gee, that was *pretty*!" Sherry said with enthusiasm. "And you can keep moving like that for twenty minutes without getting tired?"

"Just the reverse," said Donna. "Instead of working hard and wasting energy, you move slowly and build up energy inside. At the same time the concentration helps you get rid of tension in your mind. That's the real key to the whole exercise—to create a harmony between your body and your mind. I always feel super after doing tai chi."

It was obvious how true that was. All of Donna's earlier anger had dissolved during the exercise and seemed to flow out through the motions of her body. Now, with her back straight and her shoulders squared, Donna presented the very picture of relaxed composure.

"Hey, I'd like to get in on that, too," said Sherry. "Where do they teach it, Donna?"

"They have classes every Saturday at the 'Y,' " she answered.

"Wow, it'd be fun if we could practice together."

"The 'Y,' huh?" said Ron disappointedly. "Then it's only for girls, right?"

Donna patted his arm reassuringly. "No, Robinson, it's for *persons* of all kinds — you can sign up." She checked her watch again. "Oh, look," she said, "I've got to change clothes for the skateboard tournament, but I'll see you guys afterward, okay?"

She said good-by and started for home, her spirits high. As she rounded the corner and bounded up the front steps, she discovered her brother sitting on the front porch.

"Hi, Jimmy — Dad home yet?"

Her brother bristled. "Why? You aren't going to ask him to use my skateboard, are you?"

"No, I was going to get a ride—"

" — 'cause you *still* can't use it, understand?"

Donna stiffened. She clenched her fists and was about to yell back at him. But just then some words flashed in her memory: *How did you do that?* Sherry had asked, and her answer had been *Simple . . . I just didn't resist you.* All at once her face slackened and her hands relaxed.

"Okay, I can't use it. I'll borrow one from somebody."

"That's right!" the boy raved. "Because you're not going to go messing with *my* board and break it!"

"Uh-huh," the girl said mildly. "You're worried about that, right?"

"Right!"

"Okay." She gazed back at him, expressionless.

He glared back irritably — and just a shade curiously. "Well, what's with you?" he demanded. "You mean you don't even *want* it now?"

She shrugged. "It would be nice to have." Strangely, she really didn't care that much about the board. It was no big deal.

"Well, you can just—just forget it," he grumbled.

Donna said nothing.

"Anyway, you can borrow one there, right?"

"Uh-huh."

Jim was stammering. "Because, I mean, you *did* lose your own board—I mean break—I mean broke it, right?"

"Yup, I did."

There was a pause. The boy's rage was spent.

"So you'd be *super*-careful with mine, wouldn't you?"

She shrugged again. "Sure I would."

Feeling a bit foolish, Jim avoided his sister's eyes and reached for the board. "Okay, then," he said, thrusting it at her. "You *can* use it—but you'd better win a prize with it!"

"Thanks, Generous, I intend to," she said. They both grinned. Jim noticed the emblem on Donna's tee shirt.

"By the way," he remarked, "are you still doing that tai chi stuff?"

"More than you know!" she thought to herself. "Yes," she answered. "Why?"

"Good," he kidded, "it seems to be making a more civilized human being out of you."

She grinned again and nodded.

"Thanks!"

I DON'T LIKE YOUR ATTITUDE

What do you suppose the girl in the picture is reading? An editorial, perhaps? Or a letter to the editor? Whatever it is, she doesn't seem to like the opinion expressed by the writer.

While you are reading it is important that you recognize what the author's purpose or attitude is. Is he or she writing to inform? To entertain? Or to express an opinion? Most textbooks and books on factual material, as well as most reference books, are written to inform or to give information. News stories in newspapers are also written to inform. Short stories and novels, personal accounts, and humorous essays are written to entertain. Editorials and letters to the editor, as well as editorial cartoons, are written to express an opinion or to persuade readers to think or behave in a certain way. Advertising material is also written for this purpose.

Read the selections on this and the next page. Has each one been written to inform, to entertain, or to express an opinion?

The person who came up with the idea of raising transportation fares in the city should have his or her head examined. The fares are already too high, and for what? Slow, unreliable service. Broken-down equipment and drafty riding conditions. Dirty floors and torn seats. It's too bad we can't all afford to buy a car or walk to work. That would teach transportation officials a lesson.

Studies of animal behavior show that animals defend their homes and territories in a variety of ways. Some species merely behave in a threatening and noisy manner, hoping that intruders will leave. Many monkeys and birds do this. Other species will fight fiercely to defend their homes. Rats, dogs, and the tiny stickleback fish are examples. Studies have also shown that animals become more and more aggressive as their territories are crowded out by human beings.

The Daily Bee fully supports the actions of the City Council in the latest open housing dispute. No one should ever be prevented from living in any part of the city because of race or religion. We hope the Council will crack down strongly on realtors and communities that attempt to restrict housing.

When my parents came home from their vacation they immediately started looking around the house.

"O.K., where are all the animals you took in while we were away?" asked my mother.

"Do I dare sit in my chair, or will I disturb something?" laughed my father.

"This one is new," announced mother, as she pulled a baby raccoon from under the couch.

"Her mother's dead," I said defensively. "I'll let her go as soon as she can fend for herself. And the snakes can live on the porch."

"Snakes?" my parents said in unison.

"Well, I have to go to the library and do my homework," I whispered and slipped out the door.

Robin Campbell began running when she was nine years old, and she has not stopped since. Her amazing ability to run long distances at record-breaking speeds has taken her to track meets in many parts of the world, from Martinique to New Zealand to the Soviet Union. In 1974, Robin broke the world record for 600 yards.

In May 1975, Robin said good-by to her family in Washington, D.C., and set off for a "friendly competition" tour of the People's Republic of China with the United States Track and Field Team. Until a few years before, American travel to the Chinese mainland had been prohibited.

At the age of sixteen, Robin was one of the best runners in the world and the youngest member of the team of sixty-six American athletes. During the trip she made notes of her impressions of China and its people. Highlights from her China journal follow.

Robin Campbell's CHINA JOURNAL

Edited by
June M. Omura

<u>May 16</u> Canton. We were met by the first of three Chinese national teams. A very warm reception started when we got off the train. The Chinese clapped continuously for ten or twenty minutes, and we didn't really know how to react. Finally, the big wheels of the Chinese team began a hand-shaking line that ended a quarter of a mile later with about five hundred people involved.

The Chinese athletes stared at us. The women were interested in our hair. They had never seen braids on a girl's hair before. Their hair was kind of short, cut even all over and very silky. When we got together, we combed each other's hair. We made theirs into ponytails and they tried to braid ours.

The Chinese girls laughed at me, saying I'm so tall. (I'm 5 feet, 8 inches.) Except for one or two girls, they were almost all smaller than I am. We talked in sign language mostly, but when interpreters were around we went up to someone and talked about our families and schools and stuff.

My favorite food so far was sweet and sour pork. When I bit into the hot pork my face turned red. My friends thought I was choking. I suffered with the hot meat in my mouth because if I had spit it out the Chinese might have thought I disliked their food.

The Chinese all seem friendly. Big smiles. You almost thought that even if things weren't going well for them, they'd still give you those big smiles. They don't want to give a bad impression of their country.

<u>May 17</u> We tried to exchange shirts with the Chinese, but you could tell they didn't want to wear ours. They all wear the same thing. If a girl had worn one of our shirts, everybody would have looked down on her. They don't want to try to be any better than each other or show off.

CHINA

Peking

Shanghai

Canton

213

The children in China wear a lot of different colors, but the adults and the kids our age wear the same thing: black shoes, dark baggy pants, and the same kind of jacket. Our kids kept saying, "I wouldn't wear those baggy pants all the time," because they thought those clothes made the Chinese all look alike. I didn't think so, though.

The Americans just act like themselves, and the Chinese have never seen people with such ways. For instance, we don't stick together in groups, and they're always doing things as a group. They do everything on time and always march in step. When we paraded before the meet, it was raining. The Americans were saying, "Oh, my shoes" and "We're getting all wet," but the Chinese marched in step through the rain.

May 18 The Kuang Chow Museum in Canton. We walked up all five stories to the roof, where we had a beautiful view of the city. I don't know what I expected, but the buildings didn't have those funny curved tops like I thought they would. They looked just like ours, except all the buildings had big posters of Chairman Mao, Lenin, and some other people on them. (Even in the train station, we saw those posters.) From the museum I could see a tall monument, not as big as the Washington Monument back home. It was a monument to goats. Canton used to be called the City of the Goat.

May 19 They had photographers who followed us and took pictures of us while we were training and exercising so the Chinese athletes could copy us. But I don't think they should try to copy us. We have so many different track styles and so many different ways of training. They think everybody should do the same exercise. It seems to work for them, but we believe that not everybody needs the same thing. We were almost always way out in front in the races, the Americans bunched up together about fifty yards ahead of the Chinese. In a way, it was like the Nationals at home, because the Americans on the trip are the best from our country and are always the main competition here.

Many of the Cantonese are boat people who spend their entire lives on riverboats. I saw people bathing, washing clothes and dishes, getting water for drinking and household purposes, swimming, and dumping garbage all in the same water. So you can imagine how the water looked.

<u>May 20</u> Shanghai.* Our hosts took us to a commune where they raised all kinds of things: rabbits and chickens, rice and mushrooms. We visited a man who had built his own house out of cinder blocks. It was like an Abraham Lincoln cabin, but instead of logs, he used cinder blocks. He lived there with his wife, his son, his daughter and her husband, and his mother. We asked him what he did when the weather got cold, because there was no heating. He said they just piled on more blankets.

When we left, the grandmother came out of the kitchen. We told her, through an interpreter, that her home cooking sure smelled good.

<u>May 21</u> Every place we went, we saw bicycles. I just couldn't believe the things they did with their bicycles. You'd see them pulling heavy motors in a cart, or a load of produce. They'd even ride up steep hills. That's one reason I wouldn't want to live here—

*<u>Editor's note</u>: The largest city in China, one of the largest cities in the world, Shanghai has almost 11 million people. In Shanghai, as in rural China, communes became part of a national program called the Great Leap Forward, which was started in 1958. This program emphasized shared responsibility for increased agricultural and manufacturing production.

riding a bicycle every-
where you go would take you
forever to get there!

May 22 At a porcelain factory, we saw Chinese men and
women molding, carving, and
painting statues. At the
end of the tour, the guides
had arranged for us to buy
finished products. After
hearing that the statues
were all under $3.00, the
Americans went wild. I
bought twelve statues, which
cost me almost $20.00. When
buying these statues I
hadn't realized that to-
gether they weighed almost
twenty pounds. And the trip
is only half completed.

May 24 The Children's Palace in Shanghai. My favorite visit. I really enjoyed
it. The Children's Palace
is a volunteer school that
meets for two hours every
afternoon. Youngsters come
in from the country to attend—about 800 to 1000
children come every day.
What they learn they go back
and teach to their class-
mates back home. I saw them
working on a huge motor in
one room. They also study
embroidery, singing, dance,
and musical instruments.

How smart the Chinese
children are! At the Children's Palace I was assigned
to an eleven-year-old girl.
I didn't understand a word
she said, but she just
talked and talked. I got
to play table tennis with a
little boy who looked about
seven. Boy, he was really
hitting the ball fast. When
he played me, I said, "I'm
very slooooow," so he started
going very slow. He held
the paddle differently from
the way I did. And he beat
me.

I had wanted so badly to
hear the children sing.
Some days I'd wake up and
catch them singing when they
were marching to school.
They'd be blowing whistles
and marching to a certain
rhythm. At the end of our
visit to the Children's
Palace, some of the little
kids dressed up and put on
a show that consisted of

singing and dancing. I really enjoyed the Children's Palace.

May 26 Peking, the capital of China. The old Imperial Palaces and other old buildings are in the Forbidden City here. Our guides said it would be wise to stay close by because we were surrounded by 900 rooms that all look alike. We saw the rooms used by the emperor's wife in prerevolutionary times. In one room we saw a mirror that wasn't made out of glass but of shiny gold, a bed piled with silk spreads, a jewelry box made out of ivory and jade, a marble teapot, and many other valuable things. We also saw a diamond ring valued at more than $25,000. We got to see only 20 of the rooms.

One elderly woman I saw had a lot of difficulty walking. Her feet had been bound when she was a child because of an old Chinese tradition of beauty. She could only walk one or two steps before she had to stop and rest because her feet were too small to support her body.

The Great Wall of China is about two hours away from the Forbidden City by bus. When we got to it, we began on a flat part, walked a quarter of a mile, and came to some steps that went straight up. You could look up and see the sky at the top of the steps. It makes you wonder how they got anything up there. Some of the male athletes jogged along the wall for about ten miles. I don't know how they could run, because some parts just seemed to go straight up. I was tired just from walking a mile and a half in the 85-degree weather.

May 29 We saw a lot of nice things in China, and the people were really nice to us. Somewhere on the trip I saw a big poster and I copied down what it said: "Let a hundred flowers blossom and weed through the old to let the new emerge." I kind of like that.

219

The Old Men Admiring Themselves in the Water

W. B. Yeats

I heard the old, old men say,
"Everything alters,
And one by one we drop away."
They had hands like claws, and their knees
Were twisted like the old thorn-trees
By the waters.
I heard the old, old men say,
"All that's beautiful drifts away
Like the waters."

I Can Look It Up for You

Whenever people have questions about a reference book or want some help in finding facts, they turn to Ignatz Information. That's right, Ignatz, the boy in this picture. He probably knows the libraries better than the librarians.

Ignatz has several reference sources to which he directs people quite often. For instance, if you're like Rachel Read-a-Lot, who likes to find all the books by her favorite authors, Ignatz would direct you to the card catalog. In the card catalog all the books in the library are listed in three ways — by author, by title, and by subject. It's one of the best places to start, whether you're looking for information on magic or books by Charles Dickens.

This is George Pick-and-Choose. He likes to have a little bit of information on a lot of different subjects. So Ignatz will probably direct him to an encyclopedia, which will have articles on everything from the French Revolution to Quilts. But remember, the information in an encyclopedia is sometimes fairly general. If George wants more specific information, he should look for an encyclopedia on one subject, such as astronomy or animals, or he should read separate books on the subjects that interest him.

Mabel Map-Reader always wants to know things such as how Europe looked in the 1400s or how Asia looked during Marco Polo's time. Ignatz directs her to an atlas— a book of maps, all kinds of maps. In a good atlas you can find out about anything, from the mountains to the food products of an area.

Ollie Up-to-Date is the type of person who likes to have all the latest information on Academy Award winners, new sports records, current heads of nations, and so forth. Ignatz directs him to an almanac. Because almanacs are published yearly, they contain the latest statistical information available on a variety of subjects.

No matter what you want to find in a book, Ignatz can probably tell you where to start looking for it. But what if Ignatz were gone on the day you go to the library? Where would you look for some general information about the moon? Some statistics on World Series batting averages? A list of all the books in the library by Bret Harte? A map of the early colonies in America? Could you take Ignatz's place?

Harold & Burt & Sue & Amy, etc.

Casey Garber

This girl walked up to me in the hall and said, "Do you like plants?"

"No."

"Good," she said. "Take this one home."

I said, "I don't want it."

"Go on," she said, holding the pot out to me. "It's an *Aralia spinosa*. That's Latin. Just keep it for me, for a science experiment."

Larry, beside me, laughed. "He wouldn't know what to do with a plant. Actually, that's rather a nice specimen of *spinosa*. Why are you entrusting it to Mark?" (That's the way Larry talks.)

"It's a secret experiment."

"Mark'll fail, whatever it is."

I put out my hand. "I'll take it," I said.

"What are you going to do," Larry asked, "eat it for lunch?"

"Just water it twice a week and put it in an east window," she said.

"Yeah, yeah," I said. "O.K." I took the damp-feeling clay pot. The few little leaves were shiny, and there were thorns on the stems.

So I took the *Aralia spinosa* home with me, walking hunched over so that every Tom, Dick, and George wouldn't see me with this plant and start asking funny questions.

After I put it on my windowsill, I started playing my records and put on my earphones. I like my sound loud, man, but my parents have other ideas. They got into such a habit of saying "Turn that thing down, Mark" that pretty soon they were saying it before I even turned it on. So they gave me the 'phones. Now it's in one ear and *in* the other, too, and the guitars meet in the middle right over the percussion and that is where I *live*.

One day I found this article about plants that had a picture of my own *Aralia spinosa* in it, and so I read on. It said some plants like to be talked to, as long as you talk nicely.

This is when I decided to do my reading out loud. It wouldn't bother me—I would be inside the groovy sound from my 'phones and Old Spiny would be out there taking advantage of all this knowledge. If I came to any bad parts, like wars or famines, or—especially—forest fires, I wouldn't read them aloud.

So every night I plugged myself in and read to Old Spiny, and I watered him Mondays and Thursdays. I noticed that he had grown a couple of new leaves and a third was ready to uncurl, and his stems were growing very, very tall.

Sometimes Jill asked me, "How's the *Aralia*? Still alive?"

"Sure."

"I bet," she said.

Well, he was not only alive, he was thriving, but I wasn't going to argue with her. Besides, Larry was there.

Old Spiny and I really communicated. Naturally he didn't talk back, or even groan and sigh like a dog, but it was nice to have company. Even when I didn't have anything to read I still talked out loud to him, and he just sat there and grew.

Leaves, sprouts, stems seemed to pop out from him. He must love geometry was all I could say, and history and—very probably—science. I was also taking this poetry course. I needed something third period and it was that or dressmaking.

For the first few days I sat in the class with my chin in my hands and stared out the window. I was not going to like poetry and no one could make me like it. But then some of the sounds started to creep into my ears and my brain opened up and let them in. And they were cool.

We had to memorize poems and dissect them like frogs in biology, and even write some of our own. So at home I had to read poetry out loud to hear the rhythms. Old Spiny loved it. He grew to Whitman and Poe all right, but I could almost see him expanding to the rhymes and rhythms of Longfellow.

"You're getting to be a long fellow yourself," I told him one Thursday when I was watering him.

His branches had shot upward and outward and so many new leaves had appeared that I could hardly keep up with the names. The first three he had come with were Harold, Nancy, and Stephanie. But then after Burt appeared and Louise and Sue and Amy and James and Virginia and Matthew, I couldn't keep track, so I talked to them collectively.

"Leaves," I said, and then I told them what the history assignment or poem was for that night, and they listened and they grew.

I had to move the pot to the bookcase—it was too tall for the windowsill. Then, finally, to the floor.

Near the end of the year Jill said to me, "Can you bring the plant to school tomorrow? First period."

My heart thumped. I hadn't thought about giving Old Spiny back. "I don't know," I said.

"Listen, I need it. It's mine, you know."

"O.K.," I said. "Don't get excited."

"Just wait in the hall until I call you," she said.

My mom and I wrapped a sheet of plastic around him, and I sat with the pot between my knees and the long stems bent over at the top.

I waited with Old Spiny outside the science room and then the door whooshed open and Jill came out.

"O.K.," she said. "You can bring it in now." Then she stopped and threw up her hands. "Good grief!" she hollered. "What have you done?"

"Me?" I said. "What?" I looked around.

"Look at that plant!"

I did. There stood Old Spiny, tall as I was, leafy and green, holding out Nancy and James and Virginia and the others and just unrolling Albert and Frank. I didn't see anything wrong with it.

"You've ruined my experiment."

"Look, I don't understand your problem, but I'm going in there to find out." I picked up Old Spiny and carried him, swaying over my head, into the room.

The whole class started to laugh. Some even clapped. What was happening? So then they told me.

Jill had given Old Spiny to me to neglect. She had given another to Larry to care for. And she herself had taken one home to care for. (Those were the two scrawny un-dersized plants on the table.) She and Larry, since they were conscientious types, would take such good care of their plants that they would thrive. But Old-Brown-Thumb (me) would ignore mine, and the poor thing would wither.

So I told them about the reading, the earphones, and the poetry, and about how sometimes I had even put the 'phones on Old Spiny and let him listen directly to the sounds.

"Actually," I said, "I think I proved your experiment. You will probably get an A. If you talk to plants, play them some music, then they grow. Especially if you love them. I love this plant."

Jill did get an A, and she told me I could keep Old Spiny.

I told him on the way home, "Not so much poetry next semester, Spiny, or you'll grow too much and I'll have to send you to a greenhouse." But then I told him I didn't mean it.

"In fact," I said, "I'll get you a nice fern to keep you company. That's a *Filicales,* you know."

He knew.

227

Marian B. Richard

HUNGRY —FOR— GOLD

The date was January 24, 1848. The place, about fifty miles from Sacramento, California. California was not yet a state; indeed, it had been under Mexican rule until just two years before.

Try to imagine how James Marshall felt that day when, during his inspection of the newly completed sawmill that he and his crew had built for John Sutter, he saw golden specks in the running water. Looking closer, he was almost positive that he had found a gold nugget. Then he found several more. A few days later, he took the first nuggets and made the trip back to Sutter's Fort to consult privately with Sutter about what he had found. The nuggets were definitely gold, and Sutter became concerned that word of the discovery would get out. He instructed his men to concentrate on completing the work still remaining on the sawmill. They did so, but this did not stop them from looking for gold in their spare time. The fever had struck, and when the men had finished their work for Sutter, they were off to prospect on a full-time basis. The Gold Rush was on!

News of gold in the hills soon began to trickle into San Francisco, then a town of about nine

hundred people. Although many persons were at first highly skeptical, they became convinced when they saw the gold as evidence. Sailors whose ships were anchored in San Francisco Bay jumped ship, forfeiting considerable pay, to join the rush. People in all professions eagerly became gold miners. By the end of June 1848, only about one hundred people remained in San Francisco. Other California towns were hit by "gold fever" and were emptied in the same way. Buildings were left unfinished, fields went unharvested, and cattle and horses roamed wild.

Would you leave home and family and risk your life to prospect for gold? Thousands did. During 1849, more than 35,000 people took the difficult overland route to California. But the Gold Rush was by no means limited to people from the United States. The Chinese came in droves, and there were many from Spain, France, Great Britain, Germany, Hawaii, and nearby Mexico. Were it not for the Gold Rush of 1848, California's population might not have become as varied as it did.

These new miners arrived with little knowledge of how to find gold and few tools to do the job—some carried only kitchen equipment. Prices for basic supplies were high, and newcomers to San Francisco were astounded at the way business was conducted there. One man who had come by ship brought fifteen hundred dozen eggs. He was at first concerned he might not be able to sell them, but he quickly did—at a price of thirty-seven cents a dozen. When he saw that they were being resold for $4 a dozen, he bought back what he could and sold them again for $6 a dozen. Potatoes sold for $30 a bushel and flour for $75 or more a barrel. And, because it was not easy to bring in supplies, prices were even higher within the mining camps. When the only grocery was set up in a camp, the owner took advantage of the monopoly. But those who had found gold were not too unhappy to pay high prices because they felt certain that they would be able to find more.

The miners were concerned about food only when it was in short supply. During the winters the camps were frequently cut off from supplies, and sometimes the miners starved. One account tells of some miners living for more than six weeks on barley from a livery stable. From this horse feed they made barley bread, barley mush, and barley pancakes.

Sunday was generally the day that the miners took care of their few possessions, relaxed, and prepared bread for the week.

Like their other supplies, the miners' foodstuff had to be durable. No refrigeration was available, and so their foods had to be simple, easy to carry, and quick to prepare. A hungry miner did not want to waste precious prospecting time on cooking. Their mainstays were salt pork, dry beans, flour, cornmeal, coffee, tea, potatoes, onions, and sometimes rice. Miners occasionally ate meat obtained from wild animals, but if they had meat, it was usually jerked meat or dried beef. They prepared jerked meat by cutting venison into strips, salting it, and hanging it up to dry. A tired, hungry miner might even eat fried flour, which was simply flour that had been moistened and attached to the end of a stick and cooked over an open flame.

The life of a miner was a hard one. The writers of songs, plays, operas, and dances have emphasized the gold and the glitter of those times but not the hardships that many people had to endure. Many who survived the journey to California were unprepared for the rough existence of a mining camp.

Although the first California gold was found close to the surface, in time the actual gold-mining process required considerably more labor. Some miners did become rich. In the four years following James Marshall's original discovery, a quarter of a billion dollars worth of gold was taken out of the California deposits. However, most miners did not make the fantastic strikes that they had read or heard about ($36,000 in four days or $50,000 in a single day). In 1848 successful miners could sometimes find as much as $200 worth of gold a day. But in 1849 and 1850 the miners were lucky if they could bring out an ounce a day, which was worth about $16.

Unlike early settlers in our history, the miners were not seeking to establish towns or to settle down in any way. Gold was their only interest. But the miners did contribute much toward the growth of California and toward the establishment of many towns in Gold Rush country. Towns such as Nevada City (where even the streets were mined), Dutch Flat, Volcano, Coloma, and Placerville (once called Hangtown) grew up. Some of these had particularly rich veins of gold. In Volcano $90 million worth of gold

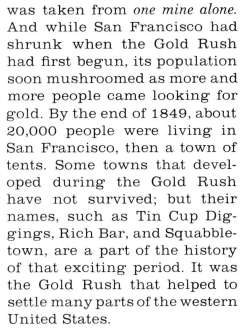

was taken from *one mine alone.* And while San Francisco had shrunk when the Gold Rush had first begun, its population soon mushroomed as more and more people came looking for gold. By the end of 1849, about 20,000 people were living in San Francisco, then a town of tents. Some towns that developed during the Gold Rush have not survived; but their names, such as Tin Cup Diggings, Rich Bar, and Squabbletown, are a part of the history of that exciting period. It was the Gold Rush that helped to settle many parts of the western United States.

There have been other gold rushes in our history. Gold has been found in Nevada, Colorado, and Alaska. But those who speak of the Gold Rush are thinking of the miners of 1848 and of the '49ers.

Picture a mining camp where living conditions are rough, foodstuff limited, and the miners are too exhausted to do any but the most basic kind of cooking. Johnnycake and cracklin' bread are two dishes that you can prepare to give you an idea of the kinds of foods miners ate.

Before doing any actual cooking, however, read the recipes that follow a few times and

think about why each ingredient was used by the miners. (Keep in mind that these are adaptations of the miners' original recipes.) For example, salt pork was popular because it kept well and the melted drippings made a good shortening to use instead of butter, which would not have been available in the gold fields. We suggest you use eggs in both breads, but it is likely that miners rarely used them because of the cost and perishable nature of eggs. If the miners had milk at all, it might well have been sour milk. Sour milk is good for baking because it helps bread to rise. There was no baking soda or baking powder, which are used today as rising agents in baking. Instead of the honey suggested here, miners might have used a sweetener familiar to them—molasses, which was far less expensive than sugar and, like sour milk, was also a rising agent for bread.

Johnnycake was originally prepared in a frying pan over an open fire and served pancake style. The name "johnny" is really a contraction of the word *journey,* a name given to this food because it was frequently prepared and eaten enroute. Both of these breads can be served from the same pan in which they are baked, just as the miners did. (But miners were not able to refrigerate leftovers as you are able to do today.)

Johnnycake ★★★★★★★★★★

1 tablespoon butter
1 egg
1 cup sour milk or buttermilk
(*Note:* Sour milk can be made
from sweet milk by adding
one tablespoon of vinegar to
the milk and stirring well.)
1 tablespoon honey
¼ cup flour
1 cup cornmeal
½ teaspoon salt
½ teaspoon baking soda

Directions

1.   Preheat oven to 400 degrees.
2.   Melt butter, set aside.
3.   Combine egg, sour milk,
and honey.
4.   Use a wooden spoon and
beat well.
5.   With wooden spoon stir
flour, cornmeal, salt, and baking soda into egg mixture.
6.   Pour melted butter into
this batter.
7.   Grease nine-inch square
pan.
8.   Pour batter into pan and
place pan in oven.
9.   Bake for 20 to 30 minutes,
or until cake is brown and has
begun to pull away from the
sides of the pan.

Cracklin' Bread ★★★★★★★★★

¾ cup finely cut salt pork
2 cups cornmeal
1½ teaspoons baking powder
½ teaspoon baking soda
½ teaspoon salt
2 eggs
1 cup sour milk or buttermilk
2 tablespoons salt pork
   drippings

Directions

1.   Preheat oven to 400 degrees.
2.   Fry salt pork over low
flame until crisp and brown.
It is now called cracklings.
3.   Drain fat.
4.   Set aside drained fat and
cracklings.
5.   Mix cornmeal, baking
powder, baking soda, salt.
6.   Beat eggs, milk, drippings
with wooden spoon.
7.   Stir egg combination into
cornmeal mixture.
8.   Add cracklings and make
sure they are well mixed into
batter.
9.   Grease a seven-by-eleven-
inch pan.
10.   Pour batter into pan and
place in oven.
11.   Bake about 30 minutes.

Some miners took their new-found wealth into the nearest town to celebrate. Restaurants and gambling houses sprang up, and even today there are restaurants in San Francisco and elsewhere in California that were founded during the Gold Rush days. One such place, the Rough and Ready Saloon, gave its name to Rough and Ready Meatball Stew, which you may also like to try. The recipe follows. When this dish was originally prepared, beer was used instead of cider. You will note that olives are one of the stew ingredients and not simply a decorative touch. Olive trees in California were originally planted by Spanish missionaries over two hundred years ago.

★★★★★★★★★ ★★★★★★★★★★

1 pound ground beef
½ pound country sausage
1 egg
½ cup bread crumbs
¼ cup chopped onion
1 teaspoon salt
1 pinch of black pepper
2 tablespoons flour
12 ounces apple cider
1 8-ounce can tomato sauce
1 cup of green ripe olives,
   pitted and cut into strips

Directions

1. Mix together the beef, sausage, egg, bread crumbs, onion, salt, and pepper.

2. Shape beef mixture into small balls.

3. Brown meatballs in a hot frying pan. (It is not necessary to add fat for browning.)

4. Remove meatballs as they brown.

5. Pour off two tablespoons of fat and discard the rest.

6. Return the two table-spoons of fat to the frying pan over low heat.

7. Add flour, a little at a time, stirring well. Brown flour.

8. Add cider and tomato sauce and continue stirring until sauce is thick.

9. Return the meatballs to the pan and simmer slowly for about twenty minutes.

10. Remove stew from heat and add olives. Stew is now ready to serve. This recipe will serve four or five people. Try either Johnnycake or Cracklin' Bread with it.

jacqueline Adato

Nathaniel Benchley is well known as an essayist, a short story writer, and a novelist. He has written for all audiences—children, young people, and adults.

He is a member of a famous American writing family: his father, Robert Benchley, was the humorist and author, and his son, Peter, is the author of Jaws.

One of Nathaniel Benchley's books, The Off-Islanders, *inspired "The Russians Are Coming, The Russians Are Coming," the popular film.*

Fathers' Day

Nathaniel Benchley

George Adams finished his coffee and stood up. "I'm off," he said to his wife as he went to the coat closet. "See you around six."

"Don't forget Bobby's school," she said.

Adams stopped, and looked at her. "What about it?" he asked.

"They're having Fathers' Day," she said. "Remember?"

"Oh, my gosh," Adams said. He paused, then said hurriedly, "I can't make it. It's out of the question."

"You've got to," she said. "You missed it last year, and he was terribly hurt. Just go for a few minutes, but you've *got* to do it. I promised him I'd remind you."

Adams drew a deep breath and said nothing.

"Bobby said you could just come for English class," Eleanor went on. "Between twelve-twenty and one. Please don't let him down again."

"Well, I'll try," Adams said. "I'll make it if I can."

"It won't hurt you to do it. All the other fathers do."

"I'm sure they do," Adams said. He put on his hat and went out and rang for the elevator.

Eleanor came to the front door. "No excuses, now!" she said.

"I said I'd do it if I could," Adams replied. "That's all I can promise you."

Adams arrived at the school about twelve-thirty, and an attendant at the door reached out to take his hat. "No, thanks," Adams said, clutching it firmly. "I'm just going to be a few minutes." He looked around and saw the cloakroom, piled high with hats and topcoats, and beyond that the auditorium, in which a number of men and boys were already having lunch. Maybe I'm too late, he thought hopefully. Maybe the classes are already over. To the attendant, he said, "Do you know where I'd find the sixth grade now? They're having English, I think."

"The office'll tell you," the attendant said. "Second floor."

Adams ascended a steel-and-concrete stairway to the second floor, and, through the closed doors around him, heard the high, expressionless voices of reciting boys and the lower, softly precise voices of the teachers, and as he passed the open door of an empty room, he caught the smell of old wood and chalk dust and library paste. He found the office, and a middle-aged woman there directed him to a room on the floor above, and he went up and stood outside the door for a moment, listening. He could hear a teacher's voice, and the teacher was talking about the direct object and the main verb and the predicate adjective.

After hesitating a few seconds, Adams turned the knob and quietly opened the door. The first face he saw was that of his son, in the front row, and Bobby winked at him. Then Adams looked at the thin, dark-haired teacher, who seemed a surprisingly young man. He obviously had noticed Bobby's wink, and he smiled and said, "Mr. Adams." Adams tiptoed to the back of the room and joined about six other fathers, who were sitting in various attitudes of discomfort on a row of folding chairs. He recognized none of them, but they looked at him in a friendly way and he smiled at them, acknowledging the bond of uneasiness that held them momentarily together.

The teacher was diagramming a sentence on the black-board, breaking it down into its component parts by means of straight and oblique lines, and Adams, looking at the diagram, realized that, if called upon, he would be hard put to it to separate the subject from the predicate, and he prayed that the teacher wouldn't suffer a fit of whimsy and call on the fathers. As it turned out, the students were well able to handle the problem, and Adams was gratified to hear his son give correct answers to two questions that were put to him. I'll be, Adams thought. I never got the impression he knew all that.

Then the problem was completed, and the teacher glanced at the clock and said, "All right. Now we'll hear the compositions." He walked to the back of the room, sat down, and then looked around at a field of suddenly upraised hands and said, "Go ahead, Getsinger. You go first."

A thin boy with wild blond hair and a red bow tie popped out of his seat and, carrying a sheet of paper, went to the front of the room and, in a fast, singsong voice, read, "He's So Understanding. I like my Dad because he's so understanding." Several of the boys turned in their seats and looked at one of the fathers and grinned as Getsinger went on, "When I ask Dad for a dime he says he'll settle for a nickel, and I say you can't get anything for a nickel anymore and he says then he'll settle for six cents. Then pretty soon Mom calls and says that supper is ready, and the fight goes on in the dining room, and after a while Dad says he'll make it seven cents, and before supper is over I have my dime. That's why I say he's understanding."

Adams smiled in sympathy for Mr. Getsinger, and when the next boy got up and started off "Why I Like My Father," Adams realized with horror that all the compositions were going to be on the same subject, and he saw that his own son had a piece of paper on his desk and was waiting eagerly for his turn to read. The palms of Adams' hands became moist, and he looked at the clock, hoping that the time would run out before Bobby got a chance to recite. There was a great deal of laughter during the second boy's reading of his composition, and after he sat down, Adams looked at the clock again and saw that there were seven minutes left. Then the teacher looked around again, and five or six hands shot up, including Bobby's, and the teacher said,

"All right—let's have Satterlee next," and Bobby took his hand down slowly, and Adams breathed more easily and kept his eyes riveted on the clock.

Satterlee, goaded by the laughter the previous student had received, read his composition with a mincing attempt to be comical, and he told how his father was unable to get any peace around the house, with his sister practicing the violin. It occurred to Adams that the compositions were nothing more than the children's impressions of their own home life, and the squirming and the nervous laughter from the fathers indicated that the observations were more acute than flattering. Adams tried to think what Bobby might say, and he could remember only things like the time he had docked Bobby's allowance for two weeks for some offense he couldn't now recall, and the way he sometimes shouted at Bobby when he got too boisterous around the apartment, and the time Bobby had threatened to leave home because he had been forbidden to go to a vaudeville show—and the time he *had* left home because of a punishment Adams had given him. Adams thought also of the night he and his wife had had an argument, and how, the next day, Bobby had asked what "self-centered" meant, in reply to which Adams had told him it was none of his business. Then he remembered the time Bobby had been on a children's radio show and had announced that his household chores included getting out the ice for drinks, and when Adams asked him later why he had said it, Bobby had reminded him of one time Adams had asked him to bring an ice tray from the pantry into the living room. The memories they have, Adams thought—the diabolically selective memories.

Satterlee finished. The clock showed two minutes to one, and Adams wiped his hands on his trouser legs and gripped his hat, which was getting soft around the brim. Then Bobby's hand went up again, almost plaintively now, and the teacher said, "All right, Adams, you're on," and Bobby bobbed up and went to the front of the room.

Several of the boys turned and looked at Adams as Bobby began to read, but Adams was oblivious of everything

except the stocky figure in front of the blackboard, whose tweed jacket looked too small for him and who was reading fast because the bell was about to ring. What Bobby read was a list of things that Adams had completely forgotten, or that had seemed of no great importance at the time, things like being allowed to stay up late to watch a fight, and being given an old fencing mask when there was no occasion for a gift (Adams had simply found it in a second-hand store and thought Bobby might like it), and having a model airplane made for him when he couldn't do it himself, and the time Adams had retrieved the ring from the subway grating. By the time Bobby concluded with "That's why he's O.K. in *my* book," Adams had recovered from his surprise and was beginning to feel embarrassed. Then the bell rang and class was dismissed, and Adams and the other fathers followed the boys out of the room.

Bobby was waiting for him in the corridor outside. "Hi," Bobby said. "You going now?"

"Yes," said Adams. "I'm afraid I've got to."

"O.K." Bobby turned and started away.

"Just a minute," Adams said, and Bobby stopped and looked back. Adams walked over to him and then hesitated for a moment. "That was—ah—a good speech," he said.

"Thanks," said Bobby.

Adams started to say something else, but could think of nothing. "See you later," he finished, and quickly put on his hat and hurried down the stairs.

Willie Morris

THE RACE

As a boy in Yazoo City, Mississippi, Willie Morris was known as a practical joker and a great baseball fan. What made him different from other people his age was that at the age of twelve he was a part-time sportswriter for his hometown paper and, at seventeen, he was a sports announcer, disc jockey, and news analyst for the local radio station. He continued his newspaper career in college.

Before you read "The Race," think about a time when you have wanted to get back at someone who teased or dared you. Is it ever fair to cheat a little to teach people a lesson they really deserve?

People rarely believe that a boy we knew ran all the way around a very large block in thirty seconds, thus breaking every track record in the world. Well, there is some truth to this story, but sometimes one has to lie to tell the truth, and I had better describe this event in a little more detail.

There was a pair of twins who lived in the town; their names were Paul and Pinky Posey. They looked so completely alike that at times even their parents could not tell them apart. They both had long red hair, they were identically bowlegged, and they had the same floppy ears and squeaky voices, and they wore the same clothes, which usually consisted of blue jeans and white T-shirts, minus shoes. They even got warts in the same places at the same time. Paul was slightly more intelligent than Pinky, but that was not saying too much. The only way we could tell them apart was that Pinky had four toes on his left foot, but seldom did anyone want to get close enough for a thorough examination.

In the summer of our eleventh year, a group of five or six boys from Greenwood, a town about fifty miles up the river, came to Yazoo for a two-week visit with their rich relatives. They were extremely obnoxious visitors, and since Greenwood was a somewhat larger town, they lorded it over us, calling us country bumpkins and the like, and acting for all the world as if they were from Paris or London or Constantinople or the lost underwater island of Atlantis. I have met many snobs in my lifetime, but, to date, these boys from Greenwood, Mississippi, still rank as the biggest.

One summer afternoon Spit McGee, Bubba Barrier, Billy Rhodes, and I were playing marbles in front of the Yazoo high school, just minding our own business, when the visitors from Greenwood walked by and decided to show us how superior they were. "Here come them Yankees from Greenwood," Spit said. "Wonder what they're gonna tell us *now?*" They proceeded to tell us how wide the main street was in their town and how big the houses were. "Why, the Yazoo River up there," one of them said, "is a lot cleaner than it is by the time it gets

down here. Up there it's blue as can be. You can even see the gars wigglin' at the bottom. Down here it's all mud. You're gettin' all our dirt." They went on like this for a few minutes. Bubba and Spit and Billy Rhodes and I ignored them and concentrated on our marbles. Finally one of the Greenwood boys said, "And you see this big fellow right here? He can outrun anybody in this hick town." The object of this superlative was a tall, hatchet-faced individual named Marsh. "That's true," Marsh said. "I can outrun anybody in town, and I can do it runnin' backwards!"

"Well, can you now?" Spit McGee suddenly exclaimed, jumping up from his game of marbles with such

vengeance in his eye that I wondered what had gotten into him to break our icy silence in the face of the visitors' provocations. "Here's bettin' you five dollars and ten moonpies that we know someone who can run around this block in thirty seconds, and it'll take your man at least three minutes to do it by Bubba Barrier's daddy's stopwatch."

"Thirty seconds around *this* block?" the leader of the Greenwood gang laughed. "That's impossible. Let's just walk around this block and see how big it is." So we all started from the front of the high school building, turned left on College Street, left on Calhoun, left again on Jackson, and a final left on Canal, arriving after a good eight or ten min-

utes' walk in front of the school again. It was not only a long block, it was the longest in town.

"Your man can't do it in thirty seconds," the Greenwood leader said. "Ol' Marsh can do it in three minutes, though, and your man can't do it in five."

"Meet us right here in front of the school this time tomorrow," Spit McGee said, "and bring your five dollars and enough extra spendin' money for the moonpies."

"We'll be here," the boy said, "and we'll make you look mighty silly."

After they had left, we all turned on Spit. "Are you crazy?" Billy Rhodes shouted.

"Shut up!" Spit exclaimed. "Just leave it up to me. It's three-thirty now. Y'all meet me right here at three tomorrow afternoon. Bubba, be sure and bring your daddy's stopwatch."

At three the next day, after a night of considerable worry, Bubba and Billy Rhodes and I showed up in front of the high school. There, on the front steps, was Spit McGee, and with him were Paul and Pinky Posey.

Spit was at fever pitch, exhibiting great resourcefulness. "Bubba, you'll run the stopwatch. Paul, this here's the place you'll start runnin'. Pinky, you come with me. The rest of you don't do nuthin' 'til I get back. And remember, Paul, once you turn the corner out of sight, you stay behind Mr. Frady's house 'til we come for you." With that, he and Pinky Posey

started walking down the sidewalk, in the opposite direction from the finish line for the race, and soon disappeared. Two or three minutes later Spit returned alone.

"Where's Pinky?" Billy Rhodes asked.

"He's hidin' in the shrubs in front of Miz Williams' house, just before he turns the corner for the home stretch," Spit said mysteriously. It was just beginning to dawn on us what Spit was up to, but before we could question him as to particulars we caught sight of the Greenwood boys coming our way.

"You mean this is the little twerp that can outrun Marsh?" the leader laughed when he saw Paul Posey, floppy ears and all, sitting on the steps of the school.

"Why, I could whip him *crawlin'*," Marsh said.

"We'll see about that," Spit said. "You run first," he added, pointing to the incorrigible Marsh. "Pick somebody from your side to run the stopwatch with Bubba Barrier so you'll know we ain't cheatin'."

Marsh lined up at the starting point, and when Spit shouted *Go* he took off at a lightning pace. Soon he was out of sight and around the corner. We all sat nervously and waited. Billy Rhodes and I exchanged glances, while Paul Posey limbered up his bowlegs and did some exercises.

Finally, about two and a half minutes later, the Greenwood runner came into sight at the opposite end of the block. "There he is!" our antagonists yelled gleefully. "Man, can't he run?" Marsh approached the finish line, and as he did so Bubba posted his time at three minutes, six seconds.

"Okay, Paul," Spit said. "Line up." Paul Posey went to the line, and with the shout *Go* he started out, legs churning, and disappeared around the first turn.

"That little twerp's so bowlegged he won't even finish," Marsh said.

"His bowlegs pick up steam after the first turn," Spit replied.

Now the Greenwood slickers sat down to wait for Paul's appearance around the final turn in the opposite direction three or four minutes hence.

To their horror, in a mere ten seconds, he appeared around that corner and headed toward the finish line.

"Faster!" Spit shouted. *"Speed it up!"* Billy Rhodes yelled. The improbable redhead, his features contorted and weary, his hair waving in the breeze, raced in our direction and crossed the finish line. I counted four toes on the left foot.

"Thirty seconds even," Bubba judged, and the boy from Greenwood who had been checking the stopwatch, by now wordless and in a state of shock, agreed. As we all patted our man on the back, the Greenwood boys stood off by themselves, shaking their heads and whispering in astonishment.

"That'll be five dollars, plus fifty cents for ten moonpies," Spit said, extending his hand. Our enemies counted out the money and then departed, too defeated to offer their congratulations. They never had the gall to face us again.

When they were out of sight, Spit said, "Let's go." Considerably more respectful of Spit McGee than we had ever been, we turned the corner where Paul Posey had originally disappeared and walked to the back of Mr. Frady's house. Paul Posey was sitting nonchalantly on the back steps of the house. "Come on, Paul," Spit said. "Let's go eat some moonpies." Spit kept three dollars for himself, and gave a dollar apiece to Paul and Pinky Posey.

CHECK THE SENTENCE

Have you ever been confused when you were talking with people because you were using a word one way and they were using it another way? This is not an uncommon occurrence. The meanings of many words depend on how they are used in sentences—as nouns, as verbs, or as adjectives. You often have to look at how a word is used before you can be sure of its meaning. For example, what does the word *rate* mean? What does it mean in each of these sentences?

How do you rate the new breakfast cereal?
At what rate are you being paid to baby-sit?
Because of her outstanding work, she rated special privileges.
Adam, the football star, really rates with the coach.

Read each group of sentences on the next page. Look at the underlined word. How do the meanings of the underlined words vary from sentence to sentence? Make sure you write your answers on a separate sheet of paper.

1. The peasant made a *demand* on the king.
2. We *demand* that you listen to our grievances.

3. The force of the water will *flush* the dirt from the gutter.
4. The edge of that step must be *flush* with the porch.
5. I often get a red *flush* on my face when I'm ill.

6. Don't *season* the soup too much.
7. Fall is my favorite *season*.

8. Can you *direct* me to town?
9. Isn't there a more *direct* way than this?

The lesson is to make sure you *use* your words in the right way. That is, make good *use* of them.

By 1800 St. Louis had become a city; New Orleans had been one for over a century. Traffic up and down the Mississippi, at first on roped or poled keelboats and barges, later by steamboats trailing the barges, steadily increased between the two once-French cities. Emigrants, German farmers particularly, spread out from the centers and began farms to supply the cities' needs. The Austins were colonizing Texas; John Law and his Scotts colony had moved northward from Louisiana to Arkansas; and the Mississippi Bubble had burst, scattering colonists westward. It was clear to everyone that the white settlers were here to stay.

It was a time of great temptation. By raiding white settlements and isolated farms and ranches, the Plains Indians could drive off horses and mules, butcher cattle when they were short of buffalo or venison, and sometimes capture women and children. The women could be put to work, and the children might be adopted by an Indian family, usually to replace a child who had died. Stories of captives are numerous; sometimes the captive actually came from another tribe, sometimes it was a frontier white child. Most of the latter seem to have adapted readily to Indian life.

Such a child was Maria James, who was found wandering alone in eastern Arkansas about 1830 by the Osages. They adopted her, and she grew up among them.

The Woman General

An Osage Legend

The little girl had wandered away from the farmyard into the woods. She was not looking for anything in particular. She found a wild grapevine and swung herself back and forth on its great rope for a while, then went on. She had no brothers or sisters to play with and sometimes she was lonely.

She heard voices ahead of her and walked toward them. Soon she saw people moving through the woods, gathering the wild grapes. There were women and children, a small group of them. She knew there were other settlers in these woods, but these did not look like anyone she had ever seen. Their language was strange, too. They must be Indians.

Her mother had warned her that the Indians stole white children, and if she ever saw any, she must go home at once. But then one of the women turned and saw her and smiled—a kind smile. Maria stood hesitating, and the woman held out a bunch of grapes. She even ate one, to show that they were safe. Maria took the bunch and ate the rest of it. She drifted with the group, and before she realized it, they had come into a cluster of mat-covered houses, all arranged to face east. She followed the woman who had given her the grapes and who stooped and entered one of the lodges. Maria followed her inside.

The woman turned and saw her, a fair-haired little girl in an old dress, barefoot, because it was not yet time for her father to go down to the river landing and trade for shoes. "You—name?" the woman asked carefully in broken English.

"Maria James."

"Where you live?"

That startled Maria. She had lost all sense of time and direction, trailing through the woods. She shook her head.

"You stay here?"

Maria stood and thought. She was not sure where home was or how to get there. Her mother would surely punish her if she went home now, but if she stayed where she was perhaps her parents would come looking for her. She had been away in the woods all day, and the kettle of soup steaming over the fire in the middle of the lodge smelled good. She nodded.

"I stay."

She stayed the rest of her life. The family she had adopted were good to her; they made clothes for her from buckskin and from trade cloth. She wore the soft-soled two-piece Osage moccasins. She learned to plait mats and sashes and to sew the big cattail mats to cover the lodge, using twisted nettle cord and a bone needle. She learned the things an Osage woman was supposed to know and do, but sometimes she was bored.

It was at such a time, when she felt idle and dull, that she saw the boys playing with their bows and arrows and asked to borrow a bow. The boys laughed at her.

"Girls don't shoot," they said.

"I'm going to," Maria answered.

"You can't. We won't let you," the boys told her.

Maria went home. She told her adopted father what she wanted, and although he, too, laughed at her, he showed her how to make a bow and arrows. "You won't play with them long," he assured her.

To everybody's surprise but her own, Maria did. She watched every step of the bow making. She saw her Osage father take a straight, seasoned length of wood from the rafters of the house, build a fire outside, and warm the wood slowly over it, turning it evenly in his hands when he did so. She watched while he began slowly and evenly to bend the wood into a curve. He measured it against her and made it long enough for her to grow into it. When the curve fitted her, he stopped.

"Now you can make your own bowstring," he directed her.

Maria went to her own supply of sinew. She had been learning to make moccasins, and there was a good-sized slab of the sinew left. She split it with the point of her knife, not as finely as she would for moccasins, and when she had a pile, she began twisting it into a cord over her thigh, as she had been taught to twist nettle fiber. When she had to join another piece of sinew to her twist, she chewed each end until they were thoroughly moist and would hold together. She went on twisting until her skin was raw and sore, but when she finished she had a cord half again as long as the bow.

"Now let it dry overnight," her Osage father told her.

In the morning he showed her how to wrap the cord around one end of the bow until it was secure. Then he showed her how to loop the other end, slip it over the head of the bow, and tighten it with a piece of bone. When it was as tight as she could make it, he lent her an arrow.

"See if you can pull it," he said.

It was a hard pull, and loosing the arrow was even harder, but Maria learned. She learned how to make her own arrows, attaching to them four straight splits of hawk quill, and she learned how to hunt.

The first time she brought down a deer and brought it home, her Osage mother was horrified. "You act like a boy," she said. "Why you're almost grown up enough to be married. You ought to be ashamed of yourself."

"Boys have more fun than girls," Maria protested.

"If you want to act like a boy," her mother said, "then do what a boy would do. Take your first game and give it to Old Lady Walking Around. She's poor and alone and needs the meat."

When Old Lady Walking Around saw Maria coming with the deer, she began to laugh. "What do you think you're doing?" she asked. "Girls don't shoot deer."

"I shot this one and I want you to have it," Maria said proudly. And she laid the deer on the ground before Old Lady Walking Around. "You are my mother's friend, and she told me to bring it to you."

"Then I thank you, and her," replied Old Lady Walking Around. "I will dry some of it for her."

From that time on, Maria hunted and rode with the men and boys, although she always dressed like a girl and wore her long fair hair loose over her shoulders, as all the women did. Sometimes the boys

would tease her about that and tell her she ought to have her head shaved except for a crest on top, as the Osage men did, but Maria refused to do that.

When she was about fourteen, and the boys her own age were going on a war party, Maria wanted to go too.

"You can't do that," her father said sternly. "No decent woman would go with a war party—only one who wanted to get away from her husband. People will talk about you. They'll laugh at you."

"I'm going," Maria declared, and she went.

She took her part in the war party as a man. There was usually a boy assigned to war parties to cook and work for the men, but Maria refused to do that kind of work. She still dressed like a woman, but she could fight like a man, and fight well, too. The men respected her.

From time to time after that, word would get back to St. Louis, from some fur trader or trapper, about a fair young woman who rode out with the Osage war and hunting parties. Nobody knew who she was, but she was seen occasionally. Not until a priest visited the camp was her identity known. By that time she could barely speak English. But she remembered her name.

"Come home," the priest suggested. "You should go back to your own people."

"These are my own people," Maria declared.

"But you are a white woman, my child. You should marry a white man and have children."

"I don't know any white men except the traders and trappers," said Maria, "and I don't want one of them. They smell bad."

Eventually the priest gave up urging Maria to change her way of life. Maria thought about what he had said, though. When her Indian father called her and said he wanted to speak seriously to her, she listened.

"Rising Star has asked for you," announced her father. "He is a good man, a few years older than you are, and will make you a good husband."

"I'll talk to him," Maria promised.

"And listen to him, too," her father warned.

Maria sat and thought about what her adopted father had said. She was as strong as any man, but perhaps there were other things in life for a woman to do. She looked around the village. None of the women rode on war parties, but they seemed happy and contented;

their faces and their voices showed peace realized and achieved. It could be that part of Maria's life was incomplete.

When Rising Star came to the lodge that evening to speak to her father again, Maria was ready to listen to him. She sat quietly on her mat, with her legs folded under her, to the right, woman-fashion. It was stiff and uncomfortable for her to sit this way—she was used to sitting like a man, with her legs straight out—but it was part of that woman's life she had decided to learn. With her head down, she listened to her father tell her of the gifts she would receive from Rising Star's family and of the horses he would give them in return.

"You will give away a great deal in my honor," she finally said.

"You mean a lot to both of us," her father assured her.

"If we marry, you can't always go out with the war parties," Rising Star said. "You can go hunting, but not fighting. Besides, if we have children, you won't be able to."

"No," Maria answered. "That would be dangerous for the child."

"That's right," Rising Star agreed. "You don't want to put the child in danger, even if you don't care about yourself."

She married Rising Star, and in time they had four children. Usually she did work in the village, but sometimes she went hunting and brought in her own meat.

The men she had ridden with did not forget her. Before each raid they consulted her, and she told them what she thought would be the best way to approach an Indian tribal settlement or a white farmstead. Usually they followed her advice and were glad she had given it. Even when she was an old, old woman, with grandchildren around her, the men came to her for advice.

By this time she was well known enough to be called "the Woman General" by the whites. They were afraid of her clever, planning mind. When she died she was buried like a man, and they piled a mound of earth over her body.

CHARGE!

A *credit card* allows someone to purchase goods and services up to a certain amount without paying for them immediately.

If you ever apply for a credit card, you will be required to provide information about yourself and your background on an application that looks something like this.

Please Print Clearly

First Name	Middle Initial	Last Name	

Social Security Number		Date of Birth Mo	Day	Year	Number of Dependents

Home Address Number	Street		Apartment Number	Years There

City	Town Post Office		State	Zip Code

Home Phone Area Code		☐ Own ☐ Rent	

Previous Home Address			Years There

Employer's Name		Your Position	Years There

Business Address Number	Street		Business Phone Area Code	Extension

City	Town Post Office		State	Zip Code

If with present employer less than 2 years, give name of previous employer.

Your Annual Salary		Amount of Other Annual Income	Source

Savings Account (Joint or Individual) Bank Name and Address			Account Number

List all debts, charge and credit card accounts held in your name, jointly, or which reflect your ability to pay.

Name and Address of Lender	Account Number	Monthly Payment	Outstanding Balance	Exact Name in Which Account is Carried

Monthly Rent/ Mortgage Payment

Applicant: I authorize Credit Services, Inc. to check my credit history and report to proper persons and credit bureaus my performance of this agreement. If I permit my spouse to use the card, performance of the account will be reported to the credit bureau in my spouse's name also. I understand that the Credit Agreement that will be sent to me with the card(s) will be binding on me after I use the card(s) or authorize its use.

Applicant's Signature		Date

Number of Cards Requested	☐ One ☐ Two	**Note:** All cards issued on this account will be in the name of the applicant only.

Name of Other User	Relationship

Answer the following questions on a separate sheet of paper, using the application form as a guide.

1. What does "number of dependents" mean? Why would the bank want to know how many dependents the applicant has?
2. Why would the bank want to know how much monthly rent the applicant pays?
3. Which spaces on this form ask you to supply information about your financial status?
4. Why do you think it is necessary to give information about your salary and bank accounts?
5. Why are you asked about other charge accounts you may have?
6. Which spaces ask you about your work background? What does "previous employer" mean?

Also make sure that you answer all the questions on the application and write your responses in the correct spaces. You may use abbreviations in some of your answers. For example, you may give your birth date in numbers, and you may use numbers to give your height and weight, if an application requires that information. You may also abbreviate the name of your state.

There are several different kinds of credit cards. *Bank cards* are issued by banks and may be used to purchase many goods and services at a wide variety of stores and businesses. *Single-use* cards are more specialized—they may be used only in certain places. For example, a department store may issue a credit card that can be used only at that store and its branches.

There are a few important points to remember about filling out an application, whether it is for a credit card or for something else. First, be sure to write *clearly.* In most cases an application form will indicate that you are to print. But even if you are not directly instructed to print, you should do so. Obviously, no one can process an application that cannot be read!

A second point to remember is that you should respond to all questions honestly. Any application form will require your signature, your promise that you've answered all questions truthfully. On the form printed here, your signature would also mean that you, the applicant, agree to accept responsibility for using your credit card properly and for paying your *bills.* Sometimes, depending on your age, it is necessary for a parent or a guardian to co-sign the application. Remember, when asked for your signature, do not print—*sign your name.*

Collection 3

262

Margery Allingham

The newspapers were calling the McGill house in Chestnut Grove "the villa Mary Celeste" before Chief Inspector Charles Luke noticed the similarity between the two mysteries. It so shook him that he telephoned the famous detective Albert Campion and asked him to come over.

They met in the Sun, a discreet pub in suburban High Street, and stood talking in the small parlor which was deserted at that time of day.

"The two stories *are* alike," Luke said. He was at the height of his career then, a dark, muscular man, high-cheek-boned and packed with energy, forcing home his points with characteristic gestures of his long hands. "I read the rehash of the *Mary Celeste* mystery in the *Courier* this morning and it threw me. Except that she was a ship and 29 Chestnut Grove is a semi-detached suburban house, the two desertion stories are virtually the same—even to the half-eaten breakfast left on the table in each case. It's uncanny, Campion."

The quiet, fair man in the horn-rimmed glasses stood listening affably, as was his habit. And as usual, he looked vague and probably ineffectual; in the shadier corners of Europe it was said that no one ever took him seriously until just about two hours too late. At the moment he appeared faintly amused. The thumping force of Luke's enthusiasms always tickled him.

"You think you know what has happened to the McGill couple, then?" he ventured.

"Heavens, no!" The policeman opened his small black eyes to their widest. "I tell you it's the same tale as the classic mystery of the *Mary Celeste*. They've gone like a stain under a bleach. One minute they were having breakfast together like every other couple for miles around and the next they were gone, sunk without trace."

Mr. Campion hesitated. He looked a trifle embarrassed. "As I recall the story of the *Mary Celeste* it had the simple charm of the utterly incredible," he said at last. "Let's see: she was a brig brought into Gibraltar by a prize crew of innocent sailors who had a wonderful tale to tell. According to them, she was sighted in mid-ocean with all her sails set, her decks clean, her lockers tidy, but not a soul on board. The details were fascinating. There were three cups of tea on the captain's table and they were still warm to the touch. There was a trunk of female clothes, small enough to be a child's, in his cabin. There was a cat asleep in the galley and a chicken ready for stewing in a pot on the stove." Campion sighed gently. "Quite beautiful," he said, "but witnesses also swore that with no one at the wheel she was still dead on course and that seemed a little too much for the court of inquiry. After kicking it about as long as they could, they finally made the absolute minimum award."

Luke glanced at him sharply.

"That wasn't the *Courier*'s angle last night," he said. "They called it the 'world's favorite unsolved mystery.' "

"So it is!" Mr. Campion was laughing. "Because nobody wants a simple explanation for fraud and greed. The mystery of the *Mary Celeste* is a prime example of the story which really is a bit *too* good to spoil, don't you think?"

"I don't know. It's not an idea which occurred to me." Luke sounded slightly irritated. "I was merely quoting the main outlines of the two tales — 1872 and the *Mary Celeste* is a bit before my time. On the other hand, 29 Chestnut Grove is definitely my business and you can take it from me that no witnesses are being allowed to use their imaginations in this inquiry. Just give your mind to the details, Campion."

Luke began ticking off each item on his fingers.

"Consider the couple," he said. "They sound normal enough. Peter McGill was twenty-eight and his wife Maureen a year younger. They'd been married three years and got on well together. For the first two years they had to live with his mother while they were waiting for a house. That didn't work out too well, so they rented a couple of rooms from Maureen's married sister. That lasted for six months and then they got the offer of this house in Chestnut Grove."

"Any money troubles?" Mr. Campion asked.

"No." The Chief clearly thought the fact remarkable. "Peter seems to be the one lad in the family who had nothing to grumble about. His firm—they're locksmiths in Aldgate, he's in the office—is very pleased with him. His reputation is that he keeps within his income and he's recently had a raise in salary. I saw the senior partner this morning and he's genuinely worried, poor old boy. He liked the young man and had nothing but praise for him."

"What about Mrs. McGill?"

"She's another good type. Steady, reliable, kept on at her job. The McGills have been gone six weeks."

For the first time Mr. Campion's eyes darkened with interest. "Forgive me," he said, "but the police seem to have come into this disappearance very quickly. What are you looking for, Charles? A body? Or bodies?"

Luke shrugged. "Not officially," he said, "but one doesn't have to have a nasty mind to wonder. We came into the investigation quickly because the alarm was given quickly. The circumstances were extraordinary and the family got the wind up. That's the explanation of that." He paused and stood for a moment hesitating. "Come along and have a look," he said. His restless personality was a live thing in the confined space. "We'll come back after you've seen the setup—I've got something really rare here. I want you in on it."

Mr. Campion followed him out into the network of trim little streets lined with bandbox villas, each set in a nest of flower gardens.

265

"It's just down the end here and along to the right," Luke said, nodding toward the end of the avenue. "I'll give you the rest of it as we go. On the twelfth of June, Bertram Heskith, a somewhat overbright specimen who is the husband of Maureen's elder sister—the one they lodged with, two doors down the road before Number 29 became available—dropped round to see them as he usually did just before eight in the morning. He came in at the back door, which was standing open, and found a half-eaten breakfast for two on the table in the smart new kitchen. No one was about, so he pulled up a chair and sat down to wait."

Luke's long hands were busy as he talked and Mr. Campion could almost see the bright little room with the built-in furniture and the pot of flowers on the window ledge.

"Bertram is a toy sales representative and one of a large family," Luke went on. "He's out of a job at the moment but is not despondent. He's a talkative man, a fraction too big for his clothes now, but he's sharp enough. He'd have noticed at once if there had been anything at all unusual to see. As it was, he poured himself a cup of tea out of the pot under the cozy and sat there waiting, reading the newspaper which he found lying open on the floor by Peter McGill's chair. Finally it occurred to him that the house was very quiet, and he put his head round the door and shouted up the stairs. When he got no reply he went up and found the bed unmade, the bathroom still warm and wet with steam, and Maureen's everyday hat and coat lying on a chair with her familiar brown handbag on it. Bertram came down, examined the rest of the house, then went on out into the garden. Maureen had been doing the laundry before breakfast. There was linen, almost dry, on the clothesline and a basket lying on the grass under it, but that was all. The little rectangle of land was quite empty."

As his deep voice ceased, Luke gave Campion a side-long glance.

"And that, my lad, is that," he said. "Neither Peter nor Maureen has been seen since. When they didn't show up,

266

Bertram consulted the rest of the family and after waiting for two days, they went to the police."

"Really?" Mr. Campion was fascinated in spite of himself. "Is that *all* you've got?"

"Not quite but the rest is hardly helpful." Luke sounded almost gratified. "Wherever they are, they're not in the house or garden. If they walked out they did it without being seen—which is more of a feat than you'd expect because they had interested relatives and friends all round them—and the only things that anyone is sure they took with them are a couple of clean linen sheets."

Mr. Campion's brows rose behind his big spectacles.

"That's a delicate touch," he said. "I take it there is no suggestion of foul play?"

"Foul play is becoming positively common in London. I don't know what the old Town is coming to," Luke said gloomily, "but this setup sounds healthy and happy enough. The McGills seem to have been pleasant, normal young people, and yet there are one or two little items which make one wonder. As far as we can find out, Peter was not on his usual train to the City that morning, but we have one witness—a third cousin of his—who says she followed him up the street from his house to the corner just as she often did on weekday mornings. At the top of the street she went one way and she assumed that as usual he went the other, but no one else seems to have seen him and she's probably mistaken. Well, now, here we are. Stand here for a minute."

He had paused on the pavement of a narrow residential street, shady with plane trees and lined with pairs of pleasant little houses, stone-dashed and bay-windowed, in a style which is now a little out of fashion.

"The next gate along here belongs to the Heskiths," he went on, lowering his voice a tone or so. "We'll walk rather quickly past there because we don't want any more help from Bertram at the moment. He's a good enough chap but he sees himself as the watchdog of his sister-in-law's property and the way he follows me round makes me self-conscious. His house is Number 25—the odd numbers are on this side—29 is two doors along. Now

Number 31, which is actually adjoined to 29 on the other side, is closed. The old woman who owns it is in the hospital; but in 33 there live two sisters who are aunts of Peter's. They moved there soon after the young couple.

"One is a widow, and both are very interested in their nephew and his wife. But whereas the widow is prepared to take a more or less benevolent view of her young relations, the other aunt, Miss Dove, is apt to be critical. She told me Maureen didn't know how to budget her money, and I think that from time to time she'd had a few words with Maureen on the subject. I heard about the 'fine linen sheets' from her. Apparently she'd told Maureen off about buying something so expensive but Maureen had saved up for them and she'd got them.

"Miss Dove says she watched Maureen hanging them out on the line early in the morning of the day she vanished. There's one upstairs window in her house from which she can just see part of the garden at 29 if she stands on a chair and clings to the sash."

He grinned. "She happened to be doing just that at about half-past six on the day the McGills disappeared and she insists she saw them hanging there — the sheets, I mean. She recognized them by the crochet on the top edge. They're certainly not in the house now. Miss Dove hints delicately that I should search Bertram's home for them!"

Mr. Campion's pale eyes had narrowed and his mouth was smiling.

"It's a honey of a story," he murmured. "A sort of circumstantial history of the utterly impossible. The whole thing just can't have happened. How very odd, Charles. Did anybody else see Maureen that morning? Could she have walked out of the front door and come up the street with the linen over her arm unnoticed? I am not asking *would* she but *could* she?"

"No." Luke made no bones about it. "Even had she wanted to, which is unlikely, it's virtually impossible. There are the cousins opposite, you see. They live in the house with the red geraniums over there, directly in front of Number 29. They are some sort of distant relatives of

Peter's. A father, mother, five daughters—it was one of them who says she followed Peter up the road that morning. Also there's an old grandmother who sits up in bed in the window of the front room all day. She's not very reliable—for instance, she can't remember if Peter came out of the house at his usual time that day—but she would have noticed if Maureen had done so. No one saw Maureen that morning except Miss Dove, who, as I told you, watched her hanging linen on the line. The paper comes early; the man who delivers the milk heard her washing machine when he left the milk but he did not see her."

"What about the mail carrier?"

"He's no help. He's a new man on the round and can't even remember if he called at 29. It's a long street and, as he says, the houses are all alike. He gets to 29 about 7:25 and seldom meets anybody at that hour. He wouldn't know the McGills if he saw them anyhow. Come on in, Campion—take a look around and see what you think."

Mr. Campion followed his friend up a narrow garden path to where a uniformed officer stood on guard before the front door. He was aware of a flutter behind the curtains in the house opposite and a tall, thin woman with a determinedly blank expression walking down the path two houses away and bowing to Luke meaningfully as she paused at her gate before going back.

"Miss Dove," said Luke unnecessarily, as he opened the door of Number 29 Chestnut Grove.

The house had few surprises for Mr. Campion. It was almost exactly as he had imagined it. The furniture in the hall and front room was new and sparse, leaving plenty of room for future acquisitions; the kitchen-dining room was well lived in and conveyed a distinct personality. Someone without much money, but who liked nice things, had lived there. The breakfast table had been left exactly as Bertram Heskith had found it, and his cup was still there.

The thin man in the horn-rimmed glasses wandered through the house without comment, Luke at his heels. The scene was just as stated. There was no sign of hurried flight, no evidence of packing, no hint of violence. The dwelling was not so much untidy as in the process of being used. There was a pair of man's pajamas on the stool in the bathroom and a towel hung over the edge of the basin to dry. The woman's handbag and coat on a chair in the bedroom contained the usual miscellany and two pounds three shillings, some pennies, and a set of keys.

Mr. Campion looked at everything—the clothes hanging neatly in closets, the dead flowers still in the vases; but the only item which appeared to hold his attention was the photograph of a wedding group which he found in a silver frame on the dressing table.

He stood before it for a long time apparently fascinated, yet it was not a remarkable picture. As is occasionally the case in such photographs, the two central figures were the least dominant characters in the entire group of vigorous, laughing wedding guests. Maureen looked positively scared of her own bridesmaid, and Peter, although solid and with a determined chin, had a panic-stricken look about him which contrasted with the cheerfully assured grin of the best man.

"That's Heskith," said Luke. "You can see the sort of chap he is—not one of nature's noblemen, but not a man to go imagining things. When he says he felt the two were there that morning, perfectly normal and happy as usual, I believe him."

"No Miss Dove here?" said Campion, still looking at the group photograph.

"No. That's her sister though, standing in for the bride's mother. And that's the cousin, the one who thinks she saw Peter go up the road."

Luke put a forefinger over the face of the third bridesmaid. "There's another sister here and the rest are cousins. I understand the pic doesn't do the bride justice. Everybody says she was very pretty . . ." He corrected himself. "*Is*, I mean."

"The bridegroom looks like a reasonable type to me," murmured Mr. Campion. "A little apprehensive, perhaps."

272

"I wonder." Luke spoke thoughtfully. "The Heskiths had another photo of him and perhaps it's more marked in that — but don't you think there's a kind of ruthlessness in that face, Campion? It's not quite recklessness — more, I'd say, like decision. I knew a sergeant in the war with a face like that. He was mild enough in the ordinary way but once something shook him he acted fast and pulled no punches whatever. Well, that's neither here nor there. Come and inspect the clothesline and then, Heaven help you, you'll know as much as I do."

Luke led the way to the back and stood for a moment on the concrete path which ran under the kitchen window separating the house from the small rectangle of shorn grass which was all there was of a garden.

A high hedge and rustic fencing separated the garden from the neighbors on the right, and at the bottom there was a garden shed and a few fruit trees; on the left, the greenery in the neglected garden of the old woman who was in the hospital had grown up high so that a green wall screened the garden from all but the prying eyes of Miss Dove who, at that moment, Mr. Campion suspected, was standing on a chair and clinging to a sash to peer at them.

Luke indicated the empty line slung across the grass. "I had the linen brought in," he said. "The Heskiths were worrying and there seemed no earthly point in leaving it out to rot."

"What's in the shed?"

"A spade and a fork and a lawn mower," said Luke promptly. "Come and look. The floor is beaten earth and if it's been disturbed in thirty years I'll eat my hat in Trafalgar Square. I suppose we'll have to dig it up in the end but we'll be wasting our time."

Mr. Campion went over and glanced into the tarred wooden hut. It was tidy and dusty and the floor was dry and hard. Outside, a dilapidated pair of steps leaned against the six-foot brick wall which marked the boundary.

Mr. Campion tried the steps gingerly. They held firmly enough, so he climbed up to look over the wall to the narrow path which separated it from the fence in the rear garden of the house in the next street.

"That's an old right of way," Luke said. "It leads down between the two residential roads. These suburban places are not very matey, you know. Half the time one street doesn't know the next. Chestnut Grove is classier than Philpott Avenue, which runs parallel with it."

Mr. Campion descended and dusted his hands. He was grinning and his eyes were dancing.

"I wonder if anybody there noticed her," he said. "She must have been carrying the sheets."

Luke turned round slowly and stared at him.

"You're not suggesting she simply walked down here and over the wall and out! In the clothes she'd been washing in? It's crazy. Why should she? And did her husband go with her?"

"No, I think he went down to Chestnut Grove as usual, doubled back down this path as soon as he came to the other end of it near the station, picked up his wife, and went off with her through Philpott Avenue to the bus stop. They'd only have to get to Broadway to find a cab, you see."

Luke's dark face still wore an expression of complete incredulity.

"But for Pete's sake *why?*" he demanded. "Why clear out in the middle of breakfast on a wash-day morning? And why take the sheets? Young couples can do the most unlikely things—but there are limits, Campion! They didn't take their savings bankbooks, you know. There's not much in them but they're still there in the writing desk in the front room. What in the world are you getting at, Campion?"

The thin man walked slowly back to the patch of grass.

"I expect the sheets were dry and she'd folded them into the basket before breakfast," he began slowly. "As she ran out of the house they were lying there and she couldn't resist taking them with her. The husband may have been irritated with her when he saw her with them, but people are like that. When they're running from a fire they save the oddest things."

"But she wasn't running from a fire."

"Wasn't she!" Mr. Campion laughed. "Listen, Charles. If the mail carrier called, he reached the house at 7:25. I think he did call and delivered an ordinary plain business envelope which was too commonplace for him to remember. It would be the plainest of plain envelopes. Well then: who was due at 7:30?"

"Bert Heskith. I told you."

"Exactly. So there were five minutes in which to escape. Five minutes for a determined, resourceful man like Peter McGill to act promptly. His wife was generous and easygoing, remember, and so, thanks to that decisiveness which you yourself noticed in his face, he rose to the occasion.

"He had only five minutes, Charles, to escape all those powerful personalities with their jolly, avid faces whom we saw in the wedding group. They were all living remarkably close to him—ringing him round as it were—so that it was a ticklish business to elude them. He went out the front way so that the kindly watchful eyes would see him as usual and not be alarmed.

"There wasn't time to take anything at all and it was only because Maureen, flying through the garden to escape out the back way, saw the sheets in the basket and couldn't resist her treasures that she salvaged them. She wasn't quite so ruthless as Peter. She had to take something from the old life, however glistening were the prospects for . . ."

Campion broke off abruptly. Chief Inspector Luke, with dawning comprehension in his eyes, was already halfway to the gate on the way to the nearest police telephone box.

Mr. Campion was in his own sitting room in Bottle Street, Piccadilly, later that evening when Luke called. The Chief Inspector came in jauntily, his black eyes dancing with amusement.

"It wasn't the Football Pool but the Irish Sweepstakes," he said. "I got the details out of the promoters. They've been wondering what to do ever since the story broke.

They're in touch with the McGills, of course, but Peter has taken every precaution to insure secrecy, and he's insisting on his rights. He must have already made up his mind what he'd do if ever a really big win came off. The moment he got the letter telling him of his luck he put the plan into action."

Luke paused and shook his head admiringly. "I have to hand it to him," he said. "Seventy-five thousand pounds is like a nice fat chicken—plenty and more for two but only a taste for a very big family."

"What will you do?"

"Us? The police? Oh, officially we're baffled. We shall retire gracefully. It's not our business—strictly a family affair."

He sat down and raised the glass his host had handed to him. "Here's to the mystery of the Villa Mary Celeste," he said. "I had a blind spot for it. It foxed me completely. Good luck to them, though. You know, Campion, you had a point when you said that the really insoluble mystery is the one which no one can bring himself to spoil. What put you on to it?"

"I suspect the charm of relatives who call at seven-thirty in the morning," said Mr. Campion.

YOUR CATFISH FRIEND

Richard Brautigan

If I were to live my life
in catfish forms
in scaffolds of skin and whiskers
at the bottom of a pond
and you were to come by
    one evening
when the moon was shining
down into my dark home
and stand there at the edge
    of my affection
and think, "It's beautiful
here by this pond. I wish
    somebody loved me,"
I'd love you and be your catfish
friend and drive such lonely
thoughts from your mind
and suddenly you would be
    at peace,
and ask yourself, "I wonder
if there are any catfish
in this pond? It seems like
a perfect place for them."

How Speed Reading Almost Ruined My Life

E. M. Hunnicutt

If this were a detective story, I'd begin by giving you the first clue. A year ago I, Martin Selby, didn't know the first thing about speed reading. I had the narrowest visual span in Mrs. Crane's English class. I sub-vocalized so much people thought I had a nervous twitch. I spent a lot of time with punctuation marks, too. I made a personal friend of every period, and an exclamation point sometimes stopped me for a full minute. Reading so slowly probably doesn't bother some people, but if your hobby is reading detective stories, it's a real problem. Now if none of this makes sense to you, don't worry. Try the second clue.

I am not a volunteer by nature. When a teacher asks, "Who has the answer to the third problem?" I develop an itching in my ankle that lasts until someone else answers the question. Or I discover an ant crawling up the wall behind me. In a tight situation I may study a crack in the wall on the chance an ant might appear.

Volunteering takes too much time. I'd rather spend my time reading a good detective story.

Not that I am a slacker. I do all my homework, but I am not an up-front type. I am a back-row type, a behind-the-scenes type, an undercover type. Which is probably why I like reading detective stories so much, when I can find the time. And that's really the third clue.

I read so slowly that by the time I'd plowed through my assignments, with all the ant-watching and ankle-scratching thrown in, I was lucky to get through one detective story a month. Which brings us to the scene of the crime.

On October seventh, Mrs. Crane asked for volunteers to learn speed reading. She said exceptional people had learned to read at fantastic speeds, but nearly all people could double their present reading speed. She didn't mention detective stories. She didn't *have* to! Bells were ringing in my head, and I raised my hand— waved it, really—like a flag of surrender.

There was quite a fuss, since I'd never volunteered for anything before. Not ever. Before it was over, Mrs. Crane had called my mother to say I was finally coming out of my shell, and for days the principal smiled at me in the halls and said, "Good show!"

So maybe I was given special treatment by the speed reading teacher who came in to teach us. The other five volunteers were ordinary, run-of-the-mill geniuses, the kind who volunteer for everything. So maybe I was singled out as the needy one for special attention. Or maybe—just maybe—I have a talent for speed reading. It's hard to imagine an ant-watching ankle-scratcher like me with a special talent. I've known detectives to come up with stranger clues, but that was in stories. This was real!

The teacher was great. He read detective stories, too—38 minutes for one book. You couldn't help admiring someone like that. The first thing he said was "Don't sub-vocalize. If you move your lips while you're reading, it makes a lot of clutter."

"Sure," I said, "like shuffling your feet when you're slipping up on a suspect!"

"Exactly," the teacher said. "And widen your visual span."

"Naturally!" I said. "If you don't see everything you'll miss important clues."

If that doesn't make sense to you, don't worry. It didn't make sense to the rest of the class, either. I began reading while the run-

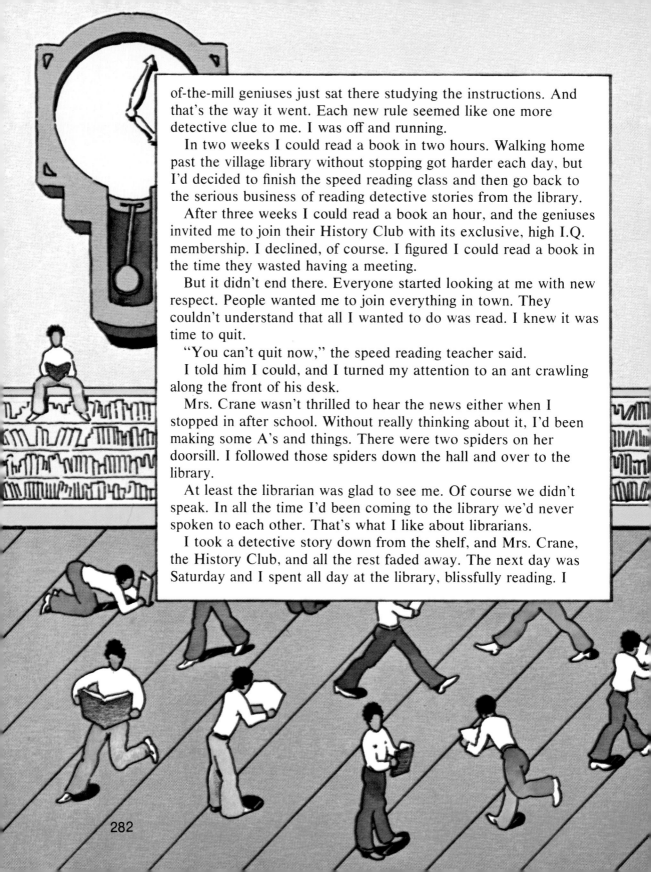

of-the-mill geniuses just sat there studying the instructions. And that's the way it went. Each new rule seemed like one more detective clue to me. I was off and running.

In two weeks I could read a book in two hours. Walking home past the village library without stopping got harder each day, but I'd decided to finish the speed reading class and then go back to the serious business of reading detective stories from the library.

After three weeks I could read a book an hour, and the geniuses invited me to join their History Club with its exclusive, high I.Q. membership. I declined, of course. I figured I could read a book in the time they wasted having a meeting.

But it didn't end there. Everyone started looking at me with new respect. People wanted me to join everything in town. They couldn't understand that all I wanted to do was read. I knew it was time to quit.

"You can't quit now," the speed reading teacher said.

I told him I could, and I turned my attention to an ant crawling along the front of his desk.

Mrs. Crane wasn't thrilled to hear the news either when I stopped in after school. Without really thinking about it, I'd been making some A's and things. There were two spiders on her doorsill. I followed those spiders down the hall and over to the library.

At least the librarian was glad to see me. Of course we didn't speak. In all the time I'd been coming to the library we'd never spoken to each other. That's what I like about librarians.

I took a detective story down from the shelf, and Mrs. Crane, the History Club, and all the rest faded away. The next day was Saturday and I spent all day at the library, blissfully reading. I shouldn't say all day. I read until seven minutes after four in the afternoon. At eight minutes after four I held my first conversation with the librarian.

"I've read all the detective stories in your library," I said. "When do you get the new ones in?"

He said they purchased one a month.

"I need one an hour," I said, "if I don't hurry."

He didn't even look surprised. I guess it's hard to surprise a librarian.

My speed reading teacher wasn't surprised either.

"My life is ruined," I said, looking him straight in the eye. Except he was looking at the wall behind me.

"Funny thing about ants," he said, "they aren't very peppy on Monday morning."

I told him I had to agree with that, but what was he going to do about my spoiled life?

Well, he gave me a talk on making a new life out of the History Club and A's on my report card, and maybe taking up basketball.

"Where's the suspense in that?" I wanted to know. "How can I begin a new life at my age?"

Mrs. Crane wasn't encouraging either. She said, "Talented people receive satisfaction from helping others." It turned out the geniuses wanted me to tutor them in speed reading and their parents were willing to pay me for the service.

"I couldn't accept money," I said.

Mrs. Crane said I certainly could. It was perfectly reasonable to accept pay for a professional service, she said, and I was a professional.

At first I wanted to laugh. Then those bells in my head started again. I did some calculations and came up with a figure for Mrs. Crane. She said, "That's a very small sum of money to ask for tutoring."

Sure it was small, like the last small clue that solves a case.

Homework is no problem now, and I've enjoyed watching the geniuses come along under my direction. A couple of them may develop into first-class speed readers.

I work with them every day after school. No Saturdays. My week's wages cover one round-trip bus ticket to the city every Saturday. The city library has 2,500 detective stories. That should get me through until three years from next February.

Skiing
IS BELIEVING

LINDA JOSEPH

Ninety-seven percent of all Americans do not ski. The strength and coordination that the sport demands, as well as its potential danger, discourage many from taking to the slopes. Yet hundreds of blind adults and children are learning to ski, thanks to a growing nationwide program sponsored by a nonprofit, volunteer organization called Blind Outdoor Leisure Development (BOLD).

During the winter of 1975, the Los Angeles chapter of BOLD participated in a five-day blind skiers' clinic given free of charge at the Kirkwood Ski Area in the California High Sierras. Chapter member Lorita Betraun, then twenty-two years old, attended the clinic and admits to being petrified the first time she attempted a run.

Skiing

"It reminded me of flying, and it was scary," she recalls. "The first time I made a run without physical contact with my instructor, I felt I was going so fast that I didn't know what was going to happen. It was like taking a fast plunge in a high-speed elevator; you know that feeling, like your heart is in your mouth."

Yet after overcoming their initial apprehensions, the BOLD skiers developed a devotion for their newfound sport.

"Skiing is like falling in love," exclaims Dora Nova, age 21, another BOLD member. "It's an incredible feeling of freedom, motion, and indescribable joy. It just blows my mind when I think about it. What's really fantastic is you don't have to see to ski."

Indeed, thanks to techniques developed in 1969 in Aspen, Colorado, the blind can be taught an activity for which vision may seem indispensable. The unique method used to accomplish this feat involves linking the instructor and the blind pupil with a 12-foot bamboo pole until the instructor determines that the pupil is experienced enough to ski alone.

It was 1969 when Jean Eymere, a former member of the French Olympic skiing team, lost his sight from diabetes. Afterward he and his fellow instructors in Aspen worked together trying to determine the best method for teaching the blind how to ski. They experimented with beepers, poles, and radios before realizing that the best method was a guide who was constantly talking and giving encouragement.

286

Eymere, who helped establish BOLD and remains one of its driving forces, believes that skiing is the most dramatic thing blind people can do. If the blind can ski, he believes, they can do almost anything else.

"Motivation of the body, which most blind people don't have, is important for the mind," he says. "You see, some blind people just sit around and concentrate too much on what is impossible, and not enough on what is possible, like skiing.

"BOLD has taken some blind skiers who had never skied before all the way to parallel turns. But how well a blind person skis is irrelevant. The important thing is they are getting turned on to something new. They are doing something bizarre, something outlandish, something absurd, for a blind person."

Pam March, a Kirkwood ski instructor, insists, "Blind skiers are easier to teach than the sighted because they are not as easily distracted on the slopes.

"Some techniques used with blind skiers are just logical extensions of basic ski instruction," Pam explains. "Verbal communication is constant. As the 'eyes' of the pupil, the instructor is continually locating her own and her pupil's position.

"Ski instructors are not only responsible for the training of a blind skier—they also are responsible for the student's life. They must be aware every second of where the skier is going and who or what is coming near. When no specific instructions are being given to the blind skier, the instructor constantly repeats the command, *'Go! Go! Go!'*

"Signs are used on the slopes advising that blind skiers are present. Each student wears a bib emblazoned 'BLIND SKIER,' while instructors use distinctive parkas. Above all, instructors evaluate each individual's capabilities—and stay within those limits."

Dora chuckles as she recalls one of her moments at Kirkwood.

"On Lift Number One for beginners, the slope drops off quite rapidly on the right side. And if you're not ready for it—wow! My instructor and I were free skiing when he told me to stop. The stopping point was directly on the edge of this drop-off. He stopped and I tried. But my skis picked up speed.

"I sat down on my rear end, and my skis just kept running until they encountered this heavy bush. By the time my instructor got to me, I was so thoroughly wrapped up in the bush that he couldn't tell which limbs belonged to me and which belonged to the tree."

Lorita outdid her friend by entangling her skis with her instructor's and falling out of the double chairlift. This happens even to advanced skiers. Hank Kashiwa, the world professional alpine racing champion, fell out of a chairlift twice in one season. And Dandy Don Meredith, the quarterback turned sportscaster turned actor, dislocated his shoulder while boarding a chairlift at Aspen a couple of seasons back.

"It was no big deal when I tumbled out of the chair," Lorita recalls. "Though I had the wind knocked out of me, I wasn't hurt. But some of the others were shaken. You would have thought I was Barbra Streisand or someone important the way they fussed over me. That part was nice."

Lorita's most exciting moment was when she skied Chair Number Six at Kirkwood, a long intermediate run bordered by a heavy growth of trees.

"My instructor and I must have looked like Fred Astaire and Ginger Rogers on skis. That's because I was so scared of this run that I wrapped my arms around his waist and held on for dear life. And when it was over, I sat right down in the snow and didn't move for half an hour. It took me that long to recover. Then we rode the chairlift back up and I conquered that run on my own."

Dora finds that skiing "is overcoming another barrier—something else that society said we couldn't do. And it has changed my inner self, too. It has increased my independence and made me a freer, happier person. After skiing, I'm ready to try anything."

Lorita has also found that her skiing lessons have taught her more than how to master a formidable ski trail.

"The goal for all blind skiers is more freedom. You don't have to see where you're going, as long as you go. In skiing, you ski with your legs and not with your eyes. In life, you experience things with your mind and your body. And if you're lacking one of the five senses, you adapt. Thanks to skiing and Kirkwood, are we ever learning to adapt!"

Skiing

BEFORE AND AFTER

Here are four commonly used prefixes.

extra-   over-   super-   ultra-

What words can you attach to them to make new words?
Do the four prefixes have a similar meaning? What is it?
On a separate sheet of paper, put one of these prefixes
before each of the words below to make a new word.

ordinary	curricular	modern
sold	fine	basic
patriot		violet

What does each new word mean? How does it differ in
meaning from the word without the prefix? How did you
know which prefix to use? What is the difference between
over- and *ultra-*?

Find and write three more words that go with each of the
prefixes above. Using as many of these words as possible,
write an advertisement for a new product.

"THIS EXTRAORDINARY ULTRAMODERN LION REPELLENT IS GUARANTEED TO GIVE SUPERFINE RESULTS."

Here are five frequently used suffixes.

-age   -hood   -ship   -some   -like

On a separate sheet of paper, add one of the first three suffixes to each word below to make a new word.

member   mother   trustee   parent   owner

Can you think of a meaning that these first three suffixes have in common? Write more words to go with each suffix.

The remaining two suffixes, *-some* and *-like*, are more similar to each other than to the other three. What do they mean? Combine one of the two suffixes with the words below to make new words. Write a paragraph or a story using as many of these new words as you can.

tiger   life   awe
irk   tire   burden
quarrel iron   child

A Self-Made Wizard

Robert C. Hayden

Not many years ago there lived an inventor of whom you have probably never heard, but this man's creations touch your life every day. If you saw a movie last week, this man's invention helped to hand you your ticket. If you had eggs for breakfast this morning, he was one of the reasons the eggs arrived fresh. The next time you enjoy an ice cream cone, in a sense you'll have this man to thank for it. His life story is one of the most amazing in the annals of American inventors: orphaned at an early age and raised without much formal education, he rose through three careers to become one of the world's foremost mechanical engineers. The name of this extraordinary man? A supremely ordinary name: Jones.

Racing Cars — A False Start

Frederick McKinley Jones was born in 1893, and for the first ten years of his life the cards seemed stacked against him.

He was an orphan for most of his boyhood. His mother died when he was only an infant, and his father died when Jones was nine years old. After his father's death Jones left his birthplace, Cincinnati, Ohio, and went to live with a priest, Father Ryan, in Kentucky. There he lived in a rectory, where he did odd jobs for the priest and attended school through grade six. When Jones was sixteen, he left the rectory and began to look for a job.

At this time, the first big automobiles were beginning to appear. Jones was fascinated by these machines and hitched a ride in one at every chance. He developed a burning desire to work with them — to use his mind and his hands and to explore the mechanical parts under the hood. He figured that the only way to do this was to get a job as an auto mechanic.

And so, without experience or much education, Jones returned to Cincinnati and convinced a garage owner that he, Fred Jones, was a skilled mechanic. The owner agreed to give Jones a tryout, and the new mechanic soon managed to prove himself at his job.

Jones had a keen, inventive mind and an ability to understand machinery. And when he came to a problem in his work that stumped him, he knew where to go for help — he went to the library and studied books on the subject that puzzled him. This became a habit of his, and he practiced it throughout his life.

Hard work and serious study paid off for the young mechanic. Three years later, Fred Jones became the foreman of the automobile shop. Now he wanted to work on racing cars. Auto racing was becoming a big sport at the time, and the successful racer needed a car that would not fall apart at high speeds. Fred and his crew could take a bare chassis (car frame), pull the steering wheel down to a sporty angle, change the gears, install a foot throttle and bucket seats, juggle some other parts around, and wind up with a racer. Jones had built a couple of speedy racers by the time he was nineteen, but his boss thought he was too young to race and so others drove his cars for him.

One day Fred could not resist the temptation to be at the track to watch one of the cars he had built. He ducked out of the garage without his boss's permission and headed for the track. It was worth it to him because the racer that he had worked on so hard and had kept in top condition won.

Fred's boss did not like the idea that he sneaked off, and so he decided to lay Fred off for a while to

teach him a lesson. This was so hard for the young racing enthusiast to take that he quit his job and headed for Chicago to see the sights of the big city.

On his way back to Cincinnati from Chicago, Fred Jones somehow boarded the wrong train. At daybreak he found himself in Effingham, Illinois. Being resourceful and curious, he decided to explore this unfamiliar town. He stayed on in Effingham and managed to land a job fitting pipes together for a heating system in a hotel. One of the hotel guests was a James Hill, who managed a 50,000-acre farm near Hallock, Minnesota. When the hotelkeeper heard that Hill was

looking for a mechanic to keep his machinery in good condition, he recommended that Hill talk with Fred Jones. Jones accepted the new challenge offered by Hill, and on a snowy Christmas Day in 1912, he arrived in Hallock, Minnesota, his home for the next eighteen years.

Steam engines, gasoline-driven tractors, hay loaders, cream separators, ditching and fencing machines, harvesters, and road graders; all this machinery and more were on the farm for Jones to work on. Mr. Hill also had several cars that had to be kept in good running order. There was plenty of work for the new mechanic and plenty of opportunity for him to learn. He turned every new problem into a learning situation. After the sun went down he spent his time reading books on electricity, engines, and other subjects, adding more to his knowledge of mechanical engineering. But he did more than just work and study. In Hallock, Jones hunted and fished with his many friends, sang in the local town quartet, and played the saxophone in the town band.

During World War I, Frederick Jones enlisted in the Army, served in France as an electrician, and earned the rank of sergeant. When the war ended, he returned to Hallock to work at a garage where cars, tractors, and farm machinery were repaired. He liked complicated jobs and would often make different parts out of scraps and pieces of old machinery. His new employer, like Jones, was a racing-car buff and together they toured the dirt-track circuit. They whipped up a racer from a Dodge frame and engine, installed Hudson "super-six" valves, a Ford Model-T rear axle, and an oil pump from a Rumley tractor. Jones raced for a number of years and set several track records at county fairground events.

But Fred was not fated to be an auto racer, as events proved one day in 1925. That day the thirty-two-year-old driver was entered in a five-mile race where three other drivers had already been killed on the treacherous track. Going into a turn at 100 miles per hour, Jones lost control and spun out, hitting a fence and clipping off several posts before the car stopped. He was knocked out and awoke to find himself in an ambulance. His injuries, though not serious, convinced him of one thing: racing cars was not for him. There had to be a less dangerous way to make a living!

"Talkies" and Tickets

His imagination and ability led him on to other adventures. As the first radios were beginning to come to Minnesota, Jones found himself surrounded by coils, tubes, condensers, and books on electronics and the science of sound. When the publisher of the Hallock newspaper obtained a radio broadcasting license, Fred Jones built the first transmitter for the station. And then he built many table-model radios for his friends in Hallock so they could listen to the new local station.

Jones also worked at the Grand Theater in Hallock, where he ran the movie projector. When "talking" movies became available, the theater owner realized that he would have to install the new, expensive sound equipment to continue to attract his customers. But he couldn't afford it. So Jones offered to build the equipment himself. Using heavy steel disks from a plow, a leather machine belt, and some other odds and ends, Jones built a sound-track unit as good as anything on the market. His device, which kept sound records in time with the moving film, cost less than $100 to make. The commercial outfits available at the time cost about $3,000.

But by 1930 most good motion pictures were made with the sound track on the film itself. Records were on their way out, and this meant that new equipment was necessary. Fred Jones again rose to the challenge and decided to design his own device for combining sound with the film. Within a short period of time, the Grand Theater in Hallock was once again in step with the modern "talking" movies.

News of Jones's invention spread, one day reaching the ears of a Minneapolis man named Joseph A. Numero, who owned a company that manufactured motion picture equipment. He was having trouble constructing sound pickup devices, and he decided to invite Jones to Minneapolis to help him. Fred accepted the offer, and in 1930 he joined Cinema Supplies, Inc.

Business began to boom. Before long, Numero's sound equipment was used throughout the upper Midwest and in eighty-five theaters in Chicago. In June of 1939, Fred Jones received his first patent, for a ticket-dispensing machine used in theater box offices. Now the ex-racing-car driver was benefiting the movie industry and contributing to the enjoyment of thousands of Americans. But little could he know that soon a practical joke and a twist of fate would launch him on a third, even more illustrious, career.

A Misunderstanding

On a hot summer night in 1937, Jones was trying to cool off by driving around a lake in Minneapolis. He stopped his car to catch a breath of fresh air. The cool breeze coming off the lake was a relief from the city's sweltering heat. But mosquitoes swarmed in on him, and he was forced to close his car windows. Then the heat inside the car became unbearable again, and so Fred Jones left the lakeside and headed home. As he drove along, he asked himself why no one had invented a device to air-condition a car.

The next morning Jones arrived early at the public library in Minneapolis. He located all the books he could find on refrigeration and air conditioning. Finding no evidence that anyone had ever developed an air conditioner for an automobile, Jones began to sketch a design for one. A week later he showed his plans to Numero, who was not impressed.

"It would be too heavy," he told Jones. "Also, it would be too expensive to make, and I don't think anyone would buy it. Besides, we're in the business of making theater equipment, so let's stick to that."

Jones put his plans for the cooler aside. But the idea stayed in his mind, and he continued to read all he could find on the science of refrigeration and air cooling.

About a year later, Mr. Numero was playing golf on a hot midsummer day with two friends, one in the trucking business and the other in the air-conditioning business. Mr. Werner, the owner of Werner Transportation Company, complained that he had lost a truckload of poultry when the ice blocks in the truck had melted and the meat had spoiled. Suddenly an idea struck him: "Why can't someone make a machine that will keep the inside of a truck cool? It seems to me that if a movie theater can be cooled off, then surely someone ought to be able to cool a truckload of chickens without having to use ice."

The air-conditioning expert explained that attempts to do this had failed so far. The jarring and jolting of a truck on the highway made it impossible for a mechanical refrigerator to work properly.

As Numero drove his ball off the fourth tee he turned to Werner and told him jokingly, "I'll build you a refrigerator for your truck."

This was quite a boast for Numero, who was in the business of manufacturing motion picture equipment. The threesome walked off the tee onto the fairway and the conversation turned back to golf. Little did Numero realize that the trucker had taken his remark seriously. And neither had he remembered Jones's idea for a car air conditioner.

A few weeks later Werner called Numero with a surprise: He had purchased a new truck and was ready for Numero to build a cooling unit for it. The same day a shining new aluminum van appeared in the parking lot of Cinema Supplies, Inc. Mr. Numero was dumbfounded. How could he make good his promise?

Learning of Numero's problem, Fred Jones decided to have a go at solving it. He went out, climbed into the truck, and took some measurements. Then he worked throughout most of the night making calculations. The next day Jones told Numero that he could build the kind of air-conditioning unit Werner wanted.

Jones knew that the earlier truck refrigeration units had been jolted into pieces. They were "big clunks," as he described them, and they took up too much space inside the truck itself. Jones had had much experience in building shock-proof and vibration-proof gadgets. After much figuring he came up with a light, compact, and sturdy unit that he thought would do the job. He installed this unit under the truck, but it quickly broke down as it became clogged with mud. So he mounted a similar unit to the forehead of the truck, above the cab, where it

would be out of the way and could use space that had been wasted. It worked!

Frederick Jones's truck cooler was a spectacular breakthrough in automotive technology. It completely changed the food transport industry, and American eating habits as well, by creating new markets for many food crops. People in Vermont could now enjoy fresh California lettuce, and Florida grapefruit began selling in Idaho. The use of frozen foods became more widespread, and during World War II, Jones's portable refrigerators even helped save lives by preserving precious drugs and medicines.

The firm of Thermo King, founded by Numero and Jones after that first practical cooler, produced many of these units. By 1949 it had boomed to a $3-million-a-year business, one that expanded its range to refrigeration on trains, ships, and airlines. Thermo King still thrives today in Minneapolis.

As for Jones, he was never satisfied with the improvements he made in his cooling units. He developed ways that kept the air around the food at a constant temperature. He created other devices that produced special atmospheric conditions to keep strawberries and other fruits from drying out or becoming too ripe in transit. Still other methods controlled the moisture in the air and air circulation.

During his lifetime, Frederick Jones was awarded more than 60 patents; 40 were for refrigeration equipment alone. Others were for portable X-ray machines and sound equipment techniques for motion pictures. Jones also patented many of the special parts of his air-cooling machines: the self-starting gasoline engine that turned his cooling units on and off, the reverse cycling mechanism for producing heat or cold, and devices for controlling air temperature and moisture.

At fifty years of age, Frederick Jones was one of the outstanding authorities in the field of refrigeration in the United States. In 1944 he was elected to membership in the American Society of Refrigeration Engineers. College-graduate scientists and engineers welcomed the chance to work with and learn from him. During the 1950s he was called to Washington to give advice on problems having to do with refrigeration. He was a consultant to both the Defense Department and the United States Bureau of Standards.

When Frederick McKinley Jones died in Minneapolis in 1961, his inventions were serving people throughout the world. He was a behind-the-scenes contributor to the luxuries of modern living.

SO YOU WANT TO PUT ON A PLAY

Karleen Schart Sabol

Do you like to act? Do you like to build things, paint things, or sew things? Do you write or sing or dance or play an instrument? Do you like to work hard, organize things, or tell other people what to do? Have you ever wondered what goes into presenting a professional play? Are you interested in getting a job in the theater someday? If you answered "yes" to any of these questions, then putting on a play may be just the thing for you.

I am an actress, and the thought of having my own theater is very exciting. One of my friends is twelve years old, and she and her friends started a theater in her barn. You don't need a barn, of course, but this is what you *do* need.

A *play*. Go to the library, get several books of plays, and pick out one that you like. If the book mentions anything about royalties, you may have to pay to present that play. The royalty money goes to the author, or *playwright*, to pay for the use of his or her material. There are lots of plays, however, for which you don't need to pay royalties. These are usually referred to as being "in public domain." You can ask your librarian to help you find one of these or, better still, you can write your own play. When you decide on a play that you like, make enough copies of it so that everyone involved with the play can have one. These copies are called *scripts*.

You need a *producer*, who will organize the whole thing. The producer makes sure you have a place where you can present your play. This can be almost anywhere — my friend's barn is great, but you can also use a garage, a cellar, a room that nobody uses much, a school auditorium, or even a lawn or a sidewalk. Just make sure you have enough space for the actors to move around — the *stage*; a place where the actors can get ready or wait when they aren't acting — a *dressing room*; and room for an audience to sit.

The producer must also take care of the publicity for your play so that people will know when and where you're planning to put it on.

Good ways to publicize your play include making posters, sending articles to the school and local newspapers, and announcing it on your local radio station.

The producer also chooses the director, the stage manager, the set designer, the wardrobe mistress or master, the lighting and sound technician, and the props person. If you will need money to put on your play, the producer thinks of ways to earn it. In other words, the producer is the boss; so make sure you get someone who is a good leader and who will stick with the job.

You need a *director* to supervise the staging, or presentation, of your play. He or she manages the *rehearsals*, when all the actors practice their lines while moving around onstage. The director tells the actors when and where and how to sit, stand, and move while they're on the stage (this is called giving them their *blocking*). The director also helps the actors figure out the best ways of saying their lines so that the characters they're playing will seem real. Finally, the director makes sure that other people working on the play do their jobs right and get everything finished by the time the play is to be performed for an audience. You'll need a director who is not only creative but is also efficient, organized, calm, and able to make decisions.

You need a *stage manager* to assist

the director. The stage manager keeps what is called a *master script,* in which he or she writes all the instructions given by the director. This means that every actor's blocking and every *entrance cue* (when an actor comes onstage) and *exit cue* (when an actor goes offstage) will be marked. All the *technical cues,* such as when the lights go on or off, when it's time for a sound effect, and when the curtain should be opened or closed, will also be marked on the master script. Then, if any questions come up during a rehearsal, the stage manager has the answers ready in the master script. During the actual performances, the stage manager makes sure that everyone is ready at the right times and that all the cues are followed. Stage managers must be efficient, on their toes, and smart.

You need a *set designer,* someone who likes to design and build things. And the set designer will

need helpers, called the *set crew*. The designer first reads the play and then decides what he or she thinks the *set* should look like. If your play is about a mad scientist, your set may be the laboratory where fiendish experiments are carried out. If your play tells of the life of a great tightrope walker, your set could suggest the inside of a circus tent. A set can be very simple; however, whatever your play is about, the set should show your audience where the action is taking place. It would be a good idea to check the library for books about how to build sets. Did you know that most of the "walls" you see onstage are made from cloth that is stretched on wooden frames and painted? These are called *flats*. The director looks at the set designer's drawing and decides if it will work. Before building begins, the director helps the set designer figure out where things like doors, windows, and staircases should be.

You need a *wardrobe master* or a *wardrobe mistress* who will get together all the clothes, or *costumes*, to be worn in your play. Sometimes, if you put on a modern play, you can wear your own clothes. But even if you do, you'll need someone to make sure the costumes suit the play and go well together. If your play calls for old-fashioned costumes, the wardrobe person does research to find out what kind of costumes should be made, bought, rented, or borrowed. There are books in the library that show the styles of clothes people have worn in different times and places. If your costumes get ripped and need to be sewn, the wardrobe person is the one to repair them. If your costumes get dirty and wrinkled, the wardrobe person has to get them cleaned. He or she must make sure that all costumes are in perfect condition before each performance.

You need *lighting and sound technicians* to get lights and sound effects just right. Sometimes one person can handle both lights and sound, sometimes two people are needed—it depends on what kinds of effects you want for your play. The lighting can be very simple; the most important thing is having enough light so that the audience can see what's happening onstage. The sound can be handled in a number of ways. Check your library for records of sound effects, such as train whistles, thunder, and screams; or find a tape recorder and record your own sounds. If you have enough people in your theater group, you can let someone stand offstage during performances banging pans or doing bird imitations or making any other sounds that might be needed. The director will tell the lighting and sound technicians to figure out the best ways of producing these effects. A warn-

ACT 2

303

304

ing: Don't play around with electric wires when you aren't sure what you're doing. Find someone who knows about electricity to help you.

You will need a *property master* or a *property mistress. Props* are all over the place. A sofa on the stage is a prop, and so is a telephone, a picture on the wall, a handkerchief, or anything else the actors use in the play. After checking with the director, the props person decides what will be needed. Then he or she makes, borrows, or buys all the props in time for the actors to practice using them before the first performance. The props person also works closely with the set designer so that the props will match the set. The property person must also check before each performance to make sure all props are in good condition and easy for the actors to find.

Finally, you need *actors* to perform in your play. You should hold *auditions.* At an audition, everyone who wants to be in the play reads some of the lines of the character he or she wants to play. Then the director and the producer, and sometimes the stage manager, decide who they think would be the best actor for each part. After choosing your cast, give each actor a copy of the script. The actors should read the whole play carefully and then memorize their own lines. Provide the actors with scripts that they can write in, because they will need to make notes of their blocking, entrance and exit cues, and any other hints the director gives them. Actors have to work very hard to make their characters come alive onstage, and you'll want people with good strong voices and lots of energy.

When you have everyone and everything you need, pick out the dates for your performances. Don't set the date for your first performance too early because you may need three weeks to a month of rehearsals, and maybe longer. The best times for performances are usually in the afternoon or early evening on weekends.

It's up to you whether or not to charge admission. My friend and her group don't charge anything, but they do pass around a hat for donations. And they always get enough money to pay the expenses for the play they are presenting and some extra to help start putting on another one.

If you don't have enough enthusiastic friends to put on your own plays but you still want to do something in the theater, there may be a professional or community theater near you. Ask them if you can be an apprentice. You will work very hard, but it's a good way to learn about theater, and you'll have lots of fun, too. Whatever you do, enjoy it — and good luck!

Anton Chekhov

A Marriage Proposal
A Joke in One Act

Translated by Theodore Hoffman

Anton Chekhov (1860–1904) is considered one of the finest playwrights and short story writers who ever lived. As a medical student in his native Russia in the 1880s, he began to write humorous articles for newspapers and magazines to help support his large, poor family. By 1886, as a practicing doctor, he had become known as a short story writer, and he decided on a literary career.

His stories and plays concentrate on people who cannot seem to understand each other. A Marriage Proposal shows the very humorous side of a breakdown in communications.

Characters

STEPAN STEPANOVICH CHUBUKOV[1]
 a landowner, elderly, pompous, but affable.

IVAN VASSILEVITCH LOMOV[2]
 healthy, but a hypochondriac; nervous, suspicious. Also a land-owner.

NATALIA STEPANOVNA[3]
 Chubukov's daughter; twenty-five and unmarried.

Scene: Chubukov's mansion — the living room.

[*Lomov enters, formally dressed in evening jacket, white gloves, top hat. He is nervous from the start.*]

CHUBUKOV (*rising*): Well, look who's here! Ivan Vassilevitch! (*Shakes his hand warmly.*) What a surprise, old man! How are you?

LOMOV: Oh, not too bad. And you?

CHUBUKOV: Oh, we manage, we manage. Do sit down, please. You know, you've been neglecting your neighbors, my dear fellow. It's been ages. Say, why the formal dress? Tails, gloves, and so forth. Where's the funeral, my boy? Where are you headed?

LOMOV: Oh, nowhere. I mean, here; just to see you, my dear Stepan Stepanovich.

[1] **Stepan Stepanovich Chubukov:** pronounced *Ste·pan' Ste·pa'nə·vich Chü'bə·kof.*
[2] **Ivan Vassilevitch Lomov:** pronounced *I·van' Və·syēl'ye·vitch Lŏ'mof.*
[3] **Natalia Stepanovna:** pronounced *Nə·tal'ye Ste·pə·nōv'ne.*

CHUBUKOV: Then why the full dress, old boy? It's not New Year's, and so forth.

LOMOV: Well, you see, it's like this. I have come here, my dear Stepan Stepanovich, to bother you with a request. More than once, or twice, or more than that, it has been my privilege to apply to you for assistance in things, and you've always, well, responded. I mean, well, you have. Yes. Excuse me, I'm getting all mixed up. May I have a glass of water, my dear Stepan Stepanovich? (*Drinks.*)

CHUBUKOV (*aside*): Wants to borrow some money. Not a chance! (*Aloud*) What can I do for you, my dear friend?

LOMOV: Well, you see, my dear Stepanitch. . . . Excuse me, I mean Stepan my Dearovitch. . . . No, I mean, I get all confused, as you can see. To make a long story short, you're the only one who can help me. Of course, I don't deserve it, and there's no reason why I should expect you to, and all that.

CHUBUKOV: Stop beating around the bush! Out with it!

LOMOV: In just a minute. I mean, now, right now. The truth is, I have come to ask the hand. . . . I mean, your daughter, Natalia Stepanovna, I, I want to marry her!

CHUBUKOV (*overjoyed*): Great heavens! Ivan Vassilevitch! Say it again!

307

LOMOV: I have come humbly to ask for the hand . . .

CHUBUKOV (*interrupting*): You're a prince! I'm overwhelmed, delighted, and so forth. Yes, indeed, and all that! (*Hugs and kisses Lomov.*) This is just what I've been hoping for. It's my fondest dream come true. (*Sheds a tear.*) And, you know, I've always looked upon you, my boy, as if you were my own son. May God grant to both of you His Mercy and His Love, and so forth. Oh, I have been wishing for this. . . . But why am I being so idiotic? It's just that I'm off my rocker with joy, my boy! Completely off my rocker! Oh, with all my soul I'm . . . I'll go get Natalia, and so forth.

LOMOV (*deeply moved*): Dear Stepan Stepanovitch, do you think she'll agree?

CHUBUKOV: Why, of course, old friend. Great heavens! As if she wouldn't! Why, she's crazy for you! Goodness! Like a lovesick cat, and so forth. Be right back. (*Leaves.*)

LOMOV: It's cold. I'm gooseflesh all over, as if I had to take a test. But the main thing is, to make up my mind and keep it that way. I mean, if I take time out to think, or if I hesitate, or talk about it, or have ideals, or wait for real love, well, I'll just never get married! Brrrr, it's cold! Natalia Stepanovna is an excellent housekeeper. She's not too bad looking. She's had a good education. What more could I ask? Nothing. I'm so nervous, my ears are buzzing. (*Drinks.*) Besides, I've just got to get married. I'm thirty-five already. It's sort of a critical age. I've got to settle down and lead a regular life. I mean, I'm always getting palpitations, and I'm nervous, and I get upset so easily. Look, my lips are quivering, and my eyebrow's twitching. The worst thing is the night. Sleeping. I get into bed, doze off, and, suddenly, something inside me jumps. First my head snaps, and then my shoulder blade, and I roll out of bed like a lunatic and try to walk it off. Then I try to go back to sleep, but, as soon as I do, something jumps again! Twenty times a night, sometimes . . .

[*Natalia Stepanovna enters.*]

NATALIA: Oh, it's only you. All Papa said was: "Go inside, there's a merchant come to collect his goods." How do you do, Ivan Vassilevitch?

LOMOV: How do you do, dear Natalia Stepanovna?

NATALIA: Excuse my apron, and not being dressed. We're shelling peas. You haven't been around lately. Oh, do sit down. (*They do.*) Would you like some lunch?

LOMOV: No thanks, I had some.

NATALIA: Well, then smoke if you want. (*He doesn't.*) The weather's nice today . . . but yesterday, it

was so wet the workers couldn't get a thing done. Have you got much hay in? I felt so greedy I had a whole field done, but now I'm not sure I was right. With the rain it could rot, couldn't it? I should have waited. But why are you so dressed up? Is there a dance or something? Of course, I must say you look splendid, but . . . Well, tell me, why are you so dressed up?

LOMOV (*excited*): Well, you see, my dear Natalia Stepanovna, the truth is, I made up my mind to ask you to . . . well, to listen to me. Of course, it'll probably surprise you and even maybe make you angry, but . . . (*Aside*) It's cold in here!

NATALIA: Why, what do you mean? (*A pause*) Well?

LOMOV: I'll try to get it over with. I mean, you know, my dear Natalia Stepanovna, that I've known, since childhood even, known, and had the privilege of knowing, your family. My late aunt, and her husband, who, as you know, left me my estate, they always had the greatest respect for your father and your late mother. The Lomovs and the Chubukovs have always been very friendly, you might even say affectionate. And, of course, you know, our land borders on each other's. My Oxen Meadows touch your birch grove and . . .

NATALIA: I hate to interrupt you, my

dear Ivan Vassilevitch, but you said: "my Oxen Meadows." Do you really think they're yours?

LOMOV: Why, of course, they're mine.

NATALIA: What do you mean? The Oxen Meadows are ours, not yours!

LOMOV: Oh, no, my dear Natalia Stepanovna, they're mine.

NATALIA: Well, this is the first I've heard about it! Where did you get that idea?

LOMOV: Where? Why, I mean the Oxen Meadows that are wedged between your birches and the marsh.

NATALIA: Yes, of course, they're ours.

LOMOV: Oh, no, you're wrong, my dear Natalia Stepanovna, they're mine.

NATALIA: Now, come, Ivan Vassilevitch! How long have they been yours?

LOMOV: How long? Why, as long as I can remember!

NATALIA: Well, really, you can't expect me to believe that!

LOMOV: But, you can see for yourself in the deed, my dear Natalia Stepanovna. Of course, there was once a dispute about them, but everyone knows they're mine now. There's nothing to argue about. There was a time when my aunt's grandmother let your father's grandfather's peasants use the land, but they were supposed to bake bricks for her in return.

Naturally, after a few years they began to act as if they owned it, but the real truth is . . .

NATALIA: That has nothing to do with the case! Both my grandfather and my great-grandfather said that their land went as far as the marsh, which means that the meadows are ours! There's nothing whatever to argue about. It's foolish.

LOMOV: But I can show you the deed, Natalia Stepanovna.

NATALIA: You're just making fun of me. . . . Great Heavens! Here we have the land for hundreds of years, and suddenly you try to tell us it isn't ours. What's wrong with you, Ivan Vassilevitch? Those meadows aren't even fifteen acres, and they're not worth three hundred rubles, but I just can't stand unfairness! I just can't stand unfairness!

LOMOV: But, you must listen to me. Your father's grandfather's peasants, as I've already tried to tell you, they were supposed to bake bricks for my aunt's grandmother. And my aunt's grandmother, why, she wanted to be nice to them . . .

NATALIA: It's just nonsense, this whole business about aunts and grandfathers and grandmothers. The meadows are ours! That's all there is to it!

LOMOV: They're mine!

NATALIA: Ours! You can go on talking for two days, and you can put on fifteen evening coats and twenty pairs of gloves, but I tell you they're ours, ours, ours!

LOMOV: Natalia Stepanovna, I don't want the meadows! I'm just acting on principle. If you want, I'll give them to you.

NATALIA: I'll give them to *you!* Because they're ours! And that's all there is to it! And if I may say so, your behavior, my dear Ivan Vassilevitch, is very strange. Until now, we've always considered you a good neighbor, even a friend. After all, last year we lent you our threshing machine, even though it meant putting off our own threshing until November. And here you are treating us like a pack of gypsies. Giving me my own land, indeed! Really! Why, that's not being a good neighbor.

It's sheer impudence, that's what it is . . .

LOMOV: Oh, so you think I'm just a land-grabber? My dear lady, I've never grabbed anybody's land in my whole life, and no one's going to accuse me of doing it now! (*Quickly walks over to the pitcher and drinks some more water.*) The Oxen Meadows are mine!

NATALIA: That's a lie. They're ours!

LOMOV: Mine!

NATALIA: A lie! I'll prove it. I'll send my mowers out there today!

LOMOV: What?

NATALIA: My mowers will mow it today!

LOMOV: I'll kick them out!

NATALIA: You just dare!

LOMOV (*clutching his heart*): The Oxen Meadows are mine! Do you understand? Mine!

311

NATALIA: Please don't shout! You can shout all you want in your own house, but here I must ask you to control yourself.

LOMOV: If my heart weren't palpitating the way it is, if my insides weren't jumping like mad, I wouldn't talk to you so calmly. *(Yelling)* The Oxen Meadows are mine!

NATALIA: Ours!

LOMOV: Mine!

NATALIA: Ours!

LOMOV: Mine!

[*Enter Chubukov.*]

CHUBUKOV: What's going on? Why all the shouting?

NATALIA: Papa, will you please inform this gentleman who owns the Oxen Meadows, he or we?

CHUBUKOV *(to Lomov)*: Why, they're ours, old fellow.

LOMOV: But how can they be yours, my dear Stepan Stepanovitch? Be fair. Perhaps my aunt's grandmother did let your grandfather's peasants work the land, and maybe they did get so used to it that they acted as if it were their own, but . . .

CHUBUKOV: Oh, no, no . . . my dear boy. You forgot something. The reason the peasants didn't pay your aunt's grandmother, and so forth, was that the land was disputed, even then. Since then it's been settled. Why, everyone knows it's ours.

LOMOV: I can prove it's mine.

CHUBUKOV: You can't prove a thing, old boy.

LOMOV: *(yelling)* Yes I can!

CHUBUKOV: My dear lad, why yell like that? Yelling doesn't prove a thing. Look, I'm not after anything of yours, just as I don't intend to give up anything of mine. Why should I? Besides, if you're going to keep arguing about it, I'd just as soon give the land to the peasants, so there!

LOMOV: There nothing! Where do you get the right to give away someone else's property?

CHUBUKOV: I certainly ought to know if I have the right or not. And you had better realize it, because, my dear young man, I am not used to being spoken to in that tone of voice, and so forth.

Besides which, my dear young man, I am twice as old as you are, and I ask you to speak to me without getting yourself into such a tizzy, and so forth!

LOMOV: Do you think I'm a fool? First you call my property yours, and then you expect me to keep calm and polite! Good neighbors don't act like that, my dear Stepan Stepanovitch. You're no neighbor, you're a land-grabber!

CHUBUKOV: What was that? What did you say?

NATALIA: Papa, send the mowers out to the meadows at once!

CHUBUKOV: What did you say, sir?

NATALIA: The Oxen Meadows are ours, and we'll never give them up, never, never, never, never!

LOMOV: We'll see about that. I'll go to court. I'll show you!

CHUBUKOV: Go to court? Well, go to court, and so forth! I know you, just waiting for a chance to go to court, and so forth. You pettifogging shyster, you! All of your family is like that. The whole bunch of them!

LOMOV: You leave my family out of this! The Lomovs have always been honorable, upstanding people, and not a one of them was ever tried for embezzlement, like your grandfather was.

CHUBUKOV: The Lomovs are a pack of lunatics, the whole bunch of them!

NATALIA: The whole bunch!

CHUBUKOV: Your grandfather was a drunkard, and what about your other aunt, the one who ran away with the architect? And so forth.

NATALIA: And so forth!

LOMOV: Your mother was a hunchback! (Clutches at his heart.) Oh, I've got a stitch in my side . . . My head's whirling . . . Help! Give me water!

CHUBUKOV: Your father was a rum-soaked gambler.

NATALIA: And your aunt was queen of the scandalmongers!

LOMOV: My left foot's paralyzed. You're a plotter . . . Oh, my heart. It's an open secret that in the last elections you brib——I'm seeing stars! Where's my hat?

NATALIA: It's a low, mean, spiteful . . .

CHUBUKOV: And you're a two-faced, malicious schemer!

LOMOV: Here's my hat . . . Oh, my heart . . . Where's the door? How do I get out of here? Oh, I think I'm going to die . . . My foot's numb. (Goes.)

CHUBUKOV (following him): And don't you ever set foot in my house again!

NATALIA: Go to court, indeed! We'll see about that!

[Lomov staggers out.]

CHUBUKOV: The devil with him! (Walks back and forth, excited.)

NATALIA: What a rascal! How can you trust your neighbors after an incident like that?

CHUBUKOV: The villain! The scarecrow!

NATALIA: He's a monster! First he tries to steal our land, and then he has the nerve to yell at you.

CHUBUKOV: Yes, and that turnip, that stupid rooster, has the gall to make a proposal. Some proposal!

NATALIA: What proposal?

CHUBUKOV: Why, he came to propose to you.

NATALIA: To propose? To me? Why didn't you tell me before?

CHUBUKOV: So he gets all dressed up in his formal clothes. That stuffed sausage, that dried-up cabbage!

NATALIA: To propose to me? Ohhhh! *(Falls into a chair and starts wailing.)* Bring him back! Back! Go get him! Bring him back! Ohhhh!

CHUBUKOV: Bring who back?

NATALIA: Hurry up, hurry up! I'm sick. Get him! *(Complete hysterics.)*

CHUBUKOV: What for? *(To her)* What's the matter with you? *(Clutches his head.)* Oh, what a fool I am! I'll shoot myself! I'll hang myself! I ruined her chances!

NATALIA: I'm dying. Get him!

CHUBUKOV: All right, all right, right away! Only don't yell! *(He runs out.)*

NATALIA: What are they doing to me? Get him! Bring him back! Bring him back!

[*A pause. Chubukov runs in.*]

CHUBUKOV: He's coming, and so forth, the snake. Oof! You talk to him. I'm not in the mood.

NATALIA *(wailing)*: Bring him back! Bring him back!

CHUBUKOV *(yelling)*: I told you, he's coming! Oh Lord, what agony to be the father of a grown-up daughter. I'll cut my throat some day, I swear I will. *(To her)* We cursed him, we insulted him, abused him, kicked him out, and now . . . because you, you . . .

NATALIA: Me? It was all your fault!

CHUBUKOV: My fault? What do you mean my fau ——— ? *(Lomov appears in the doorway.)* Talk to him yourself!

[*Goes out. Lomov enters, exhausted.*]

LOMOV: What palpitations! My heart! And my foot's absolutely asleep. Something keeps giving me a stitch in the side . . .

NATALIA: You must forgive us, Ivan Vassilevitch. We all got too excited. I remember now. The Oxen Meadows are yours.

LOMOV: My heart's beating something awful. My Meadows. My eyebrows, they're both twitching!

NATALIA: Yes, the Meadows are all yours, yes, yours. Do sit down. *(They sit.)* We were wrong, of course.

LOMOV: I argued on principle. My land isn't worth so much to me, but the principle . . .

NATALIA: Oh, yes, of course, the principle, that's what counts. But let's change the subject.

LOMOV: Besides, I have evidence.

You see, my aunt's grandmother let your father's grandfather's peasants use the land . . .

NATALIA: Yes, yes, yes, but forget all that. (*Aside*) I wish I knew how to get him going. (*Aloud*) Are you going to start hunting soon?

LOMOV: After the harvest I'll try for grouse. But oh, my dear Natalia Stepanovna, have you heard about the bad luck I've had? You

LOMOV: I think it was quite cheap. He's a first-class dog.

NATALIA: Why, Papa only paid eighty-five rubles for Squeezer, and he's much better than Guess.

LOMOV: Squeezer better than Guess! What an idea! (*Laughs.*) Squeezer better than Guess!

NATALIA: Of course he's better. He may still be too young but on points and pedigree, he's a better

know my dog, Guess? He's gone lame.

NATALIA: What a pity. Why?

LOMOV: I don't know. He must have twisted his leg, or got in a fight, or something. (*Sighs.*) My best dog, to say nothing of the cost. I paid Mironov 125 rubles for him.

NATALIA: That was too high, Ivan Vassilevitch.

dog than any Volchanetsky owns.

LOMOV: Excuse me, Natalia Stepanovna, but you're forgetting he's overshot, and overshot dogs are bad hunters.

NATALIA: Oh, so he's overshot, is he? Well, this is the first time I've heard about it.

LOMOV: Believe me, his lower jaw is shorter than his upper.

NATALIA: You've measured them?

LOMOV: Yes. He's all right for pointing, but if you want him to retrieve . . .

NATALIA: In the first place, our Squeezer is a thoroughbred, the son of Harness and Chisel, while your mutt doesn't even have a pedigree. He's as old and worn out as a peddler's horse.

LOMOV: He may be old, but I wouldn't take five Squeezers for him. How can you argue? Guess is a dog, Squeezer's a laugh. Anyone you can name has a dog like Squeezer hanging around somewhere. They're under every bush. If he only cost twenty-five rubles you got cheated.

NATALIA: The devil is in you today, Ivan Vassilevitch! You want to contradict everything. First you pretend the Oxen Meadows are yours, and now you say Guess is better than Squeezer. People should say what they really mean, and you know Squeezer is a hundred times better than Guess. Why say he isn't?

LOMOV: So, you think I'm a fool or a blind man, Natalia Stepanovna! Once and for all, Squeezer is overshot!

NATALIA: He is not!

LOMOV: He is so!

NATALIA: He is not!

LOMOV: Why shout, my dear lady?

NATALIA: Why talk such nonsense? It's terrible. Your Guess is old enough to be buried, and you compare him with Squeezer!

LOMOV: I'm sorry, I can't go on. My heart . . . it's palpitating!

NATALIA: I've always noticed that the hunters who argue most don't know a thing.

LOMOV: Please! Be quiet a moment. My heart's falling apart . . . (Shouts.) Shut up!

NATALIA: I'm not going to shut up until you admit that Squeezer's a hundred times better than Guess.

LOMOV: A hundred times worse! His head . . . My eyes . . . shoulder. . .

NATALIA: Guess is half-dead already!

LOMOV (weeping): Shut up! My heart's exploding!

NATALIA: I won't shut up!

[Chubukov comes in.]

CHUBUKOV. What's the trouble now?

NATALIA: Papa, will you please tell us which is the better dog, his Guess or our Squeezer?

LOMOV: Stepan Stepanovitch, I implore you to tell me just one thing. Is your Squeezer overshot or not? Yes or no?

CHUBUKOV: Well, what if he is? He's still the best dog in the neighborhood, and so forth.

LOMOV: Oh, but isn't my dog, Guess, better? Really?

CHUBUKOV: Don't get yourself so fraught up, old man. Of course, your dog has his good points — thoroughbred, firm on his feet, well-sprung ribs, and so forth. But, my dear fellow, you've got to admit he has two defects; he's old and he's short in the muzzle.

LOMOV: Short in the muzzle? Oh, my heart! Let's look at the facts! On the Marusinsky hunt my dog ran neck and neck with the Count's, while Squeezer was a mile behind them . . .

CHUBUKOV: That's because the Count's groom hit him with a whip.

LOMOV: And he was right, too! We were fox hunting; what was your dog chasing sheep for?

CHUBUKOV: That's a lie! Look, I'm going to lose my temper . . . (controlling himself) my dear friend, so let's stop arguing, for that reason alone. You're only arguing because we're all jealous of somebody else's dog. Who can help it? As soon as you realize some dog is better than yours, in this case our dog, you start in with this and that, and the next thing you know — pure jealousy! I remember the whole business.

LOMOV: I remember too!

CHUBUKOV (mimicking): "I remember too!" What do you remember?

LOMOV: My heart . . . my foot's asleep . . . I can't . . .

NATALIA (mimicking): "My heart . . . my foot's asleep." What kind of a hunter are you? You should be hunting cockroaches in the kitchen, not foxes. "My heart!"

CHUBUKOV: Yes, what kind of a hunter are you anyway? You should be sitting at home with your palpitations, not tracking down animals. You don't hunt anyhow. You just go out to argue with people and interfere with their dogs, and so forth. For God's sake, let's change the subject before I lose my temper. Anyway, you're just not a hunter.

LOMOV: But you, you're a hunter? Ha! You only go hunting to get in good with the Count, and to plot, and intrigue, and scheme. Oh, my heart! You're a schemer, that's what!

CHUBUKOV: What's that? Me a schemer? (Shouting) Shut up!

LOMOV: A schemer!

CHUBUKOV: You infant! You puppy!

LOMOV: You old rat!

CHUBUKOV: You shut up, or I'll shoot you down like a partridge! You idiot!

LOMOV: Everyone knows that — oh, my heart — that your wife used to beat you . . . Oh, my feet . . . my head . . . I'm seeing stars. I'm going to faint! (He drops into an armchair.) Quick, a doctor! (Faints.)

CHUBUKOV (going on, oblivious): Baby! Weakling! Idiot! I'm getting sick. (Drinks water.) Me! I'm sick!

NATALIA: What kind of a hunter are you? You can't even sit on a horse! (To her father) Papa, what's the matter with him? Look, papa! (Screaming) Ivan Vassilevitch! He's dead.

CHUBUKOV: I'm choking, I can't breathe . . . Give me air.

NATALIA: He's dead! (Pulling Lomov's sleeve) Ivan Vassilevitch!

Ivan Vassilevitch! What have you done to me? He's dead! (*She falls into an armchair, screaming hysterically.*) A doctor! A doctor! A doctor!

CHUBUKOV: Ohhhh . . . What's the matter? What happened?

NATALIA (*wailing*): He's dead! He's dead!

CHUBUKOV: Who's dead? (*Looks at Lomov.*) My goodness, he is! Quick! Water! A doctor! (*Puts glass to Lomov's lips.*) Here, drink this! Can't drink it—he must be dead, and so forth. Oh what a miserable life! Why don't I shoot myself! I should have cut my throat long ago! What am I waiting for? Give me a knife! Give me a pistol! (*Lomov stirs.*) Look, he's coming to. Here, drink some water. That's it.

LOMOV: I'm seeing stars . . . misty . . . Where am I?

CHUBUKOV: Just you hurry up and get married, and then the devil with you! She accepts. (*Puts Lomov's hand in Natalia's.*) She accepts, and so forth! I give you my blessing, and so forth! Only leave me in peace!

LOMOV (*getting up*): Huh? What? Who?

CHUBUKOV: She accepts! Well? Kiss her!

NATALIA: He's alive! Yes, yes, I accept.

CHUBUKOV: Kiss each other!

LOMOV: Huh? Kiss? Kiss who? (*They kiss.*) That's nice. I mean, excuse

me, what happened? Oh, now I get it . . . my heart . . . those stars . . . I'm very happy, Natalia Stepanovna. (*Kisses her hand.*) My foot's asleep.

NATALIA: I . . . I'm happy, too.

CHUBUKOV: What a load off my shoulders! Whew!

NATALIA: Well, now maybe you'll admit that Squeezer is better than Guess?

LOMOV: Worse!

NATALIA: Better!

CHUBUKOV: What a way to enter matrimonial bliss! Let's have some champagne!

LOMOV: He's worse!

NATALIA: Better! Better, better, better, better!

CHUBUKOV (*trying to shout her down*): Champagne! Bring some champagne! Champagne! Champagne!

CURTAIN

Haiku

Translated by Harold G. Henderson

Winter

Mountains and plains,
  all are captured by the snow—
    nothing remains.

            JŌSŌ

Spring Road

Backward I gaze;
  one whom I had chanced to meet
    is lost in haze.

            SHIKI

Loneliness

A flitting firefly!
  "Look! Look there!" I start to call—
    but there is no one by.

            TAIGI

Maple Leaves

Envied by us all,
  turning to such loveliness—
    red leaves that fall.

            SHIKŌ

In the House

At the butterflies
   the caged bird gazes, envying—
      just watch its eyes!

ISSA

WHO CALLED IT THAT?

There seems to be some confusion in the picture. The little boy is looking for an *entomologist.* The woman says she is an *etymologist,* a person who studies the origins of words. Look up the word *etymology.* From what language does it come? Look at the boy in the picture. Do you have any idea what kind of person he is looking for? If not, look up the word *entomologist.* That should give you your answer.

The English language is full of words that have been taken from many other languages. When you look up a word in the dictionary, you can tell by its etymology which language or languages it has come from, and sometimes, if the word has a long history, you can see what it has meant at different times.

In the last selection you learned the etymology of the word *macramé*. It comes from an Arabic word. Look up these other handicraft terms: *knit, appliqué, crochet,* and *quilt.* What languages do they come from? Which word comes from a word meaning "hook"? Which comes from a word meaning "knot"?

Other animal names have etymologies that tell what the animal does. A *terrier,* for instance, is a dog that hunts small animals and chases them into burrows in the earth. Appropriately enough, *terrier* comes from the Latin word *terra,* which means "earth." Look up the words *dachshund* and *dormouse.* Which animal sleeps a lot? Which animal chases badgers?

Etymologies give us an understanding of how things were first named. Animal names are one fascinating group. For instance, some animals have names that describe them in some way. The red-breasted grosbeak is a bird with a large, fat bill. *Grosbeak* comes from two French words: *gros,* meaning "large," and *bec,* meaning "beak." Look up the etymology of *porcupine.* How is the name descriptive of the animal?

GROS-BEC

Still other animals get their names from the sounds they make. This is called an *imitative* etymology, because the name of the animal imitates the animal's sound. Look up the etymologies for *cricket* and *cuckoo*. Are their etymologies imitative?

Look up the etymologies for *caribou, gecko, squirrel, oriole, nightingale, octopus, porpoise, killdeer,* and *polecat.* Which animals are named for the sounds they make? Which are named for some physical characteristics they possess? Which are named for something they do?

The English language contains thousands of words derived from well-known languages such as German, Greek, Latin, and French. But English has taken many words from lesser known languages, too. For instance, we have *coyote,* from the Aztec language, Nahuatl. *Barbecue* comes from the Haitian language. Look up the following words: *sheik, shawl, dungaree, shampoo, mazurka, samovar,* and *squash* (the plant). What languages do these words come from? What do they mean?

Some etymologies tell us that the word comes from a person's name. *Chauvinism,* which means excessive patriotism, comes from the name of a Frenchman.

Look up the etymologies for *saxophone, braille, volt, sideburns, sandwich,* and *dunce.* Just think, if you invent a famous process or an instrument or create something new to eat, you may find your name in the dictionary someday—both as an entry word and as an etymology!

Many fruits and vegetables have interesting etymologies. Whoever named dates (the fruits) must have thought they looked like fingers, because *date* comes from a Greek word meaning "finger." The *radish,* a root we eat, comes from the Latin word that literally means "root." Look up some of your favorite fruits and vegetables. What are their etymologies? Look up the words *lime* and *lemon.* What did you find out?

Look at the words on one page of your dictionary. Which word do you think has the most interesting etymology? How many languages are represented in the etymologies on that page?

MACRAMÉ PROJECTS FOR YOU

Eleri J. Reiner

I have always been interested in art. Macramé is just one of the ways I express myself. Macramé appeals to me because I can wear many of the things I design.

I am an eighth grader at Albert Leonard Junior High School in New Rochelle, New York, where I work on the school newspaper, Highlights, and play the flute in the band and the orchestra.

I like swimming, tennis, and bike riding, and I enjoy seeing new and different places. I have recently started to photograph some of the places I have visited.

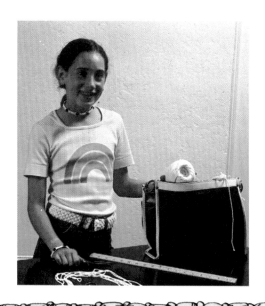

Instructions for these projects can be found on pages 332-333.

Macramé is the knotting together of wool or string of any sort to make a beautiful piece of artwork. Macramé can be done in many different forms but will never look exactly the same when done by different people. The word macramé comes from the Arabic word *migramah,* which means "ornamental fringe and braid."

The Spaniards learned the art of macramé from the Moors, and the skill spread into Southern Europe probably between the fourteenth and sixteenth centuries. The art came into England through the royal court when it was done in the late seventeenth century by Queen Mary, the wife of William of Orange. At the time of the American Revolution, Queen Charlotte, the wife of King George III, also did macramé at court.

At some point macramé must have been forgotten because it was really considered new when it was reintroduced to the English at the end of the nineteenth century. It enjoyed wide use then for both household decoration and clothing. Sailors of different countries may have helped to spread the knowledge of macramé. They knotted during their long sea voyages and, as early as the fifteenth century, used their knotted articles for barter.

327

HOW TO MAKE A HALF KNOT

One of the most important stitches in macramé is the half knot. Instead of using letters or numbers to teach you this stitch, I'm going to use colors. To do this stitch you will need four pieces of string of the same length. Tie these strings in a knot at one end. The steps are illustrated in the first photo. Put the yellow over the blue and the red and under the white. Now put the white under the blue and the red and through the yellow loop. Pull the yellow and white strings to their respective sides. You now have a completed half knot.

Next you must learn how to make this half knot into a square knot. A square knot is composed of two half knots. For your second half knot you must put the yellow over the blue and the red and under the white. Now put the white under the blue and the red and through the yellow loop. Pull the yellow and white strings to their respective sides. You now have a square knot. When the square knot is complete be sure to start the next half knot from the *left* side.

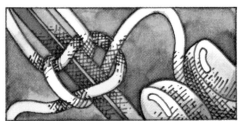

By using half knots you can make the belt and many other projects shown. *Caution:* If you are planning to put the project aside for a while, try to complete a full square knot.

GENERAL INFORMATION

1. Macramé can be done in many different colors with many different kinds of string, yarns, or rope. If you decide to use a kind of string different from the one suggested, your project may not turn out exactly as pictured here. The thickness and quality of the string will determine the look of the finished piece.

a. Number 30 string (sometimes called craft cord) is the best size for making the belt.

b. Number 21 string is good for making bracelets and choker necklaces.

c. Coarse twine can be used for making flowerpot holders and wall hangings.

d. Yarns can also be used but they are hard to handle because they have so much elasticity.

2. The rings to use for the belt and other things you will wear should be the kind shown in the picture. They are the easiest with which to work.

3. Beads can change the personality of a macramé project. They should be big enough so that the center hole can easily accommodate the number of strings (generally two) you plan to pull through. The beads you select will have a lot to do with the look of the finished piece.

With certain pieces you may want particularly showy beads. This may mean choosing beads of bright colors. With other pieces you may want to use beads that just fit into the pattern, and you would select wood-colored or wooden beads.

4. Scissors and a ruler should be part of your macramé kit.

5. If you are using number 21 or thinner string, cut each piece about ten times as long as the finished object.

6. Macramé can be worked anywhere. If you are working at home you might wish to tie the belt or project onto a chair by pulling an extra piece of string through the rings and tying that part around the chair. Some people find it easier to work when they attach the piece to a corkboard. You can do this by attaching the strings to a board with straight pins.

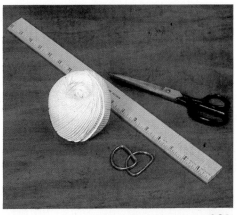

SUPPLIES FOR BELT SHOWN

One ball of macramé cord #30 (sometimes called craft cord). *Note:* If you buy a 215-foot ball of cord, you can make at least two belts.

Two semicircle rings
Scissors
Ruler

Note: Cord can be purchased in hardware stores and in hobby shops. Rings are available in hobby shops and in trimming stores.

HOW TO CALCULATE THE AMOUNT OF STRING YOU WILL NEED FOR THE BELT

You will be working with *six* pieces of string. They should be measured and folded in the following way: Take one piece of string and comfortably fit it around your waist. Measure the length of it with a ruler or yardstick and multiply that amount by eight. You will now have the length of one string. Now cut five other pieces to the same length.

HOW TO HOOK THE STRING TO THE BELT RINGS

Hold the pair of rings in one hand. Take the precut belt strings and fold them in half. Place the folded halves in front of the rings and bring the string ends behind

the rings and through the folded halves, pulling tightly.

Note: In some instances you may wish to attach your macramé to a piece of string rather than to belt rings. To do this proceed exactly as described above but substitute the holder string for the rings.

MAKING THE BELT

1. Now that you have attached the string to the belt rings you will have *twelve* strings hanging from the rings. Begin from the left and take the first group of four strings and make a full square knot (remember that is two half knots).

2. After you have done step 1, go to the next group of four strings and make a square knot with them. You will now come to the last group of four strings and your final square knot for this row.

3. To go back in the other direction (from right to left), push aside two strings on the right and take a group of the next four strings to make a square knot.

4. Go to your immediate next group of four strings and make another square knot. You will now have two strings on the left hanging free. To use these two strings you will take the two strings nearest them and make those four into a square knot.

5. Continue working across the row with groups of four strings at a time, making each group of four into square knots.

6. You now get to the right side, having worked across from the left. After that last square knot is made, remember to leave the two strings on the right hanging free. Work back to the left side again, using the two free strings and borrowing the two nearest strings from the middle square knot and making a square knot with this foursome.

7. Then make a square knot with the next foursome, and you will find you have two strings hanging free on the left. Take those two strings and borrow two strings from the closest square knot and make a square knot as you begin to work your way across the row from left to right again.

8. It is time to finish the belt when you have knotted enough belt to fit around your waist with some to spare to pull through the rings.

9. To end the belt, knot each string twice as shown in the drawing below. Cut off excess string as close to the knot as possible without cutting the knot. You now have a completed belt. Have fun wearing it.

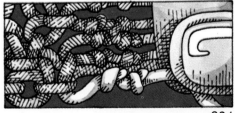

EXTRA PROJECTS

1. Choker with beads

a. Use #21 or similar string. You will need two strings ten times the width of your neck and eight to ten beads.

b. Fold the strings in half and make a knot at the top leaving enough of a loop for the bead you will use as your clasp.

c. Make ten half knots (five square knots).

d. Put the first bead through the two center strings and work a half knot around it.

e. Make ten more half knots.

f. Put the next bead on in the same way as in Step d.

g. Continue in this manner until the choker is big enough to fit comfortably around your neck.

h. Choker should end with a bead.

i. To finish choker, put the bead through the two center strings and make two knots, as shown in the drawing, with all of the strings.

2. Matching bracelet

a. Use #21 or similar string. You will need two strings ten times the width of your wrist and about five beads.

b. Follow directions for choker and end when you have enough for a bracelet.

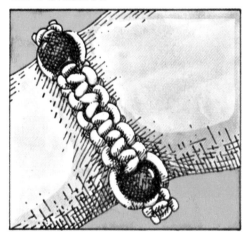

3. Lace choker with beads

a. Use #21 or similar string. You will need four strings ten times the width of your neck and five to eight beads.

b. Fold each string in half and make a knot at the top, leaving a loop big enough for the bead you wish to use as a clasp.

c. You will now have eight strings with which to work.

d. Divide the strings in half so that you have four strings on each side.

e. Make fourteen half knots (seven square knots) on each side.

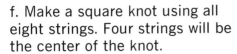

f. Make a square knot using all eight strings. Four strings will be the center of the knot.

g. Slip the first bead through the two middle strings. You will now have three strings on each side of the bead.

h. Using the bead as the center and working with the remaining six strings (three on each side of the bead), make a square knot (two half knots).

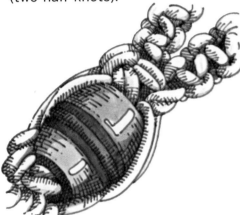

i. Separate the strings into two groups of four strings each and again do fourteen half knots on each side.

j. Again make a square knot by using all eight strings as in f.

k. Slip the next bead through the two middle strings and continue as explained in steps h through j.

l. To finish choker, put on your last bead, and instead of making a square knot around it, make two of the knots shown in the drawing.

4. Belt variation

a. Use #30 or similar string. Instead of using the belt rings use a braided piece of string.

b. Be sure to use three strings to form the braid.

c. Attach belt strings to braid in the same way you would attach them to rings or plain string (see instructions).

d. Work belt as described in the belt directions (page 330–331).

e. When belt is long enough to fit comfortably around your waist, divide the remaining strings into three groups and make them into what will be a six- to eight-inch braid.

f. Knot one section of strings to another until knots are strong and secure.

g. Trim remaining strings carefully so that you don't cut into knots.

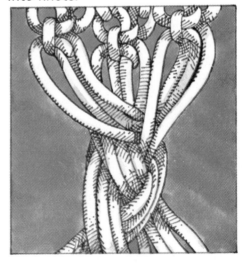

Charlotte Herman

In the 1940s, Ari Stein and his parents moved from Manhattan's Lower East Side to 2–4 Nass Walk, a building in Brooklyn within walking distance of the beach and Coney Island's famous amusement parks. On his first day on Nass Walk, Ari met Maxie, Lippy, and Brownie—the whole crowd except for Buddy, who was spending the day on Broadway waiting to be discovered by a movie talent scout. Now it's Ari's second day in the new neighborhood, and the guys are going to treat Ari to a day at Coney Island.

I woke up to a trumpet blasting out something that sounded like "The White Cliffs of Dover." On Rivington Street where we used to live, I woke up to a violin a few times but never to a trumpet. Morty Gundy used to play the violin. His mother was preparing him to become Jascha Heifetz.

My father had already left for his job in the mink shop. Before the war he drove a milk truck, and I used to go with him on his routes. Mostly I carried the unbreakables—the cheese and butter—but sometimes I even got to carry the empty bottles back to the truck.

Then the war came, and gas and tires were hard to come by. So he gave up the milk business and took this job in the mink shop. Now he sits at a sewing machine all day, sewing little minks together so some rich person can have a mink coat.

He works hard to make enough money for us to live on. He even has to work on Sunday—in spite of the Blue Laws, which say that stores and businesses have to be closed on Sunday. But like all observant Jews, my father doesn't work on Saturday, our Sabbath. It would be hard to lose two days of pay each week, so he works on Sunday instead. Every so often he gets a ticket and has to pay a fine.

"Someday the laws will be changed," my father says, "so that Jews will be able to observe their Sabbath and still be able to work a six-day week."

I got dressed and found my mother in the kitchen.

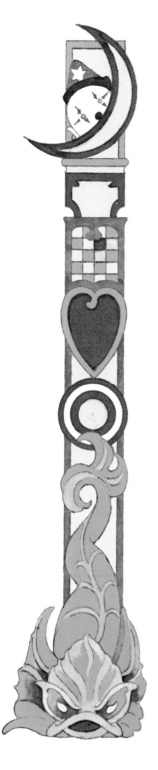

"Say, Ma, listen to that trumpet. Can I take trumpet lessons? I think I'm musically inclined."

"I should say not. Violin, yes. But trumpet, no. You'll bust your lungs."

"I don't think I want the violin," I said. "I think two Jascha Heifetzes are enough." I sat down to my favorite summer breakfast of orange juice and Wheaties— "The Breakfast of Champions." I felt like Jack Armstrong, the All-American Boy I always listen to on the radio. Then I went out.

All the guys were in the gutter playing Johnny-on-a-pony. It was Brownie's turn to jump on top of Lippy. Well, poor Lippy practically got crushed under Brownie's tremendous weight. Brownie knocked the other guys over and sent them crashing to the pavement. They were just getting up and dusting themselves off when Maxie saw me. "Hey, Ari. Come on over."

I walked over, and pretty soon I found myself standing in front of the most handsome guy I had ever seen. He was more than handsome. He was beautiful. He had black wavy hair, dark eyes, and long lashes. He was tall and slim, and even an ordinary T-shirt and dungarees looked good on him. This kid *should* have been in the movies, he was so handsome. Handsomer than Gregory Peck, even. He reminded me of somebody, I couldn't think of who.

"Buddy, this here is Ari, the new kid I was telling you about. Buddy lives on the ground floor at 2–4," Maxie told me.

"Hi, Buddy," I said. "Did you have any luck yesterday?"

"Not a bit. I walked up and down Times Square and Forty-second Street a thousand times, and I hung around some of the theaters. But I didn't see anybody important and nobody important saw me. Once I saw a real tall guy walking in front of me. From the back he looked like Gary Cooper, but when I saw his front, he was somebody else." He talked very fast, like he had to catch the words before they ran away from him.

"Maybe all the movie stars and actors are taking their summer vacations in Hollywood," Maxie said.

"That's dumb," Brownie said. "Movie stars and people like that don't work. They don't need vacations. Right, Lippy?"

"Right. They just act in movies." I figured when Lippy wasn't eating polly seeds, he could really talk.

"I wonder how Margaret O'Brien got discovered," I said.

"It's easier for girls," Brownie said.

Buddy shook his head. "I don't think so. I think it's just a matter of luck, of being in the right place at the right time. What I've got to do is walk around a lot and be seen by all kinds of people. You never can tell when an ordinary person might turn out to be a talent scout. And you never can tell where you'll be discovered. People get discovered in all kinds of places. Like elevators and drugstores."

Buddy might have gone on talking about being discovered forever if Maxie hadn't changed the subject. "So where do we go this afternoon? Luna Park or Steeplechase?"

"I want Luna Park," Brownie answered. "What about you, Lippy?"

"Luna Park," he mumbled.

"That makes two," Brownie said.

"Let Ari be the one who says where we should go," Buddy suggested. "He's the one we're treating, so we should go wherever he wants to."

"What about it, Ari?" Maxie asked. "Luna Park or Steeplechase?"

I was really tempted to say Steeplechase, just to be different from Brownie. But actually, I like the rides at Luna Park better.

"Luna Park sounds good to me," I said. "There's more rides to choose from."

"Okay, that's settled," Maxie said. "Now, how about all of us checking the alleys for empties. We can use some money for food."

"There's nothin' there, I told ya," Brownie said.

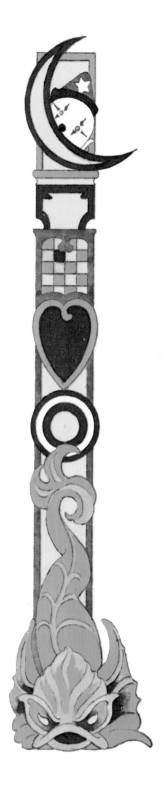

"That was yesterday. Somebody must have thrown out a couple of bottles after supper last night. Let's check again."

"While you guys go looking for bottles, I think I'll go change my clothes and clean up," Buddy said. "You never can tell who might be walking around the island."

So while Buddy was making himself even more beautiful, the rest of us went scrounging through the garbage cans, looking for soda bottles. We searched behind all the buildings on Nass Walk. There was plenty of garbage and plenty of flies—but no bottles. Then, when we were just getting ready to leave the alley behind 6–8, Lippy pulled a pair of shoes out of a garbage can. It was a pair of brown crepe-sole shoes, almost new. He held them up. "Look what I . . ."

"Lemme see," said Brownie, and he grabbed the shoes right out of Lippy's hands. "These are nice shoes. I can use 'em."

"Hey, Brownie," Maxie said. "Lippy is the one who found those shoes. Who says you can keep them?"

"Lippy don't want 'em, do you, Lippy?"

"Well . . . I . . ."

"See, I told ya he don't want 'em." Brownie ran out of the alley, yelling, "Ma, Ma, look what I found!"

Lippy just stood there with his mouth open. "It's a good thing that you're not keeping those shoes," I told Lippy. "You never know who wore them. Maybe they belonged to someone who had a contagious disease, and he threw them out when he recovered."

"Yeah," said Maxie. "They didn't look so good to me. They smelled from garbage."

We went back to Nass Walk to wait for Brownie and Buddy. In a few minutes out came Buddy Rizzo, wearing clean dungarees and a polo shirt. And his hair—it wasn't wavy anymore. It was all plastered down and wet-looking. That was it! His hair! Now I knew who he reminded me of. Rudolph Valentino. I saw a photograph of Valentino once—at my Aunt Marilyn's house. And Buddy Rizzo looked just like him.

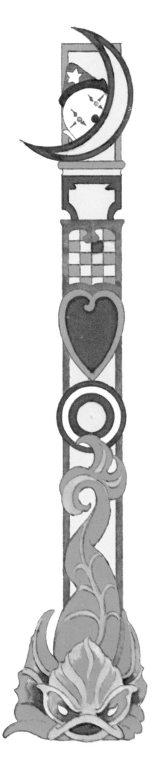

Pretty soon Brownie came bouncing out, wearing his new brown crepe-sole shoes.

"Hey, Brownie," Buddy called. "Where did you get the new shoes?"

"Found 'em," he said, puffing out his fat chest.

"They're very nice," Buddy went on, "but there's one thing wrong with them."

"What's that?"

"They're girls' shoes!" And he slapped his hands on his thighs and let out a tremendous roar of laughter.

The next thing I knew, Maxie and I were laughing and poking each other and practically rolling over in the gutter. Lippy was standing off to the side, laughing into his hand. Brownie was staring at his shoes and turning all shades of red and purple.

When the laughter finally died down, Brownie yelled, "They're not! They're not girls' shoes."

"I'll bet you they are," said Buddy. "If anybody knows about shoes, I do. And I say those are girls' shoes."

"Well, Lippy is the one who really found 'em. You found 'em, Lippy. You want 'em?"

Lippy shook his head. "No thanks, Brownie."

Brownie turned and ran back into his building, yelling, "Ma, Ma!" And boy, did we let loose! Even Lippy. He laughed right out loud this time; he didn't even bother to cover up his face.

When Brownie came out again, he was still wearing the shoes. It seems his mother wasn't about ready to let him throw away a perfectly good pair of shoes that fit him just right—almost.

He gave us all a quick look and said, "Well, what are we standin' around for? Are we goin' to Luna or ain't we?" He started walking up ahead, and then he turned around and waited for us to catch up to him.

Part of the time we walked along Surf Avenue, but mostly we walked on the boardwalk, tasting the salt air and listening to the clip-clopping of shoes on the wooden boards. The music of the calliopes mingled with the shouts of "Hurry, hurry, walk right up, come and see, come and get, nice and hot, ice cold, guess your weight and win a doll."

We passed fortune-telling gypsies and posters of bearded ladies and fire-eaters. Some of the posters looked fresh and new, while others were torn and tattered—as if they had been hanging there for over a hundred summers.

All around us were the rides. And I love the rides more than anything. I could see the parachute jump at Steeplechase, and the roller coaster rising high above us—the cars clinking and clattering up the track, then dipping and winding, carrying with them the sounds of screaming. The giant ferris wheel was going round and round, sometimes stopping in midair. I wondered what it would feel like to get stuck way up at the top. With each step we were getting closer and closer to Luna. And even though I had been there many times before, I couldn't remember ever having been so excited. I wanted to shout, "Oh, you rides, wait for me! Luna Park, here I come."

When we finally reached the main entrance, I stopped and waited for the guys to buy the tickets. But they didn't stop. They kept on walking and walking, past the entrance, around a cyclone fence, around some old shacks, and around a piece of wooden fence. I ran after them. "Hey, you guys. Where's everybody going?"

Maxie swung around and put his finger to his lips. "Sshh." They all kept on walking. At a certain part of the fence, everybody stopped.

"Okay," Maxie said. "One or two at a time. And we meet on the other side."

"Me first," Brownie said. "You come with, Lippy."

Lippy nodded. "Okay."

They sneaked along the fence and turned to see if anyone was watching. Then Brownie lifted up a loose board in the fence and barely, just barely, squeezed himself through. Lippy slipped in afterward.

"Gee, I don't know," I said. "This isn't what I had in mind."

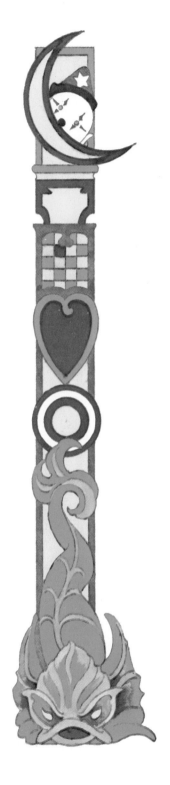

341

"You didn't really think we were going to *pay* for those rides, did you?" Maxie asked. "Who's got that kind of money?"

"But sneaking in. It's like stealing."

"No, it's not," Buddy said. "We're not taking anything from anybody. Lots of people don't get to use up all their rides, and they just throw their tickets away. We'll probably be able to pick up lots of tickets left over from yesterday."

"Yeah," Maxie said. "And if we don't get those tickets, somebody else will. Or they'll get swept up as garbage. Come on. How about it?"

"Well, okay," I said. What else could I say? They were all going, even Lippy. How could I be the only one to say no? And on my second day in the neighborhood.

"You go first," Maxie told Buddy. "I'll stick with Ari."

"If you think this is hard," Maxie said, "just try to sneak into Steeplechase. They've got a hundred times as many guards around the place. And we never once got caught."

When Buddy disappeared, it was our turn. "If anyone comes," Maxie said, "just say we're looking for the men's room."

We crept along the fence. My heart was thumping so loudly, I wondered if Maxie could hear it. I wished I was back on Rivington Street. I wished I had never heard of Nass Walk or Maxie Friedman.

When we reached the loose board, Maxie swung it to the side, stuck his head through the fence and crawled in. I glanced around a few times and started in after him. When we reached the other side, Maxie said, "See, nothing to it."

We found Brownie, Lippy, and Buddy searching the ground for the heart-shaped tickets that didn't have all the ride numbers punched out. We joined the search. To me it seemed like we spent half the morning looking for rides. But we found some good ones: The Mile Sky Chaser, Chute-the-Chutes, and The Dragon's Gorge. According to Brownie, a lot of people use up the sissy rides and throw the best ones away.

My favorite ride is the Chutes. You go up something like an elevator in a boat. Then the boat comes sliding down a wet, slippery slide—fast! And splash! Right into the water. You get soaking wet, but it feels great on a hot day.

The Mile Sky Chaser is a scary roller-coaster ride that's only fun when it's over. And The Dragon's Gorge is a spooky roller-coaster ride in pitch blackness. For me it's the most frightening ride in the park. Just the thought of it is enough to send shivers all up and down my spine.

I thought about it while the guys were searching for tickets, and suddenly the whole park felt spooky to me. I walked over to Maxie and crouched down beside him. "You know, Maxie, I've got a funny feeling about what we're doing. Like somebody's inside me, trying to warn us about something. Let's go."

"Aw, your conscience is botherin' ya," said Brownie, as he examined a ticket and threw it away. "I seen it in the movies lots of times. A devil sits on one shoulder, tellin' ya to do somethin' bad, and an angel sits on your other shoulder, tellin' ya not to do it."

"It only looks like that in the movies," Buddy said. "There isn't any devil or angel sitting on anyone's shoulder."

"Well, maybe it is my conscience," I said. "And maybe it's telling us to get out of here before something happens."

"Come on," said Maxie. "Quit your worrying and help us look for some more rides."

Right then and there I should have left. But it wasn't the easiest thing to walk out on guys I expected to be friends with. I figured the sooner I could find us some rides to go on, the sooner we could leave. So there I was, looking around and not having much luck, when a voice from above shouted, "Okay, what do you kids think you're doing here?"

We scrambled to our feet. A park guard was standing next to us. Sweat was dripping down his face. "I asked you a question. What are you doing here?"

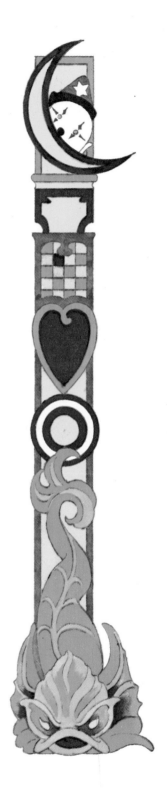

"We're looking for the men's room," I stammered. He started to laugh—a mean kind of laugh.

"Let's get out of here!" Maxie shouted.

"Run for your life!" Buddy hollered.

The guard blew his whistle, Brownie yelled, "Charge!" and we took off. We raced through the park, in and out of ticket lines, knocking into people, dodging around refreshment stands and kiddy rides. We leaped over ropes and crashed through gates, pushing and shoving anyone and anything that got in our way. And all the while, the whistle was sounding right behind us.

"Hurry, this way," Maxie called, motioning to us with a wave of his hand. We scooted around a corner and ducked into The Hall of Mirrors. We found a small, dark passageway and huddled there, panting. "There's another way out of here," Maxie said in between breaths. "At the other end of the passageways. Let's go!"

We ran through the maze of distorted mirrors. All five of us, squatty, pear-shaped, upside-down fugitives. We ran and ran. Finally we burst out of the last passageway and ran through the park until we reached the main gate. Then we nonchalantly walked out of the park and down the narrow street that led back to the boardwalk.

"Well, at least you got your wish," I said to Buddy as we were walking. "You got discovered at the island."

"I got my wish too," Brownie added.

"You didn't tell me you had a wish," Lippy said. "What was it?"

"I wished for a way to get rid of those stupid shoes."

We looked down at Brownie's stocking feet, and he wiggled his toes. "I guess I must've run right out of 'em." Then he yelled, "Charge!" And we raced off toward the beach.

When have you had a personal experience that was so astonishing, wonderful, funny, or terrible that you just had to put it down on paper? Or have you ever thought up a good plot for a story and written it? Such stories are examples of creative writing—that is, writing that does not involve reference books and research but comes from your own experience, feelings, and imagination. Most of your themes and compositions are creative writing. Your social studies and science reports are not. They may be written creatively, but they are based on facts from other sources.

"Luna Park," the selection that you just read, is an example of creative writing. We don't know whether Charlotte Herman experienced any of the events in the story. What we do know is that she wanted to write a story about a humorous experience in the lives of some children. How well do you think she succeeded? What does she think about these boys and their adventure? How do you know the author regards them warmly? Every author expresses an attitude, and this is an important element in creative writing.

Remember "Luna Park" for a minute. Then try to recall a situation in your life when you were hesitant to try something, or when you did something because you didn't want to disappoint your friends. Or, if you prefer, make up such a situation. Write a short story or theme about your experience or your idea.

Write a second story about a favorite relative or about a friend who has disappointed you. Write about your dusty, junk-filled basement or about a sunrise when you were the only one awake or about something straight out of your own imagination. Write about sadness, anger, humor, hope, or curiosity. Be creative!

348

Ann Preston

Terry Touff Cooper and Marian Reiner

"Young women of the class of 1869, welcome to the Female Medical College of Philadelphia. You decided for yourselves that medicine is a worthy and fitting channel for your energies, and that conviction has led you here. Before you lies a hard road. You are being watched and judged by a society that believes that the female who studies medicine will lose her qualities as a woman. I strongly disagree. I feel that women have the right to play a worthwhile role in the world. I believe that as long as there are women patients there must be women doctors. You will fill a vital need as you help women and men alike to enjoy the best health care possible. Watch, listen, continue to learn during your schooling and your life. I congratulate you all upon the choice you have made. It is a great and sacred work. You have a challenging and valuable career ahead of you."

Dr. Ann Preston, age 56, gazed at her audience. It seemed such a short time ago that she sat listening in this same hall, as a student in the first class at the Medical College. Since then her life had revolved around the school. Soon after graduation she became a professor at the college. And because women students were not allowed in any other hospitals, Dr. Preston worked long and hard to raise funds for a women's hospital—a place where her students could get the practical training every doctor must have. She also believed that expert nursing was a necessary part of good medical care. Thus she helped to establish a teaching school for nurses.

"I have had a good life," Dr. Preston thought as she left the podium and returned to her seat. "The sacrifices were worthwhile, although I had no way of knowing they would be. How *did* I arrive at this moment? Perhaps it all began that day in 1827." As the drone of speakers continued, Ann Preston let her mind travel back some forty-two years.

A crisp breeze rattled through the trees and day was turning into evening. As she passed the plain, white-shingled building that was her school, Ann thought, "Take a good hard look, for this may be the last time you see it." Then she remembered her father's words, "Yes, Ann has a keen mind and has learned as much as she can here in West Grove. I think she should have the chance for more education. She's fourteen and old enough now to go the twenty miles to the Quaker boarding school for girls in Chester. Ann, would you like to go?"

The challenge of a new school and new friends. "Yes. Oh yes," she had answered. And now, just five months later, it was over. She would be leaving for home tomorrow. Her throat ached and her eyes burned. "Never mind," she thought. "There are things to be done." Ann quickened her step and soon reached the familiar boarding house with its neat rows of rose bushes. She quietly opened the door, untied her bonnet, and lifted her long gray skirt so as not to trip on it as she made the two-flight climb to the attic.

Alone in her room, Ann took a rumpled envelope out of her pocket. As if she hadn't seen it before, she carefully read the address.

She pulled out and opened the letter and reread the message neatly written in her father's hand.

Dear Ann,

We are sorry that this letter must bring sad news. Your sister Lucy died yesterday. You know she was never in good health, and doctors gave us little hope for her.

Your mother nursed her these last weeks with tender care, often sitting at her bedside all night. We will miss Lucy terribly. All of this has taken its toll on Mother's frail health, and now she can barely leave her bed. We must ask you to return home to care for the boys.

Your Father

"Six boys are not too much work for me," thought Ann. "Of course I'll do as Father asks and return to West Grove."

Ann packed late into the evening, but her thoughts were with little Lucy . . . so fragile . . . and so young. When Ann finally closed her trunk, she sat down to write an entry in her journal.

March 3, 1827

Why so much death? It is only two years since Emily, my sister and dearest friend, died. She was just fourteen. Now dear Lucy, five last month, is gone. Poor Mother. And this sadness is not only ours. I've heard so often from my friends about the deaths of young women and girls. How strange it is that all six of the Peterson boys are healthy and vigorous. They've hardly suffered a sick day.

"Good-by, Ann," called her teacher as Ann boarded the train the next morning. "Remember, I'll be sending you biology and anatomy books so you can continue your studies. Good luck." The train grunted and whistled, and soon Ann's teacher was but a speck in the distance. Ann waved until she was many miles into rolling Pennsylvania farmland. Her teacher's words echoed in her mind. She would find time to study. But now she must make plans for helping at home.

The sunny colonial house didn't seem changed after the five months Ann had been away. The wide front steps were swept clean and the hickory rockers were in place on the porch. Within a few months Ann was managing the household with ease and good spirits. During the day she tended to her mother's needs, dusted her father's desk and library full of books, fed Dolly, the family horse, cooked for her brothers, and entertained them by making up stories and poems. "We want to hear 'Lola Lake and Lila Lee' again. Please," they'd beg. So Ann would recite the poem she had written for them.

Lola Lake and Lila Lee

I'm going now to tell about
   Pale little Lola Lake,
Who teased her mamma, every day,
   For candy, nuts, and cake.

She loved her sweetmeats more than books,
   And more than work or play;
I cannot tell how many times
   She ate them every day.

At last her cheeks grew very pale,
   Her teeth began to ache,
And all because she lived so much
   On candy, tarts, and cake.

Dear Lila Lee grew strong and bright
   On plain and wholesome food,
She would not eat unhealthy things
   Because they tasted good.

It was a shame, she said, to do
   Like little Lola Lake,
And very seldom would she taste
   The candy or the cake.

She loved to help her mother work,
   And many books had she,
And all her brothers loved to read
   And play, with Lila Lee.

She often, with her pennies, bought
   An orange large and bright,
And took it to a poor, sick man
   Whose name was Billy Blight.

And when he heard her gentle step,
   And looked on Lila Lee,
He blessed the child, and said, "You are
   An angel sent to me."

And Lila, then, was happier far
   Than little Lola Lake,
And had more joy than if she'd bought
   Herself the nicest cake.

In the evening, after walking with her father, Ann studied. Biology. Physiology. Hygiene. Thanks to a local Quaker, Dr. Nathaniel Moseley, Ann had an unlimited supply of science books to pore over. This routine continued uninterrupted for several years.

One autumn morning in 1834 Ann and her parents sat talking on the porch.

"Next week there is an important antislavery meeting in Philadelphia," said Mrs. Preston. "People from local antislavery societies will be forming a larger group. I am most anxious to go with Father, Ann."

"Are you sure you're feeling up to the trip?"

"I think I am, although I'm still very weak."

"Well, don't worry about the boys; I can take care of them. I'm glad you are going," Ann said. "One day I would like to be part of such an important cause and help to bring about change."

"We have already begun to help end slavery by not buying goods made by the labor of slaves and by hiding runaway slaves in our homes," Ann's father said. "But there is so much more to be done. We have to convince as many people as we can that slavery must be outlawed."

Just then the yelping of the rollicking boys disrupted the conversation. "Look at those boys, scampering around the old chestnut tree. They're having such a good time," said Mrs. Preston.

Ann turned to look. Two of her brothers shook the tree. As chestnuts tumbled down, the other boys raced around stuffing their pockets with as many chestnuts as they could find. "There are no girls playing, not one," thought Ann.

That night, after the boys had quieted down and the only sounds to be heard were the creakings of an old house settling, Ann recalled her thoughts about the day.

October 30, 1834

What fun John and Henry had up in our old tree. What freedom the boys have—out of doors in all but the worst weather. We girls, weighted down by petticoats, go from lessons to books to piano practice to needlework. Is it any wonder so many of us are stooped and pale? We so rarely see the sunshine.

Just as the slaves must be freed, so must women everywhere. We can start with freedom through good health. I'm convinced that the human body properly cared for from birth can be a source of health and vitality all through life. Women really can be taught to take care of themselves just as they're taught music and needlepoint.

A week later Ann's parents left for their meeting. The following night was pitch black—no moon, no stars. Ann had finished lighting the oil lamps in her father's library and was about to open her anatomy books when she heard scuffling and knocking at the back door. She went to the door and opened it.

"Quick. You've got to hide her," whispered a neighbor breathlessly. "She's a runaway and the slave catchers are after her. They're heading toward my house. I've got to go. I've got to find help." He vanished into the night.

Ann looked at the young black woman whose eyes were filled with terror. Her body was quivering.

"Come. Follow me and don't worry," Ann said with assurance.

Ann helped the woman dress in Mrs. Preston's plain shawl and Quaker bonnet.

"When they sold off my family, I ran away. I've been running and hiding alone for four days, and this is the closest they've come to catching me so far," the woman told Ann proudly as she dressed. "I'm going to Canada. They're never going to catch me, and I'm never going to be a slave again."

"I wish you Godspeed," said Ann as the woman finished putting two veils over her face. Then they hastily harnessed Dolly to the carriage. Both women climbed in. "Heeup, Dolly," and they started down the road toward the slave catchers.

Five men on horseback came into view and approached the carriage.

"Hold up there," ordered a gruff voice. Ann held her breath.

A head peered into the carriage. "We're wasting our time. It's just a girl and an old lady. Come on," and they raced down the road, leaving Ann and the woman to continue on their way.

Later that night, after leaving the woman at a house that had already been searched and was safe, Ann returned home physically exhausted. But she was too stirred up by the events of that evening to sleep. So she picked up her journal.

November 7, 1834

What a night this has been! I have watched a young woman—someone barely fifteen—face terrible danger boldly and courageously. I pray that she will find her way to freedom.

As for myself, tonight I discovered my own courage and strength. Now I know I can do what I've dreamt about for so many years. I can no more accept slavery than allow death and illness in women to go unchecked. I'll organize a hygiene class and convince the women of West Grove to attend. We'll discuss health care and how women can help bring about better lives for themselves and their children. Women must listen. It's time they acquired the ability to take care of themselves.

Several years passed without major calamity in the Preston household. Ann's mother continued in fragile health, while her determined nature compelled her to continue supporting and working for abolition. The boys thrived and one by one went off to boarding school.

As her duties at home lessened, Ann took on more and more community work. She earned a salary by teaching in the local school. The Wednesday afternoon school bell not only sent pupils racing home but was also the signal that brought women to Ann's hygiene class.

Ann had spent many of her evenings during the past year trying to convince West Grove women to give her class a try. West Grove was a small, closely knit community, and Ann was warmly received as she visited families to recruit students. She talked of the illnesses of many of the women and the need for an understanding of the female anatomy, diet, and exercise as the route to better health. Her neighbors listened politely, but showed little interest or enthusiasm for what she said. School was for young ones. They had no time to go to class, and they felt there was no need for women to change their ways.

Finally one or two women began to show interest, and Ann returned again and again to nurture this interest. At last six women decided to study with Ann. "Six is a beginning," she thought.

And so she began. "Tell us again what hygiene is," asked one woman. "Hygiene is personal health care beginning at birth and continuing through life." The questions were at first general, but gradually they became more personal. "Why is my daughter so listless?" "What can I do to feel stronger?"

The comfort and relief of being able to communicate their problems and concerns spread by word of mouth. Within two years the enrollment had grown from six to twenty-six. The wonderful response to the class in West Grove supported Ann's belief that women were eager for information about health care. And so Ann began recruiting students in neighboring communities.

Ann's twenty-fifth birthday approached.

"Here's an announcement in the *Philadelphia Bulletin* that may interest you," said Mr. Preston one evening. "Your old friend Lucretia Mott will be speaking in Philadelphia next week about the rights of women to lead fuller lives."

Ann looked up, her face brightening.

"You've been wanting to attend a meeting concerning an important cause. This sounds perfect. Mother and I would like to give you the fare to Philadelphia for your birthday present."

"Good. I'd like that," Ann said.

A week later Ann arrived at the hall where Lucretia Mott was to speak. A large crowd had assembled and many people were in heated debate about Mott, who was a powerful voice against slavery and for the rights of women.

"This Mott must be a very strange person," someone was saying. "A woman with such outspoken views and a career must be *very* unladylike indeed."

Just then a gentle woman, dressed in a gray Quaker bonnet and gown, came out onto the stage, stood at the podium, and carefully clasped her hands. A hush fell over the hall. In her soft voice, Lucretia Mott discussed the unfair treatment of women.

"Colleges should open their doors to women. If they won't, then new colleges especially for women must be founded. Women should be able to be doctors, lawyers, and business leaders," she stressed. "And most importantly, women must act on their beliefs."

Ann was spellbound. Someone was finally voicing what had been in her mind for years. She hadn't seen Lucretia since they had played together as children but she felt a strong bond with her.

But not everyone in the crowd did. "Women shouldn't be allowed to make decisions," called out a voice in the audience.

"They shouldn't speak at meetings, either. It's not proper," burst in another. "Lady, you're stirring up trouble."

The meeting broke up amid heated debate. By that time Ann's mind was on tomorrow. Lucretia was right. The time had come to act. That night Ann outlined her plan in her journal.

February 13, 1838

How wonderful to see Lucretia again. She has done so much with her life. She has acted upon her beliefs even in the face of scorn and ridicule. It's time that I also take my stand. I've gone as far with my hygiene classes as I can. Many questions have come up during classes that I couldn't answer. I must know more. No matter how long it takes, I will find a medical school that will admit me. I feel certain Dr. Moseley will help me. He and other Quaker doctors understand the need for doctors of my sex to minister to women.

"Of course I support women going to medical school," said the kindly Dr. Moseley. "And I especially support you, Ann. You've shown exceptional talent and sensitivity during the years you've worked in my office. But to be honest, I doubt you will be accepted by any of the medical colleges."

"I know, doctor. I know women doctors are frowned on. But we must start somewhere. Women need women doctors. I will not wait any longer."

"It may be a long, hard fight," he cautioned.

"That's fine," replied Ann in a steady, firm voice. "I am ready."

"And a long, hard fight it was," thought Dr. Preston. "I applied to one medical college after another — every college in the East." "We don't accept women as students," they said. "Finally after several years, a group of committed people saw the need for an all-women medical college. They founded the Female Medical College, and I was in its first class of eight students."

Her reverie was interrupted by clapping.

"Yes," said the speaker, "we at this college owe a great debt to Dr. Ann Preston."

GET TO WORK!

When it comes time for you to go job-hunting, you'll probably want to look for work in as many types of businesses or companies or stores as you can. Wherever you go, you will be interviewed and asked about your interests and your goals for the future. You will also be asked to fill out an employment application similar to the one shown here.

Some of the information required on an employment application is the same as that asked for on *any* kind of application form you may fill out — name, address, age, and so on. However, what is especially important to a company that may hire you is information about your education, skills, and experience. Knowledge of your background helps an employer place you in a position where you can develop your skills and learn new ones that will advance your career. The amount of experience you've had in the past may also play a part in how much money you earn when you start.

On a separate sheet of paper, answer the following questions about the employment application.

1. Why would the company want to know how much education an applicant has had?
2. Why does the company need your complete employment and salary history?
3. Answer True or False: If you've had several jobs, you're supposed to tell about the *earliest* job first.
4. In your own words, define this statement: "The State Law Against Discrimination prohibits discrimination on account of age."
5. Why do you think the company doesn't want you to include any relatives among your references?
6. Why are references necessary?
7. Write at least three questions that you think the company might ask about you when they contact your references.
8. Why would the company want to know about your future plans?

THE LESLEY CORP.

APPLICATION FOR POSITION

Date _____

Soc. Sec. No. _____

Name of Applicant _____
                   Last Name   First Name   Middle Name

Residence _____ Telephone _____

*Birth Date _____ U.S. Citizen _____ Or Type of Visa _____

Expected Starting Salary: Rate $_____ Minimum _____ Open _____

Education: (Name & Years) Vocational or High School _____ Business School _____

College _____ Major _____ Graduate School _____

Graduated from Last School: Yes _____ No _____ Date _____ Degree _____

Commercial Qualifications: Typing Speed _____ wpm   Steno. Speed _____

Other Special Abilities, Aptitudes, or Interests _____

_____

Position or Type of Work Desired _____

_____

PREVIOUS EMPLOYMENT RECORD: LIST MOST RECENT FIRST

Name & Address of Employer / Name of Immediate Supervisor	Kind of Work Done	How Long Employed	Date of Leaving	Wages Received	Reasons for Leaving

REFERENCES

Give Name, etc., of three persons, not relatives, who have known you during past five years.

Name	Address	Business or Occupation

PERSON TO BE NOTIFIED IN CASE OF EMERGENCY: Name _____

Address _____ Telephone No. _____

Introduced by _____

*The State Law Against Discrimination prohibits discrimination on account of age.

Robert Frost

The Armful

For every parcel I stoop down to seize
I lose some other off my arms and knees,
And the whole pile is slipping, bottles, buns —
Extremes too hard to comprehend at once,
Yet nothing I should care to leave behind.
With all I have to hold with, hand and mind
And heart, if need be, I will do my best
To keep their building balanced at my breast.
I crouch down to prevent them as they fall;
Then sit down in the middle of them all.
I had to drop the armful in the road
And try to stack them in a better load.

Arthur C. Clarke

WHO'S THERE?

Jacqueline Adato

When he was still a child, Arthur C. Clarke's interest in science led him to construct his own telescope and make a map of the moon. It also led him to the British Woolworth's, where he began buying science fiction magazines when he was thirteen years old. Reading one of the many science fiction stories Clarke has written is like taking a realistic journey into the future. In a story he wrote in 1945, Clarke predicted, in accurate detail, the construction of a radio–TV communication satellite. Such a satellite was actually built twenty years later.

Clarke was co-writer of the screenplay for 2001: A Space Odyssey, *which was based on one of his short stories, "The Sentinel."*

What do you think being alone in a space capsule would feel like? Why do people get frightened more easily when they are alone than when they are with other people? When has a sudden sound in the middle of the night scared you?

When Satellite Control called me, I was writing up the day's progress report in the Observation Bubble — the glass-domed office that juts out from the axis of the space station like the hubcap of a wheel. It was not really a good place to work, for the view was too overwhelming. Only a few yards away I could see the construction teams performing their slow-motion ballet as they put the station together like a giant jigsaw puzzle. And beyond them, twenty thousand miles below, was the blue green glory of the full Earth, floating against the star clouds of the Milky Way.

"Station Supervisor here," I answered. "What's the trouble?"

"Our radar's showing a small echo two miles away, almost stationary, about five degrees west of Sirius.[1] Can you give us a visual report on it?"

---

[1] *Sirius* is the brightest star in the sky.

Anything matching our orbit so precisely could hardly be a meteor; it would have to be something we'd dropped — perhaps an inadequately secured piece of equipment that had drifted away from the station. So I assumed; but when I pulled out my binoculars and searched the sky around Orion,[2] I soon found my mistake. Though this space traveler was a piece of equipment, it had nothing to do with us.

"I've found it," I told Control. "It's someone's test satellite — cone-shaped, four antennas, and what looks like a lens system in its base. Probably U.S. Air Force, early 1960s, judging by the design. I know they lost track of several when their transmitters failed. There were quite a few attempts to hit this orbit before they finally made it."

After a brief search through the files, Control was able to confirm my guess. It took a little longer to find out that Washington wasn't in the least bit interested in our discovery of a twenty-year-old stray satellite and would be just as happy if we lost it again.

"Well, we can't do *that*," said Control. "Even if nobody wants it, the thing's a menace to navigation. Someone had better go out and haul it aboard."

That someone, I realized, would have to be me. I dared not detach a worker from the closely knit construction teams, for we were already behind schedule. And a single day's delay on this job cost a million dollars. All the radio and TV networks on Earth were waiting impatiently for the moment when they could route their programs through us, and thus provide the first truly global service, spanning the world from Pole to Pole.

"I'll go out and get it," I answered, snapping an elastic band over my papers so that the air currents from the ventilators wouldn't set them wandering around the room. Though I tried to sound as if I was doing everyone a great favor, I was secretly not at all displeased. It had been at least two weeks since I'd been outside; I was getting a little tired of stores, schedules, maintenance reports, and all the glamorous ingredients of a space-station supervisor's life.

[2] *Orion* is the most conspicuous constellation in the sky.

The only member of the staff I passed on my way to the air lock was Tommy, our recently acquired cat. Pets mean a great deal to persons thousands of miles from Earth, but there are not many animals that can adapt themselves to a weightless environment. Tommy meowed plaintively at me as I clambered into my spacesuit, but I was in too much of a hurry to play with him.

At this point, perhaps I should remind you that the suits we use on the station are completely different from the flexible affairs men wear when they walk around on the Moon. Ours are really baby spaceships, just big enough to hold one person. The suits are stubby cylinders, about seven feet long, fitted with low-powered propulsion jets, and have a pair of accordionlike sleeves at the upper end for the operator's arms. Normally, however, you keep your hands drawn inside the suit, working the manual controls in front of your chest.

As soon as I'd settled down inside my very exclusive spacecraft, I switched on power and checked the gauges on the tiny instrument panel. There's a magic word, *forb,* that you'll often hear spacetravelers mutter as they climb into their suits; it reminds them to test fuel, oxygen, radio, batteries. All my needles were well in the safety zone, and so I lowered the transparent hemisphere over my head and sealed myself in. For a short trip like this, I did not bother to check the suit's internal lockers, which were used to carry food and special equipment for extended missions.

As the conveyor belt decanted me into the air lock, I felt like an Indian papoose being carried along on its mother's back. Then the pumps brought the pressure down to zero, the outer door opened, and the last traces of air swept me out into the stars, turning very slowly head over heels.

The station was only a dozen feet away, yet I was now an independent planet—a little world of my own. I was sealed up in a tiny, mobile cylinder, with a superb view of the entire universe, but I had practically no freedom of movement inside the suit. The padded seat and safety belts prevented me from turning around, though I could reach all the controls and lockers with my hands or feet.

In space the great enemy is the sun, which can blast you to blindness in seconds. Very cautiously, I opened up the dark filters on the "night" side of my suit and turned my head to look out at the stars. At the same time I switched the helmet's external sunshade to automatic, so that whichever way the suit turned, my eyes would be shielded from that intolerable glare.

Presently, I found my target — a bright fleck of silver whose metallic glint distinguished it clearly from the surrounding stars. I stamped on the jet control pedal and felt the mild surge of acceleration as the low-powered rockets set me moving away from the station. After ten seconds of steady thrust, I estimated that my speed was great enough, and I cut off the drive. It would take me five minutes to coast the rest of the way, and not much longer to return with my salvage.

And it was at that moment, as I launched myself out into space, that I knew that something was horribly wrong.

It is never completely silent inside a spacesuit; you can always hear the gentle hiss of oxygen, the faint whirr of fans and motors, the murmur of your own breathing — even, if you listen carefully enough, the rhythmic thump that is the pounding of your heart. These sounds reverberate through the suit, unable to escape into the surrounding void; they are the unnoticed background of life in space, for you are aware of them only when they change.

They had changed now; to them had been added a sound which I could not identify. It was an intermittent, muffled thudding, sometimes accompanied by a scraping noise, as of metal upon metal.

I froze instantly, holding my breath and trying to locate the alien sound with my ears. The meters on the control board gave no clues; all the needles were rock steady on their scales, and there were none of the flickering red lights that would warn of impending disaster. That was some comfort, but not much. I had long ago learned to trust my instincts in such matters; their alarm signals were flashing now, telling me to return to the station before it was too late. . . .

Even now, I do not like to recall those next few minutes. Panic slowly flooded into my mind like a rising tide, over-whelming the dams of reason and logic which every person must build against the mystery of the universe. I knew then

369

what it was like to face insanity. No other explanation fitted the facts.

For it was no longer possible to pretend that the noise disturbing me was that of some faulty mechanism. Though I was in utter isolation, far from any other human being or indeed any material object, I was not alone. The soundless void was bringing to my ears the faint but unmistakable stirrings of life.

In that first, heart-freezing moment it seemed that something was trying to get into my suit—something invisible, seeking shelter from the cruel and pitiless vacuum of space. I whirled madly in my harness, scanning the entire sphere of vision around me except for the blazing, forbidden cone toward the sun. There was nothing there, of course. There could not be—yet that purposeful scrabbling was clearer than ever.

Despite the nonsense that has been written about us, it is not true that spacetravelers are superstitious. But can you blame me if, as I came to the end of logic's resources, I suddenly remembered how Bernie Summers had died, no farther from the station than I was at this very moment?

It was one of those "impossible" accidents; it always is. Three things had gone wrong at once. Bernie's oxygen regulator had run wild and sent the pressure soaring, the safety valve had failed to blow—and a faulty joint had given way instead. In a fraction of a second, his suit was open to space.

I had never known Bernie, but suddenly his fate became of overwhelming importance to me—for a horrible idea had come into my mind. One does not talk about these things, but a damaged spacesuit is too valuable to be thrown away, even if it has killed its wearer. It is repaired, renumbered—and issued to someone else. . . .

What happens to the soul of someone who dies between the stars, far from his or her native world? Are you still here, Bernie, clinging to the last object that linked you to your lost and distant home?

As I fought the nightmares that were swirling around me—for now it seemed that the scratchings and soft fumblings were coming from all directions—there was one last

370

hope to which I clung. For the sake of my sanity, I had to prove that this wasn't Bernie's suit—that the metal walls so closely wrapped around me had never been another man's coffin.

It took me several tries before I could press the right button and switch my transmitter to the emergency wavelength. "Station!" I gasped. "I'm in trouble! Get records to check my suit history and—"

I never finished; they say my yell wrecked the microphone. But what person alone in the absolute isolation of a spacesuit would *not* have yelled when something patted him or her softly on the back of the neck!

I must have lunged, despite the safety harness, and smashed against the upper edge of the control panel. When the rescue squad reached me a few minutes later, I was still unconscious, with an angry bruise across my forehead.

And so I was the last person in the whole satellite relay system to know what had happened. When I came to my senses an hour later, all our medical staff was gathered around my bed. But it was quite a while before the doctors bothered to look at me. They were all too busy playing with the three cute little kittens our badly misnamed Tommy had been rearing in the seclusion of my spacesuit's number five storage locker.

Small Hands, Big Hands

As told to Sandra Weiner

In the fall of 1969, Sandra Weiner taped interviews with Mexican-American workers in California. This true story is based on Ms. Weiner's conversations with Doria Ramírez.

Before you read about Doria, think about the way you live. How difficult do you think your life is? Why do you sometimes feel sorry for yourself? What have you done to make your own life easier or better?

I am Doria Ramírez and I am eighteen years old. I went to school when I was ten years old and got out when I was thirteen because I had to help my parents. We used to get up at 3:30 in the morning to pick potatoes and I didn't like it. I never liked it. It was very cold. I had to leave school for another reason—I didn't have any shoes or sweater with me and it was winter.

I knew we didn't have any money so I couldn't say, "Papá, I need shoes." But when I saw all the other children with shoes, I knew that there had to be a way to change my life. I didn't want my sisters to feel the way I did. It was then that I started thinking this was not a life for the migrant worker or for *any* worker. Without shoes and warm clothes, all these Mexican-American children could not go to school. My father did not feel this way but when I used to see my younger brothers working so hard and feeling so tired at the age of thirteen, I wanted to see them have a different position in life.

We are nine in our family, and we were being paid piece rate. With a big family you can work a long day and think you are making some money. But in the winter time when there is no work it is difficult to have such a large family. My father would never take welfare. He always told us that he didn't like welfare because you had to let the governor's office know what size shoe you wore and what size underwear — and he didn't like to do this. It was too private. My mother tried to sew our clothes, but when you don't have any money you can't buy the material to sew.

The growers gave us the jobs because we were a large family. I was not afraid to ask the growers for more money because I used to see families just starving. My father asked, "Why do you always have to argue with the grower?" But there always has to be one member in a family who asks. There *has* to be one who talks too much. And I was the one. My father would say, "Don't ask for more or they will not let us work, and they will take all the money away." I said, "No, that's not enough, I don't want to live that way." He would answer, "My father lived that way and we can live the same way."

We did whatever was needed to be done on each farm, either thinning or tying or hoeing or picking. We picked almost every fruit and vegetable growing, but the hardest job that I know is working on sugarbeets. You have to leave each plant five inches apart from the others after thinning. That's very hard because you always have to bend over on your knees with a small hoe, working maybe twelve hours, and this makes you sick in the kidneys or back. You must thin the sugarbeets while they are still young plants. If you try sitting, you don't get the work done.

375

One day a labor contractor for the ranchers hired about 200 people, and I made about 32 or 33 rows that day. You have to be fast. I had gone into the field with shoes and socks but I came out without them because the blisters on my feet were paining me. I couldn't stand or move, so I went back to the car to lie down. I was already coming down with a fever. The labor contractor didn't want to pay my father and he said, "Well, your daughter has to come out and get the money. She knows how to sign her name." And even though I was feeling so sick, I was happy because I thought we were going to have so much money for the family. And all we got was seven dollars for nine people working twelve hours.

I always had to work to help my parents because I love my parents. We just stick together. This is why it's good to have a big family because together we make our own home. It's a small home but it's mine, and I don't need any other home because I have my family. We live in two rooms, a kitchen and another room, and we sleep in rows like hot dogs.

I get up when my mother starts preparing the lunches for the day in the field. She makes tacos and tortillas. The older girls help her. At night when we return home she washes the clothes and hangs up only pants on the clothes line, so the neighbors say, "You have only boys," and my mother says, "No, we have six girls and three boys." In the evenings my parents are tired and don't talk very much.

Another time I saw my father crying. That day had been a bad day for us. We had arrived in the field at 4:30 in the morning, and they had put big lights on the tractors so we could see how to pick the potatoes. And we picked all day until five o'clock in the evening. There were six of us and we earned only twelve dollars. And that was when my father wanted to cry. It was then I started to think again that I must make a change. My father said, "Now I understand you and why you are so angry at the growers."

Once I got really angry when I was working with one of the growers. We were organizing and he fired all the people who were organizing or interested in a union. When we walked from the fields everybody walked with us. But the next day the farmer found other people to work for him, and we knew it would take a long time before all the migrant workers understood about the union. It took my father a long time. Now I spend a lot of time helping to organize farm workers, and we hope the dream of a union will come true. It's just like when Martin Luther King said, "I have a dream."

I am much happier now because I am learning so much. When I was in school I didn't learn because I had to rush from school to pick cotton and I would forget English and arithmetic. I never learned to speak English in school but I learned English when I started walking on the picket lines and asking people not to buy grapes in the stores that sold them. At the first boycott they wouldn't take me because I didn't speak the language. So I quickly had to learn to speak English. Everybody who knew how to speak it helped me. I still don't know how to read or write English, but I will learn.

It is hard to believe now that we lived the way we did for so long. I remember at home on Saturdays we would all take baths and eat together and then my father would play the trumpet. My sister and my brother-in-law and my little sister played the guitar and we would sing and dance. Even though our lives are filled with so much work we love to have fun and have some happiness. You have to carry some happiness in your heart.

GRAPH IT UP

In the selection you just read, Doria Ramírez talks about joining a union. Look at the line graph on this page. The numbers going up the left-hand side of the graph represent the millions of labor-union members. The numbers going across the bottom of the graph represent years. Use this graph to answer these questions.

1. In what year were there 14 million union members?
2. In what five-year period did union membership rise from 3.5 million to nine million?
3. In what five-year period was there the largest increase in membership?
4. How many union members were there in 1970?
5. In what five-year period did membership start and end at 3.5 million with a drop in between?

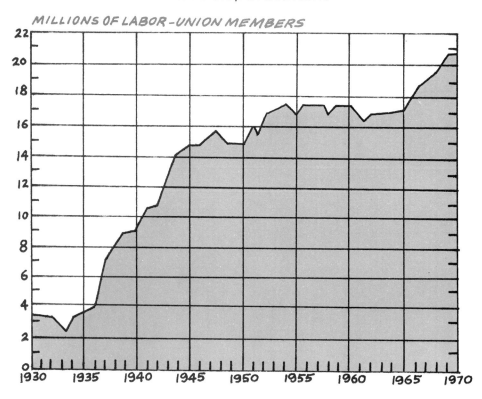

MILLIONS OF LABOR-UNION MEMBERS

The information given on the line graph can be shown in different ways on other types of graphs. On a separate sheet of paper, use the information on the line graph to make a bar graph like the one started here.

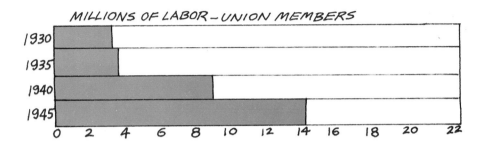

This graph shows how one infant spends her day. On a separate sheet of paper, design a graph in the shape of a pie showing how you spend your time.

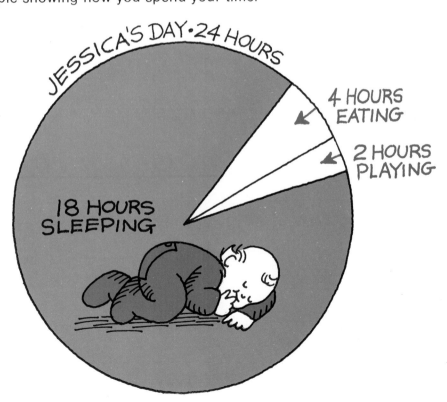

MEN OF COLOR, TO ARMS!

June M. Omura

"With silent tongue, and clenched teeth, and steady eye, and well-poised bayonet, they have helped mankind on to this great consummation. . . ." Thus Abraham Lincoln described the black men who served with the Union forces in the Civil War. Up to this point in history, the United States army had been basically a white man's institution. But by the end of the Civil War, 186,000 blacks had served the Union—almost 10 percent of the Union forces—and more than 37,000 blacks had died. Blacks served in both the army and the navy. Interestingly enough, although the army was segregated, the navy was not. Most of the black men in the Union army had been slaves in the South, but some were freedmen and some were longtime residents of the North. Black men who volunteered to serve as soldiers were assigned to all-black regiments; regimental commanders were always white.

Black soldiers took part in 449 engagements, including 39 major battles against the South. The Congressional Medal of Honor, first created during the Civil War and to this day the nation's highest military decoration, was awarded to 21 black men. This was in recognition of some of the finest fighting men on the Union side.

Being willing to fight and die for one's country, in most periods of history in most countries, has been thought worthy of the greatest admiration and praise. In the United States there have been times when brave men, not blacks alone, have had to beg to be allowed to serve and to die. At the beginning of the Civil War, when black men volunteered to fight, they were refused and sometimes ridiculed. When finally accepted, they were paid at lower rates than white men, and sometimes not paid at all.

For many reasons the North did not want to employ blacks in its army. It was a white man's army and, at first, a white man's war. But the overriding issue gradually became free-

dom for the slaves in the South. In the early days of the war, thinking that it would be over soon, the northern leadership did not want to offend the South (even though it was now the enemy) by accepting enlistments from runaway slaves or other blacks. Moreover, they did not want to offend the border states, which had not joined the Confederacy but still held slaves. Some Northerners worried that the blacks would be inferior soldiers. However, with heavy casualties among the Union troops and the realization that this would be a long war as well as a bloody one, there was an increasing need for more men. Because this was still a volunteer army, it became increasingly more difficult to find willing recruits.

Pressure for the use of black troops came from several directions, and some blacks had volunteered to serve. Some white leaders thought the black population would be a dependable source of manpower. Expecting easy promotions for commanding black units when they finally came into being, some white officers pressed for more of these units to be formed. There were also some Union officers who believed that the blacks would be as good as any white soldiers they had commanded. General David Hunter was apparently one of these officers. Colonel Thomas Higginson, a New Englander, was another.

In the spring of 1862, General David Hunter, who desperately needed more soldiers, organized a black unit known as the First South Carolina Volunteers. They went unrecognized and unpaid for three months, and the regiment was finally disbanded. In November they were reactivated and mustered into the Union army. Command of the First South Carolina Regiment, as the unit came to be known, was turned over to Colonel Thomas W. Higginson, a Boston minister, abolitionist, and Union officer, who had no doubts about his troops and who came to admire and like them beyond his initial

belief in their worth. In his memoir, *Army Life in a Black Regiment*, Colonel Higginson wrote, "Till the blacks were armed, there was no guaranty of their freedom. It was their demeanor under arms that shamed the nation into recognizing them as men."

The first black unit to serve officially was a group of southern black freedmen raised by Union General Benjamin F. Butler in New Orleans. (In 1865, in the last months of the war, the Confederacy authorized the use of 300,000 slaves as soldiers. Ironically, the bravery and the fighting skill of black men in the Union ranks demonstrated something Southerners would not admit earlier.)

General Ben Butler raised the First Regiment Louisiana Native Guards in the summer of 1862. At about the same time, Congress passed two laws that made it possible to recruit black troops. The success of Butler's Native Guards led him to call for more black units, and new ones were formed very quickly.

Meanwhile, President Lincoln had threatened to free all the slaves in the Confederate states. He finally did so in the Emancipation Proclamation on January 1, 1863. In March 1863, Frederick Douglass, the great black abolitionist, issued a proclamation of his own, calling for "men of color" to enlist. Douglass believed that black men must have a hand in winning their own freedom. He wrote, "Liberty won by white men would lose half its luster. Who would be free, themselves must strike the blow. Better even die free, than to live slaves." His words reached close to home. Two of his own sons served with the Fifty-fourth Massachusetts Volunteers.

When the Civil War was finally over, the black men who had served in the Union army had found a way to "strike the blow," for themselves and for their country, that took them part of the way to freedom.

Buffalo Dusk

Carl Sandburg

The buffaloes are gone.
And those who saw the buffaloes are gone.
Those who saw the buffaloes by thousands and
   how they pawed the prairie sod into dust
   with their hoofs, their great heads down
   pawing on in a great pageant of dusk,
Those who saw the buffaloes are gone.
And the buffaloes are gone.

Collection 4

"Papa, Papa! What's wrong? Your arm!"

Anna quickly set the baby down and hurried to help her father as he dropped weakly into a chair. His ragged coat was drenched with blood.

"Anna, find Mama and bring some water," wheezed her Papa as his head dropped to the table. Thirteen-year-old Anna grabbed a bucket and raced out the door. The hall was pitch black. She felt for the wall and fumbled her way down the stairs.

"Hurry, hurry," she thought. "Poor Papa." Anna leaped over the last few steps, raced out the door, down a dank, garbage-filled walkway along the side of the building, to the back. There she spotted Mama and a neighbor hanging up clothes on a line.

"The soot and cold will get these clothes before the sun ever does," said Mama, gazing up at the thin strip of sky barely visible between the crowded tenement buildings.

Just then she heard, "Mama! Mama! Hurry!" It was Anna racing toward her with the bucket banging against her thin legs and knobby knees. "Mama, please! Papa's home. He's hurt his arm. There's so much blood."

Bread and Roses

Terry Touff Cooper and Marian Reiner

393

Mama's face tensed. "Oh, no, no," she said over and over again as she ran past Anna and up the stairs.

The winter air cut through Anna's tiny body. She turned on the faucet, filled the bucket halfway, and lugged it back into the building. Reaching the top of the first flight, she set the bucket down. Her chest felt like it was splitting in half. "Papa, I'm coming. Just two more flights to go."

By the time she entered the apartment, Mama was cleaning the wound on Papa's arm. Six pairs of eyes watched fearfully from around the kitchen table. "It's bad, Anna. Very bad. It will be weeks, maybe months before he'll work again."

Anna Venuti knew well what that meant. She was the oldest of seven children. Her father, a tailor by trade, had left Italy looking for a better life in America. He finally found work as a weaver in the Pacific Textile factory in Lawrence, Massachusetts. It was a very low-paying job, but he was a good worker and was confident that he would soon get a better job. He was sure it was just a matter of time. Within a few months of his arrival in America, he had arranged for his family to join him. To bring Mama and their six children from Italy had taken all of Papa's savings. But this was a new world with every opportunity, and Papa felt he would soon have more money saved. In the fall of 1910, his wife and six children had arrived, carrying in two big boxes all that they owned. The seventh child was born a month later.

The Venuti family took a two-room apartment in a tenement owned by Pacific Textile. Rent was $2.50 a week. It was crowded, but Papa was sure they would soon move to a home with more space.

Anna had many dreams. One was about the new home—a dream that made living in this one easier to bear. In her dream there were no more tiny, smudged windows that opened onto another gray building an arm's length away. The new home would have giant windows opening onto a garden with rosebushes. There would be bright sunshine and clear air. Sometimes in the early morning Anna would carefully climb over her two little sisters and out of bed. With her eyes squinting so as not to break the spell, she'd cross the room and reach the kitchen window, which faced a brick wall. She'd open the window with a sweep of her arms, as if the window were ten times bigger, and whisper, "Ah, there's a chill in the air. But the sky is clear, not a gray cloud to be seen. Lovely day it is. Lovely day." Then she'd turn around and open her eyes to see her ten-year-old brother Nicola sitting up in his bed at the other corner of the room. His eyes were twinkling. She knew her dream had become his, too.

As the months passed, there seemed less and less chance that the Venutis would move. Work was very slow. Some weeks Papa worked only three days. His wages were cut—one week from $8 to $6, the next week down to $5. Still, Anna kept her private dream.

But now Anna could hear Papa's moans from the bedroom. Mama had draped his coat over a pipe to dry. "Anna," she said slowly, "you and Nicola will have to find work. Starting tomorrow. Papa has told me there are many children working in the plant. Maybe they'll have room for you."

"But school," said Anna. "What about school? I've been learning so much English. I can really speak now. Nicky, too."

"You'll have to leave school, Anna. I know. It's hard. I know you've done well. But there are so many of us here, and we've got to eat. It's the only way. If I could go myself, I would, but I've got to stay with the little ones. Please, *carissima*."

Anna stood slumped and pale in the middle of the room. She had already known the truth in her own mind. She'd leave school the way most of her friends already had. Everyone was saying that things were bad and getting worse all the time. She'd probably never get to return to school, she thought. Hearing Mama say it out loud no longer made it just a nagging fear. It was real.

Then Anna felt Mama's arms embrace her. So warm and strong. But Mama began to cry, "I'm sorry, *carissima* Anna. I know your dreams and I'm sorry," she said.

Anna slept poorly that night. She dreamt that she was

walking to school in a heavy snow storm. It was an effort to take a step. Suddenly, the snow was waist high. She'd never make it. Just then she felt a hand on her shoulder. "Anna, it's time to get up, it's already past 5:30." Mama shook Nicola, too. They dressed quickly, gulped warm tea with a drop of condensed milk in it, and were still chewing bread spread with beef suet as they put on their coats.

"Nicola, here, take Papa's hat," said Mama. "It's freezing outside, but I've only got this one hat."

"Don't worry," Anna said bravely. "I'll put my hands over my ears. I'll be fine."

"Anna, remember, start looking for work at Pacific Textile. Since they know Papa, they may help you out."

As they set out, Mama looked at her two oldest, so small for their age. Anna was draped in an old blanket roughly sewn into a coat. She wore her father's old socks on her hands. Papa's hat was so big on Nicola that he had to bend his head back to see. His coat was a made-over pair of men's trousers. He carried a small lunch bag under his arm.

Anna and Nicola headed for Pacific Textile. They'd
have no difficulty finding the mill for it was two miles
straight down Merrimac Street, the same street on which
they lived. Merrimac was already filled with many
workers on their way to the factories. Most walked with
heads down, their faces pale and weary. The mill was a
large building, almost a block in length, and enclosed by
a heavy metal-link fence. Its small, closed windows were
so grimy and dirty that they seemed to fade into the gray
of the building, giving it a lifeless look. As they approached the mill, Anna saw a line of people waiting near
the front gate.

"Nicky, you stay here in line while I go read the sign."
She walked up the line. Several women were leaning
against the fence, seemingly asleep on their feet. Others
stared blankly ahead. Few children were in line.

Anna reached the gate and read the sign:

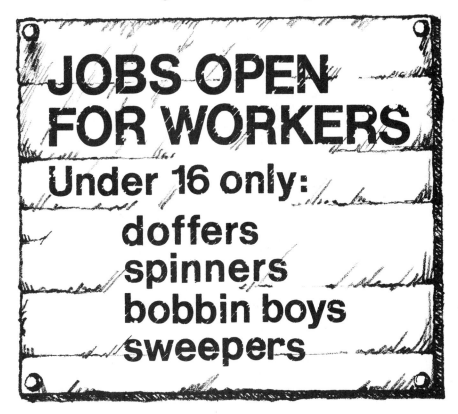

JOBS OPEN
FOR WORKERS
Under 16 only:
doffers
spinners
bobbin boys
sweepers

Confused, Anna turned to a woman at the front of the line and asked, "Why are you waiting here when the sign says there are jobs only for children?"

"I'm hoping," answered the woman. Her face was so sunken and gray. "I've been out of work for months. No money. No food. Five children. I'm hoping. Hoping."

Just then the gate swung open. In a booming voice the boss called out, "Jobs for workers under sixteen only. Everyone else away. Just workers under sixteen."

Anna watched as people in line slowly began to move away. Some remained.

"No understand. Job?" she heard a man plead to the boss.

"No work. No job. Go away."

No work, *that* the man understood. How many times had he heard those same words, Anna wondered. The words that meant no bread for this and maybe next week, a cold house, and crying children.

Anna found Nicola and grabbed his hand. "Come on," she said. They hurried to the gate and approached a small station house.

"Ya want work?"

"Yes," answered Anna.

"What's your name?"

"Anna Venuti. I think you know my father. He was one of your good weavers who was injured yesterday. He . . ."

"Nope. Never heard of him." Anna clenched her fists. Not remember Papa? But he worked so hard.

"You sure, mister? Caesare Venuti?"

"Listen, girl, I got no time to gab about your father. Ya want work, then just answer the questions. Age?"

"Thirteen," answered Anna, lowering her eyes.

"Experience?"

"None."

"O.K. You're assigned to the weaving room as a spinner. Hours seven to six, Monday through Saturday. Four dollars a week. No pay for sickness. Go into that door, leave your coat on a hook, and ask the supervisor what to do."

Anna squeezed Nicky's hand. "Wait here for me after work."

As she left, she heard the man saying to Nicola, "Name?"

"Nicola Venuti."

When Anna entered the weaving room, the supervisor had already spotted the new arrival.

"You're in charge of six rows," she shouted to Anna over the deafening cranking of the machines. "Watch them carefully. Use this brush to keep lint off the frames of the machines and be sure to put it on the table at the door when you leave today. If you see a thread break, tie the ends together quickly. Do you understand?" Anna nodded yes. "Now start and keep moving."

Anna began to walk up the first six long aisles. "What magic," she thought, fascinated. The jangling machines turned hundreds of spindles at once. On each spindle was a spinning bobbin onto which thread was wound. When a bobbin was filled with thread, a boy called a doffer replaced it with an empty one.

Anna watched her machines attentively. To her, the bobbins seemed like delicate twirling dancers, and occasionally she'd join in the dance by sneaking a twirl or two. Still, she was careful not to miss a single broken thread or a fleck of lint. Long before the lunch bell rang, she felt she knew everything there was to know about her work and could do it without thinking at all.

Anna had just ten minutes for lunch—the lunch Nicky had in his bag for both of them. But she had no idea where he had been assigned to work, and she was afraid to move too far away from her machines to look for him. So she sat and waited. From other aisles, she could hear supervisors cracking commands and warnings. "No reading." "No singing." Why not, she wondered? Who could be bothered by a song? "Two minutes left." Anna sat listlessly, listening to her stomach grumble its own commands. The bell signaling the afternoon session rang out shrilly. And in a great whirr the machines began again.

400

Hours passed. Weariness and boredom replaced what had been fascination earlier in the day. Anna's stomach growled, and her feet and back ached, so she sat down on a box to rest for a moment. "Up! Up!" ordered a figure barely visible in the dim light. "You're paid to work, not rest. Mind the machines."

And Anna was up again. Up into the stale, hot air; into a dust and lint storm that never ended.

It seemed like hours, days before the machines finally whinnied to a halt. Anna's head felt like a wad of cotton, with no feelings, no thoughts. As she shook her head to wake up, she heard the bell and saw workers—men, women, children—plod down the aisle. They mechanically took their coats and began to exit.

Anna suddenly remembered that Nicola was waiting for her, and she followed the weary procession out. A blast of freezing air knocked her awake. She neared the gate and saw a tiny nose, two sparkling eyes, and several grimy fingers poking through the fence.

"Hey, what d'ya do today?" she asked.

As they turned out the gate and started for home, Nicky answered, "I was a doffer. Nothing much happened, except there was this woman who sat near me at lunch and sang one song over and over till the supervisor made her stop. The song got stuck in my head and it's been going round and round." Nicky swayed as he sang.

> Well, you go to the mill and work your best.
> Payday comes and you get less and less.
> After so many bills what's left—not a cent.
> How you gonna pay the rent?
>
> I'm gonna starve and everybody will.
> 'Cause you can't make a living in a cotton mill.

"I was singing it as I walked out the gate tonight," Nicky went on, "and some girl said, 'Kid, that song's rubbish. Read this, and give it to a friend.'" He held out a pamphlet. Anna saw the words "Mill Worker" on the cover.

"We'll read it when we get home, O.K.? Boy, am I starved, starved, *starved!*"

"Here," said Nicola. "I saved this for you." He held out bits of bread in his grimy palm. Anna gave his hat a gentle tug.

The family was seated around the table when Anna and Nicola returned.

"Where's Papa?" asked Anna.

"In there," answered Mama, pointing to the bedroom. "The pain was terrible. He moaned all day. He's so weak. Finally, he's fallen asleep."

"Why is it so cold in here?" asked Nicky.

"Why?" snapped Mama. "Prices go higher and higher. You go to market with money in a basket and carry home food in your pocket. I bought so little. A few potatoes. A tiny bag of tea. Some canned tomatoes and cheese. And there was no money left. No money for coal. Not a cent."

The lifeless eyes of the people in the work line that morning flashed through Anna's mind as did Nicky's song: "I'm gonna starve and everybody will, 'cause you can't make a living in a cotton mill." Would it get that bad? Could it happen to them? No. It won't happen to us. She'd work hard. Night and day if she had to. They'd make it.

Mama broke into Anna's reverie. "Ah, but don't worry now. Please? We've got the spaghetti, and we'll have a little cheese and bread. Anna, Nicola, you found work? Yes?"

As Mama served the meager portions of dinner, Anna told the family about her day. Then she gobbled down her food and was finished long before anyone. She could have eaten five more helpings as quickly. "Any more, Mama?"

Mama shook her head no.

Anna swallowed hard. "It doesn't matter. I'm stuffed."

"What about that paper I brought home?" asked Nicky.

Anna turned away from the table to fetch it. She was still hungry, and she felt weak, but she'd manage. She found the pamphlet, returned to the table and, without looking up, she said, "It's called the *Mill Worker*. Some girl gave it to Nicky."

"Read some out loud," Nicky said. And Anna began.

ATTENTION
Young People of Lawrence, Massachusetts

Could you see some extra money? Jobs await you.
It is good fortune that has given you a home in
Lawrence, one of the great mill towns in the United
States.

Give up your idle ways. Earn an independent
income. Make good use of your nimble fingers.
Come to work at a Pacific Textile mill.

Why sit at home when you can be paid for easy
work in pleasant surroundings? Put your time to
good use and let us pay you for tending looms,
sweeping floors, or carrying messages. The work
will occupy your hands and leave your mind free to
think your own thoughts.

English is not necessary. You are sure to find
friends in our mills who can speak your language.
Start a new and happy life. Become a member of
the Pacific Textile family and you will see why we
are the biggest employers in Lawrence.

As Anna read, the children, one by one, slipped into bed.
Anna finished the paper and crumpled it in her hands.
"They call Nicky's song rubbish? *That's* rubbish," she
cried as she threw it into the empty stove. Anna and her
mother sat silently at the table for a moment. They
watched the last inch of the candle flicker.

"Anna, listen," said Mama, drawing her daughter close. "I talked to Mrs. Riccio downstairs today. She's taking work into her home. I'm going to try doing some here, tomorrow. Mrs. Riccio gave me the factory's ad in the newspaper. Here." She gave the rumpled scrap to Anna.

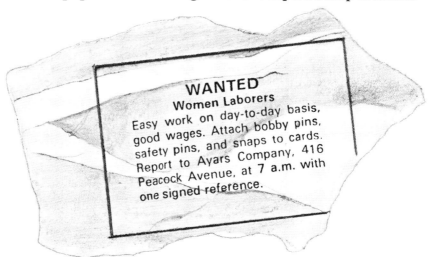

WANTED
Women Laborers
Easy work on day-to-day basis, good wages. Attach bobby pins, safety pins, and snaps to cards. Report to Ayars Company, 416 Peacock Avenue, at 7 a.m. with one signed reference.

"Each day Mrs. Riccio gets sixteen pounds of snaps and three hundred cards," Mrs. Venuti continued, straining to recall every detail about the work. "She has to attach so many snaps to each card. The company pays 14¢ for 100 cards. She says they have lots of work and I could get some. It's simple and the *bambini* can even help. Tony can work too after he sells his newspapers. It sounded good so I asked the grocer for a reference and tomorrow morning before Tony leaves for school, I'll go pick up the work. After tomorrow, I can send Tony."

Anna looked at Mama as she spoke. What with Papa's sickness and the younger children crying for food, life was hard for Mama. Anna remembered a time when Mama's cream-white face was framed by shining black hair pulled back tight and pinned into a beautiful braid. Now she looked haggard. Her once shining black hair was turning gray. She seemed so much older than her thirty-five years.

"But Mama," Anna pleaded, "you're exhausted. How can you do more? You'll get sick."

"Anna, I've got to. Only two loaves of bread this week, no meat. I can hardly buy enough food to fill your stomachs, and Papa needs medicine. It will be weeks still before he'll be able to get around."

"Mama was right," Anna thought. "It was the only way."

That night and months of nights after, Anna and Nicky returned home exhausted to the same scene — Mama, Tony, and the *bambini* working around the kitchen table. In dim light, often from only a single candle, they'd be snapping snaps or slipping bobby pins onto cards. Anna and Nicky's arrival meant a few minutes' break for dinner. Then work would resume, hour after hour, until all snaps or pins were on cards and ready to be exchanged the next morning for a new batch. Often it was midnight before Mama pinched out the candle flame.

Even with the additional $3.00 from this tedious work, the Venutis barely got by. But Papa was slowly recovering, and they had their hopes — and Anna still had her dreams.

For Anna and Nicola, days in the factory were terrible, a monotonous mix of cranking machines, spelled by shrill whistles and curt commands. The children had no idea that Friday, January 12, 1912, would be any different. At 7 A.M. on the dot the whistle signaled workers to begin. As usual, Anna went directly to her first aisle and began her work. She rushed up one aisle, dusting here, tying there, and down the next. Back and forth. Suddenly, her machines came to an abrupt halt. Anna, startled, stopped, too. She heard pounding. Was it her head? Was it her heart? She put her hands over her ears. Then she listened again. The pounding was stronger. It was from the floor above. Then the pounding came down the stairs and right into the spinning floor, her floor. The pounding and shouting were coming closer.

"All out! Get out! Strike! Strike!" A throng of people, their arms waving wildly, started down her aisle, banging on the machines with sticks, pulling bobbins off their spindles and throwing them angrily on the floor. "Out! Get out! Not enough money!"

"Leave?" thought Anna. "I can't. The supervisors will be angry. They'll start yelling, and I'll lose my job. I can't just leave." Anna huddled against a machine. More people raced by. Then one stopped. It was Mr. Kohler, a neighbor in Anna's building.

"Anna? Anna. Quick. It's not safe. You must go straight home. Find my wife. She'll explain everything." He swooped Anna into his arms and ran. When he reached the door he set her down and said firmly, "Now go. Hurry!"

"But Nicky. Where's Nicky?" Anna yelled back.

"He's gone," said Mr. Kohler. "I sent him home already. Just go and don't look back."

As Anna raced for the gate, she heard the angry shouts from the growing mob. "Short pay!" "We'll get our way or starve trying." She elbowed her way through and ran.

It was mid-morning. Merrimac Street, usually deserted at this hour, was filling with more and more people. Some loitered in small groups or watched from doorways, others ran every which way. One large crowd had gathered in the middle of the street and was stopping traffic.

Anna reached home, burst in the door and blindly blurted out a disconnected "Mama, Papa, I couldn't help it—they made me come home and Nicky and the streets filled with people and my coat is there and he picked me up and said go run and . . ."

"Anna. Anna. Come." It was Papa's soothing and gentle voice. He was sitting at the table for the first time in weeks. He pulled Anna close. She buried her face in his shoulder with a giant sigh and whispered, "Papa!"

Papa's words made the frightening morning fade. "Calm down and we'll talk. Easy, easy, *bambina*. We heard all about it. Mrs. Kohler was here and explained everything. Now easy." In a few moments Anna looked up, and for the first time noticed the family assembled around the table.

"Anna, Mrs. Kohler was handing out leaflets," said Papa. "Look, the leaflet is printed in Italian. Listen, this time I read to you."

STRIKE COMMITTEE
CALLS STRIKE OF ALL WORKERS

Strike for Bread!
  54 hours pay for 54 hours work
  No more speed-ups
  15% increase for all
  Double pay for overtime

Don't be a scab. Pitch the job. Join Industrial Workers of the World.

  Meeting—January 16th—Lawrence Common. Come with your family. Hear Joseph Ettor and Arturo Giovannitti tell us how we can beat the bosses.

Signed: William Haywood, Chairman
        Tony Russo
        Claude Biget
        Hans Kohler

        Strike Committee

409

As Papa finished, Nicola piped in, "What's speed-ups?"

"Well," said Papa, "suppose you worked as a weaver — you know, like I did before the accident. You worked well and fast — for fifty-six hours every week. Suddenly the government says that the women and girls in the factory can only work fifty-four hours a week. The bosses get very angry at this because many of their workers are women and girls. Now they can only keep the mills open fifty-four hours. But they don't want to lose the other two hours. So they make everyone work faster — they make the machines and the looms go faster so we have to work even harder. That's how they get their extra two hours. This speed-up of the machines is bad — people get hurt, the head throbs. It's too much for anyone — too much for the children in the mill. Then comes payday. The bosses reduce the pay because it is now a fifty-four-hour week. This is too much, we can't take it. We have trouble making enough money under the old way. So we say — no more work without more pay. We strike."

"But our money. And food. What . . ." began Anna.

"We'll be O.K.," answered Papa reassuringly. "Don't worry."

By night, the children were comforted and fell quickly into a deep slumber. But Mama and Papa couldn't sleep. Mama lay in bed, her hands nervously rubbing her eyes and face. "But *how* will we manage, Caesare? We've almost nothing put away. We need every penny Anna and Nicky bring home. Now we'll have nothing. And you, Caesare, a strike now, just when you are almost well enough to go back to the mill. The bosses will be angry at you. Maybe they won't take you back when the strike is over."

"Ah, Mama, we will manage. This had to happen. Workers cannot put up with being treated like animals."

Mama had stored some cans of food once when the family had a little extra money. Now she carefully rationed them over the first week of the strike. But within days there was not enough money for tea and cheese. Two weeks into the strike, Mama poured out the last drop of milk and spent the last penny.

One night as Anna climbed into bed wearing her coat and socks, she said, "Papa, Nicky and I were standing on the stoop today. We saw this bent and ragged man. Papa, it was Mr. Polti from down the block. Remember his great round face? Now he has such a look of fear, Papa, that Nicky got frightened and ran inside. But I couldn't take my eyes off him."

"Poor Theo," said Papa. "The factory he worked in closed when Pacific did. He has a bigger family than we do. A strike is hard for us all, but we are right in staying out. Don't worry, *bambina*. Mr. Kohler told me that people even in California are hearing about the strike, and they want to help us. There's been talk of opening food stations soon. We'll be O.K. Mr. Polti, too. You'll see."

The looms in Lawrence stood silent. Daily, Papa and sometimes Mama went to strike meetings, walking in subzero temperatures and entering the building through a thicket of hostile policemen. There, crowded into the small room, were hundreds of strikers, a handful of organizers, and dozens of reporters and photographers. They represented newspapers from coast to coast that were running stories about the strike. Headlines read: "High Rents Behind Lawrence Strike," "Congress to Hear of Conditions in Lawrence," "Women and Children March on Picket Lines," "Strikers Sight Victory Ahead," "Food Stations to Open in Lawrence."

Papa greeted the opening of the food stations with relief, even though the provisions given out were hardly enough to feed the nine of them. Every morning before dawn he would set out for the station. Anna liked to go with him. Mama would bundle them up, careful to cover Papa's injured arm, which was still in a sling. As they trudged through the snow, Papa would look up at the sky and say, "No gray skies and snow in Italy, Anna. You remember, yes? Just blazing sunshine and flowers—red ones and yellow ones." Papa was always remembering. As they approached the station Papa would set Anna in a corner to wait while he went to stand in line. From her hideaway she could see the legs of picketing marchers pass by. And she could hear their singing . . .

As we come marching, marching in the beauty of the
*   day,*
A million darkened kitchens, a thousand mill lofts
*   gray,*
Are touched with all the radiance that a sudden sun
*   discloses,*
For the people hear us singing: "Bread and roses!
*   Bread and roses!"*

As we come marching, marching, we battle too for
*   men,*
For they are women's children, and we mother them
*   again.*
Our lives shall not be sweated from birth until life
*   closes;*
Hearts starve as well as bodies; give us bread, but
*   give us roses!*

"Give us bread, but give us roses. Bread and roses." As Anna mouthed the words over and over, images swirled through her mind. There were blooming roses, sweet-scented and soft, caressing her hands; rose petals scattered about her and fell along a path in front of her. "Bread and roses. Bread and roses," she repeated.

One morning as Papa approached the front of the line, Mrs. Papaleo, the woman who ordinarily handed out the bread, said, "Sorry, Caesare. There's no more today. It's gone. I'm sorry." Seeing the look of anguish on Mr. Venuti's face as he turned to leave, Mrs. Papaleo called to him, "Wait. Have you seen this?" She pointed to a small story in the local paper.

> ### AID FROM PHILADELPHIA
> #### Union Bakers Offer Temporary Homes to Children of Strikers
>
> Philadelphia, Feb. 10—Union bakers of this city will adopt temporarily children of families involved in the Lawrence (Mass.) textile strike. This announcement was made today by H. Dornbloom, delegate from the local Bakers' Union to the Central Labor Union. The selection of the children has been left in the hands of the strike committee in Lawrence. Members of the Bakery and Confectionary Workers' Independent Union, who will be assessed to pay for the keep of the children, will have an opportunity to see their wards on February 19th at the tenth anniversary ball of the union.

Mrs. Papaleo added, "I'm going to send my three boys. Maybe you should send Anna and the older ones. Talk to them. They're in charge," she continued, pointing to two people across the street.

Mr. Venuti shook his head no. Send his children away to an unknown city, to strange people? He couldn't. His family was the only thing he had. They'd manage together.

He passed the empty food tables and walked toward Anna. "Anna, we're going."

Anna put aside her dreams, looked up, and smiled. But her smile faded when she noticed Papa was carrying nothing in his arms, not even a loaf of bread. "No dinner tonight," she thought.

As if Papa heard her thoughts and wanted to cheer her, he began to whistle. He was still whistling as they turned onto Merrimac Street. After a few steps he slowed his pace and stopped whistling. Something was wrong. "Where are the picketers?" he thought. A long line of women and children had been marching when he and Anna had left at dawn. Mama and Nicky were among them. Where were they now? Papa grabbed Anna's hand and raced down the block, into their building, and up the stairs. He threw open the door.

"*Gràzie Dio.* You're safe! What happened?"

Mama looked stunned. "Nicola cried himself to sleep," she said without feeling, as if that explained everything. Then she continued, holding her forehead in her hand. "We marched quietly. Only a few people sang. No trouble. And then all of a sudden..." Mama's voice broke off. She began to tremble. "All of a sudden the strike breakers were on us. They hit us and beat us with clubs. Even the children. Mrs. Kohler was hit in the face. She began screaming at them. Nicky and I pulled her away or they would have hit her again. We made it home. Some didn't."

That night Papa was awakened by Nicky's screams. "They're hitting me," he cried to Papa through his tears. "I'm scared."

Papa held Nicky close and stroked his head gently. But no amount of comforting seemed to help the child, and the nightmares continued. It was during the next few long, sleepless nights that Papa and Mama finally decided. They'd send the older children to a family in Philadelphia. At least they would be safe there, and they would have something to eat.

The next day before getting on line at the food station, Mr. Venuti spoke with the people in charge of sending the children away. On the way home Papa explained to Anna what he had done.

"Things are terrible," he said. "I worry all the time about you and Mama and the little ones. Now there is a chance for something better. I spoke with those people about sending you, Nicky, Tony, and Isabel to a safer place for a few weeks. Next Monday we'll take you to the railroad station. Someone from the union will go with you and other children to Philadelphia. Then you'll meet the family you'll stay with." Papa paused and then added, "You want to go?" hoping her answer would make him feel better about the decision. Anna wasn't sure. But she, Nicky, and Tony had never questioned their father's decisions before. Only six-year-old Isabel was concerned. "When will we come back? When will we come back?" she kept asking.

Mama's eyes would fill with tears every time she thought of their going. "It's good, it's good," she would say as if to reassure herself. "Anna will take care of them."

In February 1912, Anna, Nicola, Tony, and Isabel Venuti left for Philadelphia, leaving Mama, Papa, and the three little ones waving on the station platform. All Anna could remember about the first few days in Philadelphia was how much she slept and one incident: she had kicked Nicky under the table for taking four helpings of dinner and gulping them down as fast as he could. The rest was a blur. Slowly, though, they settled in and got used to three meals a day, fresh air, sunshine, and missing the rest of the family. One afternoon, with Nicky close by, Anna wrote home.

Dear Mama and Papa,

We are all fine. We are staying in a big house and I can see the sky from my room. When we are not here, Mr. Weber and his wife live here all alone. Mr. Weber is a baker, and this morning we had soft, fresh bread and butter—all that we could eat. Nicky says to tell you that he drank three glasses of milk without taking a breath.

Isabel and I share a room, and there is another room for Tony and Nicky. We each have our own bed, but Isabel keeps climbing in with me. I love to look out the window at the bright sunshine—just as in Italy. Right outside is a beautiful garden with trees and grass. Mr. Weber told me that in a few weeks I may see flowers there too. Here in Philadelphia we have bread and roses, just as in my dreams. We wish that you were here with us.

We miss you and the babies. We hope you are fine. Kiss the babies for us. Let us know when we can come home.

Love,
Anna and Nicky

Note: The Lawrence strike ended after ten hard weeks. The Venuti children and all the other children who had been sent away returned to their homes in Lawrence carrying gifts of toys and clothing for themselves and their families. The departure of the children had won great sympathy for the strikers. Congress held hearings, and Mrs. William Howard Taft, the wife of the President, attended these hearings to listen to some of the strikers (including children) tell of the horrible conditions in the mills and of the bloodshed and violence during the strike. The strike was considered a victory for the workers since wages were raised, overtime would be paid, and no striker would be punished. The strike did not end child labor, although it did begin to decline in the next several years. It was not until the enactment of the Fair Labor Standards Act in 1938 that child labor began to end.

Corrado Govoni

The Little Trumpet

Translated by Carlo L. Golino

All that is left
of the magic of the fair
is this little trumpet
of blue and green tin,
blown by a girl
as she walks, barefoot, through the fields.
But within its forced note
are all the clowns, white ones and red ones,
the band all dressed in gaudy gold,
the merry-go-round, the calliope, the lights.
Just as in the dripping of the gutter
is all the fearfulness of the storm
the beauty of lightning and the rainbow;
and in the damp flickers of a firefly
whose light dissolves on a heather branch
is all the wondrousness of spring.

DOUBLE
TAKE

420

DOUBLE
TAKE

DOUBLE
TAKE

423

DOUBLE TAK

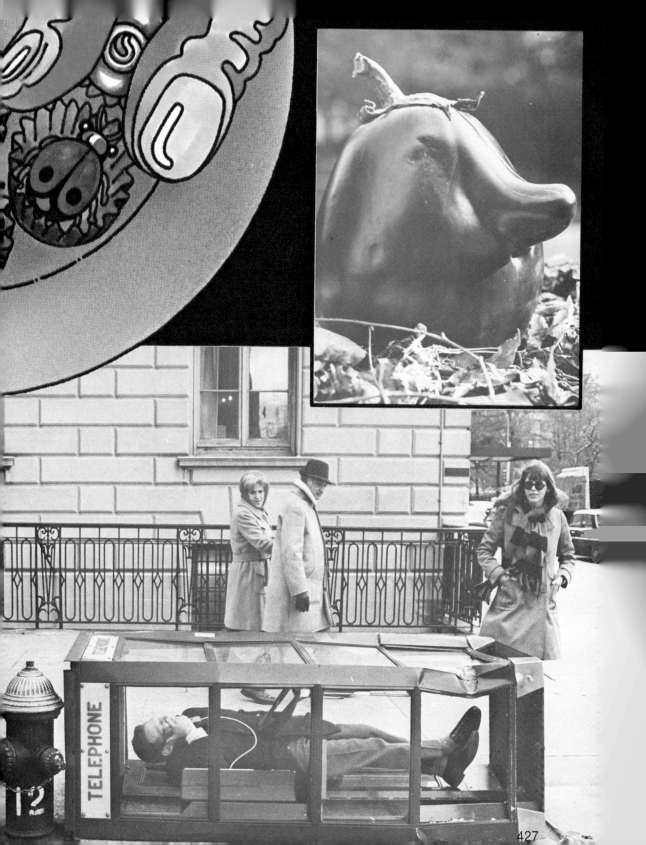

427

Jean McCord

My Teacher, the Hawk

I live on a small place about five miles out of town with my grandparents. It isn't really a farm; we've only got six acres, but we keep chickens and plant a garden, and there's lots of room to grow up in.

My grandparents are good people. Five Christmases ago, when I was ten years old, my grandfather, whom I've always called Popsie, asked me what I wanted that year.

"I'd sure like a gun," I answered, looking slant-eyed at my grandmother, who hated guns and hunting of any sort.

"Larry, you're too young for a gun," my grandmother spoke up. "You could shoot yourself. Or someone else. What would you do with one anyway?" Her mouth was pursed with disapproval, but she kept her eyes down on her sewing.

"Tin cans," I muttered. "Target practice. Lots of kids my age have guns. Jim Johnson's got a real deer rifle." This was almost a downright lie. All he had was a .22, and I knew it.

429

On Christmas morning there was a long, skinny package for me beneath the tree. I sucked in my breath. Had my grandmother relented, or was she pacifying me with a toy bow and arrow set? I ripped open the box. Inside was a beautiful Remington .22 rifle and four boxes of shells.

Popsie's face was a smiling circle. "I talked her into it," he said, nodding his head toward my grandmother, "on condition that you use it properly, of course."

"Oh, Gram." I gave her a bear hug around her short little neck. "You know I'm pretty responsible."

"Huh!" she said, grunting through my hug.

That afternoon Popsie and I went out into the cold, brown fields. Popsie had once been a pretty good hunter himself, but now a bad leg kept him from it. And, I imagined, my grandmother.

"You know, don't you," Popsie was saying, "that you never point a gun at anything or anyone unless you intend to kill them. These stories you hear about accidental shootings are all poppycock as far as I'm concerned. Everyone knows a gun is for one thing only and that is to kill. I don't mean you should ever intend to kill anyone. I'm only saying that if you ever point a gun at a person, even in fun, that's more'n likely what's going to happen."

We'd brought along some empty tin cans and Popsie set them up on a fence post. He showed me how to load the gun, how to carry it safely, and even made me practice going through a fence with it. I had to unload every time, set the gun through the wires, and then crawl through myself.

When we were potting at the tin cans, Popsie scored a hit every time, but I never even saw where my shots were going.

"It's a matter of relaxing," he kept telling me. "Everything in the world is best done relaxed. Believe me. Even work. Most of all, work."

We shot up all the shells. By the end of the day I knew what

Popsie meant. Line up the sights, relax, squeeze the trigger slowly, and no flinching when the gun goes off.

I was content with just target practice for a long time, but when I got so I could hit the cans ten times out of ten shots, I began to look around for something a little more exciting. My first chance came when Grandma came raging in from her garden.

"Those blasted jack rabbits." She slammed down a puny handful of carrots the size of my fingers. "They went right down the rows. Ate half the lettuce, all the carrot tops, and most of the beet tops, too."

It was spring now and Grandma worked her garden in the early morning and again in the evenings until the light failed. She looked like a little hunched-over scarecrow out there in the twilight.

I didn't say anything to her, but that evening after she had straightened up and put away her tools, with Popsie's consent I sneaked down to the garden and cleverly concealed myself in a clump of bushes. When the rabbits came, I could see them clearly in the wash of moonlight that lay over the land, and I picked them off one by one. Rabbits are pretty dumb. They kept coming back, and I kept getting them that night and several nights afterward. In a couple of days Grandma's garden was growing in peace. She didn't say a word to me about it. I guess she knew it was either that or lose her entire garden.

One night we were sitting around, Popsie reading his paper, and I was studying. Suddenly we heard a terrible commotion in the hen house. There is nothing in the world noisier than a bunch of frightened chickens, and they had really cut loose this time. Popsie and I jumped up, and I raced to my bedroom for my gun. We got to the hen house just in time to see a big raccoon coming out with two eggs clutched to its chest. Its startled face with those black lines on it looking like a masked bandit peered up at us in the light of Popsie's flashlight. The sight of such a bold robber who had braved squawking hens and my gun for the sake of two eggs made me laugh so hard, I fired over its head just to scare it. The raccoon dropped the stolen eggs and hightailed it to another county.

After that I gave up shooting at tin cans. Instead I roamed the countryside taking potshots at whatever flew or moved beneath my sights. I did in a lot of ground squirrels, and I don't know how many mourning doves because they just sat low on a tree limb giving out with those sad calls of theirs. Something about their mournful cries in the bright warm sunlight and the good smells of summer infuriated me, and I shot every one I could. I popped off all the blue jays, and in the back of my mind, I could hear Popsie vindicating me.

"The blue jays rob other nests, and Larry kills the blue jays. It's a balance of nature that used to be taken care of in other ways."

And, of course, with these minor triumphs, I began to swell with ambition for something really big and thrilling. I could see myself in the future as a brave hunter going to Africa and bringing down one of everything. A ground squirrel became in my imagination a rhinoceros who charged ferociously, and I brought it to its knees just three feet away from myself, and I had to keep shooting lions and tigers and such that were creeping around my tent and about to eat me up. By the time I was fourteen, I'd just about shot out every animal in Africa, from the scoreboard in my mind.

I was fifteen when the thing happened to me that changed my life forever. I know now that I'll never hunt or kill a living thing again. I'd hung up my gun in my bedroom and hadn't had time for much hunting because now there was always work to be done around the place: fences to be repaired, tinkering with Popsie's old Dodge that should have been retired years ago, and always schoolwork. Some teachers seemed to think a guy had nothing to do except make reports and write essays and study like he was making out to be a Nobel prize winner or something.

It was a Sunday morning and Grandma had gone off to services, after which she would stand around and yak a lot with old friends. I don't know what they found to talk about, but it always seemed to entrance them for hours.

Popsie came in from outside, stomping his big feet at the door to shake the mud. "There's a hawk after the chickens," he announced. "He's been around all week. Got over half of the Banty chicks already."

We looked at each other. When a person keeps livestock and animals, it becomes a duty, and a right, to protect them from predators. It's always been that way.

I went into my bedroom and unracked my gun, wondering in the back of my mind if I had lost my skill. I walked out into our orchard of old gnarled trees and went down to the far end, leaning against one of the trees to load my gun and look around.

I saw him then, floating high on air currents, almost over my head, and looking down at the grass. I saw that the mother hen with the remaining half of her little black chicks had seen him too and was clucking in a frantic manner. The baby chicks stooped close to the ground and hid their heads and bright eyes so that only their little black bottoms showed as a smudge against the earth.

I aimed through the branches of the tree as the hawk drifted sideways, riding the wind like some child's kite, loose and on its own, and when he was in my sights, I let go. With the crack of the gun and the smell of acrid smoke came a sudden change in the arrogant flight of the hawk. He slipped sideways against the wind, one wing folded under him, and the other spread out like black fingers clawing at the sky. He went into a power dive, headed straight at the ground, gaining speed every second. He hit somewhere at the bottom of the orchard.

Setting my gun down, I raced to where I had seen him smash, but though I searched every bit of brush and grass clumps, he was nowhere to be found.

When I returned to the house, Popsie raised an eyebrow at me over his Sunday paper.

"Got him," I said. "He won't be eating chicken dinners anymore."

Then I forgot about the hawk as I cleaned and racked my gun and sat down at the dining-room table with my books and papers.

The next day it rained. The day after, it not only rained, it poured down water from the sky as if someone had pulled a plug from the bottom of the ocean. Five days later it was still raining and everyone's nerves were rusty and raw. The teachers were getting so snappy no one dared do anything except bend over books and try to study in gloomy light.

On Saturday morning the rain turned itself down into a thin

drizzle, and I felt as if I had been living underwater for almost a week. I decided to take a short walk just to get out of the house for a while.

Without thinking, because it was simply easier to walk downhill, I sloughed through the dripping grass toward the bottom of the orchard. And it was while I was standing there, looking off into a light mist below our land, that I saw the hawk.

He was standing upright on spindly legs beneath a mesquite bush, and he was glaring at me out of red-rimmed eyes as if he wanted to stare me to death. I was shocked. Popsie's teaching words of five years ago hit me in the stomach. "A hunter never lets a wounded animal get away to die a lingering, painful death . . ."

Yeah! I was some sportsman. I had knocked this animal down out of his territory, the sky, and left him helpless in the pouring rain for a week. I had honestly thought him dead last Sunday, but that didn't excuse me. Standing there with the drizzle falling down my neck, I had to face up to what I really was, and it left me feeling sick and shameful.

I took a step toward the hawk, not knowing quite what I was going to do. He didn't back off; instead he set himself for a fight. He lifted one wing, shifted his weight like a boxer, and stretched his neck toward me with his beak ready like a sword. His other wing was broken at the shoulder, and it dragged on the ground with the pinion feathers all splayed and ragged. Standing tensed that way, I could see better what had happened to him. His body had shrunken in along the breastbone, and he looked more like a bundle of wet old rags than the powerful bird he had once been. I knew he was starving. And, with that thought, I also knew I had to help him.

I slipped out of my jacket, spread it wide, and threw it over him. He put up a struggle, but couldn't get at me through the heavy leather which I pulled under and around his knife-edge claws. I picked the whole bundle up carefully. I didn't know what I was going to do with him, and I was too ashamed to ask Popsie. We had a small toolshed used only for storage, so I took him there and set him on a table, trying to ease my jacket out from him. His claws had hooked into the lining and he clung to it. When I reached to loosen them, his beak plunged down and split open the back of my hand. "Well," I thought, jerking my hand up to my mouth, "I guess maybe I deserved that."

"Keep the jacket, Joe Louis," I said. "I'll fix my hand up, then try to see what you'll eat."

I sneaked into the house, wanting to bandage my hand before my grandparents saw it and asked a lot of questions. I had no stomach for answering questions right then. Fortunately they were somewhere in the front of the house, so I fixed my hand, then went to the refrigerator wondering what a hawk might eat. I took out some hamburger and a slice of bologna.

When I eased myself through the toolshed door, the hawk was stepping disdainfully out of my jacket as if he had killed it good and proper. I tossed the meat toward him, not wanting to lose another hand, and in a flash he pounced on it, ripping the slice of bologna in half, and tried to swallow the whole chunk. It stuck halfway in his throat, so he spit it out and tried the hamburger. He could handle this better, and ate it all. Then he swayed toward me, clattering his beak, as if he were really ready to fight.

We watched each other. When he saw I wasn't going to attack him again, he eased to the back of the table into a corner and hunched down, letting his eyes film over, like he couldn't be bothered with me anymore.

I left him then. At least, he was out of the rain and had eaten, probably the first time in a week.

On Sunday I fed him some more hamburger balls and left a pan of milk beside his dish of water. I was pretty sure he wouldn't know anything about milk, but I was willing to try anything.

Monday noon, at the school cafeteria, I went over to this rather big girl named Janice Allack. I'd never spoken to her before, but I knew her reputation for rescuing and finding homes for all sorts of orphan animals. I'd heard she had about fifty cats and no one knew how many dogs out at her home. She ran a regular animal-shelter league, and probably knew more about animals than anyone else around for hundreds of miles.

"Look," I said, sort of low to her, "I've got this hawk out at my home. His wing's busted. I wonder if you could come out and sort of show me what to do? You know, put it in a splint, or something?"

"Why, sure, Larry." She looked up at me over her macaroni and cheese. "I'll ride the bus home with you tonight. O.K.?"

"O.K." I went back to my lunch feeling relieved. If Janice could fix up the hawk, repair his wing so he could fly again, maybe he'd quit hating me so much, and I'd stop feeling like a low-down worm.

I rode home with Janice sitting by my side chatting happily about all the animals she had fixed up. I guess she was doing what made her feel good. I never mentioned all the animals I had killed.

"Where'd you get the hawk?" she asked.

"Oh, I found him out in the field," I said. "My grandparents don't know about him yet. I've got him locked up in the tool-shed."

"Well, there's nothing shameful about helping a wounded animal," she said, twisting sideways to look at me.

"No, I guess not," I answered, shrinking down in my seat.

We jumped off the bus and walked up the lane to my home. It had finally stopped raining, but the ground still felt like you were walking on a sodden sponge.

My grandparents were a little surprised at seeing Janice. It was the first time I'd ever brought a girl home. I guess they thought I was never going to get to that stage.

Then Grandma said, "Larry, what do you have locked in the toolshed? It's been screaming in rage all day."

Janice and I looked at each other.

"Give me some hamburger, Gram. I've got to feed it," I said. "It's a hawk."

I took Janice down to the shed and unlocked it. When we came through the door, the hawk was sitting on the highest shelf; somehow he'd managed to climb up there, knocking over everything in his way. He launched himself straight at us and the open door, but he only managed one wing stroke before he fell to the floor and spun around in dusty circles. You could see he wasn't ever going to be a tame bird.

"Oh, the poor thing." Janice knelt down beside him, and before I could yell at her to watch out, she had her hands on him, pinning both wings so he couldn't hurt himself any more. And surprisingly, the hawk held still, craning his neck around to watch Janice examine his broken wing.

When she finished, she set him carefully back up on the shelf. I thought he would strike at her, but he didn't. He just ruffled his feathers a bit in indignation.

"I don't think it can be fixed, Larry," she said gravely. "The bones are too shattered; he can't ever fly again. But isn't he a beauty? He's a redtail, isn't he?"

"I guess," I muttered. I really felt bad. She'd been my only hope of fixing up things between me and the hawk. "Here." I tossed his hamburger up beside him, but now he ignored it.

Janice spied a leather glove. She put it on and held the meat under the hawk's beak. She sure did know a lot about things, that girl. But the hawk wouldn't eat for her either.

"I don't think hamburger is exactly what he's used to," she said. "I'd try him on something else. A piece of steak maybe, cut in strips. If he won't eat that, you'd better go out and get him fresh food."

"Like what?" I croaked.

"Oh, I'd say live mice. And probably little frogs." She sounded so offhand, as if it were the easiest thing in the world. "That's what I'd do." She turned to me. "You do want to keep him alive, don't you? Have you named him yet?"

"Sure," I mumbled. "Sure. I call him Joe Louis." I showed her the back of my hand. "He's a real fighter. He might be down, but he isn't out."

"Joey," she said softly. "That's a nice name." She looked up at the hawk in sympathy. "I've got to go now. But maybe I can help you with him. Anyway, I'll come back. That is, if you want me to?" she added shyly.

"Well, sure. Sure I do. Thanks." I'd never noticed before but Janice Allack was sort of pretty. Her hair was a soft brown, and her eyes were friendly, and she had this nice feeling of confidence about her as if she really knew who she was and what she would make out of her life. She was bigger than I was, but that was just for now. I hadn't gotten all my growth yet, but I knew it would come.

She came along with me again, three days later. The hawk had refused to eat anything, even a lamb chop that I'd wheedled out of Gram. And he screeched all the time, striking out in fury at the cans of paint and tools strewn around him. The day before, I'd put him in a large cage for his own sake, and by now he had torn the sides of the cage into splintery shreds.

Janice dug into a big purse she was carrying. "Here," she said, handing me a box. "My cats bring them in, you know." She hurried outside while I opened the box. Inside were two live mice. Wow! I thought. Whew! A girl who'd actually carry mice in her handbag. That was really something.

I tossed the mice in to Joey, being a little queasy about it myself, and Joey hit like a flash of light and the mice were dead quicker than they would have been in a trap.

"That's more like it," I said, going outside. "Only you'd better wait a minute before going back in."

We leaned against the wall, looking over the land which was coming into full bloom, it being spring and all. The grass was very tall and deep green, and the fruit trees were all covered with a pink froth that looked almost good enough to eat. Birds were darting all around, carrying things in their beaks, getting ready to make nests.

Inside, in a cage, Joey sat hunched over and brooding. I was beginning to know what he must have felt, feeling the air of spring, knowing the thin, blue sky was still out there and the winds rising and somewhere, maybe, a mate looking for him.

"Larry," Janice said, looking at me, "have you ever read a story by Walter Van Tilburg Clark? It's called 'Hook.' Just 'Hook.' And it's about a hawk who gets shot down out of the sky and has to live on bugs and battle other birds. In the end he has a fight with a dog." She didn't say anything for a while, then, "I think it is really and truly the most beautiful story I've ever read." She smiled, and turned to go in. "Let's see how Joey is doing."

She stood looking at the cage. "He's terribly angry, isn't he? It must be fierce, having a temper like that." She didn't say any more, but she didn't have to. It was all there in the tone of her voice. I knew she had guessed about me being the one who'd shot him. And I also knew, somehow, that she was trying to teach me something.

"Things do happen," she was saying. "Life is never absolutely safe for any of us, people or hawks. One does what one can, and that's all." She was murmuring to the hawk, and I guess because he had finally eaten, he was allowing her to stroke the top of his head very softly. "Joey, Joey," she told him, "you'll have to learn to accept."

She turned to me. "You'd better start hunting again. Things for him to eat. Try frogs. He won't eat any more hamburger, I'm sure."

So I found myself going out at night, once more the brave hunter, only it didn't seem very noble to be sloshing around in swampy places getting covered with muck for the sake of tiny frogs. After a while, though, it got to be a pretty good game if I could restrain myself from moving or shining my light until the frogs had all started singing madly in chorus like a high-school glee club lacking only a director.

Joey didn't have to eat every day. He wasn't moving around, so his appetite had dwindled down to a mouse and two or three frogs a week. His wing healed after a while, but not so he could raise it and fly with it. He spent a lot of time preening the feathers on it, straightening them out with his beak, as if he still had hopes.

After I'd had him over four months, and managed to feed him and keep him alive, I had thought he might get to know me and be friendlier. Oh, he knew me all right. He knew I was the one to bring him food, clean his cage, put him out in the sun, and inside again. But he also remembered about the other. And he never forgave me. If I gave him the slightest chance, he was ready to rip and tear at me with claws and his wicked beak. Yet, when Janice came over to see him, he allowed her to pick him up and pet him, without once attacking her.

Still, I was getting terribly fond of him. He was a big part of my life. His complete dependence on me for food and care made me realize what it would be like to have kids to feed and all that.

And he seemed to be getting much better. His eyes lost their bitter glaze, and his feathers smoothed out and the red color came back into them. The white underparts of him were all snowy and his long curved claws seemed to get sharper than ever, if that were possible. His voice had always been loud and screechy, grating across your nerves like a piece of chalk rubbed the wrong way on a blackboard. And, as he got stronger, he screamed more.

If only I could set him free, I thought. Toss him back up there where he'd been floating so arrogantly. What were a few chickens? Popsie and I should have penned them up long ago, I told myself. It was our own fault he came around.

Janice and I were pretty good friends now. We had a common bond. I no longer considered her sort of nutty for having so many animals. In fact, I even talked Gram into taking a couple of cats off her hands.

I wrote a theme on Joey, submitted it for my English project, and got an A on it.

And every day I heard his mad screeches from the toolshed.

Janice came over one day, bringing her usual gifts from her cats. I had to laugh a little wildly. I guess I'd been spending too much time out in the swamps, not getting enough sleep, and the pressure of the last bit of school was telling on me. School would be over for summer vacation in a week. Then I'd have more time.

We walked down to the toolshed, and she went in, while I went to get some fresh water.

She came right out again and over to where I was running a hose.

"Listen," she said, squatting down by me, "Joey's dead."

We stared at each other, and my throat closed itself into a tight knot while the water ran all over my shoes.

"But he was getting better!" I cried angrily.

"He couldn't take it, Larry." She laid her hand on my arm. "It was prison to him, and he knew he had a life sentence. No way out, except one. Don't you see?"

We stood up and looked out over the peaceful countryside. The sky was empty. The chickens, poor dumb things, clucked safely to each other and rolled in the dust with no worries.

We buried him over on the top of a small rocky point where the wind blew around in rising circles, and nothing ever went there.

My life was empty for a long time.

To say he never forgave me is one thing. To say I've never forgiven myself is another. And worse. Joey escaped from his cage, his prison, but he still lives on in the back of my mind, screeching in fury. I don't think I'll ever escape from him.

GETTING A FEELING

Have you ever experienced a feeling or an emotion while reading a story or a poem? Have you ever been able to feel what the characters in a story were feeling? You may have felt frightened, sad, shocked, happy, or angry. It is most likely that the mood of the story or the poem was set for you by the author.

Establishing the mood of a piece is one of the ways in which writers involve their readers. By creating a *mood* or a *tone,* writers make their work more interesting and effective. An author's selection of words is very important to the mood of a story because many words call up certain associations in the mind of the reader. For example, read the following words: joyfully; panicky; bursting greenness; soft, soothing voice; long darkness; silently stirring; trembled; snarling; forlorn.

How did each word or expression make you feel? What mental pictures did you have as you read? Do you remember times when any or some of the words listed above could describe your own feelings?

One way an author establishes mood is by describing the surroundings, or places, in the story. For example, what mood does the following paragraph, taken from "My Teacher, the Hawk," put you in?

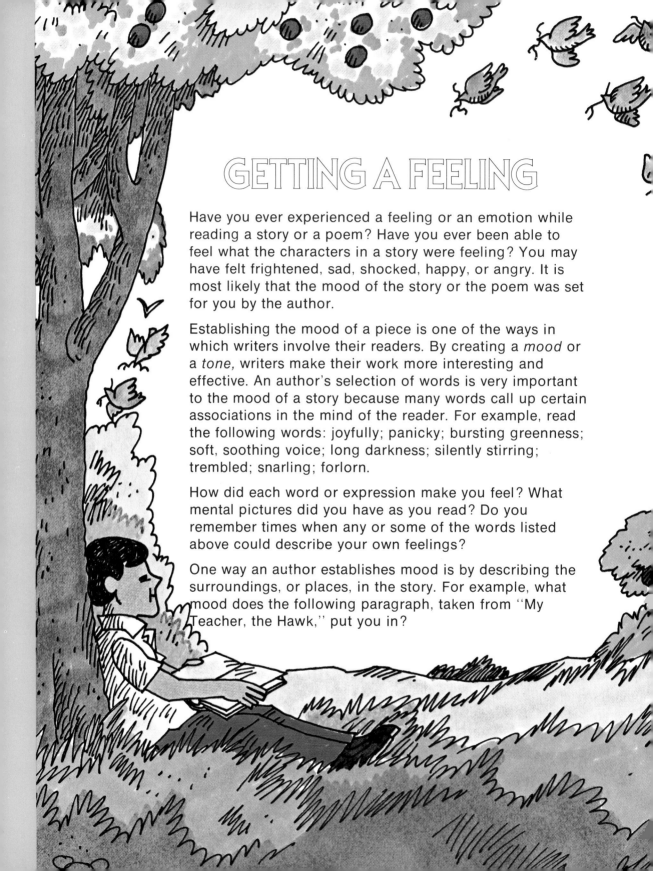

The grass was very tall and deep green, and the fruit trees were all covered with a pink froth that looked almost good enough to eat. Birds were darting all around, carrying things in their beaks, getting ready to make nests.

Would you expect much description of this sort in a story intended to terrify you? In a few sentences, tell why or why not.

Make a list with the following words as headings: suspense; happiness; fright; sadness; anger. Under each heading, write as many words, descriptions of characters, and phrases as you can think of that could be used to create the particular mood. Choose one emotion, and write a few paragraphs or a poem creating the appropriate mood. Can some words be used to set more than one mood?

Remember, the mood of a well-written piece should be consistent throughout. That is, every aspect of the story that surrounds the plot—events, settings, descriptions of characters, and their actions and reactions—will contribute to the mood of the story.

447

Alexander Solzhenitsyn
The Puppy

Translated by Michael Glenny

In our backyard a boy keeps his little dog Sharik chained up, a ball of fluff shackled since he was a puppy.

One day I took him some chicken bones that were still warm and smelled delicious. The boy had just let the poor dog off his lead to have a run round the yard. The snow there was deep and feathery; Sharik was bounding about like a hare, first on his hind legs, then on his front ones, from one corner of the yard to the other, back and forth, burying his muzzle in the snow.

He ran toward me, his coat all shaggy, jumped up at me, sniffed the bones — then off he went again, belly-deep in the snow.

I don't need your bones, he said. Just give me my freedom.

Nick Pease

ANNIE DODGE WAUNEKA

On a soft Arizona night not long ago, a woman named Annie Dodge Wauneka lay gazing out her bedroom window. It was a still night, so still she could faintly hear the howl of a coyote somewhere out on the desert. She held her gaze on the full moon, hanging large and solitary in the sky, so alone and so isolated. . . .

Gradually her lined face began to cloud over, a look of sadness creeping into her dark eyes. Her mind was roaming back to other Arizona nights of long ago, nights robbed of their stillness by a sense of fear and dread. And she keenly recalled the isolation she had felt as the hours dragged by. She shook her head slightly, trying to dislodge the thought.

The year of that recollection was 1918, and the place was the government boarding school for Indians at Fort Defiance. Eight-year-old Annie Dodge was there for the school year, together with children from a half-dozen tribes in the area. That year the school had been brought almost to a standstill by a dreadful epidemic of influenza that was sweeping the land. Throughout Arizona, the rest of the United States, and the world, more than 18 million people were dying of the disease. Each week more and more children were being sent home by the school for care. Many never returned.

Annie herself escaped with a mild case of the flu, and she put in long hours helping the one overworked nurse tend to the sick. Each morning she cleaned out the sooty kerosene lamps and placed them in hospital rooms, and during the day she carried meals and helped keep the place clean. The hard work and the constant presence of death left an indelible stamp on the young girl's mind.

Annie was born a Navajo, a tribe that counted itself among the poorest in the United States. In 1863 Kit Carson and the American troops had completed the conquest of the Navajos, and the Navajo reservation had been set up in the Arizona Territory. The people settled down to raise their cattle and sheep, but a peacetime existence brought unforeseen problems. Over the years the tribal population increased drastically, straining the food supply. More animals were raised and, as grazing increased, the valuable prairie grass disappeared, and strong winds began blowing the topsoil away. By the 1920s the reservation was becoming a desert, and its people — overpopulated, underfed, and housed in dirt-floored hogans — were falling prey to many diseases.

A courageous figure during this hopeless time was Annie's father, Chee Dodge. When Annie was thirteen, Chee was named chairman of the newly formed Tribal Council, a body set up to work with the federal government for the rights of Native Americans. As an astute politician, Chee was an effective force in the tribe's behalf. During the summers Annie always returned home from boarding school to help on the ranch, and while there she learned much about government and life beyond the reservation.

But what she learned most from her father was the value of education. This was his constant theme. One day Chee was invited to speak at the Albuquerque Indian School, which Annie then attended, and she listened carefully to his words. The world is a complicated place, he told the children, and there are now problems our traditional remedies can no longer solve. If we want our precious Indian heritage to survive, he said, we must learn new solutions and put them to use.

One of the worst problems, Annie knew, was disease. Tuberculosis was a chronic, and deadly, affliction. And an eye disease called trachoma was so widespread that her old school

452

at Fort Defiance had been converted to a permanent treatment center. If ever a problem called for greater public education — inside and outside the tribe — disease was it!

This idea grew in Annie's mind as she grew into womanhood. And as she grew, she also received a very special kind of instruction from her father. Always respectful of Navajo tradition, Chee Dodge had paid special attention to the oral ceremonies of the tribe. These ceremonies demanded an absolute exactness of speech, for to misuse a single word was to shatter the ceremonies' perfection and destroy their power. Chee's skill at speaking and translating, together with his ability to communicate with Navajos and non-Navajos alike, was his strength as a leader. It was this skill that he passed on to his daughter.

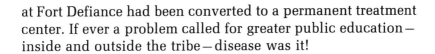

Around 1930, when Annie was twenty years old, a great controversy was stirring on the reservation. The U.S. government was proposing a law to force Native Americans to reduce their cattle herds, which were badly overgrazing the land. Naturally, most of the tribe members were outraged — cattle-raising was the Navajo way of life. They could not foresee that erosion would ruin the soil. The task of educating the people fell to Chee Dodge and other leaders. Intelligent and skilled in speech, Annie also took up the task.

When Annie first went along to meeting houses with her father, she was very shy. But Chee Dodge gave her valuable encouragement. "Don't be afraid to speak your mind," he told her, "but never lose your respect for your elders or for the old people who have lived before you. If it weren't for them and their courage, you wouldn't be here." Under his guidance she developed her natural abilities, and soon she was winning the respect of all who came to hear her.

As she gained in self-confidence, Annie also began campaigning for the issue that had long concerned her — improving the health of Native Americans. To her Navajo audiences she forcefully called for cleaner living conditions. The Navajos had heard such speeches before but rarely with such power and eloquence. For the first time, people were beginning to listen.

But just at about this time, as Annie was making progress, personal tragedy struck: the aging Chee Dodge was near death. Although father and daughter had always been close, they became even more so during those final days. Shortly before he died, Chee told her, "Do not let my straight rope fall to the ground. If you discover it dropping, quickly pick it up and hold it aloft."

The words went to Annie's heart, strengthening her determination to carry on for him. After his death she joined her Council chapter to serve as interpreter. Her spirits rose as her efforts increased, and within four years she was elected to the Tribal Council, becoming the first woman member ever chosen. The election had an amusing side as well, for one of the candidates she defeated was George Wauneka, her husband, whom she had married some years earlier. Building on that success, Annie Dodge Wauneka was appointed chairperson of

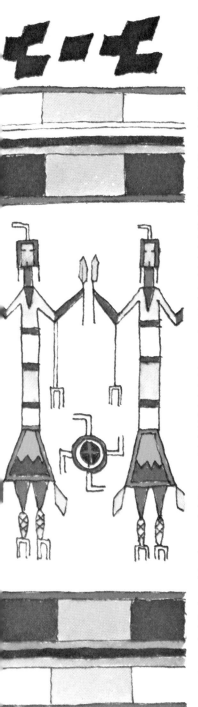

the Council's Health and Welfare Committee. And when the Surgeon General of the United States organized the Advisory Committee on Indian Health, she was invited to become a member.

Now she was really becoming a health crusader. First she concentrated her energies on tuberculosis, the scourge of the Navajo people. She began by going to hospitals and laboratories to learn all she could about the disease. For three months she studied X rays, squinted at microscope slides, and observed patients. Finally, equipped with all that she had learned, she began to visit tubercular Navajo patients to explain to them in their own language what was wrong with them and what their treatment would be. She visited private homes, persuading those who despaired to continue treatment in the hospitals. Annie wrought changes wherever she went, and no distance was too far for her to go.

Tirelessly she educated her people in better health habits. For two years she even had her own radio program to speak to her people in Navajo about health. And she used her Council position to have funds set aside for a home-improvement program. Her call for running water in the homes was a key issue. In the desert area water had to be hauled over long distances in metal drums that were often dirty – a prime reason why much illness could be traced to the water supply. But thanks to her strong campaigning, the government finally authorized the Public Health Service to construct, improve, and extend sanitary facilities for Native Americans.

Annie's work and dedication played a part in bringing tremendous changes to the reservation. Among the Navajo people the incidence of tuberculosis has been so greatly reduced that it is no longer a major problem. New health facilities are presently being built all over the 16-million-acre Navajo reservation. Furthermore, medicine men once hostile to the doctors are now working right alongside them as respected partners. How was this miracle accomplished? Again, through the unique talents of Annie Dodge Wauneka. Speaking persuasively to the medicine men, in a language they understood, she was able to convey the importance of modern medical knowledge. In communicating with the white doctors, she impressed on them the value and significance of the medicine man in Navajo life. The reconciliation has resulted in many improvements, not just in health care but in race relations as well.

Although Annie never sought personal glory, over the years she has received many honors and awards. She was named Arizona's "Woman of Achievement" by the Arizona Press Women's Association. She was also given the Indian Achievement Award for her service to humanity. As a crown to her endeavors, in 1964 she won the Presidential Medal of Freedom — the highest civilian honor our nation can bestow and the first such award ever given to a Native American. Annie proudly received the award from President Lyndon B. Johnson in the White House.

But personal recognition neither bedazzled this fine woman nor slowed her efforts on behalf of her people. Like her father before her, Annie continually stressed the need for education, but she blended with his words the feelings she held during her own lonely education far from home. "Indian parents must have a say in where schools are to be located," she declared. "We want to keep our children near us, not send them miles away. . . . Indian schools must be Indian community centers as well."

Annie continued to be a vigorous crusader. She could have, without criticism, retired to a quieter life and enjoyed the company of the nine children she raised. Instead, she found a deeper satisfaction by continuing to work with the Tribal Council for the betterment of Indian life.

On that still Arizona night not long ago, remembrances of those hard-won victories clung to Annie's mind as she lay peacefully resting. Thoughts came, too, of the challenges that remain. She glanced again through the window and saw that the moon had risen higher. No longer was she aware of its isolation. Now she thought only of its serenity and of the soft glow it cast, smoothing the harshness of the desert with its limpid light. Slowly, her features softened and composed, she drifted off to sleep.

There are several reasons why people read the newspaper. In addition to reading the latest news, people also use the newspaper as a reference tool. Some of the most common reference tools the newspaper provides are the radio and TV listings and the guide to movies.

Television	Radio	Movie Guide
Evening	**Music**	Adams Cinema
6:00 (1,3,5) News	6-8 WJSK-FM	The Soft Hello
(6) Science Hour	Symphony No 86	(6:30, 8:30, 10:30)
(9) Movie "It	Haydn.	
came from Venus"	6:05-7 WJBP AM	Baron Theater
6:30 (4) Daniel Smith	Quintet in A	The Boy Farmer
Show.	minor	(6:00, 7:00)
	Elga Holtz, cond.	

Look at the samples above. What similar information do they all give to the reader? Where in the newspaper do they appear? From your local newspaper, cut out a sample of each media listing (radio, TV, and movie) and paste them on a separate sheet of paper. Next to each cutout, indicate if it appears in the paper on a daily or a weekly basis and if it appears on the same page each time. Also indicate if in your newspaper there are any reviews or articles about individual radio programs, TV shows, movies, or plays. Note whether they are written daily or not, who writes them, and where they appear in the paper.

As another service to its readers the newspaper provides daily columns. A column may be written about anything, and there are usually several in each newspaper. Some daily columns are *syndicated.* A syndicated column is written regularly by the same person and is sold to many newspapers throughout the country. It appears as a regular feature of the newspaper. Many famous journalists have syndicated columns. Comic strips are often syndicated.

From a copy of your local newspaper, clip the articles that are featured regularly. Note who writes them and what they are written about. Columns may be about economics or politics or about less serious things. Note whether the column is syndicated or not. If it is, there will be a line saying so.

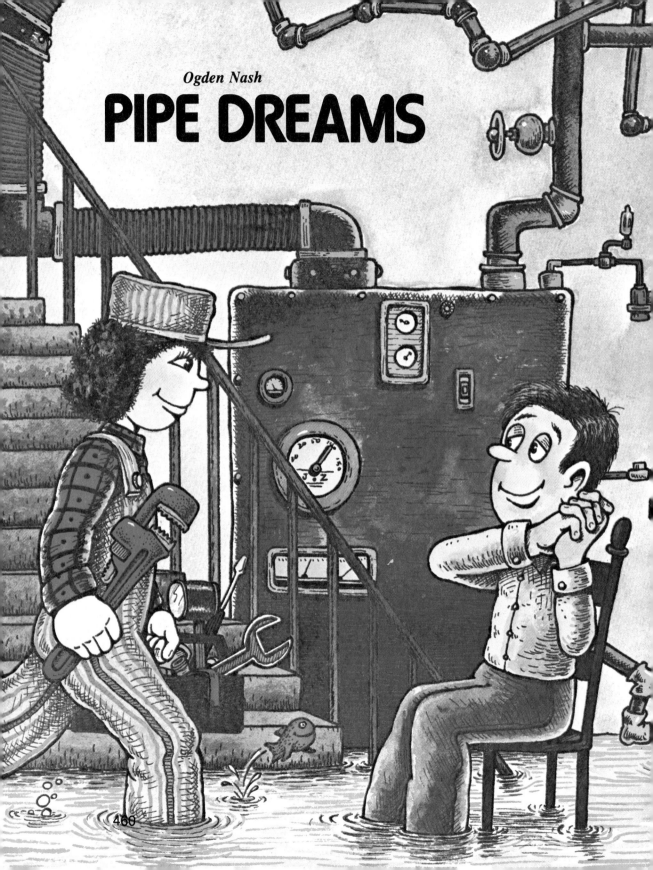

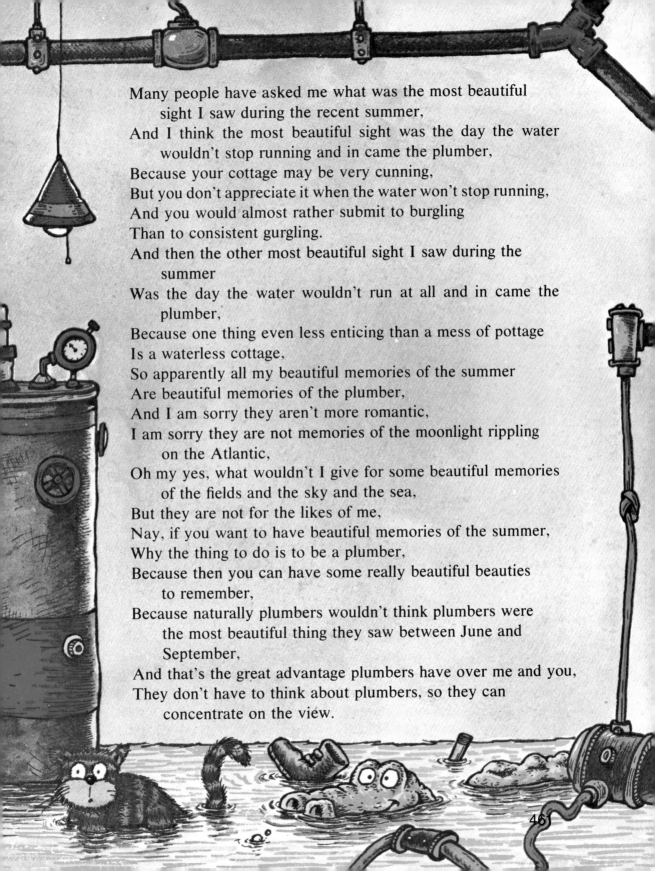

Many people have asked me what was the most beautiful
        sight I saw during the recent summer,
And I think the most beautiful sight was the day the water
        wouldn't stop running and in came the plumber,
Because your cottage may be very cunning,
But you don't appreciate it when the water won't stop running,
And you would almost rather submit to burgling
Than to consistent gurgling.
And then the other most beautiful sight I saw during the
        summer
Was the day the water wouldn't run at all and in came the
        plumber,
Because one thing even less enticing than a mess of pottage
Is a waterless cottage,
So apparently all my beautiful memories of the summer
Are beautiful memories of the plumber,
And I am sorry they aren't more romantic,
I am sorry they are not memories of the moonlight rippling
        on the Atlantic,
Oh my yes, what wouldn't I give for some beautiful memories
        of the fields and the sky and the sea,
But they are not for the likes of me,
Nay, if you want to have beautiful memories of the summer,
Why the thing to do is to be a plumber,
Because then you can have some really beautiful beauties
        to remember,
Because naturally plumbers wouldn't think plumbers were
        the most beautiful thing they saw between June and
        September,
And that's the great advantage plumbers have over me and you,
They don't have to think about plumbers, so they can
        concentrate on the view.

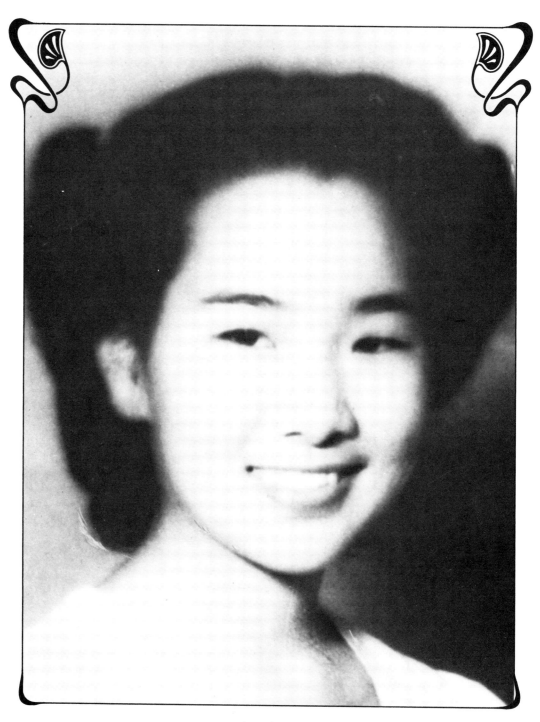

Michi Nishiura

Harriet Shapiro

MICHI

When the United States entered World War II in December 1941, fifteen-year-old Michi Nishiura was one of 93,000 Japanese Americans living in California. Her father, Tomojiro Nishiura, an immigrant from Japan, grew cantaloupes, tomatoes, cucumbers, and apricots for the owner of a 500-acre farm in a small town in the San Joaquin Valley, some fifty miles east of San Francisco. Twenty-four hundred miles to the west, on December 7, 1941, the United States fleet at Pearl Harbor in Hawaii was attacked. The following morning the United States declared war on Japan.

On February 19, 1942, President Franklin D. Roosevelt signed Executive Order 9066, which would in time consign the Nishiuras and 110,000 persons of Japanese ancestry living along the Pacific Coast to relocation centers. Along with 14,000 other Japanese Americans, Michi, her sister, Tomi, and her parents were to spend several years in the Gila (heel-a) Relocation Center in Arizona. There were nine other camps like Gila in the United States.

"Many Japanese Americans have been quiet about the internment for all these years because it's still painful to talk about what happened to us," Michi explained recently in New York City where she now lives. She was for many years a successful costume designer, and her husband is a perfume chemist. She is the author of *Years of Infamy*, a well-researched and documented history of the internment of Japanese Americans during World War II. But in her book she did not describe her own experiences at Gila. Why? Michi explains that she still feels ill at ease talking about the two years that she spent in the Arizona camp.

"Because I haven't wanted to harbor any ill feelings, I have tried to erase unpleasant memories from my mind," she says. "It becomes very difficult to reconstruct what you have tried to wipe out." It was much easier for her to talk first about growing up on a farm before the war. She lived with her family in a large, rundown house where the croquet field near the fig and olive trees was one of the few traces of elegance left over from the days when the farm was an estate.

Michi's family lived on the ground floor, and the migrant laborers whom Tomojiro Nishiura supervised lived on the floor above them. The farm's population swelled at harvest time, and its barns and toolsheds became hastily converted sleeping quarters. Some workers who had driven into the farmlands to pick crops pitched their tents in the large front yard. All the Nishiuras were out in the fields, too. There were many nights they worked straight through until dawn irrigating the vegetables. With a kerosene lantern, Michi, who looked like a skinny little boy, waited across the field in the dark at the dry end of the irrigation ditch. There she would wave the lantern as a signal to her father just before the water reached her feet. She fed the chickens and horses. Many mornings she would work a few hours before she went to school, all the time trying to prove to her father that she was as valuable as the son he had wanted when she was born. "In Japanese culture," Michi explains, "it's disastrous if a family doesn't have an heir, a male offspring to carry on the family name and help in the fields."

During summer months her morning chores involved driving the workers in the back of a Ford truck to the crops. Then she would return to look after the farm's noisy gang of cats and dogs. Whenever they could, Michi and her sister rescued kittens their neighbors had bundled into gunnysacks and abandoned on the Nishiura's road.

"They knew my sister and I had a soft heart for animals. But Mom, if she saw these castaways first, got rid of as many as she could, because we couldn't afford to feed them. I feel so guilty now that we didn't take better care of them. But we couldn't afford doctors for ourselves, much less veterinarians for the animals. When Pop fell off a ladder once and stuck a pruning shear in his thigh, instead of seeing a doctor, he got a bottle of iodine and poured it into the wound." Besides her cats and dogs, there were the family chickens, a flawed strain producing some strange-looking specimens without feathers. Michi fitted these chickens with clothes she had made, her first costume designs.

Another less peaceful world hovered outside the farm. Between 1890 and 1924 some 300,000 Asians had come to this country. Like the 1882 laws that had restricted Chinese immigration, the 1924 Immigration Act prevented any more Japanese immigrants from entering the country. Those Japanese who had come to the United States before 1924, as Michi's parents had, were called *Issei*, which means "first generation" in Japanese. Like other Asian immigrants, the Issei were not allowed to become U.S. citizens, which meant that they could not own land in many states or vote in the United States. But their children, called *Nisei* ("second generation"), were U.S. citizens because they were born here.

Eventually, the Issei and Nisei family unit made up a significant segment of the California farm-labor force. They turned swamps, deserts, and narrow strips along railroad tracks into fertile farms. By the beginning of World War II, the tiny (1%) Japanese-American minority in California was operating close to one-half of the truck farming in the state. The Japanese Americans were also small-shop owners and professionals.

At grade school Michi chose Mexican Americans and Filipinos as her friends. She explains: "Even when I was a little child my parents instilled in me *enryo*, a backing away, a shyness, especially with

Elementary school children—April 20, 1942

white people. I knew my place. Later, in high school, I was very self-conscious and terribly concerned about what people would think of me. My parents had taught me that I must not offend. They used to talk often about *haiseki,* or discrimination."

And *haiseki* did flare up around her after the war began. On December 7, 1941, the Nishiuras were sitting around the kitchen table listening to the radio when they heard that Japanese bombers had attacked Pearl Harbor. Michi found it very hard to go to school the next day because she felt she looked like the enemy. When she got there she heard the teacher tell the other students, "It's not the fault of the Japanese Americans. You are not to mistreat them."

The days and months that followed Pearl Harbor were frightening for her. "We lived in terrible dread. Japanese-American community leaders and dozens of friends and neighbors were arrested. Saying something favorable about Japan could put you on a suspect list. These raids seemed to be made to reassure the public. One family wondered if owning their grandfather's sword, a relic of the Russo-Japanese War, might make them suspect. I recall my parents going out in the middle of the night and burning books and burying things — anything that might show their attachment to Japan, such as photographs of relatives, letters, even some of their beloved art treasures. Every time Japan won a battle in the Pacific, people hated us more."

Those Japanese military successes were partially responsible for wartime legislation that affected all persons of Japanese descent, two-thirds of them American citizens. On March 2, 1942, the western halves of the Pacific Coast states and the southern third of Arizona were designated as military areas. On telephone poles signs appeared that read: "All Japanese persons, both alien and nonalien, will be evacuated from this designated area. . . ."

Michi's family and all the other Japanese Americans on the Pacific Coast soon learned what those signs meant. They were allowed six to ten days to dispose of their property and businesses. "My father had to go to a makeshift government office," says Michi, "where he was assigned a family number and told when we would be taken away. The Japanese Americans very obediently turned themselves in.

Although they thought it dreadfully unfair to have to leave their homes, they felt powerless. The Issei, as enemy aliens, had no political voice, and neither did the Nisei since most were not yet of voting age."

Packing up was an ordeal. The Nishiuras found strangers turning up at their door. "People wanted to buy our bicycles and automobiles for next to nothing, and the chickens for a quarter apiece. At that price Mom decided it would be better to eat as many chickens as we could before we left. To this day, when my sister and I talk about that period, the hurried killing and eating of our pet chickens was one of the most traumatic aspects of the evacuation. Our father and mother were losing everything they had worked for, but my sister and I had little realization of that. For us it was parting with our animals: our cats, dogs, chickens, our possum, and our parrot. Most were left abandoned. I guess that's what war is like. But these are the things that are not written up in history books."

What belongings they could not sell in time the Nishiuras stored in a neighbor's shed, hoping to retrieve them at the end of the war. Then early in the morning of May 12, 1942, a neighbor drove the Nishiuras to a nearby town where, with other evacuees, they were loaded on buses that carried them to the site of their first detention camp, the "Turlock Assembly Center." There the evacuees found guard towers, guns, and barbed wire awaiting them.

The U.S. army, which had built these camps, said that the Japanese Americans had to be protected from outraged citizens. Rules were very strict. Michi's new life was regulated with a camp head count every night at nine P.M. and lights out by ten. "In the beginning, when we had visitors, we were not allowed to touch them, and all incoming parcels were inspected. When friends brought food, the guards checked even that to be sure no guns were being smuggled in. Sometimes even the mail was checked."

After several months, Michi, her sister, Tomi, her parents, and hundreds of others were put on a train that took them to the relocation camp in Gila. They traveled two days and nights over mountains and through vast desert areas to reach their isolated new camp. Because war cargo had priority on the tracks, the trainload of

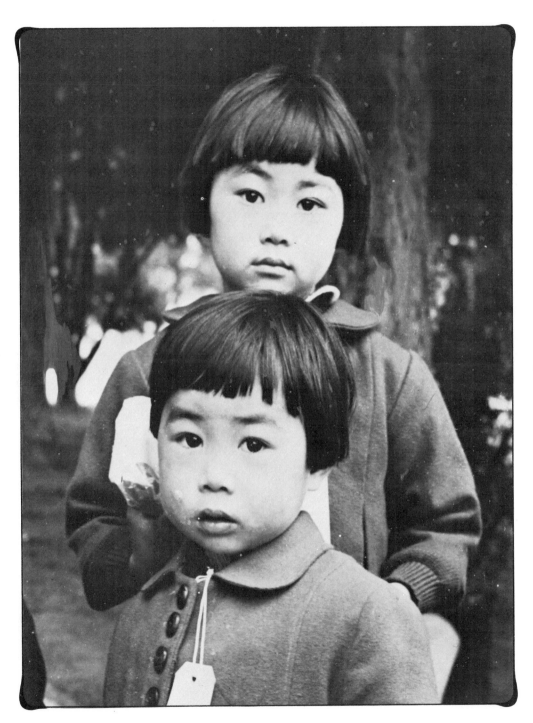

Evacuees—May 8, 1942

Gila River Relocation Center

evacuees was regularly switched to a siding and would sit for hours at a time. United States soldiers stood guard when the passengers were let out to stretch their legs.

In the desert camp at Gila, the Nishiura family was assigned an end room in Block 66, Barrack No. 12. To brighten up their new home, Mrs. Nishiura tacked a piece of colored cloth on the flimsy homemade partition that helped to divide the barrack room into living and sleeping quarters.

"It was so hot and crowded in that room," Michi says, "that some nights we slept out of doors. In the beginning, every time we took a step on the plowed-up desert floor, it was like being in a flour barrel. The sandstorms were continuous. I would end up with this loose, powdery dust all over me." Michi took to watering the room with a sprinkling can to keep it cool, but she could not keep out the sand. It was hard for the Nishiuras to adjust to the landscape—tumbleweed and cactus replaced grass and trees, and scorpions and rattlesnakes replaced the farmyard cats, dogs, and other pets. In Gila the temperature blazed up to 130 degrees. It was so uncomfortable that when people went outdoors in the middle of the day, they had to carry umbrellas and tie dampened handkerchiefs around their faces to provide some relief from the sun, the heat, and the blowing sand.

Michi's first meal at camp was a plate of beans. To vary the monotony of the meals—the starchy canned foods and an endless variety of beans—Michi and her friends would eat canned hot dogs in the Block 66 mess hall and then finish the meal with a canned desert from another kitchen. It was a while before fresh foods and leafy vegetables became available.

Most of the inmates had been farmers before they were consigned to relocation centers, and once they were settled behind barbed wire, they began farming again, this time doing stoop labor. But soon after Michi's father started to work on the 7,000-acre Gila farmland, he came down with a desert sickness called Valley Fever, which kept him in the camp hospital for nearly twenty months.

The teenaged Michi never felt resentment at being in Gila. In fact, she experienced a sense of relief, a kind of liberation for the first time. "Suddenly I was with my peers. I didn't have to feel inferior. I didn't

Manzanar Relocation Center

have to feel small. Or to face the humiliation I had begun to feel more intensely in school. I was liked for what I was, not because of what my parents did or didn't do. I had finally gained a feeling of respect, and I was managing to do the kinds of things that had been denied me, back at home, as a person who was of Asian descent.''

In the Nishiura's room in camp, Michi was still being brought up in the old-world Japanese tradition of spartan self-denial. ''Mother never allowed us to complain. It was difficult to follow this tradition, for in American schools I had been taught to assert myself as an individual. I struggled because I was trying to be the epitome of the perfect Japanese and the perfect American at the same time.''

There was a school for the Japanese-American children at Gila, but it was primitive and short staffed. Nevertheless, the Nisei teenagers put on proms, held personality contests, published yearbooks, and tried to recreate much of the world they had left behind. Michi became president of the Girl Scout troop that she organized. She set a record in Gila for selling the most $25 war bonds to Japanese-American camp workers, most of whom earned only $16 a month from the U.S. government.

''Back home I would never have established a Girl Scout troop or gone out for any office. At Gila, I was trying somehow to regain my self-respect. I thought the best way was to do my very best to prove that I was as good an American and as worthwhile a human being as those who were left behind.'' A teacher she idolized in Gila assured Michi that she would contribute more to life in America because of her experiences in the camp.

Because Michi wanted the world outide Gila to realize that the inmates were Americans, too, she organized a day-long Girl's League Convention at the camp. Invitations went out to all the state's high schools, committees sprang up, and on April 8, 1944, the camp was opened to the young conventioneers. Five hundred high school girls from Phoenix, Scottsdale, Tempe, Coolidge, Peoria, and other towns in Arizona came. They had a talent show at the large outdoor amphitheater, were given a tour of the camp, and ate together in one of the mess halls. They played baseball and volleyball in the desert sand and spent part of the afternoon discussing timely issues.

A Los Angeles softball team in Manzanar Relocation Center

Third-grade class

"These young people and a number of adult educators and dignitaries came into camp and spent a whole day with us," says Michi. "They took back to their homes the news that we were as American as anybody else. It helped turn around the feeling of distrust." And it impressed Secretary of the Interior Harold Ickes, the member of the President's cabinet responsible for overseeing the relocation centers. In a press release, Ickes referred to what Michi and her friends had accomplished in the middle of the Arizona desert. "To me it is indicative of the way the vast majority of our citizens feel, once they have the facts, toward those of Japanese descent. . . . Little children shall lead them."

From 1942 on, concerned Quakers and educators had been pressuring the federal government to release promising young Japanese Americans from the camps to attend college, and they had been urging midwestern and eastern seaboard schools to accept them.

Mrs. Nishiura didn't approve of her daughter's hopes for higher education. "She nearly sabotaged me," Michi says. "What good is it going to do you?" Michi heard over and over again. "What you need is typing and shorthand." But in March 1944, Michi went to Phoenix to take entrance examinations for Mount Holyoke College in South Hadley, Massachusetts. Just before her exam, she stepped into a drug store for a soda and was rudely turned out. The storekeeper would not serve her because she looked Japanese. It was like being back home on the farm again. The camp had shielded her from this world for a long time.

Today Michi has much difficulty recalling her arrival at Gila, but she remembers leaving. "I was full of the spirit of forgiveness and love and very grateful to the many dedicated fellow Americans who had made it possible for me to attend Mount Holyoke College on a full scholarship," she says.

Has Michi ever been back to Gila? "No. I despise deserts and the sun. For years people didn't understand why I walk in the shade." Only recently she received a letter from an admiring reader of her book, who wrote that she had just returned from Gila, and that there was nothing left but foundations and the traces of a Japanese garden.

476

Michi Nishiura

BRIGHTSIDE CROSSING

Alan E. Nourse

The leader of an expedition in "Brightside Crossing," the next story you are going to read, wants to cross the bright side of Mercury. He wants to cross at perihelion, *the point in the orbit of the planet at which the planet is closest to the sun. The word* perihelion *comes from a Greek compound made up of two elements meaning "near by" and "sun." The leader of the expedition does not want to cross at* aphelion *(the point at which a planet in its orbit would be farthest from the sun) because he wants to take the more arduous, the harder, to say nothing of the hotter, trip!* Aphelion *comes from a Greek compound meaning "away from" and "sun."*

Alan E. Nourse began writing science fiction stories while he was a medical student during the early 1950s. The money that Nourse earned through his writing paid for most of his medical training. Today when he is not working at his writing career, Nourse enjoys hunting, fishing, and climbing. His interest in climbing may have lead Nourse to think about several of the questions raised in "Brightside Crossing," questions such as the following: What do you think drives people to risk their lives climbing the world's tallest mountains? Why do some people devote themselves to breaking records and to accomplishing outstanding feats?

479

James Baron was not pleased to hear that he had had a visitor when he reached the Red Lion that evening. He had no stomach for mysteries, vast or trifling, and there were pressing things to think about at this time. Yet the doorman had flagged him as he came in from the street: "A thousand pardons, Mr. Baron. The gentleman — he would leave no name. He said you'd want to see him. He will be back by eight."

Baron drummed his fingers on the tabletop, staring about the quiet lounge. Across to the right was a group that Baron knew vaguely — Andean climbers, or at least two of them were. Over near the door he recognized old Balmer, who had mapped the first passage to the core of Vulcan Crater on Venus. Baron returned his smile with a nod. Then he settled back and waited impatiently for the intruder who demanded his time without justifying it.

Presently a small, grizzled man crossed the room and sat down at Baron's table. He was short and wiry. His face held no key to his age — he might have been thirty or a thousand — but he looked weary and immensely ugly. His cheeks and forehead were twisted and brown, with scars that were still healing.

The stranger said, "I'm glad you waited. I've heard you're planning to attempt the Brightside."

Baron stared at the man for a moment. "I see you can read telecasts," he said coldly. "The news was cor-rect. We are going to make a Brightside Crossing."

"At perihelion?"

"Of course. When else?"

The grizzled man searched Baron's face for a moment without expression. Then he said slowly, "No, I'm afraid you're not going to make the Crossing."

"Say, who are you, if you don't mind?" Baron demanded.

"The name is Claney," said the stranger.

There was a silence. Then: "Claney? *Peter* Claney?"

"That's right."

Baron's eyes were wide with excitement, all trace of anger gone. "My goodness, man — *where have you been hiding?* We've been trying to contact you for months!"

"I know. I was hoping you'd quit looking and forget the whole idea."

"Quit looking!" Baron bent forward over the table. "My friend, we'd given up hope, but we've never quit looking. There's so much you can tell us." His fingers were trembling.

Peter Claney shook his head. "I can't tell you anything you want to hear."

"But you've *got* to. You're the only man on Earth who's attempted a Brightside Crossing and lived through it! And the story you cleared for the news — it was nothing. We need *details*. Where did your equipment fall down? Where did you miscalculate? What were the trouble spots?" Baron jabbed a finger at Claney's face. "That, for instance. Why? What was wrong with your glass? Your filters? We've got to know those things. If you can tell us, we can make it across where your attempt failed—"

"You want to know why we failed?" asked Claney.

"Of course we want to know. We *have* to know."

"It's simple. We failed because it can't be done. We couldn't do it and neither can you. No human beings will ever cross the Brightside alive, not if they try for centuries."

"Nonsense," Baron declared. "We will."

Claney shrugged. "I was there. I know what I'm saying. You can blame the equipment or the men—there were flaws in both quarters—but we just didn't know what we were fighting. It was the *planet* that whipped us, that and the *Sun*. They'll whip you, too, if you try it."

"Never," said Baron.

"Let me tell you," Claney said.

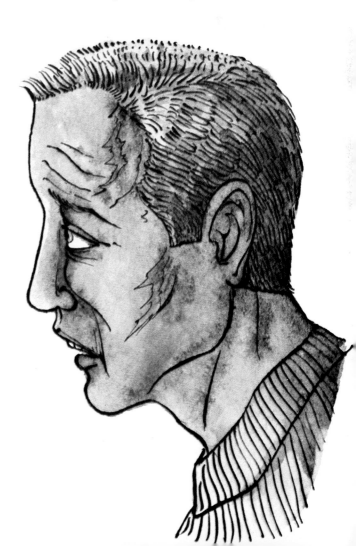

I'd been interested in the Brightside for almost as long as I can remember (Claney said). I guess I was about ten when Wyatt and Carpenter made the last attempt—that was in 2082, I think. I followed all the news stories, and then I was heartbroken when they just disappeared.

I know now that they were a pair of idiots, starting off without proper equipment, with practically no knowledge of surface conditions, without any charts. But I didn't know that then and it was a terrible tragedy. After that, I followed Sanderson's work in the Twilight Lab up there and began to get Brightside into my blood.

But it was Mikuta's idea to attempt a Crossing. Did you ever know Tom Mikuta? I don't suppose you did. No, not Japanese—Polish American. He was a major in the Interplanetary Service for some years and hung onto the title after he gave up his commission.

He was with Armstrong on Mars during his Service days, with a good deal of the original mapping and surveying for the colony to his credit. I first met him on Venus; we spent five years together up there doing some nasty exploring. Then he made the attempt on Vulcan Crater that paved the way for Balmer a few years later.

I'd always liked the Major—he was big and quiet and cool, the sort of guy who always had things figured a little further ahead than anyone else and always knew what to do in a tight place. Too many people in this game are all nerve and luck, with no judgment. The Major had both. He also had the kind of personality that could take a crew of people and make them work like a well-oiled machine across a thousand miles of Venus jungle. I liked him, and I trusted him.

He contacted me in New York, and he was very casual at first. We spent an evening here at the Red Lion, talking about old times; he told me about the Vulcan business, and how he'd been out to see Sanderson and the Twilight Lab on Mercury, and how he preferred a hot trek to a cold one any day of the year. And then he wanted to know what I'd been doing since Venus and what my plans were.

"No particular plans," I told him. "Why?"

He looked me over. "How much do you weigh, Peter?"

I told him one thirty-five.

"That much!" he said. "Well, there can't be much fat on you, at any rate. How do you take heat?"

"You should know," I said. "Venus was no icebox."

"No, I mean *real* heat."

Then I began to get it. "You're planning a trip."

"That's right. A hot trip." He grinned at me. "Might be dangerous, too."

"What trip?"

"Brightside of Mercury," the Major said.

I whistled. "Aphelion?"

He threw his head back. "Why try a Crossing at aphelion? What have you done then? Four thousand miles of butcherous heat, just to have some joker come along, using your data, and drum you out of the glory by crossing at perihelion forty-four days later? No, thanks. I want the Brightside without any nonsense about it." He leaned toward me eagerly. "I want to make a Crossing at perihelion and I want to cross on the surface. If someone can do that, that person's got Mercury. Until then, *nobody's* got Mercury. I want Mercury — but I'll need help getting it."

I'd thought of it a thousand times and never dared consider it. Nobody had, since Wyatt and Carpenter disappeared. Mercury turns on its axis in the same time that it wheels around the Sun, which means that the Brightside is always facing in. That makes the Brightside of Mercury at perihelion the hottest place in the Solar System, with one single exception: the surface of the Sun itself.

It would be a hellish trek. Only a few people had ever learned just *how* hellish and they never came back to tell about it. But someday somebody would cross it.

I wanted to be along.

The Twilight Lab, near the northern pole of Mercury, was the obvious jumping-off place. The setup there wasn't very extensive — a rocket landing, the labs and quarters for Sanderson's crew sunk deep into the crust, and the tower that housed the

Solar 'scope that Sanderson had built up there ten years before.

Twilight Lab wasn't particularly interested in the Brightside, of course—the Sun was Sanderson's baby and he'd picked Mercury as the closest chunk of rock to the Sun that could hold his observatory. He'd chosen a good location, too. On Mercury, the Brightside temperature hits 770° F. at perihelion and the Darkside runs pretty constant at −410° F. No permanent installation with a human crew could survive at either extreme. But with Mercury's wobble, the twilight zone between Brightside and Darkside offers something closer to survival temperatures.

Sanderson built the Lab up near the pole, where they'd get good clear observation of the Sun for about 70 out of the 88 days it takes the planet to wheel around.

The Major was counting on Sanderson's knowing something about Mercury as well as the Sun when we camped at the Lab to make final preparations.

Sanderson did. He thought we'd lost our minds and he said so, but he gave us all the help he could. He spent a week briefing Jack Stone, the third member of our party, who had arrived with the supplies and equipment a few days earlier. Poor Jack met us at the rocket landing almost bawling, Sanderson had given him such a gloomy picture of what Brightside was like.

Stone was a youngster—hardly twenty-five, I'd say—but he'd been with the Major at Vulcan and had begged to join this trek. I had a funny feeling that Jack really didn't care for exploring too much, but he followed Mikuta around like a puppy.

It didn't matter to me as long as he knew what he was getting in for. You don't go asking people in this game why they do it—they're liable to get awfully uneasy, and none of them can ever give you an answer that makes sense. Anyway, Stone had borrowed three people from the Lab and had the supplies and equipment all lined up when we got there, ready to check and test.

We dug right in. With plenty of funds—including some government cash the Major had talked his way around—our equipment was new and good. Mikuta had done the designing and testing himself, with much assistance from Sanderson. We had four Bugs, three of them the light pillow-tire models, with special lead-cooled cut-in engines when the heat set in, and one heavy-duty tractor model for pulling the sledges.

The Major went over them like a kid at the circus. Then he said, "Have you heard anything from McIvers?"

"Who's he?" Stone wanted to know.

"He'll be joining us. He's a good man—got quite a name for climbing, back home." The Major turned to me. "You've probably heard of him."

I'd heard plenty of stories about Ted McIvers and I wasn't too happy to hear that he was joining us. "Kind of a daredevil, isn't he?"

"Maybe. He's lucky and skillful. Where do you draw the line? We'll need plenty of both."

"Have you ever worked with him?" I asked.

"No. Are you worried?"

"Not exactly. But Brightside is no place to count on luck."

The Major laughed. "I don't think we need to worry about McIvers. We understood each other when I talked up the trip to him, and we're going to need each other too much to do any fooling around." He turned back to the supply list. "Meanwhile, let's get this stuff listed and packed. We'll need to cut weight sharply and our time is short. Sanderson says we should leave in three days."

Two days later, McIvers hadn't arrived. The Major didn't say much about it: Stone was getting edgy and so was I. We spent the second day studying charts of the Brightside, such as they were. The best available were pretty poor, taken from so far out that on blowup the detail dissolved into blurs. They showed the biggest ranges of peaks and craters and faults, and that was all. Still, we could use them to plan a broad outline of our course.

"This range here," the Major said as we crowded around the board, "is largely inactive, according to Sanderson. But these to the south and west *could* be active. Seismograph tracings suggest a lot of activity in that region, getting worse down toward the equator—not only volcanic, but sub-surface shifting."

Stone nodded. "Sanderson told me there was probably constant surface activity."

The Major shrugged. "Well, it's treacherous, there's no doubt of it. But the only way to avoid it is to travel over the Pole, which would lose us days and offer us no guarantee of less activity to the west. Now we might avoid some if we could find a pass through this range and cut sharp east—"

It seemed that the more we considered the problem, the further we got from a solution. We knew there were active volcanoes on the Brightside—even on the Darkside, though surface activity there was pretty much slowed down and localized. The trick was to find a passage that avoided those upheavals as far as possible. But in the final analysis, we were barely scraping the surface. The only way we would find out what was happening where was to be there.

Finally, on the third day, McIvers blew in on a freight rocket from Venus. He'd missed by a few hours the ship that the Major and I had taken and conned his way to Venus in hopes of getting a hop from there. He didn't seem too upset about it, as though this were his usual way of doing things, and he couldn't see why everyone should get so excited.

He was a tall, rangy man with long, wavy hair prematurely gray, and the sort of eyes that looked like a climber's—half closed, sleepy, but capable of abrupt alertness. And he never stood still; he was always moving, always talking or pacing about.

Evidently the Major decided not to press the issue of his arrival. There was still work to do, and an hour later we were running the final tests on the pressure suits. That evening, Stone and McIvers were thick as thieves, and everything was set for an early departure.

"And that," said Baron, "was your first big mistake."

Peter Claney raised his eyebrows. "McIvers?"

"Of course."

Claney shrugged, glanced at the small quiet tables around them. "There are lots of bizarre personalities around a place like this, and some of the best wouldn't seem to be the most reliable at first glance. Anyway, personality problems weren't our big problem then. *Equipment* worried us first and *route* next."

Baron nodded in agreement. "What kind of suits did you have?"

"The best insulating suits ever made," said Claney. "Each one had an inner lining of a fiberglass modification, to avoid the clumsiness of asbestos, and carried the refrigerating unit and oxygen storage which we recharged from the sledges every eight hours."

"How about the Bugs?"

"They were insulated, too, but we weren't counting on them too much for protection."

"You weren't!" Baron exclaimed. "Why not?"

"We'd be in and out of them too much. They gave us mobility and storage, but we knew we'd have to do a lot of forward work on foot." Claney smiled bitterly. "Which meant that we had an inch of fiberglass and a half-inch of dead air between us and a surface temperature where lead flowed like water and zinc was almost at melting point and the pools of sulfur in the shadows were boiling like oatmeal over a campfire."

Baron licked his lips.

"Go on," he said tautly. "You started on schedule?"

"Oh, yes," said Claney, "we started on schedule, all right. We just didn't quite end on schedule, that was all. But I'm getting to that."

He settled back in his chair and continued.

We jumped off from Twilight on a course due southeast, with thirty days to make it to the Center of Brightside. If we could cross an average of seventy miles a day, we could hit Center exactly at perihelion, the point of Mercury's closest approach to the Sun—which made Center the hottest part of the planet at the hottest it ever gets.

The Sun was already huge and

yellow over the horizon when we started, twice the size it appears on Earth. Every day the Sun would grow bigger and whiter, and every day the surface would get hotter. But once we reached Center, the job was only half done — we would still have to travel another 2,000 miles to the opposite twilight zone. Sanderson was to meet us on the other side in the Laboratory's scout ship, approximately sixty days from the time we jumped off.

That was the plan, in outline. It was up to us to cross those seventy miles a day, no matter how hot it became, no matter what terrain we had to cross. Detours would be dangerous and time-consuming. Delays could cost us our lives. We all knew that.

The Major briefed us on details an hour before we left. "Peter, you'll take the lead Bug, the small one we stripped down for you. Stone and I will flank you on either side, giving you a hundred-yard lead. McIvers, you'll have the job of dragging the sledges, so we'll have to direct your course pretty closely. Peter's job is to pick the passage at any given point. If there's any doubt of safe passage, we'll all explore ahead on foot before we risk the Bugs. Got that?"

McIvers and Stone exchanged glances. McIvers said: "Jack and I were planning to change around. We figured he could take the sledges. That would give me more mobility."

The Major looked up sharply at Stone. "Do you buy that, Jack?"

Stone shrugged. "I don't mind. Mac wanted—"

McIvers made an impatient gesture with his hands. "It doesn't matter. I just feel better when I'm on the move. Does it make any difference?"

"I guess it doesn't," said the Major. "Then you'll flank Peter along with me. Right?"

"Sure, sure." McIvers pulled at his lower lip. "Who's going to do the advance scouting?"

"It sounds like I am," I cut in. "We want to keep the lead Bug as light as possible."

Mikuta nodded. "That's right. Peter's Bug is stripped down to the frame and wheels."

McIvers shook his head. "No, I mean the *advance* work. You need somebody out ahead — four or five miles, at least — to pick up the big flaws and active surface changes, don't you?" He stared at the Major. "I mean, how can we tell what sort of a hole we may be moving into, unless we have a scout up ahead?"

"That's what we have the charts for," the Major said sharply.

"Charts! I'm talking about *detail* work. We don't need to worry about the major topography. It's the little faults you can't see on the pictures that can kill us." He tossed the charts down excitedly. "Look, let me take a Bug out ahead and work reconnaissance, keep five, maybe ten miles ahead of the column. I can stay

on good solid ground, of course, but scan the area closely and radio back to Peter where to avoid the flaws. Then—"

"No dice," the Major broke in.

"But why not? We could save ourselves days!"

"I don't care what we could save. We stay together. When we get to the Center, I want live men along with me. That means we stay within easy sight of each other at all times. Any climber knows that everybody is safer in a party than one man alone— anytime, anyplace."

McIvers stared at him, his cheeks an angry red. Finally he gave a sullen nod. "Okay. If you say so."

"Well, I say so and I mean it. I don't want any fancy stuff. We're going to hit Center together and finish together. Got that?"

McIvers nodded. Mikuta then looked at Stone and me and we nodded, too.

"All right," he said slowly. "Now that we've got it straight, let's go."

It was hot. If I forget everything else about that trek, I'll never forget that huge yellow Sun glaring down, without a break, hotter and hotter with every mile. We knew that the first few days would be the easiest, and we were rested and fresh when we started down the long ragged gorge southeast of the Twilight Lab.

I moved out first; back over my shoulder, I could see the Major and McIvers crawling out behind me, their pillow tires taking the rugged floor of the gorge smoothly. Behind them, Stone dragged the sledges.

I kept my eyes pasted to the big Polaroid binocs, picking out the track the early research teams had made out into the edge of Brightside. But in a couple of hours we rumbled past Sanderson's little outpost observatory and the tracks stopped. We were in new territory and already the Sun was beginning to bite.

We didn't *feel* that heat so much those first days out. We *saw* it. The refrig units kept our skins at a nice comfortable 75° F. inside our suits, but our eyes watched that glaring Sun and the baked yellow rocks going past, and some nerve pathways got twisted up, somehow. We poured sweat as if we were in a superheated furnace.

We drove eight hours and slept five. When a sleep period came due, we pulled the Bugs together into a square, threw up a light aluminum sun-shield and lay out in the dust and rocks. The sun-shield cut the temperature down sixty or seventy degrees, for whatever help that was. And then we ate from the forward sledge— sucking through tubes— protein, carbohydrates, bulk gelatin, vitamins.

The Major measured water out with an iron hand, because otherwise we'd have drunk ourselves sick in a week. We were constantly, unceasingly thirsty. Ask the psychiatrists why— they can give you half a dozen interesting reasons— but all we knew, or cared about, was that it happened to be so.

We didn't sleep the first few stops, as a consequence. Our eyes burned in spite of the filters and we had roaring headaches, but we couldn't sleep them off. We sat around looking at each other. Then McIvers would say how good a cold drink would taste, and off we'd go.

After a few driving periods, I began to get my bearings at the wheel. We were moving down into desolation that made Earth's old Death Valley look like a Japanese rose garden. Huge sun-baked cracks opened up in the floor of the gorge, with black cliffs jutting up on either side; the air was filled with a barely visible yellowish mist of sulfur and sulfurous gases.

It was a hot, barren hole, no place for anyone to go, but the challenge was so powerful you could almost feel it. No one had ever crossed this land before and escaped. Those who had tried it had been cruelly punished, but the land was still there, so it had to be crossed. Not the easy way. It had to be crossed the hardest way possible: overland, through anything the land could throw up to us, at the most difficult time possible.

Yet we knew that even the land might have been conquered before, except for that Sun. We'd fought absolute cold before and won. We'd

never fought heat like this and won. The only worse heat in the Solar System was the surface of the Sun itself.

Brightside was worth trying for. We would get it or it would get us. That was the bargain.

I learned a lot about Mercury those first few driving periods. I learned to read the ground, to tell a covered fault by the sag of the dust; I learned to spot a passable crack, and tell it from an impassable cut. Time after time the Bugs ground to a halt while we explored a passage on foot, tied together with light copper cable, digging, advancing, digging some more until we were sure the surface would carry the machines. It was cruel work; we slept in exhaustion. But it went smoothly, at first.

Too smoothly, it seemed to me, and the others seemed to think so, too.

McIvers' restlessness was beginning to grate on our nerves. He talked too much, while we were resting or while we were driving: wisecracks, witticisms, unfunny jokes that wore thin with repetition. He took to making side trips from the route now and then, never far, but a little farther each time.

Jack Stone reacted quite the opposite; he grew quieter with each stop, more reserved and apprehensive. I didn't like it, but I figured that it would pass off after a while. I was apprehensive enough myself; I just managed to hide it better.

And every mile the Sun got bigger and whiter and higher in the sky and hotter. Without our ultraviolet screens and glare filters we would have been blinded; as it was our eyes ached constantly, and the skin on our faces itched and tingled at the end of an eight-hour trek.

But it took one of those side trips of McIvers' to deliver the penultimate blow to our already fraying nerves. He had driven down a side branch of a long canyon and was almost out of sight in a cloud of ash when we heard a sharp cry through our earphones.

I wheeled my Bug around with my heart in my throat and spotted him through the binocs, waving frantically from the top of his machine. The Major and I took off, lumbering down the gulch after him as fast as the Bugs could go, with a thousand horrible pictures racing through our minds. . . .

We found him standing stock-still, pointing down the gorge and, for once, he didn't have anything to say. It was the wreck of a Bug, an old-fashioned half-track model of the sort that hadn't been in use for years. It was wedged tight in a cut in the rock, an axle broken, its casing split wide open up the middle, half buried in a rock slide. A dozen feet away were two insulated suits with white bones gleaming through the fiberglass helmets.

This was as far as Wyatt and Carpenter had gotten on *their* Brightside Crossing.

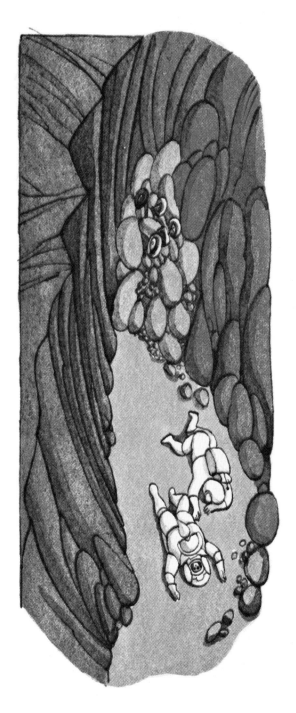

On the fifth driving period out, the terrain began to change. It looked the same, but every now and then it *felt* different. On two occasions I felt my wheels spin, with a howl of protest from my engine. Then, quite suddenly, the Bug gave a lurch; I gunned my motor and nothing happened.

I could see the dull-gray stuff seeping up around the hubs, splattering around in steaming gobs as the wheels spun. I knew what had happened the moment the wheels gave and, a few minutes later, they chained the Bug to the tractor and dragged me back out of the mire. It looked for all the world like thick gray mud, but it was a pit of molten lead, steaming under a soft layer of concealing ash.

I picked my way more cautiously then. We were getting into an area of recent surface activity; the surface was really treacherous. I caught myself wishing that the Major had okayed McIvers' scheme for an advance scout; more dangerous for the individual, maybe, but I was driving blind now and I didn't like it.

One error in judgment could sink us all, but I wasn't thinking much about the others. I was worried about *me,* plenty worried. I kept thinking, better McIvers should go than me. It wasn't healthy thinking and I knew it, but I couldn't get the thought out of my mind.

It was a grueling eight hours, and we slept poorly. Back in the Bugs again, we moved still more slowly —

edging out on a broad, flat plateau, dodging a network of gaping surface cracks — winding back and forth in an effort to keep the machines on solid rock. I couldn't see far ahead, because of the yellow haze rising from the cracks, and so I was almost on top of it when I saw a sharp cut ahead where the surface dropped six feet beyond a deep crack.

I let out a shout to halt the others; then I edged my Bug forward, peering at the cleft. It was deep and wide. I moved fifty yards to the left, then back to the right.

There was only one place that looked like a possible crossing: a long, narrow ledge of gray stuff that lay down across a section of the fault like a ramp. Even as I watched it, I could feel the surface crust under the Bug trembling and saw the ledge shift over a few feet.

The Major's voice sounded in my ears. "How about it, Peter?"

"I don't know. This crust is on roller skates," I called back.

"How about that ledge?"

I hesitated. "I'm scared of it, Major. Let's backtrack and try to find a way around."

There was a roar of disgust in my earphones and McIvers' Bug suddenly lurched forward. It rolled down past me, picked up speed, with McIvers hunched behind the wheel like a race driver. He was heading past me straight for the gray ledge.

My shout caught in my throat; I heard the Major take a huge breath and roar: "Mac, *stop that thing,* you fool!" and then McIvers' Bug was out on the ledge, lumbering across.

The ledge jolted as the tires struck it; for a horrible moment, it seemed to be sliding out from under the machine. And then the Bug was across in a cloud of dust, and I heard McIvers' voice in my ears, shouting in glee, "Come on, you slowpokes. It'll hold you!"

Something unprintable came through the earphones as the Major drew up alongside me and moved his Bug out on the ledge slowly and over to the other side. Then he said, "Take it slow, Peter. Then give Jack a hand with the sledges." His voice sounded tight as a wire.

Ten minutes later, we were on the other side of the cleft. The Major checked the whole column; then he turned on McIvers angrily. "One more trick like that," he said, "and I'll strap you to a rock and leave you. Do you understand me? *One more time —*"

McIvers' voice was heavy with protest. "If we leave it up to Claney, he'll have us out here forever! Any blind fool could see that that ledge would hold."

"I saw it moving," I shot back at him.

"All right, all right, so you've got good eyes. Why all the fuss? We got across, didn't we? But I say we've got to have a little nerve and use it once in a while if we're ever going to get across this lousy hotbox."

"We need to use a little judgment, too," the Major snapped. "All right, let's roll. But if you think I was joking, you just try me out once." He let it soak in for a minute. Then he geared his Bug on around to my flank again.

At the stopover, the incident wasn't mentioned again, but the Major drew me aside just as I was settling down for sleep. "Peter, I'm worried," he said slowly.

"McIvers? Don't worry. He's not as reckless as he seems—just impatient. We are over a hundred miles behind schedule, and we're moving awfully slow. We only made forty miles this last drive."

The Major shook his head. "I don't mean McIvers. I mean the kid."

"Jack? What about him?"

"Take a look."

Stone was shaking. He was over near the tractor—away from the rest of us—and he was lying on his back, but he wasn't asleep. His whole body was shaking convulsively. I saw him grip an outcropping of rock hard.

I walked over and sat down beside him. "Get your water all right?" I said.

He didn't answer. He just kept on shaking.

"Hey, boy," I said. "What's the trouble?"

"It's hot," he said, choking out the words.

"Sure it's hot, but don't let it throw you. We're in really good shape."

"We're not," he snapped. "We're in rotten shape, if you ask me. *We're not going to make it,* do you know that? That crazy fool's going to kill us for sure—" All of a sudden, he was bawling like a baby. "I'm scared—I shouldn't be here—I'm *scared.* What am I trying to prove by coming out here? I'm some kind of hero or something? I tell you I'm scared—"

"Look," I said. "Mikuta's scared, *I'm* scared. So what? We'll make it, don't worry. And nobody's trying to be a hero."

"Nobody but Hero Stone," he said bitterly. He shook himself and gave a tight little laugh. "Some hero, eh?"

"We'll make it," I said.

"Sure," he said finally. "Sorry. I'll be okay."

I rolled over, but waited until he was good and quiet. Then I tried to sleep, but I didn't sleep too well. I kept thinking about that ledge. I'd known from the look of it what it was; a wide sheet of almost pure zinc.

I knew enough about zinc to know that at these temperatures it gets brittle as glass. Take a chance like McIvers had taken and the whole sheet could snap like a dry pine board. But it wasn't McIvers' fault that it hadn't.

Five hours later, we were back at the wheel. We were hardly moving at all. The ragged surface was almost impassable—ledges crumbled the moment my tires touched them; long, open canyons turned into sulfur pits.

A dozen times I climbed out of the Bug to prod out an uncertain area with my boots and staff. Whenever I did, McIvers piled out behind me, running ahead like a schoolboy at the fair, then climbing back again, red-faced and panting, while we moved the machines ahead another mile or two.

Time was pressing us now, and McIvers wouldn't let me forget it. We had made only about 320 miles in six driving periods, and so we were about a hundred miles or even more behind schedule.

"We're not going to make it," McIvers would complain angrily. "That Sun's going to be out to aphelion by the time we hit Center—"

"Sorry, but I can't take it any faster," I told him. I was getting good and angry. I knew what he wanted but didn't dare let him have it. I was scared enough pushing the Bug out on those ledges, even knowing that at least *I* was making the decisions. Put him in the lead and we wouldn't last for eight hours. Our nerves wouldn't take it, at any rate, even if the machines did.

Jack Stone looked up from the aluminum chart sheets. "Another hundred miles and we should hit a good stretch," he said. "Maybe we can make up distance there for a couple of days."

The Major agreed, but McIvers couldn't hold his impatience. He

kept staring up at the Sun as if he had a personal grudge against it, and he stamped back and forth under the sun-shield. "That'll be just fine," he said. "*If* we ever get that far, that is."

We dropped it there, but the Major stopped me as we climbed aboard for the next run. "That guy's going to blow wide open if we don't move faster, Peter. I don't want him in the lead, no matter what happens. He's right, though, about the need to make better time. Keep your head, but crowd your luck a little, okay?"

"I'll try," I said. It was asking the impossible and Mikuta knew it. We were on a long, downward slope that shifted and buckled all around us, as though there was a molten underlay beneath the crust. The outside temperature registered 547° F. and was getting hotter. It was no place to start rushing ahead.

I tried it anyway. I took half a dozen shaky passages, edging slowly out on flat zinc ledges, then toppling over and across. It seemed easy for a while and we made progress. We hit an even stretch and raced ahead. And then I quickly jumped on my brakes and jerked the Bug to a halt in a cloud of dust.

I'd gone too far. We were out on a wide, flat sheet of gray stuff, apparently solid—until I'd suddenly caught sight of the crevasse beneath. It was an overhanging shelf that trembled under me as I stopped. McIvers' voice was in my ear. "What's the trouble now, Claney?"

"Move back!" I shouted. "It can't hold us!"

"Looks solid from here."

"You want to argue about it? It's too thin, it'll snap. Move back!"

I started edging back down the ledge. I heard McIvers swear; then I saw his Bug start to creep *outward* on the shelf. Not fast or reckless, this time, but slowly, churning up dust in a gentle cloud behind him.

I just stared and felt the blood rush to my head. It seemed so hot I could hardly breathe as he edged out beyond me, farther and farther—

I think I felt it snap before I saw it. My own machine gave a sickening lurch and a long black crack appeared across the shelf and widened. Then the ledge began to upend. I heard a scream as McIvers' Bug rose up and up and then crashed down into the crevasse in a thundering slide of rock and shattered metal.

I just stared for a full minute, I think. I couldn't move until I heard Jack Stone groan and the Major shouting, "Claney! I couldn't see— *what happened?*"

"It snapped on him, that's what happened," I roared. I gunned my motor, edged forward toward the fresh-broken edge of the shelf. The crevasse gaped; I couldn't see any sign of the machine. Dust was still billowing up blindingly from below.

We stood staring down, the three of us. I caught a glimpse of Jack Stone's face through his helmet. It wasn't pretty.

"Well," said the Major heavily, "that's that."

"I guess so." I felt the way Stone looked.

"Wait," said Stone. "I heard something."

He had. It was a cry in the earphones—faint, but unmistakable.

"Mac!" the Major called. "Mac, can you hear me?"

"Yeah, yeah. I can hear you." The voice was very weak.

"Are you all right?"

"I don't know. Broken leg, I think. It's—hot." There was a long pause. Then: "I think my cooler's gone out."

The Major shot me a glance, then turned to Stone. "Get a cable from the second sledge fast. He'll fry alive if we don't get him out of there. Peter, I need you to lower me. Use the tractor winch."

I lowered him; he stayed down only a few moments. When I hauled him up, his face was drawn. "Still alive," he panted. "He won't be very long, though." He hesitated for just an instant. "We've got to make a try."

"I don't like this ledge," I said. "It's moved twice since I got out. Why not back off and lower him a cable?"

"No good. The Bug is smashed and he's inside it. We'll need torches and I'll need one of you to help." He looked at me and then gave Stone a long look. "Peter, you'd better come."

"Wait," said Stone. His face was very white. "Let me go down with you."

"Peter is lighter."

"I'm not so heavy. Let me go down."

"Okay, if that's the way you want it." The Major tossed him a torch. "Peter, check these hitches and lower us slowly. If you see any kind of trouble, *anything,* cast yourself free and back off this thing, do you understand? This whole ledge may go."

I nodded. "Good luck."

They went over the ledge. I let the cable down bit by bit until it hit two hundred feet and slacked off.

"How does it look?" I shouted.

"Bad," said the Major. "We'll have to work fast. This whole side of the crevasse is ready to crumble. Down a little more."

Minutes passed without a sound. I tried to relax, but I couldn't. Then I felt the ground shift, and the tractor lurched to the side.

The Major shouted, *"It's going, Peter—pull back!"* and I threw the tractor into reverse, jerked the controls as the tractor rumbled off the shelf. The cable snapped, coiled up in front like a broken clockspring. The whole surface under me was shaking wildly now; ash rose in huge gray clouds. Then, with a roar, the whole shelf lurched and slid sideways. It teetered on the edge for seconds before it crashed into the crevasse, tearing the side wall down

with it in a mammoth slide. I jerked the tractor to a halt as the dust and flame billowed up.

They were gone—all three of them, McIvers and the Major and Jack Stone—buried under thousands of tons of rock and zinc and molten lead. There wasn't any danger of anybody ever finding their bones.

Peter Claney leaned back, rubbing his scarred face as he looked across at Baron.

Slowly, Baron's grip relaxed on the chair arm. "*You* got back."

Claney nodded. "I got back, sure. I had the tractor and the sledges. I had seven days to drive back under that yellow Sun. I had plenty of time to think."

"You took the wrong man along," Baron said. "That was your mistake. Without him you would have made it."

"Never." Claney shook his head. "That's what I was thinking the first day or so—that it was *McIvers'* fault, that *he* was to blame. But that isn't true. He was wild, reckless, and had lots of nerve."

"But his judgment was bad!"

"It couldn't have been sounder. We had to keep to our schedule even if it killed us, because it would positively kill us if we didn't."

"But a man like that—"

"A man like McIvers was necessary. Can't you see that? It was the Sun that beat us, that surface. Per-haps we were licked the very day we started." Claney leaned across the table, his eyes pleading. "We didn't realize that, but it was *true*. There are places that people can't go, con-ditions people can't tolerate. The others had to die to learn that. I was lucky, I came back. But I'm trying to tell you what I found out—that *no-body* will ever make the Brightside Crossing."

"We will," said Baron. "It won't be a picnic, but we'll make it."

"But suppose you do," said Claney, suddenly. "Suppose I'm all wrong, suppose you *do* make it. Then what? *What comes next?*"

"The Sun," said Baron.

Claney nodded slowly. "Yes. That would be it, wouldn't it?" He laughed. "Good-by, Baron. Jolly talk and all that. Thanks for listen-ing."

Baron caught his wrist as he started to rise. "Just one question more, Claney. Why did you come here?"

"To try to talk you out of killing yourself," said Claney.

"You're a liar," said Baron.

Claney stared down at him for a long moment. Then he crumpled in the chair. There was defeat in his pale blue eyes and something else.

"Well?"

Peter Claney spread his hands, a helpless gesture. "When do you leave, Baron? I want you to take me along."

502

Nicholasa Mohr

Mr. Mendelsohn

"Psst . . . psst, Mr. Mendelsohn, wake up. Come on now!"
Mrs. Suárez said in a low, quiet voice. Mr. Mendelsohn had
fallen asleep again, on the large armchair in the living room.
He grasped the brown, shiny wooden cane and leaned
forward, his chin on his chest. The small black skullcap that
was usually placed neatly on the back of his head had tilted
to one side, covering his right ear. "Come on now. It's late
and time to go home." She tapped him on the shoulder and
waited for him to wake up. Slowly, he lifted his head, opened
his eyes, and blinked.

"What time is it?" he asked.

"It's almost midnight. *Caramba!* I didn't even know you
was still here. When I came to shut off the lights, I saw you
was sleeping."

"Oh . . . I'm sorry. O.K., I'm leaving." With short, slow steps
he followed Mrs. Suárez over to the front door.

"Go on now," she said, opening the door. "We'll see you
tomorrow."

He walked out into the hallway, stepped about three feet to
the left, and stood before the door of his apartment. Mrs.
Suárez waited, holding her door ajar, while he carefully
searched for the right key to each lock. He had to open seven
locks in all.

A small fluffy dog standing next to Mrs. Suárez began to whine and bark.

"Shh—sh, Sporty! Stop it!" she said. "You had your walk. Shh."

"O.K.," said Mr. Mendelsohn, finally opening his door. "Good night." Mrs. Suárez smiled and nodded.

"Good night," she whispered, as they both shut their doors simultaneously.

Mr. Mendelsohn knocked on the door and waited; then he tried the doorknob. Turning and pushing, he realized the door was locked and knocked again, this time more forcefully. He heard Sporty barking and footsteps coming toward the door.

"Who's there?" a child's voice asked.

"It's me—Mr. Mendelsohn! Open up, Yvonne." The door opened, and a young girl, age nine, smiled at him.

"Mami! It's el Señor Mr. Mendelsohn again."

"Tell him to come on in, *muchacha!*" Mrs. Suárez answered.

"My mother says come on in."

He followed Yvonne and the dog, who leaped up, barking and wagging his tail. Mr. Mendelsohn stood at the kitchen entrance and greeted everyone.

"Good morning to you all!" He had just shaved and trimmed his large black mustache. As he smiled broadly, one could see that most of his teeth were missing. His large bald head was partially covered by his small black skullcap. Thick dark gray hair grew in abundance at the lower back of his head, coming around the front above his ears into short sideburns. He wore a clean white shirt, frayed at the cuffs. His worn-out pinstripe trousers were held up by a pair of dark suspenders. Mr. Mendelsohn leaned on his brown, shiny cane and carried a small brown paper bag.

"Mr. Mendelsohn, come into the kitchen," said Mrs. Suárez, "and have some coffee with us." She stood by the stove. A boy of eleven, a young man of about seventeen, and a young pregnant woman were seated at the table.

"Sit here," said the boy, vacating a chair. "I'm finished eating." He stood by the entrance with his sister Yvonne, and they both looked at Mr. Mendelsohn and his paper bag with interest.

"Thank you, Georgie," Mr. Mendelsohn said. He sat down and placed the bag on his lap.

The smell of freshly perked coffee and boiled milk permeated the kitchen.

Winking at everyone, the young man asked, "Hey, what you got in that bag you holding onto, huh, Mr. Mendelsohn?" They all looked at each other and at the old man, amused. "Something special, I bet!"

"Well," the old man replied. "I thought your mama would be so kind as to permit me to make myself a little breakfast here today . . . so." He opened the bag, and began to take out its contents. "I got two slices of rye bread, two tea bags. I brought one extra, just in case anybody would care to join me for tea. And a jar of herring in sour cream."

"Sounds delicious!" said the young man, sticking out his tongue and making a face. Yvonne and Georgie burst out laughing.

"Shh . . . sh." Mrs. Suárez shook her head and looked at her children disapprovingly. "Never mind, Julio!" she said to the young man. Turning to Mr. Mendelsohn, she said, "You got the same like you brought last Saturday, eh? You can eat with us anytime. How about some fresh coffee? I just made it. Yes?" Mr. Mendelsohn looked at her, shrugging his shoulders. "Come on, have some," she coaxed.

"O.K.," he replied. "If it's not too much bother."

"No bother," she said, setting out a place for the old man. "You gonna have some nice fresh bread with a little butter — it will go good with your herring." Mrs. Suárez cut a generous slice of freshly baked bread with a golden crust and buttered it. "Go on, eat. There's a plate and everything for your food. Go on, eat. . . ."

"Would anyone care for some?" Mr. Mendelsohn asked. "Perhaps a tea bag for a cup of tea?"

"No . . . no thank you, Mr. Mendelsohn," Mrs. Suárez answered. "Everybody here already ate. You go ahead and eat. You look too skinny; you better eat. Go on, eat your bread."

The old man began to eat vigorously.

"Can I ask you a question?" Julio asked the old man.

"Man, I don't get you. You got a whole apartment next door all to yourself — six rooms! And you gotta come here to eat in this crowded kitchen. Why?"

"First of all, today is Saturday, and I thought I could bring in my food and your mamma could turn on the stove for me. You know, in my religion you can't light a fire on Saturday."

"You come here anytime; I turn on the stove for you, don't worry," Mrs. Suárez said.

"Man, what about other days? We been living here for about six months, right?" Julio persisted. "And you do more cooking here than in your own place."

"It doesn't pay to turn on the gas for such a little bit of cooking. So I told the gas company to turn it off . . . for good! I got no more gas now, only an electric hot plate," the old man said.

Julio shook his head and sighed. "I don't know —"

"Julio, *chico!*" snapped Mrs. Suárez, interrupting him, "*Basta* — it doesn't bother nobody." She looked severely at her son and shook her head. "You gotta go with your sister to the clinic today, so you better get ready now. You too, Marta."

"O.K., Mama," she answered, "but I wanted to see if I got mail from Ralphy today."

"You don't got time. I'll save you the mail; you read it when you get back. You and Julio better get ready; go on." Reluctantly, Marta stood up and yawned, stretching and arching her back.

"Marta," Mr. Mendelsohn said, "you taking care? . . . You know, this is a very delicate time for you."

"I am, Mr. Mendelsohn. Thank you."

"I raised six sisters," the old man said. "I ought to know. Six . . . Believe me, I've done my share in life." Yvonne and Georgie giggled and poked each other.

"He's gonna make one of his speeches," they whispered.

". . . I never had children. No time to get married. My father died when I was eleven. I went to work supporting my mother and six younger sisters. I took care of them, and today they all are married, with families. They always call and want me to visit them. I'm too busy and I have no time. . . ."

"Too busy eating in our kitchen," whispered Julio. Marta,

Georgie, and Yvonne tried not to laugh out loud. Mrs. Suárez reached over and with a wooden ladle managed a light but firm blow on Julio's head.

". . . Only on the holidays, I make some time to see them. But otherwise, I cannot be bothered with all that visiting." Mr. Mendelsohn stopped speaking and began to eat again.

"Go on, Marta and Julio, you will be late for the clinic," Mrs. Suárez said. "And you two? What are you doing there smiling like two monkeys? Go find something to do!"

Quickly, Georgie and Yvonne ran down the hallway, and Julio and Marta left the kitchen.

Mrs. Suárez sat down beside the old man.

"Another piece of bread?" she asked.

"No, thank you very much. . . . I'm full. But it was delicious."

"You too skinny—you don't eat right, I bet." Mrs. Suárez shook her head. "Come tomorrow and have Sunday supper with us."

"I really couldn't."

"Sure, you could. I always make a big supper and there is plenty. All right? Mr. Suárez and I will be happy to have you."

"Are you sure it will be no bother?"

"What are you talking for the bother all the time? One more person is no bother. You come tomorrow. Yes?"

The old man smiled broadly and nodded. This was the first time he had been invited to Sunday supper with the family.

Mrs. Suárez stood and began clearing away the dishes. "O.K., you go inside; listen to the radio or talk to the kids or something. I got work to do."

Mr. Mendelsohn closed his jar of herring and put it back into the bag. "Can I leave this here till I go?"

"Leave it; I put it in the refrigerator for you."

Leaning on his cane, Mr. Mendelsohn stood up and walked out of the kitchen and down the long hallway into the living room. It was empty. He went over to a large armchair by the window. The sun shone through the window, covering the entire armchair and Mr. Mendelsohn. A canary cage was also by the window, and two tiny yellow birds chirped and hopped back and forth energetically. Mr. Mendelsohn felt drowsy; he shut his eyes. So many aches and pains, he thought. It was hard to sleep at night, but here, well . . . the birds began to chirp in unison and the old man opened one eye, glancing at them, and smiled. Then he shut his eyes once more and fell fast asleep.

When Mr. Mendelsohn opened his eyes, Georgie and Yvonne were in the living room. Yvonne held a deck of playing cards and Georgie read a comic book. She looked at the old man and, holding up the deck of cards, asked, "Do you wanna play a game of War? Huh, Mr. Mendelsohn?"

"I don't know how to play that," he answered.

"It's real easy. I'll show you. Come on . . . please!"

"Well," he shrugged, "sure, why not? Maybe I'll learn something."

Yvonne took a small maple end table and a wooden chair and set them next to Mr. Mendelsohn. "Now . . ." she began, "I'll shuffle the cards and you cut, and then I throw down a card and you throw down a card and the one with the highest card wins. O.K.? And then, the one with the most cards of all wins the game. O.K.?"

"That's all?" he asked.

"That's all. Ready?" she asked, and sat down. They began to play cards.

"You know, my sister Jennie used to be a great card player," said Mr. Mendelsohn.

"Does she still play?" asked Yvonne.

"Oh . . ." Mr. Mendelsohn laughed. "I don't know any more. She's already married and has kids. She was the youngest in my family—like you."

"Did she go to P.S. 39? On Longwood Avenue?"

"I'm sure she did. All my sisters went to school around here."

"Wow! You must be living here a long time, Mr. Mendelsohn."

"Forty-five years!" said the old man.

"Wowee!" Yvonne whistled. "Georgie, did you hear? Mr. Mendelsohn's been living here for forty-five whole years!"

Georgie put down his comic book and looked up.

"Really?" he asked, impressed.

"Yes, forty-five years this summer we moved here. But in those days things were different, not like today. No sir! The

Bronx has changed. Then, it was the country. That's right! Why, look out the window. You see the elevated trains on Westchester Avenue? Well, there were no trains then. That was once a dirt road. They used to bring cows through there."

"Oh, man!" Georgie and Yvonne both gasped.

"Sure. These buildings were among the first apartment houses to go up. Four stories high, and that used to be a big accomplishment in them days. All that was here was mostly little houses, like you still see here and there. Small farms, woodlands . . . like that."

"Did you see any Indians?" asked Georgie.

"What do you mean, Indians?" laughed the old man. "I'm not that old, and this here was not the Wild West." Mr. Mendelsohn saw that the children were disappointed. He added quickly, "But we did have carriages with horses. No cars and lots of horses."

"That's what Mami says they have in Puerto Rico — not like here in El Bronx," said Yvonne.

"Yeah," Georgie agreed. "Papi says he rode a horse when he was a little kid in Puerto Rico. They had goats and pigs and all them things. Man, was he lucky."

"Lucky?" Mr. Mendelsohn shook his head. "You — you are the lucky one today! You got school and a good home and clothes. You don't have to go out to work and support a family, like your papa and I had to do, and miss an education. You can learn and be somebody someday."

"Someday," said Yvonne, "we are gonna get a house with a yard and all. Mami says that when Ralphy gets discharged from the Army, he'll get a loan from the government and we can pay to buy a house. You know, instead of rent."

Mrs. Suárez walked into the living room with her coat on, carrying a shopping bag.

"Yvonne, take the dog out for a walk, and Georgie, come on! We have to go shopping. Get your jacket."

Mr. Mendelsohn started to rise. "No," she said, "stay . . . sit down. It's O.K. You can stay and rest if you want."

"All right, Mrs. Suárez," Mr. Mendelsohn said.

"Now don't forget tomorrow for Sunday supper, and take a nap if you like."

Mr. Mendelsohn heard the front door slam shut, and the apartment was silent. The warmth of the bright sun made him drowsy once more. It was so nice here, he thought, a house full of people and kids — like it used to be. He recalled his sisters and his parents . . . the holidays . . . the arguments . . . and laughing. It was so empty next door. He would have to look for a smaller apartment, near Jennie, someday. But not now. Now, it was just nice to sleep and rest right here. He heard the tiny birds chirping and quietly drifted into a deep sleep.

Mr. Mendelsohn rang the bell, then opened the door. He could smell the familiar cooking odors of Sunday supper. For two years he had spent every Sunday at his neighbors'. Sporty greeted him, jumping affectionately and barking.

"Shh — sh . . . down. Good boy," he said, and walked along the hallway toward the kitchen. The room was crowded with people and the stove was loaded with large pots of food, steaming and puffing. Mrs. Suárez was busy basting a large roast. Looking up, she saw Mr. Mendelsohn.

"Come in," she said, "and sit down." Motioning to Julio, who was seated, she continued, "Julio, you are finished, get up and give Mr. Mendelsohn a seat." Julio stood up.

"Here's the sponge cake," Mr. Mendelsohn said, and handed the cake box he carried to Julio, who put it in the refrigerator.

"That's nice. . . . Thank you," said Mrs. Suárez, and placed a cup of freshly made coffee before the old man.

"Would anyone like some coffee?" Mr. Mendelsohn asked. Yvonne and Georgie giggled, looked at one another, and shook their heads.

"You always say that!" said Yvonne.

"One of these days," said Ralphy, "I'm gonna say, 'Yes, give me your coffee,' and you won't have none to drink." The children laughed loudly.

"Don't tease him," Mrs. Suárez said, half smiling. "Let him have his coffee."

"He is just being polite, children," Mr. Suárez said, and shifting his chair closer to Mr. Mendelsohn, he asked, "So . . . Mr. Mendelsohn, how you been? What's new? You O.K.?"

511

"So-so, Mr. Suárez. You know, aches and pains when you get old. But there's nothing you can do, so you gotta make the best of it."

Mr. Suárez nodded sympathetically, and they continued to talk. Mr. Mendelsohn saw the family every day, except for Mr. Suárez and Ralphy, who both worked a night shift.

Marta appeared in the entrance, holding a small child by the hand.

"There he is, Tato," she said to the child, and pointed to Mr. Mendelsohn.

"Oh, my big boy! He knows, he knows he's my best friend," Mr. Mendelsohn said, and he held the brown shiny cane out toward Tato. The small boy grabbed the cane and, shrieking with delight, walked toward Mr. Mendelsohn.

"Look at that, will you?" said Ralphy. "He knows Mr. Mendelsohn better than me, his own father."

"That's because they are always together," smiled Marta. "Tato is learning to walk with his cane!"

Everyone laughed as they watched Tato climbing the old man's knee. Bending over, Mr. Mendelsohn pulled Tato onto his lap.

"Oh . . . he's getting heavy," said Mrs. Suárez. "Be careful."

"Never mind," Mr. Mendelsohn responded, hugging Tato. "That's my best boy. And look how swell he walks, and he's not even nineteen months."

"What a team," Julio said. "Tato already walks like Mr. Mendelsohn and pretty soon he's gonna complain like him, too. . . ." Julio continued to tease the old man, who responded good-naturedly, as everyone laughed.

After coffee, Mr. Mendelsohn sat on the large armchair in the living room, waiting for supper to be ready. He watched with delight as Tato walked back and forth with the cane. Mr. Mendelsohn held Tato's blanket, stuffed bear, and picture book.

"Tato," he called out, "come here. Let me read you a book —come on. I'm going to read you a nice story."

Tato climbed onto the chair and into Mr. Mendelsohn's lap. He sucked his thumb and waited. Mr. Mendelsohn opened the picture book.

"O.K. Now . . ." He pointed to the picture. "A is for Alligators. See that? Look at that big mouth and all them teeth. . . ." Tato yawned, nestled back, and closed his eyes. The old man read a few more pages and shut the book.

The soft breathing and sucking sound that Tato made assured Mr. Mendelsohn that the child was asleep. Such a smart kid. What a great boy, he said to himself. Mr. Mendelsohn was vaguely aware of a radio program, voices, and the small dog barking now and then, just before he too fell into a deep sleep.

This Sunday was very much like all the others; coffee first, then he and Tato would play a bit before napping in the large armchair. It had become a way of life for the old man. Only the High Holy Days and an occasional invitation to a family event, such as a marriage or a funeral and so on, would prevent the old man from spending Sunday next door.

It had all been so effortless. No one ever asked him to leave, except late at night when he napped too long. On Saturdays he tried to observe the Sabbath and brought in his meal. They lit the stove for him.

Mrs. Suárez was always feeding him, just like Mama. She also worried about me not eating, the old man had said to himself, pleased. At first, he had been cautious and had wondered about the food and the people that he was becoming so involved with. On that first Sunday the old man had looked suspiciously at the food they served him.

"What is it?" he had asked. Yvonne and Georgie had started giggling and had looked at one another. Mrs. Suárez had responded quickly and with anger, cautioning her children, speaking to them in Spanish.

"Eat your food, Mr. Mendelsohn. You too skinny," she had told him.

And that was all.

Mr. Mendelsohn ate his Sunday supper from then on without doubt or hesitation, accepting the affection and concern that Mrs. Suárez provided with each plateful.

That night in his own apartment, Mr. Mendelsohn felt uneasy. He remembered that during supper, Ralphy had mentioned that his G.I. loan had come through. They would be

514

looking for a house soon, everyone agreed. Not in the Bronx; farther out, near Yonkers: It was more like the country there.

The old man tossed and turned in his bed. That's still a long way off. First, they had to find the house and everything. You don't move just like that! he said to himself. It's gonna take a while, he reasoned, putting such thoughts out of his mind.

Mr. Mendelsohn looked at his new quarters.

"I told you, didn't I? See how nice this is?" his sister Jennie said. She put down the large sack of groceries on the small table.

It was a fair-sized room with a single bed, a bureau, a wooden wardrobe closet, a table, and two chairs. A hot plate was set on a small white refrigerator, and a white metal kitchen cabinet was placed alongside.

"We'll bring you whatever else you need, Louis," Jennie went on. "You'll love it here, I'm sure. There are people your own age, interested in the same things. Here—let's get started. We'll put your things away and you can get nicely settled."

Mr. Mendelsohn walked over to the window and looked out. He saw a wide avenue with cars, taxis, and buses speeding by. "It's gonna take me two buses, at least, to get back to the old neighborhood," he said.

"Why do you have to go back there?" Jennie asked quickly. "There is nobody there any more, Louis. Everybody moved!"

"There's synagogue . . ."

"There's synagogue right here. Next door you have a large temple. Twice you were robbed over there. It's a miracle you weren't hurt! Louis, there is no reason for you to go back. There is nothing over there, nothing," Jennie said.

"The trouble all started with that rooming house next door. Those people took in all kinds. . . ." He shook his head. "When the Suárez family lived there we had no problems. But nobody would talk to the landlord about those new people—only me. Nobody cared."

"That's all finished," Jennie said, looking at her watch. "Now look how nice it is here. Come on, let's get started."

She began to put the groceries away in the refrigerator and cabinet.

"Leave it, Jennie," he interrupted. "Go on. . . . I'll take care of it. You go on home. You are in a hurry."

"I'm only trying to help," Jennie responded.

"I know, I know. But I lived in one place for almost fifty years. So don't hurry me." He looked around the room. "And I ain't going nowhere now. . . ."

Shaking her head, Jennie said, "Look—this weekend we have a wedding, but next weekend Sara and I will come to see you. I'll call the hotel on the phone first, and they'll let you know. All right?"

"Sure." He nodded.

"That'll be good, Louis. This way you will get a chance to get settled and get acquainted with some of the other residents." Jennie kissed Mr. Mendelsohn affectionately. The old man nodded and turned away. In a moment he heard the door open and shut.

Slowly, he walked to the sack of groceries and finished putting them away. Then, with much effort, he lifted a large suitcase onto the bed. He took out several photographs. Then he set the photographs upright, arranging them carefully on the bureau. He had pictures of his parents' wedding and of his sisters and their families. There was a photograph of his mother taken just before she died and another one of Tato.

That picture was taken when he was about two years old, the old man said to himself. Yes, that's right, on his birthday. . . . There was a party. And Tato was already talking. Such a smart kid, he thought, smiling. Last? Last when? he wondered. Time was going fast for him. He shrugged. He could hardly remember what year it was lately. Just before they moved! He remembered. That's right, they gave him the photograph of Tato. They had a nice house around Gunhill Road someplace, and they had taken him there once. He recalled how exhausted he had been after the long trip. No one had a car, and they had had to take a train and buses. Anyway, he was glad he remembered. Now he could let them know he had moved and tell them all about what happened to the old neighborhood. Yes, he said to himself, let me finish here, then I'll go call them. He continued to put the rest of his belongings away.

Mr. Mendelsohn sat in the lobby holding on to his cane and a cake box. He had told the nurse at the desk that his friends were coming to pick him up this Sunday. He looked eagerly toward the revolving doors. After a short while, he saw Ralphy, Julio, and Georgie walk through into the lobby.

"Deliveries are made in the rear of the building," he heard the nurse at the desk say as they walked toward him.

"These are my friends, Mrs. Read," Mr. Mendelsohn said, standing. "They are here to take me out."

"Oh, well," said the nurse. "All right; I didn't realize. Here he is then. He's been talking about nothing else but this visit." Mrs. Read smiled.

Ralphy nodded, then spoke to Georgie. "Get Mr. Mendelsohn's overcoat."

Quickly, Mr. Mendelsohn put on his coat, and all four left the lobby.

"Take good care of him now . . ." they heard Mrs. Read calling. "You be a good boy now, Mr. Mendelsohn."

Outside, Mr. Mendelsohn looked at the young men and smiled.

"How's everyone?" he asked.

"Good," Julio said. "Look, that's my pickup truck from work. They let me use it sometimes when I'm off."

"That's a beautiful truck. How's everyone? Tato? How is my best friend? And Yvonne? Does she like school? And your Mama and Papa? . . . Marta? . . ."

"Fine, fine. Everybody is doing great. Wait till you see them. We'll be there in a little while," said Julio. "With this truck we'll get there in no time."

Mr. Mendelsohn sat in the kitchen and watched as Mrs. Suárez packed food into a shopping bag. Today had been a good day for the old man; he had napped in the old armchair and spent time with the children. Yvonne was so grown up, he almost had not recognized her. When Tato remembered him, Mr. Mendelsohn had been especially pleased. Shyly, he

519

had shaken hands with the old man. Then he had taken him into his room to show Mr. Mendelsohn all his toys.

"Now I packed a whole lotta stuff in this shopping bag for you. You gotta eat it. It's good for you. You too skinny. You got enough for tomorrow and for another day. You put it in the refrigerator. Also I put some rice and other things."

He smiled as she spoke, enjoying the attention he received.

"Julio is gonna drive you back before it gets too late," she said. "And we gonna pick you up again and bring you back to eat with us. I bet you don't eat right." She shook her head. "O.K.?"

"You shouldn't go through so much bother," he protested mildly.

"Again with the bother? You stop that! We gonna see you soon. You take care of yourself and eat. Eat! You must nourish yourself, especially in such cold weather."

Mr. Mendelsohn and Mrs. Suárez walked out into the living room. The family exchanged good-bys with the old man. Tato, feeling less shy, kissed Mr. Mendelsohn on the cheek.

Just before leaving, Mr. Mendelsohn embraced Mrs. Suárez for a long time, as everybody watched silently.

"Thank you," he whispered.

"Thank you? For what?" Mrs. Suárez said. "You come back soon and have Sunday supper with us. Yes?" Mr. Mendelsohn nodded and smiled.

It was dark and cold out. He walked with effort. Julio carried the shopping bag. Slowly, he got into the pickup truck. The ride back was bumpy and uncomfortable for Mr. Mendelsohn. The cold wind cut right through into the truck, and the old man was aware of the long winter ahead.

His eyelids were so heavy he could hardly open them. Nurses scurried about busily. Mr. Mendelsohn heard voices.

"Let's give him another injection. It will help his breathing. Nurse! Nurse! The patient needs . . ."

The voices faded. He remembered he had gone to sleep after supper last—last when? How many days have I been here . . . here in the hospital? Yes, he thought, now I know where I am. A heart attack, the doctor had said, and then he had felt even worse. Didn't matter; I'm too tired. He heard voices once more, and again he barely opened his eyes. A tall, thin man dressed in white spoke to him.

"Mr. Mendelsohn, can you hear me? How do you feel now? More comfortable? We called your family. I spoke to your sister, Mrs. Wiletsky. They should be here very soon. You feeling sleepy? Good. . . . Take a little nap—go on. We'll wake you when they get here, don't worry. Go on now. . . ."

He closed his eyes, thinking of Jennie. She'll be here soon with Esther and Rosalie and Sara. All of them. He smiled. He was so tired. His bed was by the window and a bright, warm sash of sunshine covered him almost completely. Nice and warm, he thought, feeling comfortable. The pain had lessened, practically disappeared. Mr. Mendelsohn heard the birds chirping and Sporty barking. That's all right, Mrs. Suárez would let him sleep. She wouldn't wake him up, he knew that. It looked like a good warm day; he planned to take Tato out for a walk later. That's some smart kid, he thought. Right now he was going to rest.

"This will be the last of it, Sara."

"Just a few more things, Jennie, and we'll be out of here."

The two women spoke as they packed away all the items in the room. They opened drawers and cabinets, putting things away in boxes and suitcases.

"What about these pictures on the bureau?" asked Sara.

Jennie walked over and they both looked at the photographs.

"There's Mama and Papa's wedding picture. Look, there's you, Sara, when Jonathan was born. And Esther and . . . look, he's got all the pictures of the entire family." Jennie burst into tears.

"Come on, Jennie; it's all over, honey. He was sick and very old." The older woman comforted the younger one.

Wiping her eyes, Jennie said, "Well, we did the best we could for him, anyway."

"Who is this?" asked Sara, holding up Tato's photo.

"Let me see," said Jennie. "Hummm . . . that must be one of the people in that family that lived next door in the old apartment on Prospect Avenue. You know—remember that

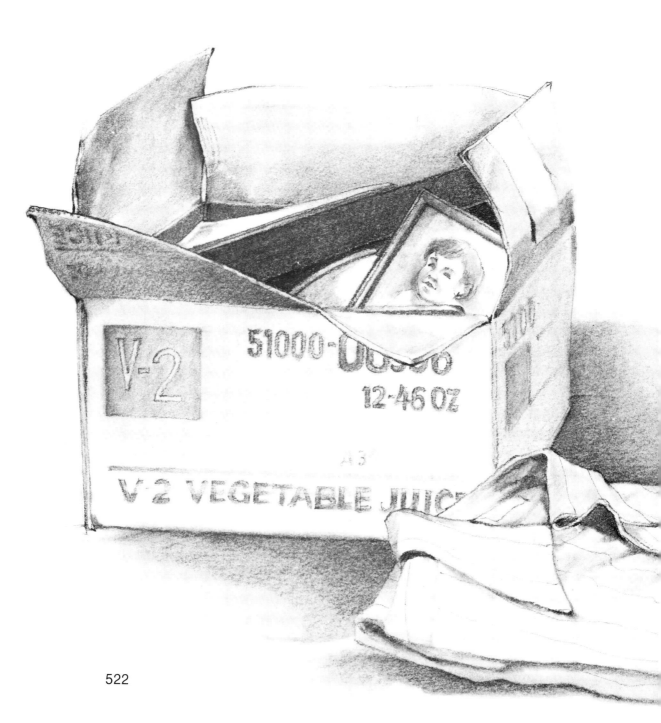

Spanish family? He used to visit with them. Their name was
. . . Díaz or something like that, I think. I can't remember."

"Oh, yes," said Sara. "Louis mentioned them once in a
while, yes. They were nice to him. What shall we do with it?
Return it?"

"Oh," said Jennie, "that might be rude. What do you
think?"

"Well, I don't want it, do you?"

"No." Jennie hesitated. ". . . But let's just put it away.
Maybe we ought to tell them what happened. About Louis."
Sara shrugged her shoulders. "Maybe I'll write to them,"
Jennie went on, "if I can find out where they live. They
moved. What do you say?"

"I don't care, really." Sara sighed. "I have a lot to do yet. I
have to meet Esther at the lawyer's to settle things. And I still
have to make supper. So let's get going."

Both women continued to pack, working efficiently and
with swiftness. After a while, everything was cleared and put
away in boxes and suitcases.

"All done!" said Sara.

"What about this?" asked Jennie, holding up Tato's photograph.

"Do what you want," said Sara. "I'm tired. Let's go."

Looking at the photograph, Jennie slipped it into one of
the boxes. "I might just write and let them know."

The two women left the room, closing the door behind
them.

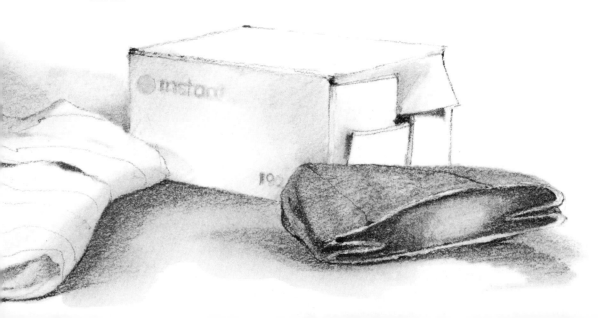

Judith Krotki

No Gnomes

There are no gnomes in Fairlawn New Jersey
or Evanston Illinois or Brigham Utah.
There are no magical beings to help you—
no elf to whisk you out of your misery
out of your growing-up aches and youthful pains
no leprechaun to transport you to another time.
There are no gnomes in Fairlawn New Jersey, are there?

Glossary

In this Glossary the letters and symbols in parentheses that follow each entry word show you how to pronounce the word. For example, **feath er** (feᴛн′ər). The symbols that may puzzle you are shown below. Each symbol is to be pronounced in the way you pronounce the spellings in very black type in the words next to the symbol.

Spaces in pronunciations show the divisions between syllables. A comma in the pronunciation means that the word or part of the word has two different pronunciations and the possible variations are given. In cases where the entry consists of two words, only the pronunciation of an unfamiliar word is shown.

As part of many of the pronunciations, the mark ′ is placed after a syllable with a primary, or heavy, accent, as in **feath er** (feᴛн′ər). The mark ′ is placed after a syllable that has a secondary, or lighter, accent, as in **i mag i na tion** (i maj′ə nā′shən). Sometimes you will see these accent marks in the spaces between syllables.

a **apple, cat**	i **itch, dip**	u **up, cut**
ā **able, day**	ī **ivy, kite**	u̇ **put, cook**
ã **air, pear**		ü **glue, boot**
ä **arm, father**	o **October, hot**	ū **use, music**
	ō **open, go**	
e **elevator, net**	ô **all, saw**	th **thin, both**
ē **each, be**	ôr **order, horse**	ᴛн **then, smooth**
ėr **earth, person**		zh **measure, seizure**
	oi **oil, toy**	
	ou **out, cow**	ə **about, occur, until**

The part of speech follows the pronunciation. The abbreviations and the parts they stand for are:

n.	noun	*conj.* conjunction
adj.	adjective	*prep.* preposition
v.	verb	*p.p.* past participle
adv.	adverb	*n.pl.* plural form of the noun

Key to other abbreviations: *esp.,* especially; *Brit.,* British; *Fr.,* French; *pl.,* plural

a bate (ə bāt′) v. to become less in force or intensity; subside

a bide (ə bīd) v. **to abide by** to accept and follow out; comply with

A bom i na ble Snow man (ə bom′ə ne bl) perhaps real, perhaps legendary creature of the Himalayan mountains, generally considered hostile to people

a breast (ə brest′) adv. alongside

a brupt (ə brupt′) adj. short or sudden in speech or manner; impolite

ac com mo date (ə kom′ə dāt) v. to have room for; hold

ac knowl edg ing (ak nol′ij′ing) adj. being aware or taking notice of

ac qui si tion (ak′wə zish′ən) n. thing purchased or received; possession

ac rid (ak′rid) adj. tasting or smelling sharp, bitter, or burned

a cute (ə kūt′) adj. having or showing keen insight

a dapt (ə dapt′) v. to change or fit to meet particular circumstances

ad min is ter (ad min′is tər) v. to give; supply

ad min is tra tion (ad min′is trā′shən) n. branch of business study concerned with the methods of managing or running an institution or team according to its special needs; management

ad mon ish (ad mon′ish) v. to reprimand gently

ad vent (ad′vent) n. coming; arrival

aer i al (ār′e əl, ā ir′ē əl) adj. growing in air rather than in soil or water

af fa ble (af′ə bl) adj. pleasant; friendly

af flic tion (ə flik′shən) n. cause of pain or distress, as death or disease

ag (ag) adj. shortened form of agricultural

ag gres sive (ə gres′iv) adj. engaging in assault and attack

air lock airtight compartment in which air pressure can be varied so as to allow for passage between places where there is a difference in air pressure

al ien (āl′yən, ā′lē ən) adj. strange; foreign; different —n. **1.** stranger; foreigner **2.** foreign-born person who is not a citizen of the country in which he or she lives

al pine rac ing (al′pīn) competition in which the skier races down an expert slope against the clock or other racers

am ble (am′bl) v. to walk at a slow, easy pace

an gry (ang′grē) adj. inflamed and sore

an guished (ang′gwisht) adj. extremely unhappy

an nals (an′lz) n. pl. historical records; history

an ni hi late (ə ni′ə lāt) v. to destroy completely and totally; wipe out

an tag o nist (an tag′ə nist) n. one who fights or competes with another

an thro pol o gist (an′thrə pol′ə jist) n. one who studies the origins and development of human beings, including their customs and beliefs

a poth e cary (ə poth′ə ker′ē) n. one who prepares and sells drugs and medicine; druggist; pharmacist

ap palled (ə pôld′) adj. shocked; dismayed

ap pre hen sive (ap′ri hen′siv) adj. afraid of what may happen; uneasy — **ap pre hen′sion,** n.

ap pren tice (ə pren′tis) n. one who is trained in or taught a craft or profession by acting as an assistant to someone in the trade for a given period of time, usually for little or no pay

A rap a ho (ə rap′ə hō) n. native American tribe living in what is now Oklahoma and Wyoming

ar is toc ra cy (ar′is tok′rə sē) n. titled and privileged upper class of society; ruling nobility

Ar kie (är′kē) n. migrant farm workers, originally from Arkansas

as sess (ə ses′) v. to tax, charge, or call for a contribution from

As sin i boin (a sin′ə bein, -boin) *n*. Chippewa word literally meaning ''one who cooks by means of, or with, stones''; used to designate a native American tribe

as tute (əs tüt′, -tūt′) *adj*. shrewd; crafty

at ti tude (at′ə tüd, -tūd) *n*. position of the body implying or reflecting a particular state of mind or intention

auc tion (ôk shən) *n*. public sale at which items are sold to the highest bidder. Since there is no fixed price for an item, its cost depends on the demand for it.

au di ence (ô dē əns) *n*. formal meeting or interview with a person of high rank or position

a vert (ə vėrt) *v*. to prevent; avoid

av id (av′id) *adj*. enthusiastic; eager

ax le (ak′sl) *n*. bar on which or with which a wheel or wheels turn

baf fled (baf′ld) *adj*. puzzled ·

bal let (bal′ā, ba lā′) *n*. any set of movements resembling dance in grace or form

band box (band′boks′) *adj*. of or like a light cardboard box used for holding hats, ribbons, or collars

ban ty (ban′tē) *also*, **ban tam** *adj*. (of fowl) miniature in size

ban yan (ban′yan) *n*. fig tree of India whose branches send out roots that enter the ground and develop new trunks

be nev o lence (bə nev′ə ləns) *n*. generosity of spirit; goodness; kindness —**be nev′o lent,** *adj*.

be sieg ing (bi sēj′ing) *adj*. that surrounds in order to capture or take by the use of force

be stow (bi stō′) *v*. to give as a gift; confer

bev eled (bev′ld) *adj*. having a slanting edge

bi car bo nate (bī kär′bə nit, -nāt) *n*. bicarbonate of soda, a remedy for indigestion

bind (bīnd) *v*. to create or impose specific legal responsibility

Black feet (blak fēt) *n*. three closely related tribes—the Blackfeet, the Piegan, and the Blood—speaking the same Algonquian language and having close political ties, living in the Plains States. *Also called* **Siksika**

blas phem ing (blas fēm′ing) *adj*. cursing God or other sacred things

bois ter ous (bois′tər əs, -trəs) *adj*. noisy and excitable; lively

boon (bün) *n*. good fortune or benefit

borne (bôrn) *p.p.* of *bear.* undergone; endured; suffered

boy cott (boi′kot) *n*. refusal to buy, sell, or use a product or deal with persons or businesses that do. This is usually an action, or campaign, done in combination with many other people

Boze man Trail (bōz′man) trail pioneered in 1864 connecting Fort Laramie, Wyoming, and Bozeman, Montana, and later used to reach gold-mining camps in Montana

brave (brāv) *v*. to meet and endure without fear; defy

brief (brēf) *v., Informal.* to provide with facts essential for a particular situation

brim ming (brim′ing) *adj*. figuratively, full or more than full (with *with*); overflowing

bris tling (bris′ling) *adj*. full of and excited about (with *with*)

brood (brüd) *n*. the young birds hatched or cared for at one time

brunt (brunt) *n*. main or hardest part

B.Sc. Bachelor of Science, a degree granted for the completion of a four-year college

---

a apple, ā able, ã air, ä arm; e elevator, ē each, ėr earth; i itch, ī ivy; o October, ō open, ô all, ôr order; oi oil, ou out; u up, u̇ put, ü glue, ū use; th thin, ⊤H then, zh measure; ə about, occur, until

program with the major work done in science or mathematics

buck skin (buk′skin′) *n.* strong, soft, yellowish leather made from the skins of deer or sheep

buff (buf) *n.* fan; enthusiast

butch er ous (büch′ər əs) *adj.* brutal and cruel; killing

ca denced (kād′nst) *adj.* having a definite measure or beat

ca lam i ty (kə lam′ə tē) *n.* catastrophe; disaster

cal cu lus (kal′kyə ləs) *n.* branch of higher mathematics using a special form of algebra

cal en dar (kal′ən dər) *n.* list; record

cal li o pe (ka lī′ə pē, kal′ē ōp) *n.* musical instrument having a series of steam whistles that are played by means of a keyboard

can teen (kan tēn′) *n.* small container for carrying water or other liquids

Can ton (kan ton′) *n.* coastal city and provincial capital in southeastern China. *Also called* **Kuang Chow**

cap i tal (kap′ə tl) *n.* money; profit

cas u al ty (kazh′ü əl tē) *n.* loss of a military or other person as a result of injury, death, or capture by the enemy

Cey lon (si lon′) *n.* island country south of India in the Indian Ocean

cha me leon (kə mēl′yən, -mē′lē ən) *n.* lizard whose skin changes color according to temperature, threat, or other factors, often serving as a means of camouflage

chap ter (chap′tər) *n.* local branch or division of an organization, club, or society

charge (charj) *n.* quantity (as of powder or an explosive) that a receptacle can hold

char ter (chär′tər) *n.* formal written document issued by a government to a group, granting it the right to organize for a specific activity and imposing on it certain rules and conditions

Chey enne (shī en′) *n.* Dakotoa word literally meaning "red talkers"; used to designate a native American tribe living on the Great Plains and famous as herders

chide (chīd) *v.* to scold mildly

chris ten ing (kris′n ing, kris′ning) *n.* Christian church ceremony in which a child is named

chron ic (kron′ik) *adj.* (of an illness) lasting a long time or recurring

cir cuit (sėr′kit) *n.* area or category as defined by a trail or route, a series of items connected by a common element: *hotel circuit, talk-show circuit*

cir cum stan tial (sėr′kəm stan′shəl) *adj.* giving full and exact details

ci vil ian (sə vil′yən) *adj.* of or relating to persons or citizens who are not members of the army, navy, or other military force

the clas sics (klas′iks) the literature of ancient Greece and Rome

clin ic (klin′ik) *n.* program offering help, instruction, or training in some special skill or field

cock roach (kok′rōch′) *n.* black or brown insect with a flat, oval body, hairy legs, and long feelers, considered a household pest

col lec tive ly (kə lek′tiv lē) *adv.* as a group; all together

col umn (kol′əm) *n.* military formation in which soldiers, ships, or the like are arranged one behind the other in one or more rows; arrangement resembling this. Distinguished from **line.**

com mend a bly (kə men′də blē) *adv.* in a praiseworthy manner

com mer cial (kə′mėr′shəl) *adj.* directed toward making money; done for profit

com mis sion (kə mish′ən) *n.* rank and authority granted by an official federal document

com mune (kom′ūn) *n.* community, often rural, set up and owned by the state, in which the people share the use and work of the land and facilities

com pos ure (kəm pō′zhər) *n.* assured self-control; calmness

com pound (kom′pound) *n.* enclosed area containing buildings or houses related in function or purpose, as an *army compound*

com pre hend (kom′pri hend′) *v.* to take in or include; encompass; embrace

con ceive (kən sēv′) *v.* to form a mental image or idea; imagine

con dens er (kən den′sər) *n.* device for receiving and storing an electric charge

con fer (kən fer′) *v.* to bestow; give

con sign (kən sīn′) *v.* to set apart; assign

con sult ant (kən sul′tənt) *n.* expert who gives professional or technical advice, usually for a fee

con sum ma tion (kon′sə mā′shən) *n.* highest possible fulfillment; completion

con ta gious (kən tā′jəs) *adj.* (of a disease) spread by contact or directly by a person having it; communicable

con trac tor (kon′trak tər, kən trak′-) *n.* one who agrees to supply persons for a job at a certain price

con tro ver sy (kon′trə ver′sē) *n.* debate over a subject about which there are differences of opinion; dispute; argument

court (kôrt) *n.* family, household, and advisors of a royal ruling power, collectively

co zy (kō′zē) *n.* padded teapot cover used to keep tea warm

crest (krest) *n.* comb or ridge, as on the head of a bird

cre vasse (krə vas′) *n.* deep crack; crevice

crop (krop) *n.* group; collection —*v.* **to crop up** to come up unexpectedly

cro quet (krō kā′) *n.* outdoor game played by using a mallet to knock wooden balls in a particular order through small wire arches set in the ground

cru sad er (krü sād′ər) *n.* person active in, or leader of, a cause, esp. for reform or improvement

curt (kert) *adj.* rudely brief

cy clone fence heavy-duty, high-wire fence

damp ened (dam′pənd) *adj.* reduced in intensity or degree; checked; deflated

deb u tante (deb′yů tänt) *n.* girl making her first official or formal appearance in high society

de cant (di kant′) *v.* to be moved like liquid being poured from one container to another

dec o ra tive (dek′ə rā tiv, dek′rə-) *adj.* serving no useful purpose, but adding beauty; ornamental

deft (deft) *adj.* quick and skillful; nimble

Deh ra (dā rä, dər′ə) *n.* town in northern India, headquarters of the national forestry service and college with a large military population associated with a training academy there

Del hi (del′i, -ē) *also,* **Old Del hi** *n.* city in northern India, next to the capital, New Delhi

de mean or (di mēn′ər) *n.* way a person acts and looks; bearing; conduct

de pend ent (di pen′dənt) *n.* person for whom one is financially responsible

de port ment (di pôrt′mənt) *n.* behavior; manner; conduct

De pres sion (di presh′ən) *n.* economic crisis of the 1930s marked by low business activity, high unemployment, and falling wages

---

a apple, ā able, ã air, ä arm; e elevator, ē each, ėr earth; i itch, ī ivy; o October, ō open, ô all, ôr order; oi oil, ou out; u up, ů put, ü glue, ū use; th thin, ŦH then, zh measure; ə about, occur, until

de scent (di sent′) *n.* ancestry; birth

de ser tion (di zer′shən) *adj.* of or related to the act of running away; abandonment

De So to (di sō′tō) trademark name for a medium-priced automobile that went out of production in 1960

de spond ent (di spon′dənt) *adj.* despairing; depressed

de ten tion camp group of buildings in which people are kept confined and which they are prevented from leaving; concentration camp

de trac tor (di trak′tər) *n.* one who belittles the achievements of, or criticizes, another

di a bol i cal ly (dī′ə bol′ə klē) *adv.* in a cruel manner, like that of a devil; devilishly

din (din) *n.* noise

dis creet (dis krēt′) *adj.* not calling attention to itself; subdued and out of the way

dis crim i na tion (dis krim′ə nā′shən) *n.* partiality, often based on prejudice, shown toward or against members of a group

dis dain ful ly (dis dān′fəl ē) *adv.* in a manner that shows scorn or contempt

dock (dok) *v.* to subtract a portion of; cut down; reduce

dom i nant (dom′ə nənt) *adj.* conspicuous or outstanding

draft (draft) *adj.* used for pulling loads

dress (dres) *v.* to prepare for cooking

driv ing force power or energy that keeps something going

drone (drōn) *n.* low, continuous humming or buzzing sound

drove (drōv) *n.* group of people; crowd

dry goods clothes, fabrics, and other related items (such as ribbons), as distinguished from other merchandise, such as hardware or furniture

due (dū, dü) *adv.* straight; directly; exactly

dump y lev el surveying instrument with a rotating telescope

dusk y (dus′kē) *adj.* of or like the color of dusk; silvery gray

e clipse (i klps′) *v.* to block the rays of and so darken or seem to wipe out (a planet or star in the sky)

e col o gy (ē kol′ə jē) *n.* relationship of living things to their environment and to each other; environmental balance

ed i tor (ed′ə tər) *n.* **1.** one who corrects, revises, or otherwise prepares written matter for publication **2.** one in charge of what shall be printed, as in a newspaper or magazine

e go (ē′gō, ēg′ō) *n.* **1.** self **2.** *Informal.* conceit

e las tic i ty (i las′tis′ətē, ē′las-) *n.* capability of being stretched; having give

elk (elk) *n.* large, reddish deer

el o quence (el′ə kwəns) *n.* effective and expressive language

em bez zle ment (em bez′l mənt) *n.* theft of money or goods entrusted to one's care

em bla zoned (em blā′znd) *v.* conspicuously decorated, as with writing or with a design

em bry on ic (em′brē on′ik) *adj.* in its early or beginning stages; not yet completed

em phat ic (em fat′ik) *adj.* given special stress or emphasis; obviously meaningful or important; striking

en camp ment (en kamp′mənt) *n.* location of temporary quarters; settlement out in the open

en chi la da (en′chi lä′də) *n.* Mexican dish made of a tortilla filled with meat or cheese, and served with a spicy sauce

en deav or (en dev′ər) *n.* great effort

en route (än rüt′, en-) *n.* on the way

en tic ing (en tīs′ing) *adj.* tempting; attractive

en to mo log i cal (en′tə mə loj′ə kl) *adj.* designed for use with insects

e pit o me (i pit′ə mē) *n.* anyone that represents the whole; essence

e quine (ē′kwīn) *adj.* of, relating to, or like a horse

er u dite (er′yü dīt, -ü-) *adj.* having wide knowledge and learning; scholarly

es ca la tor (es′kə lā′tər) *n.* motorized moving stairway

et i quette (et′ə ket) *n.* rules or conventions of conduct in a specific area or profession: *dining-car etiquette, legal etiquette;* good manners

ex clu sive (eks klü′siv) *adj.* admitting only a special or select group

ex ha la tion (eks′hə lā′shən) *n.* sigh, as of air

ex haust (eg zôst′) *adj.* referring to the mechanical or electrical means of letting off or out used steam, gases, or similar waste products

ex pe di tion (eks′pə dish′ən) *n.* journey made for some special purpose, as exploration or scientific study

ex tir pate (eks′tər pāt, eks tér′-) *v.* to stamp out or destroy completely; eradicate

ex tra ter res tri al (eks′trə tə res′trē al) *n.* being or creature not born on the earth —*adj.* concerned with regions or peoples outside the earth and its atmosphere

ex ult ing ly (eg zult′ing lē) *adv.* in a very joyous, triumphant manner

fair way (fār′wā′) *n.* area of a golf course between the tee and the twenty yards before the hole

fal con (fôl′kən, fal′-, fô′kən) *n.* any of various female hawks trained as birds of prey   **to fly a falcon**   to hunt with a falcon

fea si bil i ty stud y study made to determine whether and how something can be done

fin ish ing school private school at which girls used to complete their education before entering society

flank (flangk) *n.* side of an animal between the ribs and the hip — *v.* to be at and guard (both sides of)

flaunt (flônt, flänt) *v.* to show off

foot man (füt′mən) *n.* male servant in uniform who aids the butler in serving and cleaning and assists people in and out of carriages or cars

for ay (fô′ā, for′) *n.* short trip made for food; raid

For bid den City walled area in the center of Peking, which closed off the palaces and grounds of the former imperial rulers from the public for many centuries

for ceps (fôr′seps, -səps) *n.* tool having jaw- or armlike extensions that are used to grip or hold objects, esp. specimens

for feit ing (fôr′fit ing) *adj.* giving up or losing as a penalty for some offense or mistake

for mi da ble (fôr′mə də bl) *adj.* presenting a difficult challenge

for tune (fôr chən) *n.* **1.** chance outcome or result **2.** great wealth or riches **3.** that which happens or is going to happen to a person; destiny **4.** force that controls the universe; chance; fate **5.** good luck; success

fraught (frôt) *adj.* worked up; upset

free ski ing ski competition involving stunts or fancy steps

fric tion (frik′shən) *n.* instance of conflict or difference between two people

fri joles (frē′hōlz′, fri hō′lēz, -läs) *n. pl., Span.* beans

froth ing (frôth′ing, froth′-) *adj.* forming small bubbles at the mouth; sputtering, as with anger; foaming

frus trate (frus′trāt) *v.* to prevent from being successful; put a stop to; thwart

---

a **a**pple, ā **a**ble, ā **a**ir, ä **a**rm; e **e**levator, ē **ea**ch, ėr **ear**th; i **i**tch, ī **i**vy; o **O**ctober, ō **o**pen, ô **a**ll, ôr **or**der; oi **oi**l, ou **ou**t; u **u**p, ů **p**ut, ü **g**l**ue**, ū **u**se; th **th**in, ᴛʜ **th**en, zh mea**s**ure; ə **a**bout, **o**ccur, **u**ntil

fu gi tive (fū′jə tiv) *n.* runaway from the law

fur tive (fėr′tiv) *adj.* sneaky; secret

gab ble (gab′l) *n.* rapid, meaningless talk

Ga ble, Clark (gā′bl, klärk) 1901–1960, Hollywood movie star and idol, esp. of the 1930s and 1940s

gall (gôl) *n.* nerve

gal va nized i ron iron coated with zinc by means of an electro-chemical process in order to prevent rusting

gape (gāp) *v.* to open wide

gar (gär) *n.* long, slender fish with elongated jaws

gaud y (gôd′ē) *adj.* bright and showy in a cheap, theatrical way

ge ol o gy (jē ol′ə jē) *n.* **1.** science that deals with the structure, composition, and historical changes in the earth's surface **2.** structure and composition of the surface of a particular area —**ge o log′i cal,** *adj.*

Glouces ter shire (glos′tər shir) *n.* county in southwestern England

gnome (nōm) *n.* dwarf supposed to live in the earth guarding precious treasure

goad (gōd) *v.* to urge or drive on

gouge (gouj) *n.* hollowed-out area or hole

grant (grant) *n.* formal gift or award, esp. one given in recognition of some service, talent, or attainment, and providing for further research, study, or creation of a given project

grat i fy (grat′ə fī) *v.* to give pleasure or satisfaction to; please

the Great Be yond that which is after death; life after death

Great Wall huge stone wall extending 1500 miles along the boundary between north and northwest China and Mongolia, built originally in the third century B.C. to defend against invaders

griev ance (grēv′əns) *n.* real or imagined wrong causing anger or distress; reason for complaint

griz zled (griz′ld) *adj.* gray-haired; gray

Gros Ven tre (grō ven′tėr) *Fr.,* literally, "big belly," from the Indian sign for "always hungry, beggars"; used to designate two distinct tribes—the prairie Arapaho and the Hidatsa (or Minitari) of Montana

grouse (grous) *n.* any of several plump fowl-like game birds with spotted or streaked markings

gru el ing (grü′əl ing) *adj.* very tiring or physically punishing; exhausting

gun ny sack (gun′ē sak) *n.* sack made of strong, coarse fiber

gut ter (gut′ər) *n.* narrow channel along the edge or eave of a roof for carrying off rain water

gut tur al (gut′ər əl) *adj.* (of the voice) having a rough, grating quality

hab it a ble (hab′ə tə bl) *adj.* fit to live in

ham per (ham′pər) *n.* large covered basket: *picnic hamper*

har assed (har′əst, hə rast′) *adj.* repeatedly bothered or annoyed

har bor (här′bər) *v.* to give shelter or refuge to; hide.

Har lem (här′lem) *n.* black neighborhood in the northwest section of Manhattan in New York City

head long (hēd′lông, -long) *adv.* **1.** headfirst **2.** with great speed and force

Hei fetz, Ja sha (hī′fits, yä′shə) 1901– Russian-born American violinist

here to fore (hir′tə fôr′, -fōr) *adv.* before this time; until now

ho gan (hō′gän, -gan) *n.* traditional Navajo dwelling built of earth walls

home (hōm) *adj.* of, relating to, or concerned with one's country; in charge of or responsible for domestic affairs

host (hōst) *n.* large number; multitude

hos til i ty (hos til′ə tē) *n.* feeling of intense dislike; hatred

hu mil i ty (hū mil′ə tē) *n.* absence of arrogance and pride; meek patience

hus band ry (huz′bənd rē) *adj.* concerned with and knowledgeable about the breeding and raising of livestock, as for farming

hy po chon dri ac (hī′pə kon′drē ak) *n.* person who shows excessive concern and complains frequently about his or her health

il lus tri ous (i lus′trē əs) *adj.* distinguished; outstanding

im mu ni ty (i mū′nə tē) *n.* freedom from certain consequences; special exemption

im pend ing (im pen′ding) *adj.* about to happen; threatening

im per vi ous (im pėr′vē əs) *adj.* not allowing passage; impenetrable

im plore (im plôr′) *v.* to ask earnestly; beg

im pulse (im′puls) *n.* force that moves one to act without thought or plan; almost instinctive tendency

in ci dence (in′sə dəns) *n.* rate or frequency of occurrence

in cised (in sīzd′) *adj.* carved

in com pa ra ble (in kom′pə rə bl, -kom′prə-) *adj.* matchless; unique

in cor ri gi ble (in kôr′ə jə bl, -kor′-) *adj.* so bad as to be beyond reform or correction

in cre du li ty (in′krə dü′lə tē, -dū′-) *n.* disbelief

in cred u lous ly (in krej′ə ləs′lē) *adv.* (as of a tone of voice) expressing doubt or disbelief

in del i ble (in del′ə bl) *adj.* that cannot be erased or removed; ineradicable; permanent

in dic a tive (in dik′ə tiv) *adj.* acting as a sign or evidence (with *of*)

in dif fer ence (in dif′ər əns, -dif′rəns) *n.* lack of interest, concern, or care

in dig nant (in dig′nənt) *adj.* angry at some injustice or personal insult —**in′dig na′tion,** *n.*

in dis pen sa ble (in′dis pen′sə bl) *adj.* that which cannot be done without; absolutely necessary

in duce (in düs′, -dūs-) *v.* to bring about; produce; cause

in dulge (in dulj′) *v.* to give way to the pleasure of doing something (with *in*)

in fa my (in′fə mē) *n.* state or condition of being condemned as a great wrong or evil; public disgrace

in flu en za (in′flu en′zə) *n.* highly contagious disease, characterized by fever, headache, coughing, and exhaustion

in flux (in′fluks) *n.* steady flow

in gre di ent (in grē′dē ənt) *n.* component or part

i ni tial (i nish′əl) *adj.* occurring at the beginning; first; earliest

in quir y (in kwir′ē, -kwə rē) *n.* investigation; search

in so lent (in′sə lənt) *adj.* extremely rude or arrogant

in stall ment (in stôl′mənt) *adj.* of or related to partial payments made at regular times on money owed

in tent ly (in tent′lē) *adv.* with great concentration

in ter mit tent (in′tər mit′nt) *adj.* stopping and starting continuously; coming at intervals

in tern ment (in tėrn′mənt) *n.* act or condition of being forced to stay in a certain place; confinement, as in a prison

in tol er a ble (in tol′ər ə bl) *adj.* much too painful or dangerous to be endured; unbearable

---

a apple, ā able, ã air, ä arm; e elevator, ē each, ėr earth; i itch, ī ivy; o October, ō open, ô all, ôr order; oi oil, ou out; u up, u̇ put, ü glue, ū use; th thin, ŦH then, zh measure; ə about, occur, until

in val u able (in val′yủ ə bl, -yủ bl) *adj.* very valuable or helpful; priceless

in ven to ry (in′vən tô′rē, -tō-) *v.* to make a detailed list of

i ron i cal ly (ī ron′ə klē) *adv.* **1.** in a way that conveys a sense that the real meaning is the opposite of what is said **2.** in such a way that expresses the difference between what was predicted and what actually happened

ir rel e vant (i rel′ə vənt) *adj.* not bearing on or connected to the main point or matter at hand

ir ri ta bly (ir′ə tə blē) *adv.* in an annoyed, impatient manner

jack rab bit large hare of western North America having long ears and long, strong hind legs

jaun ti ly (jôn′tə lē, jän′-) *adv.* in a springy, carefree manner

Ka zakh (kə zäk′, kä-) *n.* citizen of Kazakhstan, the Soviet republic in central Asia

knap sack (nap′sak′) *n.* bag, usually of canvas or nylon, that is strapped over the shoulders and carried on the back

Kuang Chow (gwäng′ gō′) Chinese name for a coastal city and provincial capital in southeastern China. *Also called* **Canton**

laud a to ry (lôd′ə tô′rē, -tōr′ē) *adj.* expressing or containing praise

leg gings (leg′ingz) *n.* extra outer coverings for the legs, made of cloth or leather, and designed for outdoor wear usually reaching to the ankle

leg ume (leg′ūm, li gūm′) *n.* group of plants, as beans, peas, peanuts, or alfalfa, cultivated for food, fodder, and as natural fertilizers

Len in (len′ən) 1870–1924, Russian leader, political theorist, and founder of the Soviet Union, and its leader from 1917 to 1924. Born **Vladmir Ilich; called Nikolai**

lev el (lev′l) *n.* surveying instrument used for showing whether or not a surface is level and for measuring differences in the height or elevation of land

lib er al (lib′ər əl, lib′rəl) *adj.* generous

lift (lift) *also,* **chair lift** *n.* mechanical apparatus consisting of a chair or other device suspended from a cable that carries the skier up the slope to the top of the ski trail

lil y-liv ered (lil′ē liv′ərd) *adj.* cowardly

lim pid (lim′pid) *adj.* transparent; clear

line (līn) *n.* **1.** military formation in which soldiers, ships, or the like are arranged abreast, or shoulder to shoulder; arrangement resembling this. (Distinguished from **column**) **2.** course; direction

liv er y sta ble business establishment for the care, boarding, and rental of horses

loathe (lōŦH) *v.* to hate; despise

lop ing (lōp′ing) *adj.* with a long, uneven stride

Lou is, Joe (lü′is, jō) 1914— , Black-American boxer and heavyweight champion from 1937 to 1949

lunge (lunj) *v.* to make a sudden movement forward; lurch

lus ter (lus′tər) *n.* glory; splendor

lymph (limf) *n.* clear, nearly colorless fluid similar to blood in composition that brings nutrients and oxygen to body cells and carries away wastes; it oozes from infections or wounds

main stay (mān′stā′) *n.* main support or source of support; staple

mal let (mal′it) *n.* short-handled wooden hammer with a cylindrical head

Mao Tse-tung (mou′tse′tung′, dzu doong′) 1893–1976, Chinese leader, writer, philosopher, poet, and chairman of the Chinese Communist Party from the 1930s on

mar ket ing (mär′kit ing) *n.* branch of business study or profession concerned with methods and procedures for selling things

mat i nee jacket (mat′n ā) a morning jacket, a dressy negligee worn esp. when receiving guests informally

mat ri mo ni al (mat′rə mō′nē əl) *adj.* of or relating to marriage

me chan i cal en gi neer person skilled in scientific methods and procedures for designing, constructing, and repairing machinery

me chan ics (mə kan′iks) *n.* branch of physics that deals with the forces affecting the motion or movement of liquids and bodies

me nag er ie (mə naj′ər ē, -nazh-) *n.* collection of wild or unusual animals kept in cages or other enclosures for exhibition; zoo

mer chan dise (mėr′chən dīz) *n.* items bought and sold; wares

mes quite bush (mes kēt′, mes′kēt) thorny, dense-growing shrub or tree of the pea family found in American desert regions. The pods are used for food by cattle.

mi grant work er person who travels from one place to another to find work, usually of a seasonal nature

minc ing (min′sing) *adj.* artificial or affected

min gle (ming′gl) *v.* to mix or join together

min ing en gi neer person skilled in scientific methods and mechanical procedures for extracting coal, ores, and other materials from the earth′s surface

min is ter (min′is tər) *v.* to give knowledge, aid, or support (with *to*)

mis cel la ny (mis′ə lā′nē) *n.* collection of various items

Mis sis sip pi Bub ble money-making plan that failed in 1720 when many people withdrew their money from a company that was supposed to be developing the Louisiana Territory but was not

mo bile (mō′bl, -bēl) *adj.* easily movable — **mo bil′i ty,** *n.*

mo lest (mə lest′) *v.* **1.** to disturb; bother **2.** to tamper with, as by destructive physical contact

mol ten (mōlt′n) *adj.* melting or seeming to melt with heat

mon soon (mon sün′) *adj.* of or relating to the seasonal wind of the Indian Ocean and southern Asia that in summer blows from the southwest toward the land, bringing heavy rains with it

Moor (mür) *n.* member of a race related to the Arabs who invaded and occupied Spain from the eighth century until 1492

mo ti va tion (mō′tə vā′shən) *n.* mental or internal need or outward cause that stimulates someone to movement or action

mul ti tude (mul′tə tüd, -tūd) *n.* great numbers collected together in one place; mass, as of insects; army

mush room (mush′rüm, -rum) *v.* to grow suddenly and quickly

mus ter (mus′tər) *v.* to gather or collect (troops) officially; draft

Nav a jo (nav′ə hō) *n.* native American tribe of the Athapascan language family, living in New Mexico, Arizona, and parts of Colorado and Utah. They became sheep and goat herders and were famous for their blanket weaving

net tle (net′l) *adj.* made with or from any one of a group of weedlike plants having sharp, stinging hairs

New Guin ea (gin′ē) second largest island in the world divided into Indonesia (West Irian) and Papua, located east of the Malay Archipelago, north of Australia in the Pacific Ocean

---

a apple, ā able, ã air, ä arm; e elevator, ē each, ėr earth; i itch, ī ivy; o October, ō open, ô all, ôr order; oi oil, ou out; u up, u̇ put, ü glue, ū use; th thin, ŦH then, zh measure; ə about, occur, until

noc tur nal (nok tėr′nl) *adj.* active at night

non cha lant ly (non′shə länt′lē) *adv.* indifferently; casually

nur ture (nėr′chər) *v.* to encourage the growth and expression of; foster

ob lique (ə blēk′, ō′blēk) *adj.* not perpendicular or parallel; slanting

ob liv i ous (əb liv′ē əs) *adj.* unaware; forgetful

om i nous (om′ə nəs) *adj.* seeming or threatening evil; foreboding

op pres sion (ə presh′ən) *n.* weary feeling of being weighed down

ore dress ing physical treatment of ores, as crushing or concentrating

or na ment al (ôr′nə men′tl) *adj.* beautiful; decorative

O sage (ō′sāj, ō sāj′) *n.* member of a tribe of Sioux Indians belonging to the Siouan language family and living in what is now Kansas, Missouri, and Illinois

out stand ing (out stan′ding) *adj.* unpaid

o ver rid ing (ō′vər rīd′ing) *adj.* more important than any other; crucial

pac i fy (pas′ə fī) *v.* to reduce the strong feelings of, as by making a concession; quiet or calm down

pag eant (paj′ənt) *n.* **1.** public entertainment that presents a scene from history, religion, or legend, or of some community event **2.** spectacular parade or procession **3.** empty display; a mere show

pal pi ta tion (pal′pə tā′shən) *n.* very rapid and often irregular beating of the heart

pang (pang) *n.* sudden, short but sharp mental qualm or reservation; momentary emotional distress; sudden feeling of discomfort

pan try (pan′trē) *n.* storage room for food and items used for preparing and serving food

par al lel turn turn made with skis parallel to one another

par tridge (pär′trij) *n.* any of several plump, fowl-like game birds with white, gray, or brown markings

pat ent (pat′nt) *n.* official document from a government signifying that something is original and granting to its creator the sole right of using, producing, and selling it for a certain period of time

pee pul (pē′pəl) *n.* fig tree of India, similar to the banyan tree

pen du lous (pen′jə ləs, -dyə ləs) *adj.* hanging or drooping

pe nul ti mate (pi nul′tə mit) *adj.* next to the last

per cus sion (pər kush′ən) *n.* the various musical instruments whose tones are produced by striking, considered as a group

per ish a ble (per′ish ə bl) *adj.* liable to spoil or decay

per me at ed (pėr′mē āt əd) *adj.* spread throughout; filled

pe trol o gy (pi trol′ə jē) *n.* branch of geology that deals with the study of rocks and rock formations

pet ti fog ging (pet′ē fog′ing) *adj.* petty, devious, and mean

phys i ol o gy (fiz′ē ol′ə jē) *n.* science of the functions and processes of living things

piece rate rate or amount paid according to the quantity or number of pieces done rather than by the hour or day

Pie gan (pē gan) *n.* member of an Algonquian-speaking Blackfeet tribe living principally in Montana and Canada

pin ion (pin′yən) *adj.* of or related to the last joint of a bird's wing

pi o neer (pī′ə nir, -nēr) *n.* one who is first or among the first in a particular field

pitch (pich) *n.* black, thick, sticky substance occurring naturally in wood, coal, and petroleum, and used for waterproofing and road paving

pitch (pich) *v.* to throw over or give up

pi ti less (pit′i lis) *adj.* showing no mercy or pity

piv ot (piv′ət) *n.* turn made by the body with the weight on the toe of one foot and the heel of the other

plain tive ly (plān′tiv′lē) *adv.* mournfully; sadly; pleadingly

plait (plāt) *v.* to make by braiding

plate-rail (plāt rāl) *n.* narrow rack or shelf with horizontal bar for holding dishes upright for display

po di um (pō′dē əm) *n.* raised platform or other structure from which an audience is addressed or from which a conductor leads an orchestra

point (point) *n.* trait or characteristic of an animal, esp. one by which the excellence of a particular breed is judged

point ing (point′ing) *n.* in certain trained hunting dogs, the skill of pointing out game with the muzzle and body

pok er face face that is without expression, as those of poker players who do not want to show their hands

po ly seed *Informal.* sunflower seed

pom pous (pom′pəs) *adj.* characterized by an exaggerated sense of self-importance; pretentious

pon der (pon′dər) *v.* to consider carefully; think over

por ce lain (pôrs′lin) *adj.* of or relating to white, translucent, and nonporous ceramic ware or its manufacture

pore (pôr, pōr) *v.* to read or study with great care and concentration (with *over*)

po ten tial (pə ten′shəl) *adj.* capable of being or becoming; possible

pot tage (pot′ij) *n.* thick soup made with vegetables and meat

pound (pound) *n.* British unit of money. One pound in 1976 was equivalent to $1.67

prec e dent (pres′ə dənt) *n.* case that serves to set an example for similar situations that may arise in the future

pred a tor (pred′ə tər) *n.* animal, as a lion or hawk, that lives by feeding on other animals

pred i cate ad jec tive (pred′i kit) adjective that is linked to the verb but refers to the subject; for example, *bright* in *How bright he is; envious* in *She feels envious.*

preen (prēn) *v.* (of a bird) to clean, arrange, and smoothe (the feathers) with the beak

prey (prā) *n.* habit of hunting and killing for food: *beast of prey*

pri mate (prī′māt, -mit) *n.* any member of the highest order of mammals

pri mor di al (prī môr′dē əl) *adj.* primitive; original; basic

pri or i ty (prī ôr′ə tē, -or′-) *n.* preferential treatment given in time, order, or importance

pro duce (prə düs′, -dūs) *v.* to prepare a program for the public, as by developing an idea, hiring performers, and getting money to pay for making it — *n.* (prod′üs, prōd′, -ūs) farm products, esp. fruits and vegetables sold at market

pro fes sion al (prə fesh′ən l, -nəl) *adj.* **1.** done as a means of earning a living, esp. when such activity is not usually done for money **2.** made up of such professionals, as opposed to amateurs

pro mot er (prə mōt′ər) *n.* one who arranges a sporting event or lottery, as by getting necessary funds for its presentation

pro pul sion (prə pul′shən) *adj.* driven by fuel vapors ejected by the engine in one direction, forcing the plane to move in the opposite direction

pros pect (pros′pekt) *v.* to search; explore

---

a **a**pple, ā **a**ble, ã **a**ir, ä **a**rm; e **e**levator, ē **ea**ch, ėr **ear**th; i **i**tch, ī **i**vy; o **O**ctober, ō **o**pen, ô **a**ll, ôr **or**der; oi **oi**l, ou **ou**t; u **u**p, u̇ **p**ut, ü **g**lue, ū **u**se; th **th**in, ᴛʜ **th**en, zh mea**s**ure; ə **a**bout, **o**ccur, **u**ntil

prov o ca tion (prov'ə kā'shən) n. something that stirs one up; cause of anger or attack

pu ny (pū'nē) adj. of inferior size and number

purse (pèrs) v. to draw together; pucker

pus tule (pus'chül) n. small inflamed swelling containing pus

quar ter (kwôr'tər) n. place or region, esp. when unspecified

ques tion (kwes'chən) n. **in question** under discussion or consideration

quill (qwil) n. hollow stem of a feather

rang y (rān'jē) adj. slender and long limbed

rap ids (rap'idz) n. pl. part of a river where the current moves swiftly due to a sharp drop in the riverbed

rec on cil i a tion (rek'ən sil'ē ā'shən) n. settlement of differences; process of coming into harmony

re con nais sance (ri kon'ə səns) n. examination or survey to obtain information

re cruit (ri krüt') v. to get to join or enlist

rec to ry (rek'tər ē) n. priest's residence

re dress (rē'dres, ri dres') n. act of compensating for or remedying some wrong done or injury suffered

re flec tion (re flek'shən) n. serious and weighty thought

reg i ment (rej'ə mənt) n. military unit, commanded by a colonel, which is composed of three battalions and forms part of a division

reg is trar (rej'is trär, rej'is trär') n. official or office of a college or university responsible for keeping records, as of students enrolled, grades, and the like

re hash (rē'hash) n. review of old material

rel ic (rel'ik) n. object having interest because of its age or associations; souvenir; keepsake

re luc tant ly (ri luk'tənt lē) adv. in an unwilling manner

re o ri ent (rē ô'rē ənt, -ō-) v. to place (oneself) in a new relation to a situation; to change and become used to a different point of view or understanding

re pel (ri pel') v. to force or drive back

re port (ri pôrt, -pōrt') n. explosive sound or noise made by the firing of a gun

re source ful ness (ri sôrs'fəl nəs) n. skill and creativity in dealing with a situation or condition

re spec tive (ri spek'tiv) adj. related or belonging to each; own

rés u mé (rez'u mā) n. summary

re tail (rē'tāl) adj. of or relating to items bought singly or in small quantities directly by the consumer

re ver ber ate (ri vèr'bər āt) v. to echo

rev er ie (rev'ər ē) n. daydream

rip tide (rip'tīd) n. strong seaward current that returns water from waves breaking against the shore

roost (rüst) v. to sleep or rest on a perch or in a nest

root crop any plant having roots underground, as carrots or beets, grown primarily for food

root ing (rüt'ing, rut'-) adj. digging small roots out of the earth with the snout

routed (rout'əd) adj. completely defeated

rud der (rud'ər) n. broad, flat, movable piece of wood or other material attached at the bottom end of a boat, used for steering

rue (rü) v. to feel sorry about; regret

run (run) n. ski trail or slope

rus tic (rus'tik) adj. made of unfinished wood

sab o tage (sab'ə täzh) v. to interfere deliberately with so as to destroy the effort or activity of

sal vage (sal'vij) v. to save from loss or ruin

Sal va tion Ar my international Christian charitable group founded in 1865 and organized on a military model

San Joa quin (san wä kēn′) river and county in central California

sap ling (sap′ling) *n.* young tree

sap per (sap′ər) *n., Brit.* soldier trained or employed in the construction of trenches, fortifications, or the like

scab (skab) *n.* worker who will not join a labor union or join with striking workers; worker who crosses a picket line

scaf fold (skaf′ld) *n.* any framework or structure, esp. a temporary one

scald (skôld) *v.* to burn with hot liquid or food

scan dal mong er (skan′dl mong′gər) *n.* one who spreads scandal or malicious gossip

scarp (skärp) *n.* cliff or steep slope

scoff (skôf, skof) *v.* to express disbelief or annoyance; make fun; mock

score (skôr) *n.* set or group of twenty; twenty

scourge (skėrj) *n.* any sweeping or widespread means of suffering, esp. some natural disaster, as an outbreak of disease

scout (skout) *n.* person employed to hunt for and employ new talent, esp. in sports and entertainment — **scout′ing,** *adj.*

scrab bling (skrab′ling) *n.* scratching sound or movement made with hands or claws

se clu sion (si klü′zhən) *n.* place shut off from view or otherwise set apart

se cure (si kyür′) *v.* to get or obtain

seeth ing (sēŦH′ing) *adj.* surging, as if boiling, or as a result of inward agitation

seis mo graph (sīz′mə graf, sīs′-) *adj.* taken from the instrument that records the direction, intensity, and duration of an earthquake

se lec tive (si lek′tiv) *adj.* that which is careful in what it chooses

se mes ter (sə mes′tər) *n.* half a school year; term

sem i de tached (sem′ē di tacht′) *adj.* having a side wall in common with another building

se ren i ty (sə ren′ə tē) *n.* clarity and peacefulness

Ses qui cen ten ni al Ex po si tion (ses′kwisen ten′ē əl eks′pə zish′ən) elaborate display and collection of exhibits that marked the 150th anniversary of the United States

sewer (sü′ər) *n.* underground pipe or channel for carrying off waste water and garbage

shad y (shād′ē) *adj., Informal.* of a dishonest or illegal character or reputation

sheaf (shēf) *n.* bundle of things of the same sort tied together

shy ster (shī′stər) *n., Slang.* unethical, disreputable lawyer

sight (sīt) *n.* device on a gun aiding the eye in lining up the barrel on target

Sik si ka (sik′sə kə) *n.* Indian name of any one of the three closely related Algonquian-speaking Blackfeet tribes of the Plains states. *Also called* **Blackfeet**

sin ew (sin′ū) *n.* tough cordlike fiber of an animal that joins muscle to bone and is used as sewing or stringing material

siz ing (sīz′ing) *n.* paste or pastelike mixture used to stiffen and glaze clothing

skep ti cal (skep′tə kl) *adj.* inclined to doubt; questioning; disbelieving

skir mish (skėr′mish) *also* **skir mish ing** *v.* to engage in a minor fight with another group; said esp. of a small group detached from the major force

slea zy (slē′zē) *adj.* of poor quality; thin or flimsy

---

a **a**pple, ā **a**ble, ã **air**, ä **arm**; e **e**levator, ē **ea**ch, ė**r ear**th; i **i**tch, ī **i**vy; o **o**ctober, ō **o**pen, ô **all**, ô**r or**der; oi **oil**, ou **out**; u **up**, ů **p**ut, ü **g**lue, ū **u**se; th **thin**, ŦH **then**, zh mea**s**ure; ə **a**bout, **o**ccur, **u**ntil

slick er (slik′ər) *n., Informal.* sly, clever person

slough (slou) *v.* to move or walk (on muddy ground)

sod (sod) *n.* earth

sod den (sod′n) *adj.* filled with water or moisture; soaked through

so no rous (sə nô′rəs, son′ər əs) *adj.* full, rich, and impressive in sound

soot y (sut′ē, sut-) *adj.* colored or darkened as with dust or particles from burned fuel

spar tan (spär′tn) *adj.* simple and highly disciplined and courageous

spe cies (spē′shēz) *pl., -ies. n.* plant or animal understood as classified in a certain category because of characteristics it shares with other related forms

spec i men (spes′ə mən) *n.* one thing considered representative or typical of a group, class, or species; example

spelled (speld) *adj.* relieved or interrupted

sphere (sfir) *n.* range or extent

spin dle (spin′dl) *n.* rod or pin or a spinning machine holding the bobbin on which the thread is wound as the fiber is twisted or spun

splayed (splād) *adj.* spread or extended

split (split) *n.* thin, small strip, as of wood or other material

spouse (spous, spouz) *n.* husband or wife

squeam ish (skwēm′ish) *adj.* overly sensitive or particular; easily sickened

stand ing (stan′ding) *n.* particular status, grade, or condition

sta tion ar y or bit fixed position or point along a planned path

stem (stem) *v.* to stop or dam up (the flow of)

steppe (step) *n.* vast treeless plain in southeastern Europe and Asia

sti fling (stī′fling) *adj.* holding or keeping back

stone-dashed (stōn dasht) *adj.* decorated with inset stones

stoop la bor farm work involving back-breaking bending

stores sched ule list of supplies, as of food or equipment

strat e gy (strat′ə jē) *n.* plan to achieve a specific goal or advantage

styl ized (stīl′īzd) *adj.* conforming to the rules and conventions of a particular art, rather than to nature and reality

su et (sü′it) *n.* the hard fat from around the kidneys and loins of cattle

Suf folk (suf′ək, -ôk) *n.* county in eastern England

su per im posed (sü′pər im pōzd′) *adj.* placed one on top of another

su per la tive (sə pėr′lə tiv) *n.* statement that expresses someone's capacity to surpass all others

sup pressed (sə prest′) *adj.* kept or held back; restrained; muffled

surge (sėrj) *v.* to move or flow in a wavelike motion

the sur ger y (sėr′jər ē) *n., Brit.* doctor's office

sus pect (sus′pekt, səs pekt′) *adj.* open to suspicion; suspected

swarm (swôrm) *n.* large group or great number of insects flying or moving about together. —*v.* to move or fly about together in great numbers

swel ter ing (swel′tər ing) *adj.* very hot

sym met ri cal ly (si met′rə klē) *adv.* so that the size, form, and design of two halves are exactly the same

ta boo (ta bü′, tə-) *n.* restriction or ban, as on the use of some object or place, or on some act considered sacred or cursed

ta co (tä′kō) *n.* Mexican dish made of a fried tortilla filled with ground beef, cheese, or chicken

tac tics (tak′tiks) *n. pl.* procedures or methods used to achieve a goal, specifically in military combat

tal on (tal′ən) *n.* claw of a bird of prey

ta ma le (tə mä′lē) *n.* Mexican dish made of corn meal, minced meat, and red peppers, wrapped in cornhusks, and cooked by steaming or roasting

Tan gan yi ka (tan′gen yē′kə) *n.*·former country in east Africa; originally a British territory, it achieved independence in 1960, became a republic in 1962, and united with Zanzibar in 1974 to become Tanzania

tan nin (tan′ən) *n.* yellowish or brownish acid substance found in the wood or bark of many trees, used for tanning hides and in preparing ink and rubber

teach er's college college specializing in training students to be teachers

tech nique (tek nēk′) *n.* manner or method of performing the activity of a particular field or sport; technical skill

tech nol o gy (tek nol′ə jē) *n.* practical or industrial application of scientific knowledge

tee (tē) *n.* small mound or peg on which a golf ball is placed for the first shot at each hole

teem (tēm) *v.* to be filled, crowded, or overrun; swarm (with *with*)

tell (tel) *v.* to have or produce an effect

ten dril (ten′drəl) *n.* leafless, threadlike coiling part of a climbing plant that gives support by twining around or attaching itself to an object, as a wall, tree trunk, or trellis

ten e ment (ten′ə mənt) *n.* poorly maintained and overcrowded walk-up apartment building or rooming house that is usually in a poor, slum area

thick et (thik′it) *n.* huge crowd, created as by bushes growing close together

throng (thrông, throng) *n.* crowd

throt tle (throt′l) *n.* pedal regulating the valve and flow of gasoline vapor to an engine

toil (toil) *v.* to move with difficulty, pain, and weariness

to pog ra phy (tə pog′rə fē) *n.* all surface features of a place or region

tor til la (tôr tē′yə) *n.* Mexican round, flat pancake or bread made of corn meal and water and used in preparing tacos and enchiladas

tor tu ous (tôr′chủ əs) *adj.* full of twists and turns; winding

tote (tōt) *v., Informal.* to carry

trade cloth cloth bought from white traders

trans it (trans′sit, -zit) *n.* **1.** being moved from one place to another **2.** surveying instrument with a movable telescope that is used to measure angles

trans mit ter (trans mit′ər, tranz-) *n.* apparatus that produces and sends signals from a radio

trans port (trans′pôrt) *adj.* of or related to conveying or carrying goods from one place to another

trap pings (trap ingz) *n. pl.* ornamental blanket covering the harness and saddle of a horse

trau mat ic (trô mat′ik, trou-) *adj.* of, related to, or characterized by severe and long-lasting effects of a deep hurt or shock

tra vois (trə voi′, trav′oi′) *n.* vehicle used by Indians for carrying loads, consisting of two poles tied with netting, the V-shaped end harnessed to the horse, and the other end dragged along the ground

trek (trek) *n.* long and difficult journey

tri um phal (trī um′fl) *adj.* victorious;

---

a apple, ā able, â air, ä arm; e elevator, ē each, ėr earth; i itch, ī ivy; o October, ō open, ô all, ôr order; oi oil, ou out; u up, ủ put, ü glue, ū use; th thin, ҭн then, zh measure; ə about, occur, until

truck farm ing farming in which vegetables are raised for market

tu ber cu lo sis (tü ber′kyə lō′sis, tū-) *n.* infectious disease in which small swellings caused by bacteria may affect any organ of the body, esp. the lungs and joints

tu ber (tü′bər, tū′) *n.* thick part of an underground stem

tur moil (tėr′moil) *n.* commotion; disturbance

ul ti mate (ul′tə mit) *adj.* last; final

un checked (un chekt′) *adj.* not stopped in progress

un hood (un hüd) *v.* to remove the covering that is used to blind (a falcon) when it is not pursuing game

un pol lut ing (un′pə lüt′ing) *adj.* that does not damage, harm, or contaminate the environment or the ecological balance of something

un taint ed (un tānt′əd) *adj.* having no trace of corruption or decay; pure

un wit ting ly (un wit′ing lē) *adv.* not knowingly; unintentionally

up end (up end′) *v.* to turn on end

Val en ti no, Ru dolph (va′len tē nō, rü dolf) 1895 – 1926, Italian-born American Hollywood star and movie idol of the 1920s, known especially for his good looks

valve (valv) *n.* movable part of a device that controls the flow of liquid, gas, or other material by closing or partly closing off a passage

var i a tion (vār′ē ā′shən) *n.* change or difference in design; the extent to which something is different

vau de ville (vô′də vil, vōd′vil) *n.* theatrical show consisting of a variety of short performances, including singing, dancing, juggling acts, comedy routines, and the like

Ve la Spur (ve′lä spėr) southernmost part of the constellation of Argo

venge ance (ven′jens) *n.* desire to hurt or punish in return for hurt received

ven i son (ven′ə zn, -sn) *n.* flesh of a deer, used for food; deer meat

ver an da (və ran′dah) *n.* large, open porch on the ground floor, usually having a roof and railing, and extending along one or more sides of a house

ves i cle (ves′ə kl) *n.* small sac filled with lymph; blister

vet er an (vet′ər ən, vet′rən) *adj.* having extensive experience

vil la (vil′ə) *n., Brit.* suburban house, the name for which is meant to suggest a large and luxurious estate

vin di cate (vin′də kāt) *v.* to clear from suspicion of guilt or wrongdoing; justify

vir u lent (vir′yə lənt, vir′ə-) *adj.* extremely harmful; very poisonous

void (void) *n.* empty space; vacuum

want (wont, wônt) *n.* lack

wash (wosh, wôsh) *n.* thin coat or layer of some coloring medium or substance, such as ink or paint

well sweep device for drawing water from a well with a long pole or lever to raise or lower a bucket

welt (welt) *n.* skin raised by a branch or whip lash

whim sey (hwim′zē) *n.* playful humor

winch (winch) *n.* machine for lifting or pulling, having a drum with cable around it turned by a lever or crank

WPA *Works Projects Administration,* a former federal agency (1935–43) responsible for creating public projects to relieve unemployment caused by the Great Depression

"Y" abbreviated form for *YWCA* or *YWHA,* Young Women's (Christian, Hebrew) Association, an organization providing educational and recreational activities for its members

zith er (zith′ər) *n.* musical instrument having thirty to forty strings, stretched across a hollow wood sound box, which are plucked with a plectrum and the fingers

zo ol o gist (zō ol′ə jist) *n.* expert in the science that deals with the structure, development, and classification of all forms of animal life

PROPER NAMES

Ca es are (chä′zä rə)

Dor i a Ra mi rez (do′ryä rä mē′rəs, ram′ər ez)

Gor gon zo la (gôr′gən zō′lə)

Her mi one (hėr mī′ə nē)

Jean Ey mere (zähn ā mer′)

Ju li o Suar ez (hu′lē ō′ Swär′ez)

Ni co la (nik′ə lə)

Rah moon (rä′mün)

Ven u ti (ven′u tē)